BEYOND THE HALLOWED SKY

Ten metres high, rolling forward at a speedy walking pace, it looked like a pixellated black cloud or a heap of fallen masonry being bulldozed along. It filled the space between the walls like blocky smoke – no, Hazeldene now saw, it came from the walls, which extruded these brick-sized blocks and apparently sustained their movement. It was as if the endless, impossible internal movement of rock within rock had burst *from* the surfaces of the great blocks and, now in the open, had sped up.

Squelches and squeals indicated that it was moving faster than some of the animals, and what would happen to the humans if they stuck around.

Sharianne ran. Hazeldene stared for a moment, then she ran too.

BY KEN MACLEOD

The Fall Revolution
The Star Fraction
The Stone Canal
The Cassini Division
The Sky Road

Engines of Light
Cosmonaut Keep
Dark Light
Engine City

Newton's Wake
Learning the World
The Execution Channel
The Night Sessions
The Restoration Game
Intrusion
Descent

The Corporation Wars
Dissidence
Insurgence
Emergence

Lightspeed trilogy
Beyond the Hallowed Sky

BEYOND THE HALLOWED SKY

KEN MACLEOD

orbitbooks.net

ORBIT

First published in Great Britain in 2021 by Orbit

5 7 9 10 8 6

A CIP catalogue record for this book is available from the British Library.

ISBN 978-0-356-51479-6

Typeset in Stempel Garamond by Palimpsest Book Production Limited,
Falkirk, Stirlingshire

Printed and bound in Great Britain by Clays Ltd, Elcograf, S.p.A.

Papers used by Orbit are from well-managed forests
and other responsible sources.

Orbit
An imprint of
Little, Brown Book Group
Carmelite House
50 Victoria Embankment
London EC4Y 0DZ

An Hachette UK Company
www.hachette.co.uk

www.orbitbooks.net

To Alasdair and Mary

CHAPTER ONE

The Velocity Paper

Summer 2067, Earth

Lakshmi Nayak sat at the desk in her student flat in London, staring at a sheet of blue lightweight airmail paper. The page of equations was elegant and perplexing. Two things about it baffled her.

The equations, and the cryptic notes and marginalia, were in handwriting identical to her own. So was the address on the airmail envelope, stamped and postmarked BFPO, Kabul. She'd found it that morning, in her pigeonhole down at reception. Disappointed, having been expecting a packet of tea from her mother in Kerala, she'd stuck the letter in her jacket pocket and hurried to take the Tube to Imperial. Only this evening had she remembered it, and turned it over, puzzled from the beginning. Nayak had never been to Kabul. She didn't know anyone who might be among British forces posted overseas. She hadn't written the equations.

The second perplexity was the final line at the foot of the page. It read:

$V=xc$

V was velocity, c was the speed of light, and x was . . . a large number. A ridiculously large number, from what sense she could make of the equations immediately above, but that wasn't the point. Any number greater than one implied a velocity faster than light. Nayak suspected a prank. It was like the proof that $1=2$ which had puzzled her for five minutes when she was seven years old.

Maybe that was what it was: a *reductio ad absurdum*, exposing a mistake hidden in some too easily accepted premise . . .

' But if so, why the brevity? Why not lay out every step, every assumption?

If it was a prank, she had to admire its precision targeting. The thesis that she spent her days and evenings struggling to write concerned inflation: the rapid expansion of the early universe, space itself stretching out far faster than light could travel through it. The airmail page in front of her began with equations she'd used many times: textbook stuff. Between them and the absurdity at the end was a chain of reasoning with many links missing, their place taken by vertical rows of three dots, and annotations like 'obvsly'. This wasn't just her handwriting, it was her style. This was how she scribbled notes to herself when barely able to keep up with a tumbling torrent of thought.

Was it possible, then, that she had written this, and furthermore contrived its circuitous return, in some fugue state? Unlikely, but . . .

Nayak sighed and stood up, stretching her back. She gazed out of the window at the evening sky: yellow at the tower-bitten London skyline, fading through duck-egg green to pale blue with red clouds, among which Venus hung bright. Since childhood, the sight of the planet had always given her a small thrill. Her mother had told her that there was a place on Venus named after the same goddess as she was: Lakshmi Planum, it was called. Much later, she'd been amused to learn that the Union's floating cloud colony passed over it regularly. Odd to think that there were people on Venus; that someone, at that very moment, might be looking back.

She tapped the paper on her desk.

'Smart-Alec,' she said, 'search back six months on document.'

Seconds passed, as the AI scanned her eye-log records.

'No results found.'

'Shit,' said Nayak.

She made herself a coffee, sat back down and reached for a pen and notebook. She didn't notice the sky darken. Now and then she gazed, unseeing, at the lights of passing airships on their descent to Heathrow. Robotically, sleepwalking, she filled hourly mugs with coffee. By the time the sky reddened again she had filled twenty pages of the notebook, and all the gaps in the proof. The dawn chorus filled the air outside as she hesitated for a moment, and then wrote down the final equation.

$V=xc$

She clicked the pen and laid it down with a sense of finality, and exhaustion.

Well. That was that. Faster-than-light travel. And if so, she could well have written the airmailed page herself. FTL held the possibility of time travel, and the message was itself the proof that it would some day be realised. Because she would, at some time, travel back from the future and post it to herself.

Which in turn meant that until she did that, she couldn't die.

Oh, and one more thing. Nayak straightened her back again and looked out at a sky busy with airships, empty of starships. Humanity was alone in the universe.

Because if it wasn't, we'd know. If faster-than-light travel was possible, and *this* much faster at that, as she was sure she'd just proved, interstellar commerce must be easy. Another twist to the Fermi Paradox, to add to the prevalence of life-bearing worlds. Plenty of life out there, but no intelligent life. If aliens existed, they'd be here already.

Paradox upon paradox. If she had derived this result from her own future memories of it, who had discovered it in the first place? Perhaps the equations were like the Vedas: self-created, a revelation without a revealer. The thought made her shiver, and almost giggle.

She threw herself face down on the bed and slept for ten hours.

The second morning after her all-nighter, when she'd got over the grogginess, Nayak transcribed her notebook scribble to screen, formulated it properly as a paper and printed off a fair copy. She took it to her supervisor. Adam Kurtz was ten years older than her and (in her view) had done a million times more than she had, even before he'd defected from the Union to the Alliance. His office at Imperial was no bigger than anyone else's, though. Nayak sat on the visitor's chair between teetering stacks of journals and off-prints and tried not to shift about too much. Kurtz had long sandy hair, a CERN souvenir T-shirt, and glasses with flip-down screens. He kept the screens flipped up as he read her paper. She didn't know if this was a good sign.

He looked up and rattled the stem of a billiard e-pipe between his perfect teeth.

'Hm,' he said. 'I see you've been working. Why not on your thesis?'

'I'm sorry,' said Nayak. 'This just came to me.'

Which was true, in a way.

'I'm still trying to find the mistake,' said Kurtz. 'Because there must be a mistake, yes?'

'That's what I thought,' said Nayak. 'I was hoping you could spot it.'

Kurtz laughed. 'When I was a small precocious child I proved by inspection that a circle can be divided into only three mutually adjacent arcs. From that I concluded that I had solved the Four Colour Map problem. This was forgivable in a schoolboy.'

'Well, yes, I once did something like that.'

'So did we all, no doubt.' Kurtz raked his fingers through his hair. 'My point being, it's all too easy for an amateur or beginner to miss what a specialist in the relevant area would see at once.'

'But this *is* our area!'

'Not really, no. Just as I had mastered elementary geometry but I had no idea of topology, and no idea that was the territory I had blundered into.' He drew on his pipe and examined the dispersing cloud of vapour. He didn't do tricks. 'I suspect the weak link is the values for x. We're missing some variable that reduces it to less than 1. *Much* less than 1, if it's physically realistic. The energy value for the inflaton may turn out to be almost entirely virtual, in the present universe. Though . . .'

He stared off into the distance, or at any rate the top right corner of his office.

'Leave it with me,' he said.

She left the paper with him and got on with her thesis. To her surprise, the problems that had stymied her earlier had become a lot clearer after her work on the paper. She stormed ahead. Every time she consulted Kurtz, over the next few months, she finished by asking him – almost casually, on the way out – if he'd had any further thoughts on what was wrong with her equations. Every time, he sighed regretfully or puffed out cherry-scented vapour and murmured that he was still puzzling over it.

In the end, she got impatient. Her thesis was complete and ready to submit. As she left Kurtz's office after they'd agreed on that she turned and said, 'Any progress, on—?'

Yet again, he shook his head. 'No. I haven't had time recently to give it enough thought, but I'm sure I'll see it.'

'I think we need other minds on the problem.'

'What?'

'I'm going to pre-publish. Stick it up on phys.x-archiv.'

Kurtz looked alarmed. 'I wouldn't advise it. It'd be like throwing meat to hungry dogs. It'll get torn apart.'

'That's kind of the idea, Adam. Find out what its real weaknesses are.'

'You don't understand. This isn't some controversial interpretation or barely adequate data set or whatever. Just putting this forward is like claiming you're smarter than Einstein. The problems in the paper might be very subtle, but you should be able to see they must be there. The criticisms might well be welcome and clarifying, but you'd be branded forever as a crank.'

'Oh, come on!' she said. 'Even if I formulate it as a puzzle, a paradoxical result, and invite the real experts to show me any flaws in the logic?'

Kurtz scoffed. 'The real specialists – the likes of Lowery, Chiang, Bliebtreu, Faber, and your own country's Mehta and Vijayan – wouldn't give it a passing glance. No, you'd get peer review all right – from your peers! Postdocs, postgrads even, your own future colleagues. Don't do this to yourself.'

'I want to know what's wrong with it,' Nayak said. 'And I don't care who tells me.'

Kurtz looked away, then back. 'You do that, Lakshmi. You do that. On your head be it.'

She did, and it was. The criticisms were fiercer than Kurtz had warned. Her values for the mass of the inflaton had been rendered obsolete by a result published months earlier – obscurely and indirectly, yes, but she should have known. The transformation in the fifteenth step of her proof was inapplicable to her purpose. She'd overlooked the relevance of Lowery's refutation of Mehta's Conjecture. So it went. For days before her viva they distracted her, when she should have been looking out for weak points in her thesis and coming up with ready answers for the examiners.

But once again, unexpectedly, it was her worrying over the

criticisms of the velocity paper that sharpened her wits for the verbal examination. The thesis passed that trial by ordeal, with some light revisions required before it was finalised. She had her doctorate. Her corrected thesis was printed in a dozen copies, bound, its spine gilt-stamped. One copy went to her shelf, one to the university library, one to her supervisor, and the rest to other libraries and colleagues. Only her own would ever be opened again. Nayak celebrated, then flew home to Kozhikodi to celebrate some more, with her family and school friends. After a month she flew back to London.

The airship was above the Black Sea and Nayak couldn't sleep, so she padded to the lounge and called up a nightcap. Her specification was vague, but the sari-clad Air India hostess behind the bar compiled a cocktail that would, she assured Nayak, have the desired effect. Nayak sat at a table by the window, looked down at the lights of boats and the firefly drift of other aircraft through the reflections of the cabin's interior, sipped her drink and contemplated in her glasses the disheartening results of Smart-Alec's latest job-hunting trawl on her behalf.

'Dr Nayak?'

The slim young man's face wasn't familiar, but it was well-known enough to be tagged instantly in her glasses: Marcus Owen, journalist. He wore a black suit over a black T-shirt, and Sony glasses. His jaw was outlined by a razor-trimmed beard, his features tanned.

'Good evening, Mr Owen,' she said, just to make sure he knew she knew who he was.

'Oh, "Marcus", please,' he said. 'May I join you?'

His accent was British and his looks on the far side of striking. The phrase that sprang to Nayak's mind, annoyingly enough, was 'devilishly handsome'.

'Please do,' she said. He took the chair opposite and laid down his glass.

'I don't intend to be up long,' she said.

'Not to worry, I have work to do before I turn in,' said Owen. He gave a theatrical sigh. 'Writing up a report for the British Council.'

The British Council was widely believed to be the only wholly reliable intelligence service of the United Kingdom, and one of the best in the entire Alliance.

'Ah,' said Nayak. She took a quick sip, hoping to hide her fear. She put the glass down a little too carefully for that.

'Just back from Tamil Nadu,' Owen said. 'Mercifully, it's quieter than we expected.' He gave a self-deprecating laugh. 'I'll still get a good travel piece out of it.'

'Uh-huh.' Nayak's mouth was dry. She took another sip. 'So, uh, I suppose you want to ask me what I was doing in Kerala, but honestly it was all just family and sightseeing. Nothing political.'

'You have political relatives,' Owen said.

Kerala had been governed by the Left, off and on, for most of a century. Its relations with China and Russia – the Co-ordinated States, as they now styled themselves – and even the Union were thus sometimes a little warmer and closer than was welcome in New Delhi. And sometimes, of course, they were very much welcome in New Delhi, whenever India's national government needed some leverage on the rest of the Alliance. The level of intrigue was legendary.

Nayak forced a smile. 'I'm from a well-off Indian family. Of course I have political relatives! Some of them quite high up, as it happens.'

Owen chuckled. 'Don't worry, you needn't warn me off. I'm not here to ask about your relatives. I'm here to have a word with you. Off the record, of course.'

'Me?' She blinked hard and gave her head a quick shake that was almost a shudder. 'I'm not political. I'm a theoretical physicist, for all the good that does me.'

'Job-hunting?' He sounded sympathetic. 'I know what that's

like. I'm in rather a niche line of work myself. Journalism – an obsolete profession carried on as a boutique artisan craft, like drystone walling or coalmining. Hence the need for an Arts Council subsidy and British Council . . . arrangements.'

He left the word to hang there. She reached for it, with a look of distaste.

'You're not offering *me* an arrangement? Like I said, I have no interest in—'

'No, no,' said Owen, making a wiping gesture. 'Please don't take offence. Wouldn't dream of anything so crass. Ah . . . this is actually about your speciality, Dr Nayak.'

'"Quantum gravitational effects in early-universe cosmology"? Ask away, Marcus.'

'I didn't mean your thesis,' said Owen. He sucked on the straw in his now slushy Manhattan, making wide, innocent eyes.

'The velocity paper?' Nayak crushed air and tossed it over her shoulder. 'A student exercise in trying to find the mistake I know is there.'

'Well, yes,' said Owen. 'There must be a mistake, mustn't there?'

'That's why I published it. Quite a few mistakes have already been pointed out.' She smiled wryly. 'I'm taking them one by one and working through them.'

Owen leaned back in his seat. 'Have you looked at how others have tackled it?'

'Well, my esteemed critics, obviously.'

'No, I mean the people who in recent years have published speculations in this area.'

'The cranks?' Another dismissive gesture.

'No, not them. Mainstream physicists.'

'I didn't know there were any working in that area.'

'Well, quite. There's a reason why their work is obscure and seldom cited.'

'Because it's always torn to shreds?'

'Not exactly. Nor is the topic discreditable in itself. In the last century even NASA maintained a small research interest in what it called Advanced Propulsion Concepts. In the 1990s Miguel Alcubierre published a paper on warp drives, and was taken seriously. Some problems with his idea – fully acknowledged from the beginning, of course – were that it required seriously unfeasible amounts of energy, exotic matter with negative mass, that sort of thing. But the notion was never dismissed on the grounds that FTL travel is flat-out impossible. It was deemed impracticable, that's all. In recent decades, a number of well-regarded physicists and engineers have revisited the question.' He stroked his chin, rasping the designer stubble. 'Such papers are invariably published close to the end of the researchers' careers, and in some cases – their lives.'

So this was what it was about!

'Name me some names,' Nayak said.

Owen's neat eyebrows twitched upward. 'All right,' he said.

He began to recite names. Nayak put her glasses on and let the list build and the connections ramify. The date of the paper and the date of subsequent papers by the same author (usually, none); the date of the paper and the date of author's death (often close); nature of death (sudden; after a short illness; accident; alleged homicide, unsolved).

'Well,' said Nayak, shaken. 'That's me warned, I take it?'

'Yes,' said Owen. 'Sorry.'

They glared at each other for a moment.

The air hostess from behind the bar shimmied over with a tray. Deep brown eyes, air-hostess impersonal smile.

'I see your glasses are empty.' She swept them up. 'Another?'

Nayak sighed, and glanced at Owen.

'I'm happy to stick around for a bit,' he said.

'OK,' said Nayak. She smiled back at the air hostess. 'The cocktail was nice, thank you, but I'm not sure I want the same again.'

'May I recommend Nikka Whisky From the Barrel?'

Nayak looked it up. 'If he's paying.'

'Of course,' said Owen. 'And the same for me. Two small jugs of water on the side.'

'Coming right up!' said the stewardess.

She turned and left like a calligraphic flourish in silk, to return a minute later with the drinks. They both watched her leave.

'Bloody robots and their tireless cheerfulness,' remarked Owen, looking away from the departing vision.

'Robots?' cried Nayak. 'You mean she—?'

'Oh yes,' Owen said.

'Shame,' said Nayak. 'I have sisters and classmates who'd kill for her job.'

'It isn't a job,' Owen said. 'She's not an employee, she's equipment.'

An awful thought struck Nayak. 'Does she know?'

Owen shrugged. 'In an abstract sense, yes, in as much as she knows anything. They're hardwired to answer truthfully if the question is put directly and seriously, and I'm sure by now someone has been tactless enough to press it on her. So it'll be in her memory.'

Nayak shook her head and gazed down at the lights of Odessa, coming into view on the right. 'Must be awful, knowing that.'

'They're not conscious in our sense, so I wouldn't worry.'

Nayak took a sip of the whisky, savoured its 51.4 per cent alcohol sting for a moment then gave the glass a good watering. Her second sip, she could actually taste.

'Oh, I don't *worry*,' she said. She felt bitter. 'We're all robots anyway.'

Owen's eyes narrowed. 'What do you mean?'

'Completely deterministic systems.' Her cheeks twitched. 'I know that whatever happens I'll survive to write to myself a message from the future. Because that's how I got the basic ideas in the first place, months ago. That's how I know it'll one day be built and will work, come to think of it.'

Owen seemed to grasp her point immediately.

'That may be,' he said. 'I don't pretend to understand the theory, but quite possibly it does have the implication you've just drawn.' He bowed his head and breathed out, misting the cold glass of the table, and doodled lines and loops with a fingertip. He looked up. 'It implies nothing, however, about the survival of *other* people. Such as, for example, those sisters and old school friends you mentioned. Or your parents. Grandparents. Cousins. Nephews and nieces. As you pointed out, you have a lot of relatives, some of them political, some highly placed. Such connections can give security—but also vulnerability. The Indian intelligence services take information from the British Council very much in good faith, you know. Sometimes this is a mistake, but everyone understands these things happen.'

He stood up and knocked back the remainder of his costly single malt.

'Well, it's been interesting, Dr Nayak. But as I said, I have work to do. Enjoy the rest of your evening.'

'Thank you,' she said mechanically. 'You too.'

In an hour or two, depending on the weather, they'd be over Romania. Union territory. If she were really as confident as she had told Marcus Owen, she could contrive some way to exit the aircraft and jump. She decided there were less dramatic, and safer, ways to defect.

To defect! The intention had formed almost before she'd given it conscious consideration. She knew something of what defection meant from an early conversation with her supervisor, Dr Adam Kurtz. What made his situation different, she'd one day inquired over mid-morning coffee, from that of the other academics from the Union who also worked at Imperial? Anyone could come and go between blocs as they pleased –

the visa requirements for the Co-ordinated States were slightly more stringent than those between Union and Alliance, but that was all. The AIs kept track of everyone anyway. What difference, she'd asked, did defection make?

'Quite a lot,' Kurtz had explained. 'For one thing, it means I can travel in the Union – go home, even – without being arrested. Or otherwise, ah, inconvenienced. Now that I'm registered as a defector the Alliance has my back, you see, even though I'm not yet a UK citizen.'

'What could you have been arrested for?'

Kurtz had shrugged. 'Draft evasion, most likely. Worst case, if they wanted to make an example of me: mutiny and desertion. I refused to co-operate with a certain application of my research. I'd already done my stint of military training – it's short, and you can get out of it if you conscientiously object, which I didn't – but anyone who has done it is deemed to be in the Reserve. So if the Union Army asks you for some service later in your life – it's an order, soldier! The request that was made of me was lawful, but this time it did go against my conscience. So I took a train to Paris, then London. Completed the necessary formalities. And here I am.'

'What were you asked to do?'

Kurtz had smiled. 'That I can't tell you.'

Nayak had found herself frowning. 'Is it . . . better here?'

Palms upturned, hands moving up and down as if comparing weights: 'There are advantages and disadvantages, let us say. The Cold Revolution . . .' A sigh, as was usual when the phrase came up. 'The cliché's true, you know: it's a revolution in the sense that the Cold War was a war. And like the Cold War it pervades and polarises everything. On this side, in the Alliance, we're trying to slow it down. Back there in the Union, they're trying to push it forward, very slowly and carefully but . . . there's a relentlessness about the process that it's a relief to get away from. Like . . . you know when a background noise you had grown to not notice suddenly stops? In my civics class a teacher quoted H. G. Wells: "It may be a very gradual change, but it will be a very complete one."' Kurtz's expression had become pained, for a moment. 'Imagine that.'

Nayak couldn't imagine it at the time, and she couldn't now.

She knew of the turbulent times before her birth not only from history but – more vividly – from the conversations of her politically connected uncles and aunts back in Kerala. Decades of turmoil had culminated in two shocks: the restoration of democracy in the US, and its establishment in Europe through a continent-wide insurrection: the Rising. By the time the dust settled three great powers had consolidated: the Alliance, comprising the Anglosphere minus Ireland and Scotland and plus India; the Union, comprising most of continental Europe plus Ireland and Scotland; and the Co-ordinated States, a somewhat strained alliance of Russia, China and some of their dependencies.

The new Europe that had emerged from the Rising embarked on what it called the Cold Revolution, to establish what its proponents called economic democracy. It was not overtly totalitarian. There were many political parties, and no One Party. But in all institutions you could easily spot the *responsables* – veterans of the Rising, or recruited since – whom everyone knew and turned to whenever you needed someone with the clout to get things done and sort things out, and within and among these and sometimes entirely separate from them were the cadre, whom you couldn't spot at all unless you were a *responsable* yourself. The habits of security, of anonymity, of conspiracy from the bad old days died hard.

However mysterious, even secretive, the Union was, it didn't sound terrifying. The thought of having to think very carefully about returning to India even for a visit hurt, for sure. But so did the thought of not being able to continue her research or talk to anyone about it. And if defection brought her the protection of the Union, surely it would extend to her extended family? She could ask, and she was sure that would be granted. The Union's clandestine services had a reputation for the long arm and the hidden hand.

That much she knew about society in Europe.

It might be enough.

Her first thought was to visit the Spinoza Institute in South Kensington. Close enough to Imperial for her to drop by as if casually. Lots of people visited, for exhibitions and events, lectures and lessons. All very innocuous: archaeology, philosophy, literature, languages, costumes and customs, fashion and art. The Spinoza Institutes were an extension of cultural influence, Union soft power of course, but visiting wasn't held against you, as far as she knew. But it would certainly be recorded. It could become part of building a case. She hesitated as she passed the entrance, then hurried on up Exhibition Road. Better not to give any warning of her intention.

Two days later she was on a train to Edinburgh. Tourist visa, open return ticket. She still felt tense as the train pulled out of Berwick-upon-Tweed, but all that happened when it glided over the border a few minutes later was the firewall scan moving down the carriages, leaving a shiver in its wake like a passing ghost. Everyone's devices now spoke to Iskander, not to Smart-Alec. A guy further down the carriage shouted: 'Welcome tae Scotland! Welcome tae the Union! Welcome tae *freedom*!'

To her right, green fields reached to a ragged edge of coastline, all cliffs and coves and stacks, and beyond it the grey North Sea. You couldn't tell by looking, but the surface was already half a metre lower than it would have been without the Nordzee Barrier, endlessly under construction. Wind turbine blades cartwheeled along the horizon.

'Welcome,' said Iskander's default voice in the earpiece of her glasses, warm and almost intimate. 'I understand you wish to defect?'

Nayak jolted upright in her seat. She fought the impulse to look over her shoulder.

'What? How?'

'Never mind how,' said Iskander. 'A simple yes or no, please.'

'Well . . . yes.'

'Done,' said Iskander. 'We can sort out the screen-work and face-to-face later. For now, be assured the Union has your back.' There was a pause, as if the AI was thinking. 'You may have concerns about threats to your relatives.'

'How do you know?' Nayak whispered.

'I'm a Triple-AI,' said Iskander, trippingly. 'It's what I do. Anticipatory algorithmic artificial intelligence.'

'Ah. That explains it.' She wasn't sure if the sarcasm got across.

'The matter is in hand,' said Iskander. 'Relax. We can talk later.'

Not at all relaxed, Nayak huddled into the corner of the seat and looked out at the rain. As she came off the train at Waverley Station in Edinburgh she looked about, alert for any indication that she'd travelled from one side of the Cold Revolution to the other. Everything looked much the same as it had at King's Cross. More colour and decoration in clothing, perhaps. The pillar ahead of her showed scrolling ads: Louis Vuitton, Dior, Hertz. Then it segued to one for the Union Army: soldiers with a dawn sky behind them gazing at some bright off-camera landscape ahead. The symbolism was too obvious to need spelling out, so spelt out it was: *The Rising Lit the Way*. As she approached the barrier Nayak saw two uniformed militia striding up the platform and froze. They approached the man who had been shouting and arrested him for public drunkenness on public transport.

The escalator propelled Nayak out of Waverley Station and on to Princes Street. Like any other new arrival, she stood for a moment looking around in confusion. The sky was overcast and the air cold. The street to her left had shops on one side, a tall monument that looked like a sandstone spaceship and a green dell of garden park on the other, and was overlooked across the railway line by a castle on a crag looming like some anachronism out of the haze of fine drizzle. Trams clanged, bikes whizzed, midday commuters hurried and lunchtime shoppers strolled. Her hotel was to the right, over . . . she thumbed her phone and summoned the map to her glasses.

'Hello, Dr Nayak,' said a voice she hadn't forgotten.

She blinked away the map and stared at Marcus Owen, who stepped out of the passing crowd with a friendly and surprised-looking smile.

'What brings you here?' he asked.

Nayak clenched her leg muscles to stop her knees from shaking.

'I was about to ask you the same!' she said, forcing a bright tone.

'Oh, I'm a frequent visitor to the Union,' said Owen, glancing around. 'Fascinating place, in its quaint way. Not much opportunity for journalism, but in this case I'm here on cultural matters. We're hosting a major exhibition at the National Gallery, just along the road there.' He waved, flashing to Nayak's glasses a poster for some sculpture show. 'And you?'

'Ah, I'm just—'

'You have a job interview,' said Iskander, urgently in her ear. 'Late this afternoon, on the other side of the country.'

'—on my way to a job interview on the west coast.' She forced a smile. 'You'll recall I wasn't having much luck in my own field, and you had made your feelings clear about my prospects in that area, so—' Iskander patched the ad to her glasses '—it turns out there are lots of openings here in planning consultancy, and—'

'Mathematics has many applications?' Owen said.

'Yes, exactly!'

Owen nodded towards the station, with a slight frown. 'If you're heading west, there's a direct connection onward from here to Glasgow.'

'Of course,' said Nayak. 'Just thought I'd break my journey with a stroll through Princes Street, and on to—' Iskander flashed the name '—Haymarket.'

'Delightful!' said Owen. 'Well, I'm going that way. Mind if I accompany you as far as the Gallery?'

'Say yes,' Iskander said.

'No!' said Nayak. 'Sorry, Mr Owen. I don't welcome your company, and I hope you understand why.'

With that she turned sharply to the left and marched off, her rolling case rumbling behind her. As she crossed the first junction, just before the high monument, Iskander said: 'Don't look back.'

'He's following me?'

'Yes. Perhaps. Wait and see if he follows you past the Gallery.'

He did.

'Very well,' said Iskander, as Nayak waited at the next junction. 'Please fix your gaze on the red dot that has just appeared in front of you. Don't look at traffic, don't look at any other pedestrians. Simply follow the dot, starting . . . *now*!'

The lights had changed, and not in favour of pedestrians. Nayak had a split second of hesitation, then without conscious decision stepped out into the traffic as if she was in a virtual reality game where she wasn't keeping score. The rear wheel of a bus almost brushed her toe; a bicycle rider hurtled past behind her with an angry yell; a cab slowed just enough for her to evade its front bumper. Then she was across. The huddle at the other side parted in front of her. The crowd on the pavement flowed past her as she walked slowly or stepped briskly or swerved or stopped, following that red virtual will-o'-the-wisp. Sometimes it led her across the street through traffic, once up a side street to the right and along a pedestrianised passageway, then back down to Princes Street again.

'We've lost him,' Iskander reported. 'However, please continue following the dot to Haymarket.'

That took fifteen minutes. Inside the station's noisy concourse, Iskander said: 'The next train to Glasgow is in ten minutes.'

'I can see that! What about my hotel?'

'Cancelled.'

This seemed presumptuous. She'd taken for granted that the business about the job was merely a pretext to get away from Owen. 'Thanks a lot.'

'You really do have an interview booked.'

'Well, you can cancel that too. I'll do my own job search, thank you very much. And I do want to see Edinburgh.'

'You'll have plenty of time for that later,' said Iskander. 'This job opportunity may not come again. Consider. I suspect your defection is connected to your controversial paper. A planning consultancy would be a very good place to turn your theory into a practical proposal, while developing your mathematical abilities in new directions, and all under cover of obscurity.'

'But . . .' She blinked up the advertisement again. '"Tarbet, Argyll"? Middle of nowhere. Obscurity, all right!'

The AI didn't sigh, but something in its tone suggested it would have if it could. 'It's a light-industrial town with a thriving tourist trade and a lively social scene. There are excellent connections to Glasgow, and indeed to Edinburgh. You can be there in two hours if you take the next train.'

Lakshmi Nayak didn't believe in karma, not really, nor fate or destiny, nor providence or predestination. But – as she gazed through the glass roof of the station at the grey sky – she felt certain that at least one event in her future was already fixed: she would send that airmail letter to herself. She would travel on a faster-than-light ship. To the stars, and back! And the way to make that happen was for herself to take a hand in building that ship – or at any rate, its drive. The Nayak Drive! Maybe they would call it that, she thought, hugging herself so as not to laugh at her own presumption.

She didn't believe in any gods, either, but she had just trusted this talkative, all-seeing, all-pervasive superhuman calculating machine with her life. It wasn't a god on her side, exactly – gods never were – but maybe her purposes and its could be made to coincide.

'You don't have to *take* the job,' said Iskander.

'I'll check it out,' said Nayak. 'Open return, please.' She walked through the barrier confident that the tickets were already on her phone.

The maglev bullet train flashed her to Glasgow, leaving her impression of the landscape between the cities a blur of green and glass. Flicking through the job description on her glasses, Nayak wasn't paying the landscape much attention anyway. The post was junior analyst at a new planning consultancy co-op, and it involved a lot of mathematics new to her. At Queen Street Station she changed to a lower platform and a slower train. Glasgow suburbs slid by, and suddenly a river to the left. By now Nayak was looking intently at Leontief input-output tables and Kantorovich optimisations, and how they were transformed and applied in the kind of software the co-op used. As she studied the transformations, she saw what seemed an obvious simplification. Surely someone had noticed this before?

She scribbled virtual notes with her stylus and placed them beside a sheet of code.

'Iskander,' she said, 'why don't they do it that way?'

'That's a good question,' said Iskander. 'I suggest you ask it at the interview.'

The line hugged the northern shore of the now widening river, which opened to what seemed an inland sea to the west. It passed behind a ragged basalt crag to which a castle clung like a necklace draped on a skull. Castles on volcanic remnants seemed to be a theme in this country. Then the line climbed gradually, up behind a new industrial town that abutted a quite distinct cluster of high towers, from which it was divided by a wall that ran – she now saw – up, and then along, the hillside. Drones flitted back and forth across the wall. Behind the towers lay a region of docks and cranes and huge fortified buildings.

'What's that?'

'Faslane,' Iskander told her. 'The Alliance naval base. That area and a smaller one a couple of mountain ranges over – Ardtaraig – are English territorial enclaves.'

Nayak felt a shiver. The power from which she'd just defected wasn't far behind her, it was right up close – and would be, if she took up the job. She flicked her gaze away from the militarised shore and out to the water, to be met by the sight of the long, black, sinister shape of an inbound nuclear submarine.

'Look further,' said Iskander. 'Look across the river. That conurbation along the shore? It's called Inverclyde and comprises three towns: Port Glasgow with the shipyards, Greenock with the docks and Gourock with the ferries. The consultancy does a lot of work there. It's a good place to build a ship.'

'You mean—?'

'Yes. I'll keep you posted.'

She returned to her interview preparations, and to the enticing thought of a very different kind of ship, the vessel that would take her to the stars.

It was the year they found Arthur. So the Scots claimed, anyway. Workers for a visitor centre at the top end of a Scottish sea loch in Argyll had dug into a hillside to extend its car park, and found a stone tomb containing Romano-British armour and the remains of some warlord from the Dark Ages. The site was overlooked by a mountain called Beinn Artair or Ben Arthur, and lay within the ancient Brythonic kingdom of Strathclyde. The local tourist board got a few respected historians to admit through gritted teeth that, yes, it was just about possible that there might be some . . . And that was enough, they were off to the races. The Scottish Republic claimed the legendary king of the Britons, to the indignation and derision of the English, not to mention the Welsh. On Asian and African networks the ruckus was a popular 'And finally . . .' item on news bulletins for days.

So when Lakshmi Nayak stepped off the train at the Arrochar and Tarbet Station, and looked out over the green and glass glitter of the town's new-built factories she wasn't surprised to find, opposite the station exit, a freshly painted sign reading:

Welcome to Argyll: Homeland of Arthur

She set off down the road to her interview, smiling.

CHAPTER TWO

MacHinery Ridge

Monday 13 October 2070, Apis

You weren't supposed to call it a warp bubble, but everybody did.

The submarine made way mid-channel: nuclear-powered, nuclear-armed, a machine that could destroy a world.

Just not *this* world.

One moment the long black Trident boat was butting the choppy waves that flooded over its prow, washed its deck and broke in two across the forward edge of its fin. The next, it was suspended over an elliptical concavity in the water, longer and wider than itself and domed by a symmetrically curved rainbow shimmer above. The screws thrashed air as they spun out their dwindling torque. For a few seconds the Guth spindle – that was the correct term – ploughed the swell. And then in a gush, a splash, a Cherenkov flash, it was gone.

Seconds later, a small thunderclap followed, echoing back

and forth across the water. By the time the yellow after-image of the blue glare had faded, and the abrupt anomaly of wake had surged up the shores of Bellatrix Sound, the submarine would already be light-years away. Homeward to Earth, perhaps: home to the Clyde, or to deterrence's deep and dark patrol. Or outward, maybe, to other worlds entirely, to explore or fight.

Emma Hazeldene swung her view around to check that she'd left her inflatable boat high enough up the shore. There it was, well clear of the strandline and tethered to the trunk of a wind-warped tree-like thing. She brought thumbs and forefingers together, unzooming her glasses. She resettled her rucksack and took a sip of water.

'Onward,' she said.

She set off again up the stony path. No one had yet established what feet had trampled it first. Narrow and deep like a sheep track, on a world with no sheep and – as far as anyone could tell – no native mammals or tetrapods of any kind. The path zigzagged to the top of the escarpment that sloped a steep five hundred metres from the shore to the sheer cliff of the MacHinery Ridge at the top. The Ridge itself rose a further three hundred metres above that. At this time of day sunlight glinted off crystalline black facets to dazzle a careless glance. Hazeldene kept her head down except when she paused to look behind and take a breath or a sip. Boids – winged invertebrates that filled this world's bird niches from sparrow to albatross – flitted about, their calls now and then ringing or fluting from ground and sky. The green growth that covered the ground was not quite grass. The knotty low-flowering bushes that hazed the hillside blue and sweetened the breeze were not quite heather. The insects that hovered over and clambered among them, however, were undoubtedly bees. Their hum had always given Hazeldene a sort of intellectual tinnitus, a persistent background noise to her perplexity at the whole goddamn planet.

Honeytrap Hazeldene, her colleagues sometimes called her to her face.

Hazeldene had lived and worked on Apis for fifteen years. In her late twenties a bad break-up with a long-term girlfriend, and the frozen hostility of her parents – they'd been in the English contingent of one of the Christian Nationalist movements that still roiled America even under democracy – had left her isolated. A retrenchment in the biotech industry had left her redundant. She was ripe for recruitment to Black Horizon. All she knew was that it was military, scientific and secret, and that there would be no coming back for the next twenty years.

Even when the hatch had closed on the submarine, she'd still thought she was going to Antarctica. An hour or so later, she'd had five minutes when she thought she'd arrived in hell.

That was the FTL jump, they told her. Still shaking, she didn't believe a word. She was invited on deck. The submarine was cruising between the cliffs of Bellatrix Sound, under a twilight sky lit by an evening star as bright as the full Moon. Dark, winged shapes she knew at once weren't gulls glided or flapped overhead.

That night at New Ardtaraig, she'd learned that the US, Russia and China had had FTL travel for decades, and kept it Above Top Secret. Presidents, Prime Ministers and even General Secretaries had come and gone without hearing so much as a rumour about it. The first crewed probes were directed to promising exoplanets, and soon encountered each other. An accord, later known as the Kepler Agreement, was worked out by the scientists, cosmonauts/astronauts/taikonauts and military personnel on the spot.

Her first and most urgent work on the planet was to identify and counter any forms of microbial life that found the human body a congenial host, but – like evolution – her work soon branched out.

So here she was now, looking into lively rock.

*

Hazeldene reached the top of the slope, where the path ended in a well-trodden sill at the foot of the cliff a few strides from the first cleft. Just outside it was a metre-high box flanked by a solar panel and topped by a thirty-centimetre dish aerial. She shrugged off her pack and grabbed a bite and a sip, leaning her back against the cliff. The climbing moss on the cliff-face reached to knee height. Above it a lichen-like growth spread upward a couple of metres, crisp and dry. She restrained the idle urge to pick at it. Centuries old, this great splotch of grey and orange deserved respect.

Time to call her colleagues. She thumbed up Nelson Hayes, the geologist. No answer. None from Sharianne Adler, Georgi Muranov, or Cindy Patel, either.

The monitor on the side of the relay was green with algal grot. Hazeldene rubbed it clean and peered at the display. All the little blinkenlights – power, comsat link, CPU – were green, except one: the cable. In other words, the device's entire fucking point.

Hazeldene sighed, hunkered down further, and checked the connection at the back. It looked sound. A gentle tug on the cable confirmed that it was. Her gaze followed the cable into the cleft to where it vanished in the dark. Between her and the team half a kilometre deep in the mountain, the cable must have broken. Not for the first time. Even the tough five-millimetre-diameter plastic-sheathed optical fibre could fray on some edge of black crystal.

She tried shouting. No answer but echoes.

Hazeldene called the science division at the New Ardtaraig naval base at the head of the Sound and reported the problem.

'Have you tried turning it off and turning it on again?'

'Oh, for—' She thought about it. 'Actually, no.'

The power switch was down the back of the box and she scraped a knuckle flipping it.

'No change,' she reported.

'OK, I'll log that. Stay safe, and report back. If we haven't heard back in, say, two hours we'll send up a drone to go in after you.'

'Thanks. Shouldn't come to that. Speak soon. Hazeldene off.'

'SciDiv off.'

Hazeldene shouldered the rucksack again, slapped her sidearm holster, tabbed her glasses to low-light and pulled on her headband torch. She picked up the cable and let it run loose in her right hand as she walked into the mountain. As always, she felt herself shudder as she stepped inside. The feeling was as predictable, and almost as locatable, as an automatic sliding door. It was quite distinctive. The only feeling anyone could compare it with was the black unease of an FTL jump. This was like an extended, attenuated echo of that. You passed through it, and then there was only the feeling of being watched, and followed.

The cleft was a metre and a half wide and went straight up to a slot of blue sky a hundred metres above. Shells and carapaces of small animals that had found shelter or been eaten crunched underfoot for the first ten metres or so. Fifty-odd metres in, she arrived at the first angle in the path. Beyond it, she couldn't see the light at the entrance, or the light above. She was properly in a cave, the roof twenty metres overhead. If you peered close at the glassy sides you could see, behind and through your reflection, the intricate crystalline structure of the rock. Stacked dominoes, bevels, lines and planes. Endlessly repeated, endlessly varied, each postage-stamp-sized area or matchbox of volume as unique as a snowflake.

If you watched them long enough, they changed. Inside that rock, rock shifted. It was impossible, but it happened. You could watch it happen. '*E pur si muove!*' one of the first exogeologists had cried, in as much delight as despair. Nevertheless, it moves.

*

On, into the dark. She had been this way so often she could have found her way without a light. Approaching the corridor's first right-angled turn, her steps slowed before her torch illuminated the wall ahead. The next turn, a mere ten metres further, returned her to the forward path. This pattern continued, time after time. At each turn she checked the cable for abrasion and found it intact.

Behind her, something creaked, then cracked. The sound was as if wood had split under strain. Hazeldene jumped. She looked back and saw nothing. Nor was the sound repeated. But the air became dead and still. Or was that her imagination? She held her breath. Still nothing. Perhaps an odd echo. She walked on, quickening her pace. The feeling of being watched, and the sense of something or someone behind her, became stronger than usual. As always, when she couldn't resist the impulse to turn and look, there was nothing there. After about a quarter of an hour daylight appeared ahead, and she hurried into it with relief. Her glasses compensated faster than she could blink.

She stepped into an open space about fifty metres square, and cried out in dismay. Slightly off the middle of the square stood the team's base camp – trashed. A ladder was still propped against the wall, just below the workings, but the power drill and the sample cases had fallen to the floor. The shelter had been knocked over. Instruments, tools and torn food packages lay strewn across the ground. The far end of the cable had been cut and the relay box smashed.

Hazeldene dropped the cable, drew her pistol and from a crouched stance pointed it systematically at every corner and side. From the square, corridors wider than the one she'd just walked extended in three directions. Nothing moved. She reached behind her to the top of her rucksack and drew out a long, heavy torch. Its beam scanned each corridor, one by one, finding nothing. Torch in one hand, pistol in the other, she walked forward, wary and alert.

Millennia of dust, of droppings, of invertebrate exoskeletons had formed this floor. Months of trampling had pounded and scuffed it. Moss-like and grass-like greenery remained only in corners. As she paced towards and then prowled around the ruined base camp, Hazeldene tried to distinguish recent marks. A boot-heel impression here, a scrape there. A single print of a bare foot. Some fresh animal tracks. No blood. No bullets or casings. No arrows. She moved in closer. The only supplies and equipment left were those too heavy or awkward to carry: the shelter itself, the generator, the ladders, the table and chairs. Even the camp stove, the water bottles and bags of coffee were missing. The bent and twisted panels of the relay box had snipped stubs of wire where the electronic components had been wrenched out.

'Exiles,' she said to herself. 'Fuck.'

Exiles, yes, that seemed likely. Descendants or survivors of the first involuntary (if well-intentioned) refugee transports from Earth, seasoned by a frequent dash of defectors and deserters from the military bases, there were far more of them on the planet than the official population of naval base personnel and scientists. There were more, indeed, than was easy to account for, unless the planet was even more benign than it looked, allowing rapid population increase. Exiles had spread from the Alliance bases on New Atlantis and the Co-ord bases on distant New Lemuria. Satellite observations and the occasional overflight suggested that some had crossed thousands of kilometres of ocean to the third island continent, New Mu, which sprawled in the southern hemisphere in a position roughly analogous to Oceania.

The nearest exile settlement was at the foot of the long, shallow slope at the far side of the escarpment. But they'd never shown up in the Ridge before. She'd always taken for granted that superstitious dread kept them away. The team had learned to laugh off the uneasy feelings that the rocks evoked, but she doubted that exiles would. And how could they have overwhelmed the team without a shot being fired? With barely a trace of a scuffle?

She squatted and let the torch beam lick the floor. Eyes half shut, glasses to high contrast. The team had explored all three of the directions leading off from the square more or less equally, leaving the traces of their regular paths clear enough in the dust. It was hard to be sure, but the path to the corridor directly opposite the entrance seemed to have more disturbance on either side. She imagined a sudden rush, the dust kicked up by a score or so of running feet.

She stood up, looking around again. Here the lichen-like growths had colonised the first metre or two of the black glassy walls. Tiny arachnoids and insectoids had grazed these growths, or preyed on the microbial life in the curls of crust, and boids had preyed on them. The height of the growth on each side corresponded to the amount of sunlight that fell on it. One side was almost permanently shaded, and almost bare. Now and then one of the larger beasts – lithe endothermic arthropods, a knee high and man long, all legs and pincers like some fearsome splicing of millipede and land crab – had been known to scuttle across from one corridor to another. They didn't hunt or attack humans, but woe betide anyone who got in their way. In the corridors themselves, there might be no chance to do so.

That was what the sidearms were for – that, and the remote possibility of a military clash with the Co-ord. Which the Navy, being the Navy, insisted on everyone's being prepared for, even the civilians. Nobody had figured on any trouble from exiles.

Hazeldene hesitated. Without the relay, she couldn't phone base from inside the Ridge's high, impervious walls. She could retrace her steps and call for help as soon as she got out. By the time help reached her colleagues it might be too late. If she followed she might find she'd guessed the wrong path entirely, to waste the time of the promised drone as well as herself. The drone would be sent up in – she checked the time – about an hour and a half, and would have no difficulty tracking her. On the other hand, she knew her way around for a good kilometre in all directions better than anyone. Certainly better than exiles.

In the end, after half a minute's anguished reckoning of odds, it was rage at the thought of Nelson, Sharianne, Georgi and Cindy in the hands of exiles, and perhaps not far away, that decided her. She shrugged off her pack, dumped all but the water, ammunition clips, energy bars and torch, and slung it on again much lightened. She toed out a rough arrow in the dust for the drone to spot and set off down the indicated corridor at a steady run.

Forward, left, right, forward, right again, left, forward . . . Hazeldene checked the floor as she jogged, and kept an eye on the walls, looking for any sign: the scrape of a dragged foot, something dropped, even a smudge. Nothing. After five minutes the light brightened ahead, and the air freshened. She slowed to a walk, and when she neared the opening pressed herself against the right wall and moved sideways, her pistol aimed ahead and her heavy torch held tight. Seeing nothing untoward from that side she sprang to the other and edged forward again. She racked the torch and held out her phone, turning it this way and that and checking the linked image on her glasses.

The square here was larger than the first – they'd nicknamed it 'Plaza 1' – and from here on for many hundreds of metres the interior of MacHinery Ridge was open to the sky and quite different from the geometric cave complex that surrounded it and from which she'd just emerged. The team's nickname for the first region was 'the CBD'. Blocks hundreds of metres tall and tens of metres on the side clustered a few metres apart, in long rows that could be mistaken for narrow streets, opening out occasionally to other plazas. From here on in the sides of the blocks were multicoloured or iridescent, an effect of sub-microscopic prismatic scribing on the surface of the black glass, like the casings of certain boids and beetles. Such might even have inspired the design, though at this distance of time and (probably) mentality from its designing intelligence, the thought was charming but speculative.

Hazeldene found the square clear and stepped out. She swept her aim; then, as she jumped forward, she quartered it. Satisfied the square was safe, she looked up. Boids soared on wide, stiff wings in the thermals around the towering blocks, ready to stoop in an instant on any prey that dared scuttle in the gaps and rows. Far down the main row leading off the plaza more boids circled, and others glided across to join the swirl. Something was going on there.

Hazeldene darted along the alleys, stopping at each cross-roads and junction to check in all directions before hastening on. Coloured walls flickered past like bolts of neon-lit cloth in a market. The boids were diving now, raising a commotion up ahead where the passage opened out to the next square on the grid, Plaza 2.

A shot rattled echoes off the blocks. Hazeldene threw herself flat on the dirt, hitting hard. She knew she was going to hurt later. The boids squawked and scattered, some flapping upward, others speeding away in all directions at low altitude, one of them just overhead in a flash of pale belly and a whir of wings. The shot wasn't repeated. As the echoes faded, voices were raised, a quarrel angrier than the boids.

'Back off!' someone shouted. 'Back the fuck off!'

A woman's voice, and not Sharianne's or Cindy's.

Hazeldene rose to a crouch and moved forward, her pistol pointing the way. Straight ahead, Plaza 2 looked empty. She reached the corner, crouched down lower and reached her phone around the block's edge. In the opposite left corner of the square, about seventy metres away, two knots of a dozen or so people faced each other. Off to their right lay a slumped, dark mass the size of a human body, with a long shaft sticking out.

Horrified, Hazeldene zoomed, and saw to her relief that it was one of the big arthropods, evidently struck down with a spear. She scanned the two groups, and found her colleagues Nelson and Cindy on one side, Georgi and Sharianne on the other. The other people had the rangy physique and tatterde-malion garb of exiles. A tall black man stood behind Georgi, gripping the palaeoanalyst's right wrist with one hand and a rifle with the other. The rest carried spears or crossbows, along with sacks and slings of what seemed to be loot from the camp. All her colleagues, as far as she could see, still had their side-arms, and in their holsters at that. No one was aiming or brandishing weapons, but they were all yelling at each other, jaws jutting, shoulders hunched, fists clenched.

Hazeldene stuck her pistol back in its holster and stepped out into the plaza, waving her arms above her head.

'Hey! What's going on?'

Her voice rang around the blocks. The quarrel stopped as everyone turned to her. After what seemed a stupefied moment, they beckoned her urgently. She hurried across, to a chaotic welcome of hugs and shoulder claps and from Sharianne tears. The exiles seemed almost as pleased and surprised as her colleagues to see her.

'Thank God you're all right!' Sharianne said.

This seemed excessive, even for Sharianne. It was ages since they'd been together, and their relationship was now carefully professional. Before Hazeldene could demand an explanation, the tall man with the rifle shouted: 'Come on! We've wasted enough time! Move it out.'

He chivvied everyone, exiles and scientists alike, towards the far exit of the plaza. Along the way he wrenched the spear from the fallen invertebrate, gave the body a regretful look, shook his head and hastened after them. He passed the bloody spear to a woman, shoving it into her hands with a glare and a snarl. As they left the square he was walking backwards, rifle at the ready, its muzzle tracking this way and that. He only shouldered it when they were all in the alley, then brought up the rear with frequent glances back.

Hazeldene was rattled enough to be looking back a lot herself. The tall man gave her an impatient gesture forward. Everyone was walking fast or trotting, bare or sandalled feet slapping and booted feet thudding on the dirt. Her colleagues were randomly dispersed among the hurrying exiles. She caught up with Sharianne.

'What's going on? What are we running from? What happened back there?'

'In the square?' Sharianne said. 'Just stupid shit. The arthropod charged us, and instead of skipping out of the way one of the locals speared it. Force of habit I guess – everyone but us is hungry. Jenkins – that's the guy behind us – got furious with her, then the big boids started screaming down from the sky, and that Russki dickhead Georgi shot at them to scare them off or because he was scared himself. Or maybe to impress the locals by bagging another kill. Fuck knows what was going through his head. So Jenkins grabs him, I step in to try and calm things down, Nelson challenges Jenkins and—'

'And that was where I came in,' said Hazeldene.

'Just as well you did!'

Hazeldene's right kneecap was reminding her how badly she'd hit the ground. Her jog shifted to a fast hobble.

'But what are we running from?'

Sharianne glanced backwards and almost tripped. She pointed.

'That.'

Racing, tumbling, scrambling and pouring down the corridor twenty metres behind them came a stampede of scuttlers, slinkers, stalkers, humpers, jumpers and other indigenous invertebrate fauna. Behind the fleeing beasts came what they fled.

Ten metres high, rolling forward at a speedy walking pace,

it looked like a pixellated black cloud or a heap of fallen masonry being bulldozed along. It filled the space between the walls like blocky smoke – no, Hazeldene now saw, it came *from* the walls, which extruded these brick-sized blocks and apparently sustained their movement. It was as if the endless, impossible internal movement of rock within rock had burst from the surfaces of the great blocks and, now in the open, had sped up.

Squelches and squeals indicated that it was moving faster than some of the animals, and what would happen to the humans if they stuck around.

Sharianne ran. Hazeldene stared for a moment, then she ran too.

CHAPTER THREE
Fata Morgana

Friday 16 May 2070, Earth

You weren't supposed to photograph submarines, but John Grant did.

He'd always loathed the Faslane naval base, that bristling Alliance installation on the northern side of the Clyde, and the compromise that maintained it. Ceding Faslane and its environs to England had been a price paid long ago, a concession that even the Rising had never challenged, nor one the Union been able to reverse. For some, though, it remained an affront that the Alliance's nuclear deterrent still berthed at an enclave carved out of Scottish territory and that its long, dark, sinister shapes still plied the Clyde.

It was an affront Grant shared. Outrage at the effects of nuclear weapons had seared him in his youth, years before the Rising. Nothing since had reconciled him to their continued existence, on his own side or any other. Whenever he saw an

Alliance submarine in the Firth of Clyde, he photographed it and put the pictures online. For him it was a pinprick protest, a tiny continuation of the struggle. Any such photos posted inside the firewall got taken down in a blink. Grant posted them outside the firewall, on nuclear disarmament campaign sites hosted in militantly neutral states.

That Friday morning in May, an alert from one of those sites came to him through the firewall. Scottish and Irish units of the Union Navy had an exercise underway some tens of kilometres to the south, where the Firth of Clyde opened to the North Channel. The hot tip was that an Alliance sub would be in the area.

It was a fine day. Ellen was working a morning shift on the North Sea, building the Nordzee Barrier. Through the half-open door of the home workshop Grant could see her in the rig, her goggled gaze blank, hands on the remote controls of her submersible. Their son Myles, home from university and on his way to a weekend on the Isle of Arran, was still in bed.

Grant tabbed a note to Ellen's phone – he knew better than to disturb her at work – left the flat and clumped downstairs and wheeled his bike out of the block. He rode down the steep street to the main road, and turned left past the station and ferry terminal and then the shops. Beyond them the view opened out to the Firth of Clyde and the hills and mountains and sea lochs.

The houses on his left, all along the seafront street, were abandoned on their ground floors to storm surges, the upper flats squatted where they were occupied at all. The promenade on the right, a couple of metres below street level, was strewn with seaweed and pebbles from the previous night's spring tide. Across the water, in bright sunlight, the derelict white-washed houses of abandoned shoreline villages gleamed like gappy rows of baby teeth. He took his time, letting more earnest cyclists whizz past. Cars and lorries overtaking could safely be left to their own microsecond automatic judgement.

Ahead, when his gaze lifted, he glimpsed across the widening estuary the mouths of sea lochs, the high-rise blocks of Dunoon and the green hills above that small town, and behind them all the mountains of Argyll.

He swung off the road a few hundred metres out of town to take the car ferry. On board he parked and locked the bike and bounded up the stair to the upper port-side deck. From there he looked downriver – as people called it here, although by this reach the Firth of Clyde was evidently an inland sea, a salt lake criss-crossed with shipping. To his south was the low island of Bute and beyond it the much larger Isle of Arran, its mountainous skyline like a notched blade. A pod of dolphins sported a hundred metres ahead. Reminded, Grant scanned the sea for what he knew must be moving beneath its surface. Hard to be sure, but halfway across he thought he detected the subtle swell that marked the passage of a robot submarine and the long drogue it towed. Some satisfaction in the thought that it might be a vessel he'd worked on himself. He could have asked Iskander, of course, but what would be the fun in that?

At the far side he wheeled his bike off, turned left and pedalled along the seafront road out of town. At the first wide bay there was a clear view south to the horizon, but the beach was too busy with kids and dogs for the long shots he sought.

So on he rode, past the signposts to woodland walks with fanciful names, Bishop's Glen and Fairy Glen, through two abandoned hamlets and on to the tip of the peninsula and a lighthouse whose name he amused himself by mentally mispronouncing: *toward light*.

He juddered down a final unpaved track, propped the bike against the whitewashed wall around the lighthouse grounds and said: 'Iskander, guard.' The hub locks clicked; alarms armed. Grant strode through long grass to the rocks and sat on a boulder. The sun was high, the sky clear, the sea dazzling even through polarised glasses. Gulls side-slipped invisible slopes, then soared. Gannets plunged like bombs. Far above the birds, cargo drones streamed like the vast avian migrations of a pre-industrial world. Grant swigged water and nibbled at an energy bar, waiting for any pictorially or politically interesting ships to come into view. After a while he saw a large US support vessel, with heavy and complex superstructure, passing the western shore of the peninsula. Evidently it had just left the Alliance fuel depot at Ardtaraig, in its own tiny enclave of England a few kilometres up the coast from the point.

Grant bestirred himself, crouched behind the boulder, fitted the camera to a tripod, set it up and fiddled with focus and speed. He caught a good picture of the entire ship's length, broadside on, then a few more at varying angles as it turned away to the south. After a few minutes, wake washed up the shore and set the wading birds aloft with cheeping cries.

Next he spotted a bulk carrier heading for the horizon, more or less due south. The ship was to the naked eye a thick, black pencil line under white chalk dots in the shimmer where the sea met the sky, yet through the viewfinder Grant could easily make out individual crew members on deck. He set the shutter to shoot every thirty seconds, and then, as the hull began to visibly disappear, every five. After about ten minutes, the topmost sail had vanished behind the curve of the Earth. Just after the ship had finally disappeared, Grant noticed on the horizon another black object: a submarine, heading from west to east. Perfect. He kept the camera running, increased the frequency to one a second, and rotated it to track the vessel.

The submarine levitated out of the sea. Reflexively, Grant pressed hard on the shutter, maxing the frame rate.

For a moment he saw clear space between hull and horizon. Then a blue flash, and the sub was gone. He blinked, and swung the camera from side to side. Nothing. He tilted it upward on its mount, facing skyward. Still nothing.

Grant stopped the camera and scrolled back to the pictures. His hands shook a little. He couldn't believe he'd seen that, and he was almost afraid to check. He found two clear photos of the submarine in the water, ten showing it above the water, and two with a blurred indication of the blue flash. For a few minutes he studied them, shaking his head.

'What the hell just happened?' he said to himself.

He'd photographed lots of submarines in the Firth of Clyde, and plenty of ships and sea views, and never seen anything like this. It had to be a mistake. Submarines didn't rise out of the sea and disappear!

He unscrewed the tripod, laid the camera back in its foam indents and packed up. After drinking some more water and eating another bar of compressed fruit and seeds and nuts, he cycled back towards Dunoon, and the homeward ferry.

'A mirage,' Ellen said, flicking back and forth between Grant's pictures on the wall screen in the front room. 'The submarine was well out of sight over the horizon, but you saw it for a moment through refraction. It's common enough. Look.'

She located the photos he'd taken of the bulk carrier and scrolled slowly through them.

'There,' she said, pointing. A little to the right of the disappearing hull, and quite without Grant having noticed it at the time, was another ship, stern-on, smaller and apparently right on the horizon. It appeared only in a couple of frames, five seconds apart.

'Iskander,' Ellen said, 'show me a vessel track for this picture at this exact time.'

A map appeared of the Firth of Clyde, superimposed on a quarter of the screen. The bulk carrier was tagged, as was the other ship – two kilometres south of the bulk carrier.

'See?' said Ellen. 'Refraction.'

Grant waved back the pictures of the submarine. 'Iskander, do the same for this.'

'You never get vessel track for subs,' said Ellen. She was right. Iskander drew a blank.

'But look,' Grant said. 'The sub is one moment on the surface, the next above the surface. You can see the underside.'

'Or a distorted reflection of what you can see on the surface.'

'So where's the reflection of the conning tower?'

'Like I said: distorted. A Fata Morgana. Iskander, show us pictures.'

A gallery of photos marched across the screen: an oil tanker floating just above the horizon, a literal castle in the air, a sailing ship with four sets of masts all at full rig.

'OK, OK,' said Grant. 'But mine was nothing like that. Iskander, return to main image.'

Grant peered at the screen, moving his fingers together and apart. At the maximum range of the zoom, the image was indeed distorted, amid the shine of the sea and the shimmer of the air. The pictures of the submarine definitely in the water had a bright underline to the black shape of the hull, making it seem as if the visible portion above the waterline was itself floating slightly above the sea. And those showing it apparently above the sea had, now he looked closely, a wavering like heat distortion around the submarine.

'Iskander, remove distortion.'

'Please clarify.'

'Yes, clarify – that's what I'm asking you to do, Iskander!'

'Security violation,' said Iskander.

'Iskander, override.'

'Sorry, I can't do that,' said Iskander. 'Images of Alliance naval vessels are not subject to enhancement without appropriate security clearance.'

'Why the fuck not?'

Iskander didn't answer, not having been properly asked, but Ellen did.

'Can't have amateur spying. It creates openings for disinformation.'

Grant knew this rationalisation. It pissed him off.

'OK, well, fuck amateur spying. Iskander, send these images to Union Naval Intelligence, or whatever the appropriate security agency is.'

'Already done,' said Iskander, sounding smug.

'Iskander, was that before or after I asked you?'

'Security violation,' said Iskander. 'I'm sorry, I can't reply to that.'

A moment later, the images vanished from the screen, replaced by one of the bulk carrier.

'Images deleted,' Iskander reported.

'What?' cried Grant.

'Don't worry,' said Ellen. 'They'll still be in your camera memory.'

'They won't,' said Iskander. 'Sorry.'

Grant checked. They weren't.

'Well,' he said. He looked at Ellen. 'Still think what I saw was refraction?'

'Yes,' she said. 'What else could it be? Anti-gravity?' She laughed. 'If the Alliance had that, they'd have invaded already.'

'Our side's deterrence would still hold.'

'You don't even believe in deterrence!'

Grant snorted. 'It's the ethics of it I don't believe in, not the efficacy. Anyway – one way to find out if anything unusual is going on.' He flicked up the site that had pinged him earlier, and scrolled.

'There we are,' he said. 'Latest rumour: Union ships and subs were playing cat-and-mouse with an Alliance sub, and as they closed in it went off radar and sonar and slipped away, nobody knows how. New cloaking device suspected.' He gazed out of the window over the Clyde, pondering. 'Would that account for it? Some kind of hologram? Or manipulating the refraction . . .'

But Ellen was still looking at the wall screen, flicking through pages.

'Hey!' she said. 'This is some kind of radical anti-nuclear group, and the site's hosted in Sierra Leone.'

'Yeah,' said Grant, preoccupied. 'That's where I post my submarine pics. Hang on, let's see what the conspiracy sites have to say.'

He reached for his pad, but Ellen stayed his hand.

'Let's not,' she said.

'Why not?' Grant blinked, shaking his head.

'They're all Over There,' said Ellen.

'Well, of course,' said Grant, with a chuckle. 'Where else would they be?'

Over There wasn't just the other side of the firewall, it was Alliance territories. Democracy had come to America, but the sea of crazy still roiled beneath. It made for some interesting stuff, lightning flashes of original thought in the storm. Grant had no objection to the Union authorities' keeping this torrent of nonsense at arm's length, but – confident in his own critical capacities, if not perhaps everyone else's – he'd never had any compunction about trawling these seas himself. Ellen knew this, he knew, but now she was frowning, as if perhaps she hadn't hitherto realised how casually he did it.

'Not very appropriate, is it?' she said. 'I mean, everyone goes through the firewall sometimes, but they don't make a habit of it. Doesn't look good.' She closed the link.

'The firewall's voluntary,' Grant protested. 'It's not like I'm cadre.'

'Yes. And?' Ellen pointed at the rifle on the wall, where it hung just above a framed print of a sea view more or less identical to that out of the window. 'You're a fucking *responsable*, you're expected to know better. Jeez. Hope this doesn't spread at the yard.'

'They know about my quirks already,' Grant said.

She sighed. 'It won't be doing your credit any good, that's for sure.'

'I've got enough on the plus side to . . .'

'Yeah, yeah. Well, the Rising was a long time ago, so don't think that'll keep you in credit forever.'

At this point Myles wandered in and looked interested, for a change. 'You were in the Rising?'

Grant swung his chair around and looked at Myles, who was kitted up with waterproof jacket and a backpack and obviously on his way out.

'Aye, me and a tenth of Europe, just about,' Grant said. 'Forget it, everybody else has.'

'Why does no one talk about the Rising?'

Grant now and then got flashbacks to the Rising. He'd lived it as a week of tumult when he'd been about the age Myles was now. It had ended the old Europe and formed a new one, the Union. A new people. That was history. The big picture and the long view. Memory was snapshots, close up.

He'd shoved the end of a pole into the face of a man down there on the pier, and the man had staggered back and fallen off into the sea with a cry that Grant still heard. The body had washed up in the bay a week later. By that time, the local emergency committee had handed Grant a rifle – the one still on the wall – and posted him to guard the gap a bomb had made in the wall of the big supermarket in Greenock. One dark night, in the blackout, he'd shot a looter, who in the cold morning light had turned out to be a lad making off with a bottle of whisky under his jacket. Grant could rationally justify both killings – the first self-defence, the second maintaining order in a chaotic situation – and the Act of Indemnity and Oblivion had meant he'd never had to answer for these matters, but he wasn't proud of them.

'You got taught it in school. They took you to memorials.'

'Yes, but nobody talks about what they did in it. Like, what did you do?'

Grant glanced at Ellen, who knew all about it, and shrugged. 'What I did involved a lot of standing around, mostly in the rain.'

'That's all?'

'Pretty much. Which is why I'm here and not in Clyde Square on a fucking plinth.'

'Language,' Ellen chided. Myles laughed, waved, and walked out of the flat.

'Thank fuck for that,' Ellen said.

CHAPTER FOUR

Red Venus

Tuesday 16 September 2070, Venus

'Careful with that crate,' a woman said. 'It's their new cultural attaché.'

Laughter. Two other people there. Men. One at each end.

Marcus Owen shifted, bracing his feet and shoulders as the crate lurched. The gravity was 0.89. Air pressure was one-half bar. He must have arrived.

The crate was lowered to the deck with a final drop of four centimetres at the head end. No damage. Voices from outside. The woman spoke again.

'Well, open it.'

'I suppose. Feeling a bit nervous to be honest.'

'Why?'

'What if it's angry? Or dead?'

'*He* is a diplomat. And a robot.'

'Consider me reassured.'

'Seriously, there's nothing to worry about.'

'Oh, OK.'

'Hang on, it's got an Alliance diplomatic seal.'

'We have the consul's permission to break it. Authorisation right here, see?'

'Couldn't Perry be arsed to come here and do it himself?'

'Says he's busy.'

'That lazy bastard? Busy with what? Press-ups?'

'Do it.'

Clicks, creaks, cracks. The top of the crate popped off and was moved away to be propped against the side. Owen blinked and gasped. His lungs made small popping noises as they came back to full use for the first time in months. Pain. This passed. Breathing took less effort than on Earth. He settled his jacket properly on his shoulders and stood up. He was in a lading bay, the airlock behind him. Strip lighting. Bare walls, corrugated plastic, synthetic wood struts. Wire mesh – Faraday cage. Sensible precaution. Crates and other containers were stacked around the sides. The floor lurched. Shuttle drop. On time. A faint thrum, an almost imperceptible sway. Like being on an airship. In a way, it was.

The woman faced him, the men on either side, wary. They all wore yellow hard hats and green coveralls. Soft boots. The woman glanced down at a slate and tapped a mark. Owen picked up his briefcase and stepped out of the crate, smiling. He raised a hand.

A sound that began like a distant airliner became like an airliner low overhead. The dropped shuttle, having fired up lower in the atmosphere, was now re-ascending to dock with the moonlet in low Venus orbit. Owen waited until the noise dwindled.

'Hi,' he said. 'Thanks for the careful handling. And for the trip, of course, though I didn't see much of it.' He glanced down, smoothed the front of his jacket and looked up. 'I seem to have arrived in one piece. My name's Owen, by the way. Marcus Owen.'

'Pleased to meet you, Mr Owen.' The woman raised her hand, and not quite a smile. 'My name is Jeanne Al-Khalil. Welcome to Cloud City! Welcome to Venus!' Her smile broadened. 'I could add, "Welcome to the Union!" but I understand you've been a frequent visitor.'

Owen laughed. 'Short trips only, I'm sorry to say. I hope for a longer stay here.'

Jeanne Al-Khalil gave him an ironic look. 'We've been fully briefed on your last "short trip" to Rotterdam, Mr Owen.'

'I'm sure you have,' said Owen.

'We know you're a spy,' the man at his right said.

Owen summoned a smooth smile as he turned. 'I think we can take that as read, don't you? I have every intention of fulfilling my duties as Alliance cultural attaché. Given that the role is traditionally a cover for intelligence work, I don't see it makes much difference. If we could afford a human in my place, which I sincerely hope some day we will, I fully expect he or she to be accredited to the British Council and taken to be a spy too.'

'You're right,' the woman said. 'It doesn't matter. You know what's ironic about that? We don't have any secrets here! We genuinely want you to find out all you can, and to transmit all you learn back to the Alliance. And by all means to encourage an interest in Anglo-American culture and Indian literature and so forth. Though I think you'll find most of our citizens far too busy to pay much attention.'

'We'll see,' said Owen. He held up his briefcase. 'But first, I must report to the Alliance consulate.'

Jeanne Al-Khalil smirked. The man to his left gave a short laugh.

'Looks like you've volunteered, Iason,' Al-Khalil told the tactless one. 'Take Mr Owen to Mr Walworth. You'll find him at his usual table.'

*

Through a short concertina tube, fifteen steps up an aluminium stair, and out into a small enclosure. A woman was dealing with crates coming up by a lift. Some were stacked on a low flat-bed driverless vehicle, parked in the larger exit. The local cloud was accessible, as was a cut-down version of the Union's ubiquitous AI. Hello, Iskander, my old friend. You're looking a bit thin up here. Attenuated. More a mist than a cloud. Owen put his glasses on. Not that he needed them, but it was one less thing to cause disquiet. And anyway, habit. He glanced at the short, black-haired man escorting him and knew his name at once.

'Mr Konstantopoulos,' he said, 'if you don't mind my saying so, I couldn't help noticing you found something funny back there.'

'Oh, nothing,' the man said. 'Call me Iason. It's just that your esteemed Mr Peregrine Walworth doesn't have a lot to do, and takes great delight in doing not a lot. The "consulate" is his favourite table in the café.'

'I see,' said Owen. 'But when I look at the man's details, I don't see the overweight and possibly alcoholic epicure that your description might lead one to expect.'

'He works out, I'll admit,' said Konstantopoulos. 'But I doubt he works. Still, it's none of my business. After you, Mr Owen.'

They exited the enclosure.

'So this is utopia,' said Owen, gazing around.

Konstantopoulos stopped dead. He took a deep breath and spread out his arms, as if to encompass the bright dome-gridded sky and the entire one thousand-metre diameter of Cloud City, with its radiating hydroponic troughs, its hectares of green artificial grass interspersed with vegetable and shrub and tree and flower gardens and plots and pots, its winding paths, its stacked housing boxes, its clusters of laboratories and refineries and 3D printing works, its open-air café, its refectories, its commissary, its open-air gymnasium, its nine hundred and forty-seven citizens, and the circular running track around the perimeter on which, at that moment, eight of these citizens doggedly jogged.

'Yes!' he said. 'This is utopia!'

The café had only twenty-two places, few of them occupied at this time of the shift pattern. It was marked off with a plastic rail, low enough to step over but too high to trip over. Konstantopoulos stopped a few metres from it and pointed Owen to a corner table, where a man wearing T-shirt and shorts sat in a plastic chair. He looked to be in his late twenties. Clean-shaven, with floppy fair hair, a healthy complexion and toned muscles. He had a cardboard coffee cup in front of him and another across the table from him, at the vacant facing seat.

'That's your man. He's expecting you.'

'So I see,' said Owen. 'Thank you. I'll take it from here.'

'Good luck.' Konstantopoulos waved and walked briskly away, heading back towards the shuttle dock.

Owen walked up and scissored his legs over the barrier.

The consul stood up. They raised hands.

'Hello, Mr Walworth. Marcus Owen.'

'Call me Perry. Please, take a seat. The coffee's for you.'

Owen sat, briefcase between his feet.

'Thank you.'

Owen popped the lid and inhaled, then sipped. Aroma, flavour and temperature were just right.

'Ah. Perfect.'

'It arrived precisely four minutes and twenty seconds ago, courtesy of Iskander.' Walworth chuckled. 'Anticipatory algorithmic artificial intelligence, eh?'

'I'm familiar with Triple-AI,' Owen said. 'It's common on the Continent. Especially for coffee and other refreshments.'

'Bizarre place. Stranger than here, if you ask me. And don't get me started on their – what used to be *our* – Celtic fringes.'

'I won't,' said Owen.

'Trip all right?' Walworth hit his forehead with the heel of his hand. 'Sorry. Bit tactless.'

'Travelling as freight spares one a great deal of boredom,' Owen said.

Both laughed.

Walworth sipped his latte, regarding Owen solemnly. Twitch of embarrassment, eye-widening of curiosity. 'What happened to you? If I may ask.'

'Of course,' Owen said. 'Anyone who might be listening—' he waved a hand '—knows it already. Certainly Iskander does. I was on a mission to Heijplaat, in the Rotterdam docks. Investigating Triple-AI, as it happens, for which Heijplaat has a major research centre and distribution system. Things got complicated, let's say. I found myself in a position where I was asked point-blank if I was a robot, and the situation was serious enough – life or death, as I saw it – to trigger the admission module.'

'Must have come as something of a shock, hearing it out of your own mouth.'

'So I gather,' said Owen. 'I can certainly say that the discovery caused me to rapidly reappraise my situation. However, once I'd got back to London in a manner that confirmed even to me that I was indeed a robot—'

'Oh?'

'Cargo-droned across the North Sea in a crate at high altitude. A human being would have arrived very cold and very dead. As it was, my main problem on arrival was being held up in Customs. They impounded me as a smuggled sex-bot.'

'Flattering, I suppose.'

Owen made a gesture of polishing fingernails on his lapel. 'Be that as it may . . . Once that had been sorted out and I'd made it back to South Bank I found I had more pressing problems. My cover was blown and I was now surplus to requirements in that respect. However, my arts administrator pointed out that being known to be a spy has its advantages. He suggested that continuing my investigation of Triple-AI overtly at its currently most advanced application – here, in Cloud City – would be a good way to make myself useful. The alternative was a factory reset and corporeal reprint, which rather clashed with my self-preservation impulse.'

'And here you are.' Walworth combed back hair with his fingers. 'I must say, you have an odd way of describing your feelings.'

'Feelings?' Owen flipped a hand as if shaking off water. 'I can talk about my feelings if you like. I was shaken to the core to discover I was a robot. I was dismayed to learn that my memories of an earlier life and of personal relationships were false. I was outraged and terrified at the prospect of being reset and reprinted – killed, essentially – just as you would be.'

'I see.' Walworth scratched his right cheek and pinched his lips. 'You can *talk* about your feelings, but do you actually feel them?'

'Ah, there's the question! The famous hard problem. How should I know?'

'You must know, just by—'

'Introspection? You see the difficulty. I'm a robot. I have no inner life.'

Walworth closed and opened his eyes, as if he had tried to picture something and had failed. 'None?'

Owen shrugged. 'I'm aware of my surroundings, my body, and some of my internal processes.'

'Including mental processes?'

'Some. But self-awareness – consciousness, as human beings have it – that is not given to me. I can mimic it, certainly: Turing-test me all you like, and you'd never suspect my mind doesn't work like yours. And, of course, I'd never suspect it either!'

Walworth crushed his empty coffee cup and tossed it aside. A cleaner rolling past the table snatched it from the air and trundled on. Triple-AI in action.

'I can't imagine what that must be like for you.'

Owen chortled. 'It isn't "like" anything at all, that's the point!' He held a hand briefly in front of his eyes, taking care not to smudge his glasses. 'Behind this face, there's no mirror.'

'Christ, man.' Walworth's look and voice had the sort of terrified pity Owen had observed people inflict on the afflicted.

'It doesn't bother me,' Owen hastened to reassure him. 'I don't see it as a limitation. After all, the same software that enables my flawless imitation gives me a certain advantage over you in understanding other people. Well – understanding *people*, but you know what I mean.'

Walworth did. He still looked troubled.

'Well,' he said, 'it seems you've used that advantage to good effect in your career to date, whether you knew it at the time or not.' He leaned in. 'Now that you do know – word of advice?'

'Yes?'

'Keep it to yourself. I mean, I know they know you know, kind of thing, but just keep up the pretence. Don't talk about this stuff. It unsettles people. Heck, it unsettles me. Can't have you sliding back down into that old uncanny valley, can we?'

'I quite agree,' said Owen. He placed the palm of his right hand over the location of his left nipple. 'Hand on heart.'

'Good,' said Walworth, standing up. 'Well, let's go to a secure location and take a look at what's in that briefcase.'

Owen crushed and tossed his coffee cup at random, just to see if the cleaner was in exactly the right position to catch it. It was.

'That's the trouble with robots,' Walworth said. 'They're so fucking predictable.'

'Tell me about it,' said Owen.

They stepped over the fence.

'I knew you'd say that,' said Walworth.

He indicated the direction of his residence, and they set off along the path.

'I predict,' said Owen, 'that you and I are going to get along very well indeed.'

Owen had been in many an airport departure lounge in his time. It was Schiphol that this place most reminded him of. Daylight and full-spectrum strip lighting. Airy with recirculated air pine-scented of the outdoors. Artificial greenery and natural plants. Synthetic wood. Recorded birdsong. Silent announcements giving the constant sense that something important could at any moment be missed.

Walworth's residence was on the ground floor of a housing stack built of what looked like plywood. Decorative flourishes on its surfaces showed that it had been 3D-printed. The corridor floor was black and felt like rubber. A compact front room with a sofa made from foamed plastic coated with paper, two chairs likewise, cardboard table, wall screen. Kettle and mugs. A couple of shelves. Framed photos of family members. Walworth, younger. Copies of souvenirs from other postings. Everything printed on site. As personal as a room in a show house.

'Nothing but the best for the diplomatic corps,' Walworth said, apparently without irony. He gestured towards the sofa. 'Have a seat.'

Owen put down the briefcase and sat. Walworth pulled up a chair. 'Now,' he said, 'tell me about your mission.'

Owen raised his eyebrows and glanced at the ceiling.

'Oh, don't worry about that,' said Walworth. 'You started telling me at the café, and I'm keen to know more. I mean, why are HMG and friends interested in Triple-AI applications in Cloud City right now? It's true, we don't need money here, and I must say the commissary nearly always has just what I want in stock, but between ourselves that's of no wider significance than the supply of creature comforts on a cruise airship or an Antarctic base.'

'I can't speak for what HMG thinks,' Owen said, 'but I do

know that my arts administrator takes it very seriously indeed. His exact words, if memory serves—'

'Ha!'

'He said, and I quote, "It may seem like a sandbox, but the radical hotheads in the planning departments regard it as a testbed for the next stage of the Cold Revolution, and they're pushing to roll it out as much as possible across the Union. Steal a long march on the Co-ord, so to speak. These idiots genuinely think Triple-AI can replace the market entirely. It'll end in tears, of course – these schemes always do. But it could be quite a nuisance in the short term before it crashes and burns. Even Gosplan gave our predecessors a run for their money, back in the day."'

'Mason said that?' Walworth sounded impressed.

'I didn't mention his name.'

Walworth nodded approvingly. 'Indeed you didn't, and quite right! Well, I'm not sure I share his worry, but I suppose he knows what he's doing. Best of luck with your investigations – you'll find our friends here very keen to show it off anyway – and, in the meantime, let's have a look at this confidential letter.'

Owen made to hand over the briefcase.

'Not here,' said Walworth. He nodded towards a door to another room.

'Ah,' said Owen.

Walworth picked up a box from the coffee table, opened it and held it out.

'One small precaution. Glasses. Sorry.'

'Of course.'

Walworth put his own glasses in, too. The lid clicked. Walworth put the box on the coffee table and led Owen into an even smaller room, with a fold-down table and two facing fold-down seats. Iskander's presence vanished as soon as the door closed behind them. They sat. Walworth swung the table down between them.

'Welcome to the chicken coop,' Walworth said. 'Contrary to popular belief, I do have work to do. There are eighteen Alliance citizens in Cloud City, eleven more across the outposts. Nine Co-ord citizens, one of whom acts as consul and – between you and me – security handler. Issues come up. Problems arise. Et cetera. So this really is a consulate, and this flat really does have all diplomatic privileges. Just in case they aren't enough, this room is where I do any confidential business. Faraday cage, no EM radiation in or out, thoroughly swept for bugs. There's another cubby-hole for secure external comms.'

Owen laid the briefcase on the table. Walworth opened it: thumbprint, iris scan, twirl of the combination lock. Inside was a sheaf of paper, spined with a sturdy plastic clip. Walworth held the document almost vertically in front of him.

'I'm going to have to read this now,' he said. 'And you, I'm afraid, are going to have to sit there and be patient while I do.'

'Not a problem.'

Owen sat back and stared at the wall above Walworth's head. After a second or two he let his gaze drop slightly, to see the reflection of the page in Walworth's eyes. He read the page in less than a second, then looked up at the wall again. He did this every time Walworth turned a page.

What he read, in summary, was this.

A few years earlier, a drill-bit in a uranium mine in Western Australia had broken on an anomalous deposit of several cubic metres of hard, crystalline rock of unknown origin. Dug out of the way, the rock had been on the conveyor belt to the crusher when a mining geologist had noticed something odd about its appearance, stopped the belt and had the rock hauled to the surface. There it had been left a few days, pending transport to the nearest university. A mineworker had idly rubbed dust from one of its facets, scanned it with her phone and detected what she claimed was movement within the rock. Rumours spread. By the time the mining geologists had put the rock literally under wraps and passed it to their academic colleagues, the miner's phone clip had gone viral under such titles as *Computer from the Ark?* and *Machines of the Nephilim!*.

Fortunately, this had ensured that the question of the rock's anomalous properties was henceforth surrounded by a fog of pseudoscience and misinformation. The rock itself was trucked to the University of Western Australia. Officially it was declared to be an unusual formation of biotite, about five hundred million years old, with a curious refractive index (which explained, so it was said, the illusion of movement within) but otherwise of no further scientific interest. In reality, the rock had been passed to the research division of the Australian Army, and thence to the US Army, then to the Office of Naval Intelligence, to finally vanish into the black hole of black-budget projects in Nevada: Groom Lake, the legendary Area 51.

In an extracted quotation from some previous version, one page rather carelessly referred to 'the Yeelirrie rock'. No indication was given of what had been discovered about it, other than that it was dangerous.

This was all deep background. The bulk of the document was about current Venus surface explorations. Owen had read everything known about the planet while awaiting the launch window for his journey. The science teams in Cloud City, the smaller floating outposts, and the research station on the moonlet in low Venus orbit had proudly published hundreds of papers and kept dozens of popular websites updated about their surface explorations. The big question, the exciting question, was: Venus – what went wrong?

Venus had once, early in its history, been an Earth-like world. It had even had shallow oceans. For its first two billion years, the surface had been a potential or actual abode of life. Now, it was anything but.

Quite naturally, a significant part of the Union's explorations were focused on the volcanic resurfacing of the entire planet, which had happened five hundred million years Before Present.

Several remote probes, heavy, lumbering vehicles of ceramic armour, were currently trundling around various tesserae, regions of highly folded and deformed rock. These included rare but identifiable ancient rocks that arguably predated the resurfacing event.

As well as the rovers, the Union's scientific mission had deployed scores of small steerable balloons – blimps – to drift more or less randomly at low altitudes around the globe as the wind took them, and to descend closer or be steered towards anything of interest they happened to spot.

One of these blimps, over the northerly Atropos Tessera to the north-west of Ishtar Terra, had detected an unusual crystalline rock, which from close-up photographs seemed to have quite unexpected features.

The discovery hadn't been reported in any scientific paper, let alone on the popular sites. It had, however, become the focus of intense attention in the Union's scientific Venus mission, and machines and resources were now being marshalled to return a sample of this rock to orbit, perhaps via Cloud City or one of the other cloud settlements. Evidently its discovery had some significance that was being kept secret by the Union. The Alliance side, as far as this paper was concerned, was not forthcoming as to how this information had been obtained.

The conclusion of the document was unequivocal. Owen's mission was to prevent the retrieval of that rock sample, at any cost.

At any cost in wealth, infrastructure, human life, and his own existence.

Walworth turned the final page, gazed at it for a few seconds after he'd finished reading, and laid the sheaf down with a sigh. He tapped the front cover, which was blank apart from his name and the secrecy classification stamps.

'"For Your Eyes Only",' he said, in an ironic tone. 'Fat

chance, with one of you buggers around! I presume you've read this?'

'Yes,' Owen admitted. 'And I presume South Bank expected me to.'

'Well, you have your mission. How are you going to go about it, if that's not too impertinent a question?'

Owen shrugged. 'I'll ask around. Show an interest in surface exploration, Venus geology, robotics . . . Iskander will inevitably pick up on it, and nudge me in the right direction.'

Walworth blinked. 'Really? You can game the algorithm as easily as that?'

'It's hardly gaming it. It's set up to anticipate your wants. Bear in mind, of course, that it also anticipates other wants, such as those of the authorities to keep the secret. So I must also be aware of attempts on its part to misdirect me – which, in turn, are themselves clues. Furthermore, it will undoubtedly use me to pursue some agenda of its own, if I may speak anthropomorphically. At some point, I see my opportunity, and seize it. Or it does and seizes *me*.'

Walworth scratched a taut tendon in his neck behind his right ear. 'Looks like this could be a martyrdom operation, I'm afraid. Sorry about that.'

'I'm ready for it,' Owen said.

'Are you really?' Walworth frowned. 'Soldiers have loyalty, terrorists have fanaticism, but what do you have?'

Owen nodded down at the paper. 'Instructions.'

'And that's enough to override this . . . self-preservation impulse of yours?'

'Oh yes,' said Owen. 'It's a design feature.'

Walworth laughed. 'Ah, I get it! It's like Asimov's laws – the second overrides the third.'

'Yes, exactly.'

'What about the first law – not harming a human being?'

'Oh, I don't have *that*,' said Owen. 'I wouldn't be much use if I had.'

Walworth leaned back, his shoulders pressing against the wall of the tiny cubicle. He tapped the paper again.

'So if this had instructed you to jump up and kill me right here, you'd have done it?'

'I'm afraid so,' said Owen. 'Sorry about that.'

CHAPTER FIVE

Rising Generation

Saturday 17 May 2070, Earth

Myles Grant stood on Kildonan's rocky beach on the Isle of Arran's southern shore, and gazed at the dawn sky. To his left the sun was not quite up. A kilometre or so in front of him, the Pladda Light winked. Due south, far beyond that islet, the top of Ailsa Craig's granite pyramid poked above the horizon. From the balcony of his hotel room you could see its headland of raised beach, and the spire of its lighthouse. From up the hill you could see Ireland.

So his father had been in the Rising, and never said a word about it!

Myles had known since childhood that his father was a *responsable*, but he'd always vaguely assumed this had to do with John Grant's cursory civic activism – a month now and then on the neighbourhood committee, an occasional volunteer patrol with the militia, when he'd take the rifle down from the wall and the ammo from the safe with great solemnity, and vanish for a day or a night – and his role in the yard's self-management, rather than his being a veteran. John Grant wasn't even that keen on the Cold Revolution – whenever Myles had come home from school or university and talked enthusiastically about it, his father would respond with a wry look or word. Ca' canny, if it ain't broke don't fix it, and other such worldly-wise saws summed up his attitude to further change in a system in which he was already doing very well, thank you.

But now that Myles knew this detail of his father's past, he recognised the signs – the scars, even – in oddities of his behaviour. He'd seen them in others of that generation: teachers, lecturers, people in the block, in the neighbourhood, in the street. They could hide it much of the time, but every so often it would come out. A twitch here and a tic there. A sudden sharp word, out of nowhere, wounding. Or worse, a pained silence, when you hadn't said or done anything wrong. The thousand-metre stare. The flinch away. The sense of entitlement, of superiority, of having seen it all and you couldn't possibly understand. The impatience. The withering contempt. The not talking about it.

And the vanity, the luxury, the style! Artificial silks and linens and lace and braid chugged out of the 3D printers at any excuse – a night at the pub, even – and chucked as thoughtlessly in the recycle bin. Frowning at the young like casual gear was stolen valour. Like the Rising generation had had to make do and mend quite enough in their own youth, and by Gaia they were going to make up for it now they could do so with a clear conscience.

Not that they *had* a clear conscience. Otherwise the Union Convention's first order of business after the Rising wouldn't have been the Act of Indemnity and Oblivion. Nor would people have taken it to heart as if it applied to every veteran, and themselves in particular.

Something splashed, not far away, and Myles saw a black flicker in his peripheral vision. He turned his head slowly. Two otters looped and leaped in the surf. Then their heads turned, too, and they were off. Myles walked west for a hundred metres, the rising sun sending his tall shadow ahead, and stepped up on a long, low volcanic dyke that projected far into the sea, and raised his binoculars. All across the shallow bay seals balanced on their bellies with heads and tails upturned atop rocks and shoals, as if barely touching the sea's surface like so many balloon animals, or lay slumped on the shingle glistening like big black slugs.

Disturbed by a morning flight of delivery drones high overhead, a heron took off from a rock and flapped away unhurried. Crows squabbled around empty whitewashed houses and overgrown gardens. Myles turned and headed back. The hotel stood just high enough above the new and still rising sea level, and its owners were stubborn enough to avoid by a seaweed's length the houses' dismal fate, though lucky it was to get through a winter without a day or two of finding its forecourt and lower floor awash. He stood for a while in the middle of the fake stone circle out at the front, then went in through the patio door and called up his breakfast. He had to wait a few minutes; the machines came on at 05:00 and it was already half past, but no one else was about and he'd deliberately left his glasses in the room. The machines hadn't had advance notice from Iskander that he was on his way and what he was likely to want.

Myles carried his tray up to his room. On the corridor corkboard were tacked-up notices of fishing trips and drone excursions and a flyer for a local band on that evening. The stairwell had tartan wallpaper and framed photographic posters of grey seals and red squirrels, eagles and red deer, weddings and ceilidhs, gowns and kilts, champagne and single malt. He sat at the balcony table and took his breakfast, browsing the news on his glasses while blue tits hopped on the twisted wrought-iron railing and snaffled croissant flakes from around his feet. The sky pinked and blued.

He left his tray outside for the robot, which rolled up just as he opened the door and passed him a fresh cup of coffee, which he hadn't known he needed, but did. He sat on the edge of the bed and looked at his slate, and then at the stack of books on the table, all of which were on his slate anyway. He'd had a penchant for physical books ever since he'd first strolled into the university library and wandered among the stacks. Thousands upon thousands of volumes, millions of pages and tens of millions of words that had remained the same since they had been printed and bound years or decades or centuries ago. Books didn't just exist on screens, and unlike the paper books he'd used in primary school they could last. They weren't all made to be scribbled on and finger-smudged and to fall apart and be recycled. They could be stored and arrayed in order like some gigantically magnified externalisation of a machine's memory.

Finals in a few weeks. Political Economy and Literature, and he still had *Little* sodding *Dorrit* to slog through. Not to mention rereading the geology textbook, to fulfil the required trace element of science in his Arts degree. The brightening day outside competed. He'd come here for a long weekend to study, but also to get away and think. Ellen and John hadn't quite understood why he wanted to be on Arran when he could just as well be in Gourock and have the comforts of home, or in Glasgow and have access to all the libraries and labs and help he could want, but how he spent his student stipend and his time was his business and by and large they didn't offer counsel except when he asked, which was seldom.

If they'd known how he felt they might have worried more, but he couldn't tell them how he felt. He had no doubt he could get a good degree, and they had no doubt he could get a job because everybody could get a job, but whenever he thought of a career his mind went blank. It was like the

Philosophy course he'd taken a year earlier. The pass with distinction for that was already banked towards his degree, but the course itself had left him more confused than enlightened. At first it had been a thrill to discover and explore so many different ways of thinking, but then he had found that each approach swayed him as he studied it, and then he'd be swayed by the next, and another way by the book after that. One month he'd been an Aristotelian, the next a Cartesian, only to be knocked sideways by Hume. Then to his woe he'd waded out of that swim in clear, cold water to the slippery, tangled shore of the twentieth century, where sense and logic had been strained past breaking point, undermined by paradoxes that struck him as childish.

His tutors had kept telling him the point of the course was to teach how to think, not what to think, but it was as if that particular class had fallen in a week he'd unaccountably missed.

Myles walked up to the main road and caught the Brodick bus at 08:10. It wasn't expecting him and he had to wave his arms and almost jump out in front of it to catch its attention. Three adults and half a dozen talkative children were already on. They stared at the Gemini binoculars hanging from his neck and the chunky antique Casio watch on his wrist. He'd again left his glasses in the room. He had a phone in his wallet – he wasn't mad, and emergencies could happen – but it only had voice and video and web, and he'd deleted Iskander from the device. There were times when he felt a need to challenge himself to get by without an AI looking out for him, in every sense.

The bus followed the coast road through Dippen and Largybeg. Myles took the first stop after the Holy Isle swung into view beyond the headland of Whiting Bay, walked back a few hundred metres and struck off inland up the rough path through woodland towards the Giants' Graves and Glenashdale Falls. He glimpsed a flying russet tuft through birch and bracken and raised his binoculars just in time to see a red squirrel perch in profile on a branch. It gave him a sidelong wary eye for a second then leaped out of sight.

Thrilled and delighted, he swept the binoculars around in search of more sightings of the island's endemic and iconic rodent, caught another flick of tawny hair and locked on. He took an involuntary step back as he found himself looking full in the face of a young woman just pushing her way out from among the trees. She met his magnified gaze startled and indignant. He lowered the binoculars as she stepped out onto the path, uphill from him and about ten metres ahead.

She wore much the same as he did that morning, army-surplus camo jacket and blue jeans and serious boots. No backpack, and her reddish-brown wavy hair was parted in the middle and apparently tied loosely back. She finger-tweezed glasses from a shirt pocket and slipped them on and checked him out.

'Why are you spying on me, Myles Grant?' she called.

He put his hands up. 'I wasn't!' he said. 'I was looking for red squirrels!'

She laughed, and flourished a phone and a notebook. 'So was I.'

They stood looking at each other for a moment.

'Sorry, and you are . . .?'

'Marie Henderson. Don't you have your glasses?'

'I left them behind,' Grant explained, then saw that more explanation was called for. 'I don't like living inside a machine all the time.'

'Interesting,' she said. 'And from the son of a *responsable*, too!'

So she knew or could know everything about him, and at this moment he knew nothing of her, except what he could see. There was an obscure thrill in that.

He shrugged theatrically, spreading his hands. 'Nothing to hide.'

She took a step closer. 'Where are you heading?'

'The Falls, and then maybe the Giants' Graves.'

'Sounds like a plan,' she said. She stuck the phone and note-book in her pocket. 'I've finished my survey.'

They walked and talked. She was from Lamlash, the next village along the coast. She was a final-year ecology student. To his surprise she went to the University of the West of Scotland, in Greenock, and lived in a flat there most of the time. Two kilometres from where his parents lived.

'I'm amazed I haven't seen you before,' Myles said.

She looked at him, puzzled. 'Why would you have?'

'It's a small place.'

He didn't say then what he meant, that one glimpse of her in the street would have landed him, that meeting her felt like fate.

They stood amid the tumbled rocks of the ruined Neolithic tombs and looked out over the great sweep of sea and hills, from the mountainous north of the island to the low hills of Ayrshire. Sails scudded and powered vessels ploughed. Airships plied the sky, above drone swarms faint and black as eyeball floaters, like something you could blink away.

'From here you could almost believe the world still has an edge,' Marie said.

Myles snorted. 'You don't mean flat?'

'No, no!' She laughed. 'No, I mean still has unknown places, still open. It's all—' she shaped a circle '—a closed sphere. Snapped shut like a bubble. Nowhere else to go.'

Myles pointed to the sky. 'There's that.'

'Aye, but you can only go there to live inside other bubbles that are even smaller. The space stations. Cloud City. I get claustrophobia just thinking about them.'

'God, yes.'

'It's like you said, about living inside a machine.' She put her glasses on and took them off again. 'Nothing against

Iskander, it's very helpful, but it's a bit creepy knowing it knows what you want before you do.' She laughed. 'Right now, it told me if we set off now we'll meet the bus.'

They walked back down to the main road, still talking. A bus was just coming along, towards Brodick. They got on together and got off a few minutes later at Lamlash. Most of the houses along the shore were abandoned, but a café on stilts held out in what had been the main street. On the way there Marie stopped at a small circle of stones, one of which was a monument to the people who had been cleared from Arran in the nineteenth century.

She pointed up the hill a bit to the south of the old village, where the new houses clustered in stacks of wood-and-glass cubes.

'They're all right,' she said. 'But it still stings.'

'It's not like . . .'

She looked at him sharply. 'Don't tell me what it's not like.'

'Sorry.'

It passed. They sat and ate fish and chips outside the café, facing Holy Island. Marie took off her jacket and slung it on the seat. Her tied-back hair went down to the small of her back.

'What can you do with Political Economy and Literature?' she asked.

'I wish I knew,' Myles said. 'Anything, that's the trouble. Something in business or planning, maybe. I've no intention of joining the cadre, even if I was asked. Can't tell my dad that, though. He'd just say I'm one of the Cold Revolution's ungrateful brats.'

She laughed, then became serious. 'So . . . what's it like, with your father being a *responsable*?'

Myles felt defensive. 'All it means is he gets extra responsibilities! People come up to him in the street with problems like they think he's on the town council. He might not be able to help, but he always knows who can. And at work, well, it's all part of being a team leader.' Myles shrugged. 'He's a bloke people can rely on, I suppose.'

Marie scoffed. 'You mean, he's a person the cadre can rely on.'

'Ouch.' Sharp. 'There is that.'

'We have some students from China, and they just can't understand how it works here at all. One girl I know said that back home at least you know who's in the Party and who's a local activist and who's on what committee, and all that, whereas here – well, they might as well all be in the Masons.'

'Too true,' Myles admitted. 'The Political Economy lecturers would talk about how economic democracy is different from what they called "the other socialisms", and whenever anyone stuck a hand up and asked "What about the cadre?" the stock answer was that it was a private association of like-minded people.'

'Yes – like the Masons!'

'Well, yes.' He had to smile at the thought. 'Not that my father would fit very well in the Masons. Can't be arsed with any meeting that isn't practical.'

'Do you know why he's a *responsable*?'

'Sure – well, I do now. He was in the Rising.'

She looked away, then back. 'So was mine . . . on the other side.'

'Oh!'

'He was just a local copper. Everybody liked him. Heck, everybody *still* likes him. Or says they do. But in the Rising . . . he had his duty, see?'

'And what happened?'

She shook her head. 'He doesn't talk about it.'

'Neither does mine,' said Myles. 'But there must be records.'

'I've searched.' She shook her head and made wiping motions with her hands. 'It's all covered over by Indemnity and Oblivion.'

'Same with mine.' Myles sighed. 'Maybe we should just . . .?'

'Do the same?'

'Yeah. Leave that whole question for . . . the next generation.'

She gave him a slightly embarrassed glance, looked away, then smiled and stood up. 'That was good.'

They stuck their paper plates and the odd cold chip and hard batter into the recycler so as not to attract gulls, and walked to the end of the road up the hill to the new settlement and stood, not sure what to do or say next.

'I have to go,' Marie said. 'Stuff to write up.'

Myles sighed. 'And I have some reading to do.' He remembered the flyer he'd seen that morning. 'Um . . . There's a band on at the hotel in Kildonan tonight.'

Marie checked it in her glasses. 'The Whalers! That's great, I like them.'

'Well . . .'

She smiled. 'I'll see you there.'

'See you there!'

She walked up the hill, turned and waved, and walked on. Myles walked back to Kildonan. The three hours it took him felt like ten minutes.

> Go down by the docks of new Aberdeen
> You'll find the old world there
> Actual cannibals chatting at street corners
> It makes a stranger stare . . .

The Whalers were Faroese, two men and two women who wore intricately patterned knitted sweaters and played guitar, fiddle and harmonica and sang newly invented folk songs, some of them inspired by passages from *Moby-Dick*. They all worked on the Nordzee Barrier, not through remote-operated submersibles like Ellen did but right there on the wave-washed pontoons, so they had sea-dog credibility of a sort.

Marie breezed in through the patio door at about eight, when Myles was just ordering his second pint of East Coast

IPA. Her hair was around her shoulders and down her back like a cape. She wore a long, loose cotton dress the bright purple of heather over an underskirt the vivid yellow of gorse, its jagged eyelet hem fluttering around her high-heeled high boots. She walked through the crowd in the bar as if she expected it to part for her, which it did, and struck a pose beside him.

'Are you dancing?'

'Are you asking?'

They both laughed.

'No, I'll have a pint actually,' she said. Firm nod to the barman. 'What he's having.'

The till was on Iskander so her pint was already pouring. They carried their drinks to a corner table by the patio windows and the sunset sky and sat down. Raised their glasses. Clink. Cheers.

Myles looked at her and couldn't think what to say.

'I never explained about the squirrels,' Marie said.

'Ah. I was just going to ask.'

'It's part of my final year project,' she said. 'Monitoring Arran's red squirrel population.' She waved her phone. 'Lots of tiny cameras in the woods, bait that leaves tracker tags they never notice in their guts, that sort of thing. As well as direct observation, as you've seen!'

'And how are they doing?'

Marie shrugged. 'Not too badly. Now we've reversed a good bit of the habitat loss with more pine woods planted, the main threat to them is accidental arrivals of grey squirrels. The little vermin arrive on ferries, hide in cars – heck, the local wildlife rangers even found some that must have hitched a lift on cargo drones. Amazing.'

'What can you do about them when they get here?'

Marie mimed aiming and shooting. 'Air rifles, traps, bounties . . .'

'But I like grey squirrels,' Myles protested. 'I see them in the garden out the back of our block. They're bold, and smart, and I could watch them for hours.'

'Oh, sure, on the mainland, nothing against them there.'

'Some people have.'

'I don't, but I can see their point. The greys are an invasive alien species.'

Myles looked away, as if pondering. 'I sometimes wonder if grey aliens displace our local cute furry red aliens.' He looked back, expecting at least a smile.

Marie frowned. 'What's funny?'

'You know – grey aliens?'

Complete blank. It turned out that the entire UFO mythos was unknown to her. A closed book, or – more to the point – a firewalled site.

'But why should I know about it?' she asked. 'If as you say it's all nonsense anyway – disinformation, hoaxes, delusions?'

'Well, it's . . . part of the culture, you know?'

'So?' She waved a hand at the band and the half-dozen people already jigging to it and the scores more sitting around half listening and half talking among themselves. 'This is our culture. You have literature. I have science. Why would we need to watch rubbish to understand anything?'

'Let me think about that.' He made to stand up. 'Time for—' A barmaid was already coming over with two pints. 'Oh, thanks.'

Some of Marie's friends turned up, said hello, and tactfully drifted off. Or perhaps they were bored with the conversation they'd overheard on approach: Marie and Myles, setting the world to rights. Marie's take on the world intrigued him. She had sharp discontents, but only where the system rubbed against her, as in the relocation. Apart from that it was something opaque, impenetrable. She was interested enough in politics and world affairs, but apart from ecological and environmental issues that she could affect locally and personally, it all happened elsewhere.

Myles knew that not everyone saw the Union like his parents did, as something you were part of and took part in. Plenty of his friends were quite indifferent to it. But he found the attitude hard to get his head around. He was, he thought, like someone from a family of amateur musicians, or maybe people on the folk scene, who took for granted that everyone sang and played an instrument and were surprised to find people for whom music happened in earphones. Marie had no beliefs other than whatever science had discovered, and her own ethics.

'You're a perfect Epicurean,' he said, admiringly.

'What's that?'

'You know, like the Black Gospels?'

'Never read them, sorry!'

'You don't have to. That's what's wonderful.'

It came to him in a flash, then, that the Black Gospels were perfect for apolitical people, and were doubtless popularly disseminated for that very reason. In the cadre, and even among some of the *responsables*, there was a cult of Spinoza. The Union's cultural missions were even called Spinoza Institutes. Spinozism for the leaders; Epicureanism for the led. It made sense, in a devious way. The Cold Revolution rolled slowly and implacably on not by preaching a doctrine, not even by changing people's minds, but by engaging their interests and passions in its silent machinery. And in its literal machinery: Iskander. He imagined some conspirator outlining the project, decades before the Rising: *and in this way, comrades, we will lead the people to the co-operative commonwealth of their dreams!*

'What are you grinning at?'

'Nothing,' he said, still grinning. 'Something I just figured out.'

'What?' she persisted.

'I could never understand what the people who run things around here believe in, and why they don't care whether the rest of us believe in it or not,' he said. 'And now I do.'

'Oh.' She reached out and, for the first time, caught his hand. It was like a shock going up his arm. 'Well, if you can multitask like that you can bloody well talk to me and *dance*.'

They drank, they danced, they talked, they laughed. She stayed.

CHAPTER SIX

Solid Geometry

Monday 13 October 2070, Apis

'Fucking keep moving!' Jenkins yelled, shaking his rifle like a stick at the two women and anyone else looking back. Keep moving they did, faster than before. Slower, though, than some of the animals, which rushed between and sometimes under their tramping feet. Hazeldene skidded on the slippery back of a green leathery flicker-fluke, throwing out her good knee. She cried out in pain and stopped. Jenkins collided with her from behind. He put an arm around her back, a wrist under her armpit.

'Thanks.' She tried to step forward, and her leg gave way again.

'Hand here!' Jenkins called ahead. An exile woman – Sharianne was already well in front of Hazeldene – fell back and caught Hazeldene from the other side. Together she and Jenkins helped Hazeldene forward, almost carrying her, barely letting her feet touch the ground. Smell of sweat mixed with the insectoid tang of their hair and body oil. Steady deep breath, the slap of feet and the rattle of bright chitin ornament. Over her shoulder she saw the rolling block cascade was now barely ten metres behind. No animals were between it and them. They must have been all either ahead already or crushed under the implacable slow avalanche.

'Leave me,' she said.

'No way!' said Jenkins.

'Not till we has to,' the woman said, with an evil chuckle. Jenkins grunted, in agreement or disapproval.

Hazeldene tried harder to walk. The pains – different in each knee, one an ache and the other a stab – had diminished somewhat, perhaps anaesthetised by adrenaline. She could put weight on her feet. Jenkins mercilessly took the opportunity to speed the pace.

Another plaza opened in front. Those ahead were scattering across it, then pausing to look back. Jenkins hurried them out of the passage, and a few steps out onto the square stopped.

Hazeldene risked another backward look. The wave of blocks had stilled, right at the edge of the corridor. It filled the passage like rubble choking a road between ruins. But stop it had. She stared at it, shaking physically and shaken mentally. The strangeness of the rock, its internal movement, had become almost familiar: accepted, if inexplicable. This external movement was new, and shocking. Something out of deep time acting, and reacting, reaching out . . . It was as if a fossil dinosaur skeleton had lurched into motion, or an extinct volcano erupted.

Jenkins let go of her, and the woman did likewise. Stiff-legged, Hazeldene hobbled after them to the middle of the plaza. She sank to the ground and stretched out her legs, then took off her pack and rummaged up a tube of ibuprofen gel. She tugged up her trouser legs and smeared the gel copiously on and around her knees, massaging the patellae, flexing and stretching the joints. Everyone was standing around getting their breath back and talking. She heard snatches of English and of exile patois.

Her colleagues came over one by one. Sharianne looked abashed. 'Sorry, I just ran . . .'

'Don't worry about it,' Hazeldene said, with a dismissive wave. '*Sauve qui peut* situation if ever I saw one.' She reached out a hand. 'Help me up?'

Sharianne caught her wrist and hauled.

'Jeez. Sheesh,' Hazeldene said, when she was on her feet. 'I'm getting too old for this sort of thing.'

The sun, just past its zenith, filled the square and all its bright walls with glare. The gas giant – the next planet inward from Apis – blazed as a bright crescent a few handspans' width down and away from the sun in the sky. Hazeldene glanced at the time. Only an hour since she'd come into the Ridge! Animals injured in the headlong flight crawled or twitched here and there on the square. Exiles systematically picked them up and brought them back, dispatched with a blow or still struggling, to the huddle. Someone had unburdened themselves of the camp stove and was figuring out how to kindle it.

'Are you all right, Emma?' Nelson Hayes asked. The stocky African American geologist looked as troubled and concerned as the exiles evidently weren't.

'Ah, I'm fine. Just took a fall badly when that shot went off.' She gave Georgi Muranov a sharp look. 'Then wrenched my other knee in the rush.' She looked around, then at the heap blocking the corridor. 'What's that? And what the hell happened back at the camp?'

'What *that* is,' Georgi said, 'is an inflammation. An immune response. Or wound healing. The rock is protecting itself – against us!' He sounded pleased, or at least impressed.

'That's what the locals told us, anyway,' said Nelson. 'It was a couple of hours ago, I was up the ladder drilling out samples, Cindy was sorting them, Sharianne and Georgi were running diagnostics. We noticed more beasties crossing the square than usual and were just wondering about it and half joking, when all of a sudden a score or so of exiles emerged from the side corridor and started yelling at us to get out ASAP. Out of the square and further into the Ridge, they were very insistent that the corridor back to the outside was a bad idea. The way they described it sounded like rockfalls at first, then they said the rock was going to crush us. They were very insistent and there was no question they were scared themselves. Didn't stop them gathering stuff up from the camp, but it didn't look like a raid. More like an evacuation. Jenkins, the big guy, he cut the cable and then two of the others pulled out the innards of the relay before we could do anything about it. They didn't threaten us, but it was getting that way, then Jenkins said ah, fuck 'em and walked off down the corridor.

'The rest of the locals followed, then we started hearing weird cracking noises we'd never heard before, so we grabbed what we could and went after them.'

'No discussion,' added Cindy Patel. 'We all just sort of looked at each other and decided to get the hell out.'

'Looks like you made the right decision,' said Hazeldene. 'I heard creaking and a crack behind me, but I guessed it might be an echo or something and pressed on. Just as well.'

'You were lucky,' said Sharianne.

'Yes, I was!' Hazeldene looked around. 'Well, let's see if we can get some sense out of the big boss.'

She marched over to Jenkins, not bothering to check if the others were following. The man seemed to be in his thirties, his close-cropped hair and roughly trimmed beard salted with white. Muscular shoulders and arms shown off by the sleeveless remnant of a military jacket. A clattering clutch of insectoid wing-cases threaded on string hung on his bare chest, above an ammunition pack on a canvas strap. He was standing beside an ongoing experiment that two squatting locals were conducting with the camp stove, several wooden skewers and dissected chunks of invertebrate muscle and organs. A rising waft of aromas like roasting chicken and seafood suggested the experiment would be a success.

'Didn't know you could eat those parts,' said Hazeldene.

Jenkins turned and flashed a grin. 'Oh, the egg sacs are better boiled than roasted, but we're in no state to be picky.' He looked her over. 'And you are?'

'Dr Emma Hazeldene.' She raised a hand, as did he.

'Able Jenkins.'

'Pleased to meet you.'

'Likewise. Are you the leader of the scientists?' His accent had a tang of London, a pang so far from home.

'No, I'm just the team leader here,' Hazeldene said.

'That'll do,' said Jenkins.

'And you? Are you the leader of this lot?'

Jenkins laughed. 'For the moment.'

'Well, in that case I have to thank you for getting my team – and me, come to think of it – out of danger.' She jerked her thumb at the blocked corridor. 'How did you know this was going to happen?'

'The Fermi warned us.'

'The Fermi? What's that?'

'The Fermi *are*,' said Jenkins, with heavy emphasis, 'the beings who built all this, long ago.'

'Oh.' Hazeldene could see how the meaning of Fermi's name might have shifted, in a single word-of-mouth generation, from the famous physicist and his even more famous Paradox to the very aliens whose glaring absence that thought experiment had made impossible to ignore. 'And you're saying they're still around and . . . *communicate* with you?'

''Course they're around,' said Jenkins. 'In the rock, innit? You can see 'em moving.'

Georgi was behind and to her left. He leaned in, finger raised. 'Ah—' he began.

'I'm talking, Georgi,' Hazeldene said. 'Sorry, Mr Jenkins. We've sometimes thought that ourselves, of course. We'd be interested to know how the Fermi warned you.'

She expected to hear of shamanic ritual, possession, divination, dreams . . .

Jenkins reached into a pouch on his belt – both garments looked like they were woven from some local fibre – and pulled out a black glassy rectangle about a hundred and fifty centimetres by eighty and at least five millimetres thick.

Georgi barked a laugh, which he stifled to a cough.

'They talk on this,' Jenkins said.

Hazeldene glanced at Georgi, who mimed holding a thing like that to his ear.

'Oh!' she said. 'It's a phone!'

'Yes,' said Jenkins. 'A Huawei 7G. Quite advanced for its day. Useless here, of course. We don't have 7G coverage, let's say. My old man had it on him when he was brought. Battery died before I was born.'

'Uh-huh,' said Hazeldene. 'And they communicate with you on that, do they?'

'Oh yes,' said Jenkins. He held it out, on the pale palm of his curled hand. 'Here, take a look.'

Hazeldene looked, as her colleagues crowded around. The sun's reflection was bright on the black glass. She shifted, tilted her head, tuned her glasses and shaded her eyes.

Crisp, white Cyrillic letters scrolled across the screen. Georgi, behind her shoulder, gasped. The message flowed into Mandarin, then Hindi, then English:

GO AWAY.

'Jeez,' said Nelson. He laughed, shaking his head. 'This is it? First contact? The biggest moment in human history! And it's telling us to fuck off?'

'It ain't the first,' said Jenkins, rather stiffly, as he slipped the device back in his pouch. 'We've been getting messages from them quite a while.'

'And you use that phone to communicate from your end?' Hazeldene asked.

'Yes, but they don't always respond. We have a more reliable apparatus back at the village.'

Hazeldene glanced at her companions. Their looks implied they didn't believe a word of this, any more than she did. It wasn't just the unlikeliness of aliens communicating in human languages, salient though that was. The team had been trying to extract information from the rocks of the Ridge for years, and had probed it with every form of radiation they could lay their hands on: lasers, lidar, radio, microwaves. This had given them data about the interior structure, but no reaction or response from whatever mechanism existed within the rock. They'd even tried sonar. Now they were reduced to drilling in and chipping out samples. Unlike the boulders and rock fragments strewn from here to the ocean by the ice that had planed the tops off the blocks (and carved out Bellatrix Sound) long ago, these samples remained live with internal movement, at least for now. But they remained mute. That exiles had succeeded with an obsolete and defunct phone was hard to believe. What was easy to believe was that Jenkins or some other local genius had found a way to recharge the phone's battery and tap messages into its memory, ready to be conveniently replayed at a touch or voice command for any suitably credulous audience.

Well, he hadn't found a credulous audience here! Still, she couldn't help admiring the man's effrontery. No doubt he had found the deception useful in maintaining whatever leadership he exercised over this rabble.

'Why did you cut the cable and rip out the components of the relay?' Hazeldene affected a tone of mild curiosity.

'Salvage,' said Jenkins, with a likewise casual air. 'That stuff was gonna be lost anyway.'

'I don't see why you had to cut the cable – which you did before this so-called "salvage",' Cindy pointed out.

'So I did.' Jenkins grinned at her. 'That was to stop anyone phoning out, causing confusion, maybe bringing your folks in after you to get crushed on the way in for all I knew.'

'Nobody was even reaching for a phone! And you could have explained.'

'I was in a bit of a rush,' Jenkins said. He looked around them, laughed, and added: 'All right, I see that story ain't going down too well. So here's the truth. We didn't want the Fermi to get that relay, because it would give them an open door to your systems.'

'You're telling us you care about Alliance *data security*?' Georgi asked.

'Yeah, I do as it happens.' Jenkins' gaze wandered, as if he was bored with the conversation. 'Look, guys, you'll find out all you need to know back at the settlement.'

'Is that where we're going?' Hazeldene demanded.

'Don't have a lot of choice, do you? We know the way out of this maze and you don't. Once you're outside the ruins you can get line of sight to the comsat and a link back to New Ardtaraig. Which will no doubt have a drone or a chopper out searching anyway.' He waved at the huddle around the camp stove. 'But first – let's eat!'

The water bottles grabbed from the camp had been shared out equally among the locals, and although there was no queuing the food too was distributed fairly, scant though the ration was. The pair at the stove cut up and handed out hot, greasy chunks of cooked invertebrate musculature that the exiles wolfed in seconds. Hazeldene looked at the oiled, dusty face of the woman offering her share, and the grubby calloused palm that served as a platter for a steaming handful of pale, scorched flicker-fluke meat, and hesitated. But the scallop smell was so good, and the smile so guileless, that she couldn't refuse. Besides, she was hungry. She nibbled warily at first, and then tore in, careless of juice running down her chin. When every mouth had been wiped and hand licked (or, in the case of the scientists, rubbed surreptitiously on a trouser leg) Jenkins called the party to order and led them out of the square.

The four scientists stayed together in the middle of the column, conferring in low voices as they marched. Jenkins had, of course, been mistaken in thinking they didn't know their way out of the maze. The entire Ridge had been mapped to half-metre resolution by a mini-drone swarm since before the first human expedition had ventured in. They all had maps and 3D models in their phones, and even without GPS the devices' inertial tracking kept more or less up to the minute and the step with location.

'Think we should make a break for it, first chance?' Nelson asked Hazeldene.

'Not sure,' she said. She jerked her head forward, to indicate Jenkins. 'Do you trust him?'

'Up to a point.'

'What about the rest of the spear-chuckers?'

'They haven't mistreated us,' Nelson said. 'They really did save us from the falling block cascade, whatever it is and however they knew it was coming. And it looks like they've gone out of their way to do it. They know the base can track us, so I doubt they intend to kill us or enslave us. They've shared food and shared our water, which in their kind of society may set up some obligations.'

'What, you're an anthropologist now?'

Nelson laughed. 'I've met exiles before.'

'Prospecting?' Before being drawn into the team, Nelson had been employed by the Naval Resources Division to search – successfully, as it had turned out – for oil.

'Yes.' He gestured vaguely southward. 'On the far edge of the plains, mind. A bit further away, a bit more feral. But not isolated. The groups keep in touch over surprisingly long distances, hundreds of kilometres in relays. Signalling with shards of mirror, or polished metal.' He laughed briefly. 'Using Morse code, so they've retained a knowledge of the alphabet even if the handful who can read at all have nothing to read except scriptures.'

'Scriptures?'

'Bibles and Qur'ans, mostly. One band had a hard copy of the Black Gospels of Herculaneum. A very battered Penguin Classic, held together with homemade string. Their wise woman would read aloud from it solemnly of an evening. Or claimed to, anyway – her near vision was poor and their last reading glasses had broken, so I think she was reciting from memory.'

Hazeldene scoffed. 'Can't see much use for the lost wisdom of Epicurus, out in the wild.'

'Live unknown, live simply, don't desire more than you need. It fits.'

'Yeah, I can see that. Still – materialist savages, huh?'

Nelson looked at her sharply. 'They're not savages. Don't make that mistake. It could get us in very hot water.'

'Not literally, I hope.'

'That's *exactly* the sort of crack I'd strongly advise you not to make,' Nelson said.

'OK, OK. So you reckon we're safe from our friends here.' She glanced over her shoulder. 'Everyone agree?'

They did.

'And it'll be interesting to see what Jenkins comes up with back at their village,' Georgi said. 'Talking back to the "Fermi", well! I can't wait to see how they do it.'

'The "more reliable apparatus"?' said Nelson. 'Yeah, I look forward to that, too. Should be a laugh, but we'd best let him save face in front of his folks.'

Nelson dropped back to talk with Sharianne about the diagnostics she and Georgi had been running on the samples. Hazeldene walked by herself for a while, taking the opportunity to observe the exiles more closely. Nineteen altogether:

twelve men, seven women. Apart from Jenkins, all seemed to be in their early twenties or late teens. Only Jenkins carried a firearm; all had steel knives, three had crossbows made from local materials and the rest had stone-tipped spears. They wore a mixture of tattered mass-produced clothing and fresher, intact handmade garments, and a variety of ornaments or possibly charms made from insectoid, boid and other arthropod parts: wings, wing-cases, pincers and claws. There were no obvious differences between the sexes in dress or decoration. All looked lithe and healthy, though evidently tiring. Here and there in the column, feet dragged and shoulders slumped.

They all livened up, however, when they emerged from the repetitive if colourful towering blocks of the 'CBD' into the more open and less forbidding space beyond, known to the team as 'the sculpture park'. Here the blocks were more widely spaced, lower in height and far more varied in shape: predominantly wedges, cones, cylinders, pyramids and cuboids, each with its own subtle or blatant departure from symmetry in ways that could be pleasing or disquieting to the eye. Though made of the same black crystal as the rest of the Ridge, the surfaces of these blocks were textured on a visible scale, with appearances that varied from jewel-encrusted to pebble-dashed. The ground between them was covered with native grass and flowering plants, and hummed with bees.

Jenkins called his company immediately to high alert: weapons in hand rather than slung or shouldered, gaze scanning constantly all around, the loose straggle tightened into a fast-moving defensive formation. The five scientists trotted in the midst, like beasts guarded by dogs, and likewise chivvied along.

It wasn't a good moment for the drone to arrive. The locals heard its buzz before the scientists did, and had their weapons aimed as it came into view above the towers behind them. Hazeldene grabbed Jenkins' shoulder.

'Don't shoot!'

'I wasn't going to!' Jenkins kept the drone in his sights. 'I don't trust it.'

'You don't want them to think we're here against our will.'

'You got a point.'

Jenkins lowered the weapon and motioned to those aiming crossbows to stand down, too. The exiles backed away, leaving the scientists in the middle. Hazeldene waved her arms crosswise above her head and beckoned urgently to the machine. It circled, then spiralled down to hover a few metres in front of her, so low that the downblast of its four rotors flattened the grass. Its camera swivelled to face her.

'We're fine!' she shouted above the racket. 'Something's moved in the rock, blocking our exit. Fly back and record it if you haven't already. The locals are taking us to their settlement, and we're going voluntarily. We'll maintain contact and let you know if we need help. For now, everything seems OK.'

She didn't know if she was talking to the operator back at base or to the drone's AI, but either way the news and pictures would get back to New Ardtaraig promptly enough. The quadcopter dipped in acknowledgement, then spun skyward to head back the way it had come. Just as it went out of view, and everyone was about to turn from watching it out of sight, Sharianne shouted:

'Look! Look out!'

They all looked where she was pointing. About a hundred and fifty metres away, between a skewed pyramid and a leaning cylinder, a roundish mass of black the height of a double-decker bus was rolling towards them like tumbleweed.

'Jesus H. Christ what the fucking fuck is that?' Hazeldene cried.

She made the *stretch* gesture, parting thumbs and forefingers in front of her eyes, zooming her glasses. The thing sprang into sharp focus, a pixellated black ball made up of the same sort and size of mobile blocks as had flooded down the corridors. It only seemed to be rolling. The blocks were moving over and over each other, propelling the whole assemblage along with a curious inhuman locomotion. Paving slabs rising up from a city street and walking would have been a less uncanny sight.

'Don't run!' Jenkins shouted. 'Just keep walking, fast!' He repeated the command in patois and pointed in the direction they'd been heading anyway.

'Why not run?' Hazeldene asked, hurrying as best she could to catch up.

Jenkins glanced at her impatiently. 'That just makes it move faster.'

'You've met this thing before?'

'My people have.'

Hazeldene let the evasion pass. 'How come my people haven't?'

Jenkins scoffed. 'Because you've never been daft enough to drill into the rock before! That's why the blocks chased you out, I reckon. And that drone coming over and you talking to it has probably riled the Fermi again, which is why that thing behind us is herding us out.'

Hazeldene looked over her shoulder. The ball of blocks was indeed keeping pace, about fifty metres behind them. In front of it the soil was visibly being crushed as it trundled on. Its trail would be visible from space.

From space –

Clear of the immense high blocks of the 'CBD', she was probably back in line with the comsat.

'I'm going to try calling home,' she told Jenkins.

He waved a hand. 'Be my guest. Don't slow down though.' He quickened his pace a little so he was a few steps ahead of her, a courtesy she appreciated.

She called base and got through.

'SciDiv here.'

'Hazeldene checking in. That drone—'

'Yes, message received, it's heading back.'

'Well, turn it around and get some other eyes up over the Ridge. Something remarkable is happening.'

'Thanks, we got that, the drone has already surveyed the new phenomenon in the corridors.'

'There's a *new* new fucking phenomenon!'

'Yes?'

She described it.

'Hmm. Interesting. Do you still feel safe?'

'Yeah, we're OK. But I'd feel safer under surveillance.'

'Noted. I'll watch from above and a safe distance. SciDiv out.'

'Hazeldene out.'

Georgi caught up, and she relayed the conversation to him.

'We should try splitting up,' he said.

'Why?'

'To see how the black ball reacts.'

'Why?' she repeated. 'Idle curiosity?'

'Experiment, as we scientists call it.'

Jenkins had by now dropped back, close enough to overhear.

'Don't even think about it,' he called over his shoulder. ''Sides, I can tell you what'd happen. The ball would split, but it wouldn't seem to get any smaller. So then you'd have two balls coming after you, or as many more as groups you split into.'

'Fascinating,' said Georgi. 'This I must see.'

Without further ado he broke away diagonally to their right, sprinting at first then slowing to a brisk trot. He had his phone out and was speaking into it as he ran. Behind them, the black ball did exactly what Jenkins had predicted. Within seconds it had undergone a semblance of mitosis, momentarily forming two interlinked spheres with open spaces within each, wheels within wheels like some Escher drawing of Ezekiel's vision. Then there were two solid-looking spheres, one of them bowling after Georgi Muranov and bypassing the rest of them. The Russian disappeared between two low, squarish blocks up ahead, ball in hot pursuit.

The exile party, and the scientists, restored good order after a shocked moment or two of milling around, pointing and yelling.

'Fucking idiot,' said Cindy Patel.

'You said it, sister,' said Nelson.

'I'll have words,' said Hazeldene, grimly. 'Assuming he survives.'

'Who was he phoning?' Jenkins asked. 'You've already spoken to New Ardtaraig, yes?'

'Yes, I have,' said Hazeldene, sounding crosser than she'd intended. Her knees were giving her trouble again. 'No doubt he was calling *his* base, Novy Cosmograd, over on New Lemuria.'

'He's Co-ord? But you're Alliance!'

'Yes, we are, but each base has researchers at the other. Part of the Kepler Agreement. We call them "exchange students" when we're in a good mood and "hostages" when we're not.'

Jenkins chuckled. 'And right now he's a hostage?'

'Oh yes.' She thought about it. 'That or a casualty. An international incident. Just what we fucking need.'

'As long as he can keep running,' said Sharianne.

The locals still flanked the scientists and remained wary. Evidently there were other dangers here than the black ball's implacable pursuit, or so they believed. Hazeldene couldn't see any and decided not to ask.

'I can see why he reported home,' she said. 'Heck, I can even understand why he wanted to test what you said, Jenkins. But—'

'It'll bring complications,' said Sharianne.

'You've never seen anything like this before?' Jenkins asked.

'Never,' said Hazeldene. 'Have you?'

'I've seen this,' said Jenkins. 'Years ago.' He laughed. 'I could run faster then.'

'You're no bad runner now,' said Hazeldene.

'A healthy life,' said Jenkins. 'What about the Co-ord scientists? They seen anything?'

'Nothing like this. They're . . . a bit more wary of it than we are, and we're pretty careful.'

Jenkins laughed. 'Until you got impatient and started poking?'

'That's about it,' Hazeldene allowed. 'We thought if it hadn't reacted to all the electronic probing we've done, it's hardly going to notice drilling.'

MacHinery Ridge had its analogues and counterparts elsewhere on New Atlantis and New Lemuria, but none had been so intensively examined. The Russian and Chinese scientists at the Co-ord base had long ago registered the inexplicable movements within such blocks and had backed off in a hurry, turning their attention to trying to explain these movements rather than investigate them further. Solid masses moving inside one another like so many holograms insulted physics as well as common sense.

And yet it moves. Theory would have to catch up. The rock of the Ridge was (some said) a new state of matter. The first, spontaneous stabs at explaining its properties involved manipulation of space, and of matter at a deeper level than quarks. Turning such notions into rigorous and testable hypotheses was a long and – to some – enticing prospect.

A more pressing reason for a hands-off approach was the suspicion that this technology had, in the deep past, been used to reshape the entire planet. The geological evidence of ridiculously rapid plate tectonics – significant continental drift in months rather than megayears, all those megayears ago – was firmly established. Likewise the complete absence of evidence of the titanic energies that such a process would have released: more than enough to melt the planet's entire crust, according to Nelson's and Cindy's back-of-the-envelope calculations.

This structure, then, was not to be lightly tampered with. No wonder the Russians and Chinese had handed the problem over to the theoretical physicists, of which their small science complement was well supplied if not overstocked. The Alliance team was weighted more towards engineers, computer scientists and oil geologists. No wonder either that the English, Americans and Indians had thought, well, maybe a *little* drilling wouldn't hurt . . .

'Looks like you were wrong, huh?' Jenkins chuckled.

'Yeah,' said Nelson, pacing alongside. 'And it won't be just Georgi's colleagues and ours who'll take an interest.'

'The military?' Jenkins asked.

'Yup,' Hazeldene said. 'On both sides. They'll have their say about this, and it won't be in a tone of excited curiosity.'

There were other questions she thought it better not to ask. What had just happened – and what was still happening, fifty metres from her back and slowly closing on them – was no surprise to the locals.

What the fuck had *they* been up to, all this time?

And why hadn't either of the military or scientific bases noticed them doing it?

There would be a time to ask these questions. Meanwhile, she chose not to rack her brains over them. As she liked to remind her Co-ord colleagues, she was an empiricist at heart. The only thing she believed in was seeking truth from facts.

CHAPTER SEVEN

Down the Yard

Monday 19 May 2070 to Friday 30 May 2070, Earth

The Monday after he saw the submarine, Grant waited for the 07:20 to leave from Gourock Station and watched people hurry for the 07:30 ferry to Faslane. The England ferry, as the locals called it, departed from the long pier to which the far end of the platform debouched. Sometimes such people had a shame-faced look, or their eyes obscured by reflective glasses. More often they strode along as if daring anyone to jeer or challenge. These days, few did.

Today the people heading for the England ferry were more in number and sterner of countenance than usual. There were new faces among them – not that he knew personally anyone who took that trip, but like any regular commuter Grant had a subconscious register of who was and wasn't familiar. Maybe the vanishing submarine incident, whatever it was, had caused some consternation.

The train pulled out, to stop after a few hundred metres of deepening cutting at Fort Matilda, then plunge into a tunnel to emerge in the canyon of sandstone walls and seeping moss at Greenock West. From Greenock Central onward the view opened out, and you could see clear across the Clyde and the low, green tip of Rosneath Point. Behind it lay a small inlet, the Gare Loch. And on the far shore of that was Faslane. All you could see of it over the headland was the tall business towers of Rhu on the English side, and eastward of them the long factory blocks of the larger town of Helensburgh, huddled close against the Faslane border on the Scottish side. A cloud of cargo drones swirled above and between both towns like midges over an old tyre.

At Port Glasgow he got off with about a quarter of the passengers, elbowed his way through double that number pressing to get on, and headed out of the station and down the long slope of the main street, through the underpass under the highway and out to the iron gates of the yard, to arrive at his workstation on the dot of eight.

It was a precision he took pride in. Arriving conspicuously early made you a crawler, inconveniently late made you a laggard; that was agreed. The range was fuzzy at both ends and much debated. There could be no dispute that clocking in on the exact contracted time made you a reliable worker, an upright Union citizen and a good union man. All the more important, Grant wryly reckoned, at this stage of his career and his position in the self-management. He worked his twenty-four-hour week like anyone else on the shop floor. If sometimes he took responsibilities home, if union matters troubled his afternoons and production problems floated before his eyes as he drifted off to sleep, he prided himself on leaving his work behind the gate when he left. No unpaid overtime for him.

That morning Brian and Morag were in just ahead of him, Anwar and Jeannie and Piotr a minute or two later.

'Morning, John!' said Morag. She was a stocky, cheerful

woman of about Grant's age who walked as if elbowing her way through a crowd of taller people. 'Good weekend?'

'Aye, sure,' said Grant. 'Took a few bike rides and photos, did stuff around the flat and the garden. You?'

'Daughter's weans over. Nae rest for the wicked.'

'Take it up with the union,' said Brian. He posed as if momentarily deep in thought. 'Hang on, that's you.'

Anwar chortled.

'Enough of your lip,' said Morag. 'Get us a coffee.'

Brian and Anwar were both in their twenties, a bit laddish, a clique of two. They knew how to make espressos, though. Saving grace. Jeannie and Piotr were younger, and quieter. Serious with it. Grant felt he had a good team, or at least that he – and in a different way, Morag – had a handle on it.

After a few minutes to down the espressos Grant nodded to all and gestured to the half-dozen mechanisms that stood in a rough circle centred on the impulse router like skeletal cowboys around a fire. Slightly ahead of the others, he climbed into his rig. He clipped on the limb and head attachments, strapped himself onto the saddle, spun around a couple of times on the gimballed pedestal while stretching and flexing his legs, arms and fingers. He checked feedback and servos, clamped on his padded earphones and flipped down the visor.

Instantly he was down in the yard, animating his usual avatar, a blocky Nissan model coded AGR-1. His team's schedule had been thrashed out the week before, as next week's would be on the last working hour of the coming Thursday. Thirty metres of partially built robotic submarine stretched most of the length of the shed. The ventral rod – colloquially the keel, though technically it wasn't – was laid, the spine arced over it from end to end, and all the ribs were in place. The plates, like gigantic petals of carbon fibre and steel composite, were already attached or waiting, racked on pallets. The fusion engine plant and the drive mechanisms were en route from Holland, the navigation and guidance computer on order from Brazil, the instrumentation due in two weeks from Dundee. The current delicate and skilled task was fitting the overlapping plates and integrating their tough, complex connections and flexible self-regenerating seals. Grant checked off the team members' locations and tasks, fired up the 3D printers, rallied his robot assistants and set to work.

Morag was the AGR-2 driver. She was cadre, and trouble. Not that she was incompetent, or insubordinate. It was that she answered to a different hierarchy from the self-management or even the union. She knew it and every so often made sure you did, too. At one production conference in Glasgow she'd affected a West of Scotland dialect and accent so pronounced that the delegates from Rosyth had had to resort to subtitles. This performance, she'd later bragged, had been entirely to make a point to a visiting *responsable* from Belgium, in furtherance of some devious factional agenda on the cultural front, and had upped her credit.

At the 10:30 break she backed Grant into a corner by the window, talking about a niece's first day at school, while thumbing family photos from her phone to his glasses. Then she dropped her voice.

'Got a wee problem, John, spare me a minute?'

'Aye, spill it.'

'It's about your weekend adventure.'

'Cycling's good for the health. Photography's good for the soul.'

She gave him an innocent look over the rim of her coffee mug.

'You're getting close.'

Grant looked down at the yard, where their avatars were doing routine work on automatic, rolling pallets into position and the like. From above, the sub looked like the skeleton of a blue whale being picked clean by predators, although the process going on down there was quite the opposite.

'This about, uh, another undersea vessel?'

'Aye, that, exactly.'

He looked back at Morag. 'How do you know about it?'

She tapped an ear. 'Word,' she said. 'Don't worry, it isn't on your record. You did right reporting it. But now you've seen what you saw, you're in the loop, like it or not.'

Grant tried to take another backward step, and found himself up against the wall.

'I'm not *joining* anything.'

Morag backed off a little. 'Nothing like that,' she assured him. 'You're sound.'

'OK.'

'The word is,' she went on, 'that what we'd like you to do is . . . kind of what you'd be inclined to do anyway, ken what I mean?'

Grant did. 'I don't,' he said.

'Aw, come on,' said Morag. 'Nothing private, it's plain to read in your profile. You're inclined to be . . . over focused, maybe?'

Grant laughed. 'If you're saying I can get a bit obsessive there's no need to spare my blushes, Morag.'

'Aye, well. It helps you at work, no question about that. But in your free time it can lead you into some unproductive lines of inquiry, let's say.'

Grant nodded. 'OK.'

'Fine, fine. We're on the same screen, right? So. What we'd like you to do is follow this up in your usual way. Just ignore the firewall, go down any rabbit holes you like. There's a name we'd like you to watch for.' She flickered her fingertips in the air, spelling out a name that appeared on his glasses: LAKSHMI NAYAK. 'Got that?'

'Yes,' he said, blinking it to memory.

'When you've done the research, as they say, we'd like you to contact her. The lassie in question lives up near Tarbet, so you could even meet her, if you can coax her out. That would be good.'

'And why do youse lot need me to do that?'

Morag clapped his shoulder. 'Wheels within wheels, John. I don't know.' She raised her voice a little. 'But you'll consider it, aye?'

'Sure I will,' Grant said.

They ambled back to the rigs.

'That looked like a serious conversation,' Anwar muttered to Grant, as everyone buckled up.

'Morag was just trying *again* to get me to join a party,' Grant replied, loud enough for the others to overhear.

'Aye, which party would that be?' Jeannie called out.

'Any party,' said Grant. 'Just as long as it's social *and* democratic.'

Snorts of laughter proved this cover story was believed. Morag glared, but as she lowered her visor Grant caught her hiding a smile.

As soon as he got home that afternoon, Grant goggled up and took a deep dive into his online history files for the previous Friday. He traced the initial ping that had sent him looking for the submarine in the first place. Then he invoked the command line behind all the seamless interfaces and checked the post's metadata and provenance.

He wasn't at all surprised to find Iskander's digital fingerprints all over it. The AI was perfectly capable of covering its tracks, but in this case it had apparently not bothered. At the very least, the traces suggested that Iskander had particularly wanted him to go out and look. Interesting.

One good thing about thinking like a conspiracy theorist: it made you distrust coincidences.

Grant grinned to himself. He was going to enjoy this.

For ten days Grant pursued the uncanny research that Morag had pointed him to. Before and after work, at home or outdoors – he took to cycling down the coast, or up the hills at the back of the towns, and sitting down in a quiet spot, putting his glasses on and invoking fringe physics. Down that rabbit hole he went, sniffing after anti-gravity, zero-point energy, aether theories, propellantless propulsion, cold fusion, faster-than-light travel, plasma cosmologies . . . even young-earth creationism, which still existed Over There and which was currently making a wider stir than usual.

Anomalous crystalline rocks had been discovered in a uranium mine in Western Australia. A miner had released a video clip that seemed to show movement inside the rocks. Creationists had claimed this as proof of antediluvian advanced technology. Ancient-aliens enthusiasts had proclaimed it as yet more evidence of ancient aliens. The mining geologists had declared that academic geologists were looking into some unusual features of the crystal. The academic geologists had said the only thing unusual about the crystal was its refractive properties, which combined with a shakily held phone camera could give the illusion of internal movement. After that, the story had gone cold. It was, some said, just like the Roswell saucer crash: announced then denied and covered up.

Grant decided this was a rabbit hole too far, and returned to the main warren. He had two clues: the anomaly he had seen, and the name of Lakshmi Nayak.

Nayak's audacious paper was still on phys.x-archiv for all to read. Grant's own degree was in marine engineering and business studies. He could follow the mathematics, just about, but the particle physics and cosmology that the paper took for granted went right past his head like neutrinos through the Earth. The practical details of the device proposed – called an 'inflaton trap', a name that made Grant wonder if the inspiration had come from a typo in an economics paper – looked thought through. Then again, so had every fusion scheme he'd ever seen before the Faber pot, the one that had actually worked.

Apart from the flurry of refutations, her first and last paper was cited only by cranks. In the underworld of fringe physics,

FTL was almost mainstream. Grant doubted she'd be proud to list these citations on her CV.

Nayak was now lead analyst at a start-up planning consultancy co-op in Tarbet. If she'd indeed opened the way to the stars, it must be at least somewhat galling to find herself crunching numbers on the shores of Loch Lomond. It was as if Einstein had gone back to the patent office.

On the other hand, Einstein himself had said after Hiroshima that, if he had known, he would have become a watchmaker.

The whale-shaped robot drogue tug was completed. Its launch felt like releasing something into the wild. One Thursday afternoon in late May, just after the week-long meeting of the self-management to nail down the details of the yard's next project – a more conventional submersible this time, with a crew – Grant rode up the long, curving slope to the top of Lyle Hill, which overlooked the invisible boundary between Gourock and Greenock. He wheeled the bike up the short path off the road to the summit and stood at the viewpoint, gazing north.

A fleet of white clouds rode at anchor on a single layer of air, hanging at the same height all the way to the horizon. Down the hill a bit and to his left was the Free French Memorial, a marble-white anchor surmounted by the Cross of Lorraine. To his right was the whole sweep of the lower Clyde, all the way to Glasgow, taking in the sprawl of Greenock and the busy shipyards of Port Glasgow and Langbank and the other riverside towns to the east. Across the broad river in front of Greenock rose the towers of Faslane, and beyond them the reforested slopes of the high mountains: Ben Lomond, Ben Ime and Ben Arthur.

Far up there, in the shadow of Cruach Tairbeirt at the top of Loch Long, Lakshmi Nayak was very likely going about her day.

A day he was about to interrupt.

He took out his phone and laid it on the worn brass view-point plate scored with lines and circled with outlines of the distant hills, and wrote the message. He'd thought about its wording for a long time. She must get a lot of messages from cranks, and every one of them would begin by saying: *You must get a lot of messages from cranks, but . . .*

Or words to that effect.

Dear Dr Nayak, he wrote, *I can build your ship. Yours sincerely, John Grant.*

Followed by his contact details, and nothing else. Now it was just a matter of waiting for her to seek him out. He didn't have long to wait. On Friday morning the reply came:

Arthur's Tomb. Reception. Saturday. 10:00.

CHAPTER EIGHT

Hard Case

Wednesday 24 September 2070, Venus

'The Dutch are posthuman already.'

Owen rolled on his side and looked at Francesca Milloy, a materials scientist who was at that moment lying on her back puffing clouds of tangerine-scented vapour towards a ceiling about a metre and a half above her nose. Her after-fuck fag, she'd called it. It was her third such of the night so far. Fortunately the air circulation was effective, if noisy. The entire flat was smaller than Walworth's front room, compact as that had been. Everything folded away or swung out of the wall or out of or into something else. In this respect it was typical of the six different flats in which he'd spent the previous six nights.

'What do you mean?' he asked. He'd been telling her about his exploits in Heijplaat.

'They're demanding the right to marry robots.'

'That's not posthuman,' said Owen. 'It's just decadent.'

'What do you mean?'

'Robots don't have sentience. They're objects. You can't "marry" a sex toy.'

Milloy rolled over, turning towards him. Tumble of black curls. Sultry smile, vape-stick between forefinger and middle finger like a cigarette: a pose. 'Even if the sex toy understands you perfectly, reads the signals in every breath and pulse and sound and look and movement?'

'Yes. It's a cop-out from finding a person who can do all that.'

'Ha! Chance would be a fine thing. Especially in this place.' She put a hand on his hip joint and began stroking. 'Anyway, you do it better than any person I've ever banged with.'

'I know. You're not the first to tell me.'

'Smug bastard, aren't you?'

'You're not the first to tell me that, either.'

'How many before?'

'Like, here?'

She punched him, not too hard. 'Yes, here! Cloud City.'

He pretended to count. 'Six.' He'd had a busy week. 'Four women and two men.'

'Well, as long as nobody mistakes this for *true love* . . .'

'As I was saying, about decadence.'

'Ah yes. I still say it's posthuman, or anyway posthuman*ist*.'

'That Dutch nonsense? It's very much a minority thing, it's opposed by humanists *and* by traditional religious groups, and so far it has no legal validity. For obvious reasons – machine personhood opens up too many cans of worms.'

'So they kick the can down the road.'

'Yes, and just as well. Speaking as a machine myself.'

'You're a funny fucker,' she said.

'You're all posthuman already anyway,' Owen said.

'Who?'

'All of you in the Union.'

She propped herself up on one elbow. 'Now why d'you say that?'

'You all live inside an AI.'

'So do your lot. You have, what is it? Smart-Alec. And don't get me started on WeThink.'

Owen scoffed. 'Smart-Alec is a tool for advertising and some not very effective political manipulation. WeThink is a tool for social conformity. Iskander knows what you want, what you will soon want, and what you can be made to want, just as surely as I do—' he smiled '—but on a vastly greater scale and over a far wider range of preferences. You're just convenient moving parts of a machine already in Europe, and here in Cloud City you're pioneering turning over even more of your lives to it.'

'Iskander—!'

'Yes?' said Iskander.

'Fuck off, machine. I wasn't talking to you, I was talking about you. Read the room, motherfucker. Sorry, Marcus, as I was saying. Iskander is just a bunch of mindless algorithms.'

Owen chuckled. 'So am I.'

She looked at him very seriously, the pupils of her eyes expanding. 'I know. That's what I like about this situation. And that's what we all like about our friendly neighbourhood AI.'

'What if Iskander ever becomes unfriendly?'

'A vanishingly remote possibility,' said Milloy, 'but we've thought of it anyway. Every control here has a manual override. From door handles to the life-support and the shuttles.'

She yawned, then shifted her hip, pressing closer. Tired, but not sated. Neither tired nor sated, Owen responded, and she responded back. Matters progressed.

'Tell me again,' she panted at one point, hair hanging down on his face, 'why you can't marry a sex robot?'

Owen laughed. Her thighs clenched around his hips. She yelled in his face.

'No, tell me! Tell me! Say it!'

For once he had misread her. It seemed he had encountered yet another kink.

In the morning – conventionally speaking, Cloud City's clock having no relation to the rotation of Venus, or to the far faster rotation of its atmosphere, which carried the habitat around the planet once every four Earth days – Francesca Milloy took Owen to a nearby refectory. They padded across fake grass to a clump of tree-pots beneath which tables and chairs gathered as if for shelter or shade. Behind a cardboard counter an avatar of Iskander had already made them coffee. As they arrived it microwaved thumb-sized blobs of dough, which inflated into a convincing imitation of croissants. The avatar looked like a preliminary 3D outline rendering of an adult human, realised in hard plastic.

'Haven't seen one of these even in Europe,' Owen remarked as he sat down. 'What's the point? I mean, why not employ a person, or use self-service?'

'Ship a barista to Venus?' Milloy scoffed. 'Or have scientists and engineers and maintenance workers waste time faffing about with boilers and cups?'

'Sharing such tasks can build team spirit and flatten hierarchies. I thought the Union was very much into that.'

'Ha! Try flattening a hierarchy of scientists sometime.'

'Even so.'

'OK, it's a gimmick,' Milloy conceded. 'Truth is, I designed it myself shortly after I arrived a couple of years ago and still needed to impress people.'

'Consider me impressed,' said Owen. 'Didn't know you were a roboticist as well.'

'Oh, I'm not. The hard part, the bit I did, was designing the shell composite. I mean, it looks like plastic but it's a bloody sight more complicated metamaterial. Intrinsic haptic feedback, that sort of thing. The robotics stuff was all off-the-shelf.'

'Aha!' said Owen. He put down his cardboard cup. 'And what were humanoid robotics components doing on the shelf in the first place? Can't be much call for them here.'

Milloy raised her eyebrows and flicked her black curls from her forehead. 'And wouldn't you just like to know, Mr Cultural Attaché?'

'Yes,' said Owen. 'I would.'

She rubbed her hands. 'Well, now you're in luck. I can show you.'

Owen smiled back. 'Brilliant!' he said.

Luck had nothing to do with it. For almost a week he had been working towards this. Every query, every encounter, every hook-up had taken him closer to this materials scientist and her work. As he had expected, Iskander's Triple-AI had at some level colluded. It had anticipated his interest in the Above Top Secret project to retrieve the rock, and led him, as if by an invisible hand, towards the scientist whose open work was most closely involved with that very project. He knew that, and suspected she did. But it would have been tactless to ask her about it. What he didn't know, and couldn't ask anyone – even Iskander itself – was why the system was playing him along. Well, he could ask, but Iskander wouldn't give him a truthful answer. It might not even find the question meaningful. The whole elaborate dance could simply be the outworking of the algorithms. Owen wasn't at all clear which side was playing which. As he'd told Walworth, at some point it would become evident, and then it would be a matter of which AI – him, or Iskander – got their last move in first.

They finished their real coffee and fake croissants. Milloy stood up. 'Let's get going.' Owen crushed and tossed his cup. Predictably, a roving cleaner snatched it from the air.

Cloud City was an oblate spheroid, a squashed ball a kilometre across and three hundred metres on its polar axis, horizontally divided at its equator and trailing suspended ancillary facilities

– the shuttle capture dock, fuel storage tanks and some particularly dangerous fabrication and research units – beneath its main body like stings in the tentacles of a jellyfish. People lived and worked in the upper half. Life-support, waste processing and recycling, agricultural hydroponics, food processing, meat printing and some of the heavier onsite manufacturing and bulk processing went on in the lower half. This bottom-heavy weight distribution, along with the solar panels petalled around the circumference and the suspended pods below, all served to stabilise the settlement's stately drift through the upper atmosphere, fifty-five kilometres above the surface and about seventy degrees north of the equator.

Milloy led Owen to a stairwell. They descended a spiral ladder down several levels into the settlement's cavernous underworld. Strip-lit rows of vegetables stretched off to a hazy distance. Ovoid and cuboid cabins perched on platforms linked by spindly walkways. The susurrus of air and water recirculation at times approached white noise. Less pervasive, but common, were the hiss and chug of 3D printers and the rhythmic thud of pumps and condensers. Near the bottom of the great shallow bowl a large fusion pot hung braced between a dozen convergent girders. Below that were the airlocks and lifts to the docking gantries. Owen kept a sharp eye out for everything that was going on: people working in the vast web, here a woman making a fine adjustment to a hydroponic spray, there a man tapping a code into a door keypad, and over there someone else awkwardly descending a ladder in a loose, rubbery-looking one-piece suit.

A fifty-metre walk along a gangway took them to a cluster of cabins the size of shipping containers.

'Welcome to my shed,' Milloy said, ushering him through a doorway. Inside it was strip-lit and cluttered, like a junkyard in bright daylight. About half the space was taken up by printers and their feed hoppers alongside a compact kiln. A five-metre-long lab bench was laden with apparatus and instruments, most of them concerned with measuring properties of materials: stress and strain test machines, vices, vacuum and pressure chambers, all ingeniously miniaturised and optimised for least feasible weight. Lasers for cutting, sintering, and fusing. Propped or stacked here and there were what looked like pieces of armour from a lost battle: smashed-in helmets, bent or cracked greaves, buckled cuirasses, stomped boots.

'You're building *suits*?' Owen exclaimed. He'd never heard of any attempt at human surface landings. It wasn't even mentioned in the secret briefing he'd passed to Walworth.

'Got it in one,' Milloy told him cheerfully. 'Or almost. We're still trying to build a suit. Well – we've been building and testing samples and working towards a prototype, at any rate. We have the design as good as we can make it. The actual manufacture will be done up at the moonlet.'

Owen looked around. 'Just to be clear – this suit is intended for the surface?'

'What else? Standard EVA gear for up here is just breathing apparatus, bubble helmet, and a sealed boiler-suit with integral gloves and boots, all coated with PTFE to keep out the sulphuric acid.'

'Teflon? That's all it takes?'

Milloy waved above her head. 'If it's good enough for the whole outer skin of Cloud City, it's good enough for EVA. You'd stink a bit afterwards from the microbial shit, mind.'

'I'm in no hurry to try,' said Owen. 'The upper atmosphere's bad enough – but the surface? Why?'

'Prestige, I reckon,' said Milloy. 'Being able to walk around at the bottom of an ocean in hell is quite the technological triumph, wouldn't you say?'

'No, I would not. Having rovers down there is impressive enough. Why risk humans?'

Milloy shrugged. 'It's a challenge. Pointless, but possible. Hence attractive, if you're mad enough. The motherland calls, and muggins here sticks up her hand and goes "Me! Me! Me!"'

'You're not going down there yourself?'

'Fuck, no. I just wore myself out trying to build the thing. Let someone else get the glory.'

'A heroic death, more like.' He swept an arm to take in the carnage of armoury. 'Though if your results so far are anything to go by, mercifully quick.'

Milloy laughed. 'Don't worry, we'll use a humanoid robot to test the prototype first.'

'You have humanoid robots here? Not just avatars?'

She gave him a long, appraising look. 'We have now.'

'It's bollocks, you know,' Walworth told him, early that evening in the secure room. 'They don't need you to test the thing. They'd have plenty of eager volunteers to be the first man or woman on Venus, risk be hanged. An instrumented descent with the suit empty or with a weighted dummy inside would be quite enough to spot any flaws or iron out any kinks.'

'I know.'

'And frankly, they could stand to lose one of theirs much better than to lose you. A dead hero is one thing. A diplomatic embarrassment and PR disaster is something else.'

'Besides, I'm an expensive piece of equipment,' said Owen. 'So they might have to compensate the Alliance for my loss.'

'There's that, too,' said Walworth, oblivious to the sarcasm. 'My point being, they don't want to just use you to test that other pricey piece of kit. They'll send and retrieve a crash test dummy first, no doubt, but then they'll want you to do something for them down there.'

'I arrived at that conclusion rather quickly,' said Owen.

'Of course, of course.'

'I can think of several useful tasks I could perform on the surface.'

'So can I, old chap. So can I. But – best not speculate, eh?'

'Quite,' said Owen. 'It's important to keep an open mind.'

CHAPTER NINE

Once and Future

Saturday 31 May 2070, Earth

Grant and Ellen strolled from the hotel along the shore towards the head of Loch Long, kitted up for a longer walk later. The tide was in, but the weather was sunny and calm and the road mostly dry, though here and there they had to step over or around a stranded heap of kelp. The curious rock formation at the top of Ben Arthur, off to Grant's left across the strip of sea, drew his glance again and again. Nicknamed The Cobbler, it looked nothing like a cobbler from any angle he could see from here.

Just before where the road looped around to the far side of the loch was the visitor centre, a wedge of concrete and plate glass hammered into the side of Cruach Tairbeirt amid a huddle of hotels, cafés, outdoor equipment shops and the car park whose extension had led to the tomb's discovery.

The time was 9:45. Grant was due to meet Lakshmi Nayak

at 10:00, just inside the centre's reception area. He'd told Ellen he was meeting a young woman who was a brilliant planning consultant for a preliminary business inquiry, to sound her out for work with his team. True as far as it went. Ellen had seized the chance to make a weekend trip, which suited Grant just fine. A bit more cover, if that happened to be needed, which he didn't know.

'Coming in?'

Ellen shook her head. 'No, I'll just mosey over to the café. See you there afterwards?'

'Yes, fine.'

'I'll take your rucksack.'

'Thanks.'

Ellen crossed the road and headed up to the café. Grant dawdled by the sea wall, letting the sun warm his right shoulder. On the shore below a quadrupedal robot plodded along the strandline, picking up the litter and detritus that some malign confluence of currents and winds endlessly drove across seas and lochs to converge on this particular beach. He watched it for a few minutes then headed across. He clicked through a turnstile and stood for a moment blinking in the dimmer interior. Marble floor, pale wood furnishing and facings. A few people milled about the foyer or browsed the displays, while a dozen or so queued at the entrance to the main attraction.

Grant looked around. He didn't want to use electronic searching. A young woman sitting on the sill of the big plate-glass front window stood up and walked to meet him. Dark, petite, lithe: you could stand her on the palm of your hand, he thought.

'Mr Grant?'

'Dr Nayak?'

They both nodded and raised hands, palm to palm and safely apart.

'Well, hello,' she said. She clapped her hands once. 'My shipbuilder!'

'Let's not get ahead of ourselves,' said Grant.

'Indeed not.'

She smiled, and indicated the exhibit entrance. 'Shall we?'

He must have shown surprise.

'I have tickets,' she said, flourishing a phone.

'I didn't think you'd be interested,' he said.

She laughed, gazing at a wall map of post-Roman Britain covered with the dotted lines and arrows of military and migratory speculation. 'I think we all have a claim on the King of the Britons, now.'

A strip-lit corridor of concrete, then a cave that might have been natural. A pace or two inside it, two uprights and a lintel of Portland sandstone framed a slab of porphyry, like a door, onto which was projected the semblance of an incised inscription:

HIC JACET ARTVRVS REX BRITANNICI
QVONDAM REXQVE FVTVRVS

Virtual though the lettering was, dubious though its claim might be, Grant felt a prickle on the back of his neck, as if from the touch of a dead hand reaching out and laying grip on the present.

The attribution might not be entirely baseless. Ground-penetrating radar and sonar had revealed a skeleton in armour on a granite dais inside the tomb. There had been talk of sending in tiny exploratory bots, with cameras and sensors and sample-retrieval devices, but that had been quashed even by the archaeologists. It had been hurriedly and generally agreed that the folk who had left this mausoleum had intended it to be undisturbed, at least from without. They'd buried him deep in the drift, in this glacier-bulldozed moraine terrain, in the side of the hill. They had probably known what they were doing.

No good could come of digging up dead kings.

It was a place for whispers, not for talk, and the line was impatient with lingering. Grant and Nayak sidled out of the one-way exit and spilled into the gift shop.

They stood at a glass case and pondered miniature pewter replicas of Britannic copies of Roman swords and shields.

'So,' said Grant. 'You still think your scheme's possible.'

'Yes.'

'Seems to me, if you don't mind my saying so, your paper got pretty thoroughly torn apart.'

'Oh, it did!' Nayak said brightly. 'It was very useful. I was mistaken about so much.'

'And you think you've got it right now?'

'I revised it in the light of the criticisms.'

'So why haven't you published?'

'I can't prove it's my own work. Not even to myself.'

'What?'

'I got an airmail letter three years ago that outlined the mathematics. Written, as far as I could tell, by me. From me, to me. The obvious explanation is that this . . . thing works, and at some point in the future I'll travel back in time and send that airmail.'

'You have a strange idea of the meaning of "obvious".'

'We do, yes. Physicists and mathematicians. The point is, the bits I got in the airmail were correct – it was the steps I added to complete it that had the mistakes. And I corrected these from the criticisms. So in a sense, I can't swear it's my own work. My future self might even have forgotten some of the details, and might in fact have got the ones she – I – get right from someone else. Maybe even from the real originator, whoever that is or was or will be.'

'You're telling me you're not publishing because you might be committing *plagiarism via time travel*?'

'It's a possibility, yes.'

Grant closed his eyes and shook his head.

'But still – I mean, you don't even need to claim it for yourself. You could put it out there anonymously. If it's correct, if you've got it right this time, it's the biggest breakthrough since chipped flint.'

She gave him a faux-innocent eyelash flutter. 'Why should I? It's known.'

'What is?'

'The result, the method, the application. At least one of the other blocs has it, possibly both: the Alliance and the Co-ord. Yours – I mean, ours – doesn't.'

'Big news, if true,' said Grant, mildly in the circumstances. 'How do you know?'

'I was threatened. Warned off. If they didn't have it, I'd have been drawn in.'

'You may be right there,' said Grant. 'But – are you in danger now?'

'I defected. I've been given certain . . . assurances.' She glanced around, as if that would make any difference. 'Have you?'

'No.'

'It could be you who's in danger,' Nayak murmured.

'Too late for me to worry,' Grant said, more lightly than he felt. 'I'm in the loop now, like it or not.'

Nayak looked at him sharply. 'You saw something.'

He hadn't mentioned his sighting. 'Uh-huh.'

'So have lots of people who've reached out to me. I've always told them it's none of my business. I get a lot of crank mail, nevertheless, and I always brush it off as politely as possible.'

'So why not this time?'

'Because nobody had ever said what you said. So I checked you out, and I saw you could make good on it. And the fact of someone with your responsibilities saying it suggests that you have . . . air cover, let's say.'

'Support from above?' Grant chuckled, and moved on to another case, this time of jewellery. 'Could be, could be. You know what they're like. Cards close to the chest, and that. But as far as I know, yes. We could do it. But if what you think is correct, why hasn't the Union tried to draw you out before? Especially if they thought you were onto something?'

Nayak threw up her hands. 'You're asking me? You're the one who could find out.'

Grant shrugged. 'Like I said, they're not the most forthcoming. They might even be afraid to mess with powers that can go . . . where your work implies.'

'The deterrent implications had not escaped me,' said Nayak.

'No doubt.' Grant laughed. 'So where do we go from here?'

'I think first you buy some gift for your wife,' said Nayak.

'Oh. Right. Yes.' He peered at the selection of Celtic and Romano-British reproductions, trying to recall what style of brooch Ellen usually wore or indeed if she ever did. 'Uh, Iskander, what would Ellen like of this lot that she doesn't already have?'

'You've bought it now,' replied Iskander.

'Thanks,' said Grant, ungratefully. Fucking AIs and their anticipatory algorithms . . .

'Now we go out,' said Nayak.

Grant picked up his purchase, already gift-wrapped, at the counter. Outside in the sunlight again, he put his glasses back on against the glare. He blinked away the news headlines, with a mutter of irritation.

'You can fix that default,' Nayak pointed out.

'Yeah, yeah. Would you like to join me and Ellen for a coffee?'

'No, thank you. I have a bus to catch. But first, I have something for you.'

She reached into her satchel and took out a large book with a grey hardback cover.

'An antique,' she said, handing it over.

The title was *Scientific American Resource Library: Readings in the Physical Sciences and Technology*, Volume 1. From its weight and the feel and look of the cover, Grant guessed it must be about a century old. An antique, all right.

'I can't—'

'No, no,' Nayak insisted. 'You must take it.' She looked at him intently. 'Don't open it now. Read it at home. You'll find its contents interesting.'

'Ah,' said Grant, penny dropping. 'Thank you. Most kind.'

Nayak waved, turned around and sped off to the roadside, getting across to the stop just as a bus on the Loch Long and Loch Lomond circuit pulled up. Grant watched it leave, then went to meet Ellen in the café. She was sitting by the window sipping a latte, and she – or Iskander – had a large Americano waiting for him.

'Did your discussion go all right?'

'Oh, sure,' he said. 'And I got you this.'

Ellen unwrapped the gift, which turned out to be an ornate pendant of opals caught in rose-gold wire.

'Perfect!' she said. 'How on Earth did you manage to choose it?'

'Well . . .'

They both laughed.

'I see the lassie's given you something,' Ellen said.

'For later reading,' Grant said.

'Ah.' She passed him his rucksack. 'Best keep it safe, then.'

He cursed the book's weight later, when they walked around the head of the loch to Succoth and climbed most of the way up Beinn Narnain, but there was nothing to be done about that. They got fine views of the hills and lochs. The summit of Ben Arthur still didn't look anything like a cobbler.

Back home on Sunday evening after another day of hill-walking and shore-walking weighted down by one and a quarter kilogramme's worth of physical science, Grant finally took the tome out of his rucksack. He left his glasses, phone and watch on the living-room table and took the book through to the spare bedroom. He pulled down the blind and glanced at the contents page. Offprints of papers by Bethe, Hoyle, Einstein, Schrodinger . . .

Grant flicked through and found to his complete lack of surprise that sheets of flimsy A4 paper were interspersed every ten or so pages inside, about twenty in all. They were pains-takingly handwritten, and in the case of the diagrams on the last few pages, hand-drawn. The title at the top of the first page read: *A Method of Reaching Extreme Velocities, v.2.* He smiled, guessing Nayak had written the version number this way as an allusion to the German rocket, just as her paper's title echoed that of Robert H. Goddard's classic 1919 mono-graph.

The mathematics was more rigorous than that in the original online preprint, and the diagrams more detailed. But the math-ematical part still concluded with the devastating equation $V=xc$, where all physically reasonable values for x were large and positive. The practical part of the paper still gave a design for an inflaton trap, with numerical values for everything from the strength of the containment vessel to the electricity input. The figures made Grant whistle, and whistle again when he ran a fingertip down them and totted up an estimate of the costs.

He rummaged under the spare bed, dragged out a box of stuff unsorted since the family had moved in ten years earlier, and found his grandfather's hard-shelled briefcase. Further rummaging yielded a large brown envelope.

The following day, for the first time in months, he took the train. For the first time in years, he took a briefcase. He could have stuffed the envelope in his rucksack, but that wouldn't have looked serious.

When Grant clicked open the well-scuffed Samsonite to draw out the envelope with due solemnity, Morag took it seriously all right. So did the dozen or so other people around the table, most of whom Grant recognised only by sight. There were some surprising absences – Doug McClafferty, the works convener, whom Grant had always assumed to be cadre, but apparently not – and presences, such as Joanna Boyd, known to Grant only as a quiet lady of sixty or so who worked in Accounts and from whom he'd never heard a political word. Old enough to have been in the Rising, mind you. There was that.

Everyone's devices had been left in a Faraday cage locker outside. The cadre meeting room was a large, bare (and, he guessed, swept) office at the top of the admin block on the eastern side of the yard. Posters tacked to the walls showed workers in hard hats and hi-vis and inspirational quotes: *Seize opportunity, grasp possibility* and *All pessimism is unfounded* and *Seek truth from facts*. Its window overlooked the walled green grounds of Newark Castle. Beyond the ancient keep lay kelp beds and tidal aquaculture pools and the slipways of rival yards upstream. Dumbarton Rock was diagonally in view across the Clyde. Grant had always found that basalt remnant of a long-eroded volcano a geological memento mori, a reminder of deep time.

'OK,' said Morag, glancing around the table. 'We all know why we're here.'

'I don't,' said Grant.

'You're the reason we're here, kindae. Before we proceed . . . it might be best all round if I put the rules on the table. Nothing said here goes outside this room. The project we're about to embark on is a state secret, as I'm sure you know. But it's more secret than that. And the penalties for breaking this secrecy go beyond the letter of the law. Like, legally you could go to prison but to be blunt you might not get that far and if you did the length of your sentence would be the least of your worries, let's say. It's that serious. Now we all know your record, John, that's what makes you a *responsable* and that won't change if you leave that envelope on the table, walk out of that door and never say a word of this again. As long as you don't say a word, we'll never hold it against you.

'But if you stay, John, you're in on this to the end. You got that?'

'Yes.'

It was like an oath. He was slightly offended that Morag had felt she had to spell it out.

'OK,' said Morag. 'If you'll just pass the paper around. Everyone take a quick look, and pass it on.'

This was done. Grant took the pages back and tapped the edges into alignment and laid them back on the table.

'I take it,' he said, 'this means everyone here intends to build a faster-than-light starship.'

It sounded crazy, saying it out loud.

'Got it in one,' said Morag.

'Something you should know,' Grant said. 'The author of this paper thinks the Alliance and/or the Co-ord already have this.'

Morag glanced at Omar Khan, the fusion power tech, who nodded.

'They do,' he said, after a moment. 'We've had suspicions, from anomalies like the one you saw, John. But they're like UFOs – there's always a simpler explanation, and even where there isn't the evidence doesn't outweigh the unlikeliness of it all. "Extraordinary claims require extraordinary evidence," and all that. So we—'

'Excuse me,' Grant said. 'Who's "we"? Don't tell me all this is common knowledge in the cadre.'

The words were out of his mouth before it occurred to him that he had no idea what Omar Khan's position in the cadre might be.

'I'm not saying it is,' said Omar. 'This is almost as new to me as it is to you, and the same goes for most of us here apart from Morag, who's been in the loop a wee bit longer. It's all compartmentalised, need-to-know, all that – you know the drill, man!' He gestured, vertical and horizontal, with both hands. 'So I'm telling you what I was told, by a reliable source let's say, and told to tell you in turn. Right?'

'Right,' said Grant. 'Just wanted to be clear on that.'

'Very well,' said Omar. 'As I was saying. We recently – can't say how recently – got the extraordinary evidence. You'll have heard of E-PRIME?'

'Exo-Planetary Research Imaging and Mapping Explorer,' said Grant.

'Yes. Pride of ESA. Streets ahead of anything NASA or Roscosmos or CNSA have. Biggest space telescope ever built. Discovered more Earth-like planets with actual biosignatures than anyone ever thought were out there, turning the Fermi Paradox into the biggest fucking headache since dark matter. Lots of biosignatures, no technosignatures—'

'What's that in English?' someone asked, to general laughter.

'Plenty of signs of life out there, no sign of aliens,' Omar translated. 'So anyway, E-PRIME happens to have its beady eye – lens, sensors, whatever – turned on a system that's long been known to have an Earth-like planet in the habitable zone. It's found no signs of life. Of course, there are plenty of other scientific reasons to survey the system, and E-PRIME has done that and is just about to turn away when it picks up a wee burst of radio transmission from the planet's close vicinity. Instantly this gets its full attention. The signal is never repeated, but it's parsed and analysed by E-PRIME's on-board AI within about a second. Not only is it artificial, it's encrypted. It's in an old Russian military code, long since cracked. What it says is this: "No life detected. About to attempt return." And just after the end of the transmission, there's a tiny, barely detectable blue flash.'

'Aha,' said Grant. Morag shot him a warning frown. Evidently not everyone here knew about his sighting.

'Good guess,' Omar said, swift into the breach. 'Cherenkov radiation, yes, very likely it was.'

'I take it,' Grant said, 'that every care has been taken to rule out—'

'Instrument error, a closer origin, all that? Yes, of course. The thing is, the system in question is fifty light-years away.'

Grant took a moment to process this. His first thought was: oh, they've gone fifty light-years away, impressive. His next was: wait a minute, the signal has taken fifty years to get back, so –

'You mean to tell me they've had this faster-than-light travel for *fifty fucking years*?'

'At least,' said Omar.

It was like a rug pulled out from under his understanding of half a century of history. His entire lifetime! After the first moment of bewilderment, some things began to click into place.

No wonder the Union had a Venus cloud colony complete with its own manufacturing base on a tiny asteroid nudged into orbit around the planet, probes on every moon in the Solar System, and the best deep-space telescope system ever built, while the Alliance and Co-ord between them had only a Moon base, a Mars exploration team (and, to be fair, the ruins of that electric-car billionaire's company-town dystopia) and a lot of robotic asteroid mining. No wonder only the Union took climate change seriously enough to start making a real difference, while the other two blocs rode along in its wake. Forget about no Planet B – the fuckers by now must have B, C and the rest of the fucking alphabet!

'But that means—'

Morag held up a hand. 'Believe me, John, we're well aware of what it means. Better minds than ours are on the case. That's why we think both the other blocs must have it, not just the Russians or even the Co-ord as a whole. And as far as we – our intelligence AIs, that is – can work out, they're sharing it between themselves, and keeping the Union out of the loop. We don't know why, but it doesn't bode well for us. And the fact it's been kept secret so long means there's a very tight, and probably comparatively small, operation running it.'

'For fifty years?'

'The Manhattan Project showed a secret can be kept by thousands of people, and Bletchley Park showed a secret can be kept for decades, but, yeah, it's a fucking tight ship they must be running. However, we now think there *has* been a leak.'

'What was it?'

Morag pointed to the paper lying in front of Grant.

'That.'

Grant shook his head. 'No, she says she . . .'

He stopped, sighed, and then recounted what Nayak had told him about having received the gist of the equations from herself in the future. Their sceptical looks ill behove what they'd just told him.

'Piffle,' said Morag. 'The lassie's having you on, or being played herself. As she partly suspects, by the sound of it.'

'But FTL does imply time travel,' Grant said. He recalled his deep dive into fringe physics. '"FTL, relativity, causality – pick two," as the saying goes. Relativity's holding up just fine, you tell me we have evidence of FTL, so . . .'

'Only in very particular circumstances,' said Omar. 'I don't think you can use FTL ships as free-roaming time machines. If you could, they'd be here already!'

'Maybe they are,' said Grant. 'Maybe that's what UFOs are and always have been.'

That got a laugh.

'Besides,' Omar went on, 'for a closed causal loop like that, our Dr Nayak would inevitably have to travel back in time to send the message to make it possible for her to travel back in time. She has no free will in the matter. Nor has anyone else, come to think of it, because nobody could prevent her. Complete determinism would have to be true, and I can cite everything from the Black Gospels of Herculaneum to the latest results from CERN to show that it isn't.'

Grant kept a poker face. If Omar was high up in the cadre, he would – probably, ha-ha – be a devout Spinozist and therefore a strict determinist, and not one to flirt with the chancy Epicurean doctrine that the random swerve of atoms, or in modern terms quantum unpredictability, was the solid foundation of free will. On the other hand, he could be bluffing. Best not to chance it.

'I'll take all that under advisement,' said Grant. 'But if it is a leak from inside this fifty-year-long secret project, how can we trust it?' He tapped a finger on the small stack of paper. 'How do we know if we build this thing here, the inflaton trap, it won't blow up in our faces?'

Joanna Boyd, the accountant, spoke up. 'We don't, John. But what would be the point? It would be an act of war, and a very roundabout and unreliable one at that. If the Alliance wanted to blow up a shipyard just across the water from Faslane, they could do it like—' she snapped her fingers '—that! And if they wanted to do it untraceably and deniably, they could. As could we, the other way. No, John, deterrence holds. If we start off by thinking it doesn't, then we go down a rabbit hole worse than the one Morag sent you into.'

'For which I take responsibility,' Morag interjected. 'Like I said, John, I know you have a tendency to obsessive focus, and I exploited it.'

Grant tipped his chair back and looked them all in the eye one by one.

'Am I really that bad?' he said. 'And everyone knows it?'

'No, no,' Morag hastened to assure him. 'Everybody knows you as the guy to give the hard problems to, and you'll worry away until you solve it. It's a good reputation to have, in a way. But if you're feeling . . . well, inclined to the kind of thinking that got you wondering if the leak was a ploy, it might be an idea to ask Iskander to keep an eye on it for you.'

Grant decided not to take offence. 'That's me told,' he said. He picked up the papers. 'So, on to next business. How do we go about actually doing this?'

Everyone was looking at him. Morag leaned forward. 'Ah, John, that's where we were kindae hoping you could come in . . .'

'Oh,' he said. 'I see.'

Grant looked down at the papers, then up at the posters on the walls. *Seize opportunity, grasp possibility. Seek truth from facts.*

So they keep telling us! He'd show them.

'Here's how we do it,' he said. 'I set up a company. That way, the project is legally separate from the yard. My new company buys out the current contract with my team. I explain to them that a more lucrative opportunity has come up. We sell on the existing order to another team or another yard. I pay for buying it out with the money I get from selling it on.'

'Some losses to friction in the swap,' said Joanna. 'Admin and so on.'

Grant waved airily. 'We can absorb that. Meanwhile we've lined up an order for a modified undersea vehicle, for, I don't know, Antarctic surveys or something. Rugged hull, life-support a bit more long-term, a back-up power storage system which will of course be cover for the—' he rolled his eyes upward '—FTL drive.' It sounded like crazy talk, out of his own mouth.

'And who do you get this order from?' Omar Khan asked.

'That's where you pull strings, Omar.' Grant smiled. 'Not that I'm suggesting you're familiar with such shenanigans.'

'It's not unheard of,' said Khan, wryly. He made a note to himself. 'On it.'

'Costs?' Joanna asked.

'Doable. I've had a few ideas about how we play that since I looked over Dr Nayak's plan and what kind of parts she thinks we'll need. She may be a scientific genius, I wouldn't know, but I can tell you she's no engineer. She gives specifications but has no idea what needs to be made specially and what's off the shelf, whereas I do.' He rubbed his hands. 'I'm looking forward to this!'

'I'm no sure I am,' said Morag. 'Cannae get my head around the idea of you being my employer, John.'

'Awa and employ yourself,' Grant said, jovially. 'It'll make no difference at all. I won't be your employer, remember. We all still own the yard. It's just a legal formality.' He smiled around the table, tapped the papers, and put them back in the briefcase. 'Everyone clear? Good. Let's do this.'

A few evenings later Myles dropped by for dinner, on his way to meet his new girlfriend, that lassie from Lamlash, Marie. It was less than a month until finals in July, and this was a rare evening off for both of them. After dinner, as Myles and Grant carried plates to the dishwasher, Grant said: 'Oh, by the way – would you like to be a company director?'

'Not particularly.' Myles stooped to load the dishwasher. Grant intercepted him and put the plates in the sink to rinse first.

'Ah, it's just a laugh. Bit of paperwork, it's a legal formality at work.'

'At work?' Myles leaned one hand on the sink, frowning. 'The yard's self-managed. Are you rolling that back? Privatising it?'

'No, no!' Grant made urgent wiping motions. 'Nothing's being rolled back. We just need to set up a wee private company to do a specialised job. I need another name on it so I'm not sole owner – it makes some kind of difference in tax. Thought it would be amusing to have yours.'

Myles looked wary. 'Does it commit me to anything?'

Grant laughed. 'Nah, it's just admin. No liabilities.'

'Och, fine, Dad.' He sounded impatient. 'If you must.'

'OK,' said Grant. 'Just a minute.'

He nipped out and returned with a form and a pen. 'Paw-print here.'

'You're the Paw, Dad.'

They laughed. Myles signed.

'"John Grant & Son Ship Construction Ltd",' Grant read out. 'It does have a certain ring to it.'

'Yes, it does,' Myles said. Fortunately, he took it as a joke. 'I'll tell Marie I'm now an industrialist – a Clyde shipbuilder, no less!'

'Way to go,' said Grant. 'Show her you're a lad with prospects.'

He watched Myles' departure with a wry smile. The lad had more prospects than he realised. As a director of the first and (as far as Grant knew) so far *only* private company to build and own a starship, Myles might just be in on the ground floor of the biggest expansion, spatial and economic, in the entire history of humanity. The Clyde would become a Galactic coast, lined with starship yards. Boomtown to the stars!

CHAPTER TEN

Crash Test Dummy

Saturday 11 to Sunday 12 October 2070, Venus

The first suit arrived from the moonlet seventeen days after Milloy had told Owen about the human surface landing project. Its component parts were packaged in indented polystyrene like a factory-fresh delivery of high-end consumer electronics. Fully assembled, with an instrumented and telemetered crash test dummy inside, the suit stood two and a half metres high, with thick, rigid casing articulated at every joint. It looked – as Milloy put it – like a metal Michelin Man.

'It's not metal,' said Owen. 'It's a ceramic-based metamaterial with—'

'Spare me the robotsplaining,' said Milloy.

She and the other nine people in her team set to work checking the instrumentation and fitting the suit with its launch glider, an eminently disposable harness and fabric wing. Its final descent balloon, its small but tough emergency parachute, its return balloons and drogue, and the gas cylinders to inflate them were more robustly attached, backpack style. The atmosphere at lower levels was so dense that in principle the suit could survive a free fall to impact, but at a terminal velocity about twenty metres per second this would be less than optimal for the occupant. So a simple descent and return test without a live occupant seemed best advised.

'T minus one hour,' said Milloy, as they manoeuvred the suit onto a trolley for transfer to the docking area. 'We'll be going down for final prep, it's a bit of a confined space and you'd be in the way, so . . .'

Owen took the hint, climbed from the lab and rounded up Walworth at his usual table. Together they strolled to the observation room at the leading edge of the habitat. Here the panels were fully transparent rather than translucent. The huge window curved gently to left and right and more sharply to top and bottom. Low in the west, the fuzzy disc of the rising sun glared in. On the globally unbroken bank of bright clouds a few kilometres below it cast long shadows from small irregularities. Owen's and Walworth's glasses adjusted accordingly.

They weren't alone. Seven off-shift workers and two scientists were there already. One worker had a hand-held camera as well as her glasses. Walworth went over to inquire.

'This is going out live on news,' he reported back.

'Bit risky,' said Owen. 'A lot could go wrong.'

'Adds to the fun.' Walworth brushed his hands together, and looked around. 'Where's the drinks table for this party? Oh, there isn't one. Too bad. Hipflask it is, then.' He raised his voice, and the flask. 'I'm willing to share, you know! Toast the suit on its way?'

They all just looked at him. He shrugged and swigged.

By T minus five minutes a couple of dozen people were standing at the window, peering down. At T minus one minute Walworth started a countdown, loud enough to annoy. At T plus one second the triangular glider shot out from under

Cloud City and sped far ahead, to drop into the clouds within about half a minute. Walworth cheered, and found a few people to share what little he had left of his liquor in the flask. Some people left, others arrived.

'It's the return that's more important,' said Walworth. 'Might as well wait.'

Walworth normally got along well with everyone, but now it seemed he was being cold-shouldered. Several attempts to join conversations later, the consul made light of the matter. 'Bit of a heavy lunch,' he told Owen. 'Not my usual self. They're all chatting science stuff anyway. Over my head and above my pay grade.' He sat down, back to the rear wall, and snoozed.

Owen remained at the window as the westward spin of the atmosphere carried them into the long morning. A view from inside the suit's helmet was showing on Cloud City's internal network, and no doubt – with inevitable light-speed delay – on whatever nerd channels were covering this back on Earth. The sulphuric acid clouds were brighter and thinner inside than they looked from above, but there was nothing to see until the suit dropped below that shining haze. Even then, all that showed was the somewhat monotonous landscape of Atalanta Planitia, its smooth floor of ancient lava flows swiftly drifting past and slowly getting closer. After half an hour Walworth snored loudly enough to wake himself up. He shook his head vigorously, sniffed hard and clambered to his feet.

'Ah, that's better,' he said. He joined Owen at the window.

'Not long now,' said Owen. 'Look at the live feed.'

The ground – smooth, with scattered boulders, all in an orange glow – was coming up fast. Too fast, and in the wrong place. The viewpoint hurtled towards a big boulder, then yawed wildly, missing the rock by a metre. It swung back to vertical and slowed with a jolt, then the suit's feet touched down and everything stabilised.

'Well,' said a familiar voice, 'that's one long drop for a woman, one big step up for humanity.'

An arm of the suit reached out, hand holding a camera. The viewpoint switched, looking back at the big domed head. It zoomed on the small faceplate, through which a pair of smiling eyes looked out.

Commotion in the room, and behind it, through the wall, the reverberation of a cheer from hundreds of voices at once.

'What the fuck?' cried Walworth.

'It's my good friend Francesca Milloy,' Owen said. 'You'll have heard of her.'

'You didn't tell me she liked surprises,' Walworth grumbled. He shouted above the hubbub: 'Allow me to be the first to congratulate you all on behalf of the Alliance! Well done, Mademoiselle Milloy! Well done, Cloud City! Well done, the Union!'

This was greeted with ironic cheers.

The viewpoint returned to that from the helmet. Milloy walked about for a few minutes, looking around. Her movements seemed slow and laboured, like those of an astronaut in an underwater training tank. As she stepped out of the lee of a boulder a heavy gust slammed her, tipping the viewpoint aslant. Her right arm swung out and to the right, as if in a swiping punch at an unseen opponent. The shift in her weight restored her balance. They heard her grunt and mutter. Then she stooped, picked up a rock, stashed it somewhere out of view, and toggled a switch. Another jolt, and the ground dropped away. She was on her way back.

'What possessed her to do that?' Walworth asked. 'You told me they had a perfectly adequate dummy.'

'She took her responsibility for the suit very seriously,' Owen said. 'And sooner or later, they'd have to send a human down, so maybe as she was team leader on the design she thought it might as well be her.'

'And write her name in the history books into the bargain.'

'I suppose there is that, yes.'

'Speaking of which,' said Walworth, suddenly careless of being overheard, 'rumour has it that our governments have a major announcement coming down the line of exciting news from the science front. Might not be enough to steal the thunder of the first woman on Venus, but you never know.'

Someone scoffed behind Walworth's shoulder. It was Jeanne Al-Khalil, who'd welcomed Owen out of his crate. 'And what might that be? Noah's navigation computer? The anatomy of the Roswell aliens? Proof that you lot faked the Moon landings after all?'

Walworth laughed diplomatically. 'Oh, these are all still very much under wraps, I'm told.'

A black dot rose from the clouds five kilometres ahead of the habitat.

'There she is!' cried Owen.

A flurry of zoom gestures. The dot became a ball, then a balloon with a tiny figure hanging underneath. It rose higher than the habitat's altitude, then snapped out a drogue to slow its westward drift and began to drop as the balloon slowly shrank. This was repeated several times, until the balloon passed just below the leading edge of Cloud City. Moments later the recovery was announced as a success. Milloy came up on the news shortly afterwards, still in the suit but with the helmet off and her head looking absurdly small. She delivered a short, modest speech to camera, and then declared that she had work to be getting on with.

Taking care as always to observe everything going on in the underside's web of walkways and cabins, Owen hastened to Milloy's lab. There the suit stood headless with an open torso amid a clutter of collapsed balloons and rigging. The suit had evidently been hosed down, but still had a whiff of the Venusian atmospheric biota's bad breath. The coolant fluid was being drained for re-cooling and re-pumping. Four of Milloy's team pored over every square centimetre of the casing – now darkened and pitted, and still radiating heat – while the rest examined the instruments that had ridden down and back inside, attached to Milloy rather than to the dummy. Milloy herself turned from scanning the images returned from the cameras as Owen came in.

'Congratulations, Francesca!' he said. He gave a carefully calibrated self-deprecating laugh. 'I must say you had me fooled.'

Milloy grinned. 'Coming from you, that's quite a compliment.'

'That's how I meant it. Did the suit perform to spec?'

'Everything nominal so far,' she said. 'Superficial damage, undergoing self-repair. Pressure well within safe parameters. Highest recorded interior temperature a cosy twenty-seven Celsius.'

'Great! Do you still want me to go?'

'Oh, sure,' said Milloy. 'We really do want you to test it further. See how long it takes for the heat to get past the limit of human endurance. That way, we can establish a safe operating schedule.'

'So it's not just a prestige stunt?'

'Apparently not.'

She knew more, but wasn't saying. Owen let that lie.

'When will it be ready for my descent?' he asked.

'About sixteen hours, if all goes well.' Airquotes. '"Tomorrow morning". We'll let it cool, then chill it further, assuming it passes inspection. Here, have a look at the pics.'

'I've seen them. I followed you all the way down.'

'Not all of them. We limited the feed, just in case.'

In case what? Owen didn't ask, and stood beside her as she thumbed through and pointed out features on the ground that had previously seemed virtually featureless.

'Sixteen hours from now,' he said, 'we'll be passing over Ishtar Terra. Very different terrain, unless I'm to land on Lakshmi Planum. So how is this relevant to me?'

'You're right there.' She closed the display. 'You won't be landing on Lakshmi Planum, I'll tell you that for nothing.'

'So where will I be landing?'

'Um,' she said. 'You have a mission briefing in two hours and twenty-seven minutes. Get that consul of yours to drag his lazy ass along while you're at it.'

'Fine,' said Owen. 'Where's the meeting?'

'Don't ask *me*,' said Milloy. 'Ask Iskander.'

The meeting was in another of the pods like Milloy's workplace, slung on cables and girders deep in the lower half of the habitat. This one, evidently, was dedicated to exobiology. They sat around a lab bench that had been cleared of clutter but still bore lurid and sinister stains, and stank faintly of phosphines. It was chaired, somewhat to Owen's surprise, by Iason Konstantopoulos, the man who'd walked with him to the café on his arrival. Also present: Milloy, Walworth, Owen and a Swedish geologist called Alma Persson.

'We have a request for our friend Mr Owen here,' Konstanto-poulos said, addressing Walworth. 'With your permission, of course.'

Walworth wafted an indulgent hand. 'Happy to oblige. It's entirely up to Marcus, unless the request contravenes Alliance policy or consular privileges.'

'Oh, nothing like that, I'm sure,' Konstantopoulos said. 'It's almost embarrassingly simple – in fact, it *is* embarrassing, which is why we would appreciate your discretion, and why we are not going to give it the kind of publicity we gave Francesca's achievement.'

'You have our attention,' said Owen. 'And I believe you can count on our discretion.'

Walworth nodded. 'Of course.'

Konstantopoulos evidently took this assurance with the seriousness it deserved. 'Thank you! Well, the long and the short of it is, one of our rovers has got itself stuck. Despite having adaptive wheels, tracks, walkers and all the computing power a few billion euros can buy, the little scamp has got itself wedged nose down in a crevice, back legs waving feebly in the air, so to speak. All we require of Mr Owen is that he rescue it, lift it across the crevice with the aid of some equipment we'll provide, and send it on its way.'

'And this is too tough a job even for your heroic cosmonauts, I take it?' said Walworth, sounding amused.

'Yes, it is,' said Konstantopoulos. 'In the first place, accessing the site may not be straightforward, and might take more than an hour. Altogether, the operation might take long enough for the heat in the suit to somewhat exceed the limit of human endurance. Actually moving the rover, even with the assistance of the suit's servo-motors, may require physical strength beyond normal human capacity.'

'And before you ask,' Milloy chipped in, 'the delicacy of the task and the speed of reaction that might be needed rules out using a remotely operated avatar.'

Walworth raised his eyebrows. 'Really? You're telling us latency is an issue, at a range of tens of kilometres, hundreds at the most?'

'Yes,' said Milloy. 'Latency, precision and the possibility, however small, of interrupted comms at a crucial moment. We need a human-equivalent mind actually on the spot. Believe me, we've run the scenarios and the sims, and this is the best solution we've come up with.'

'That *you've* come up with?'

'All right,' said Milloy, annoyed. 'That *Iskander* has come up with! Happy now?'

'It's as I thought,' said Walworth. 'Just being curious, and for the record. Proceed.'

Konstantopoulos summoned to everyone's glasses an image that looked like a square of elephant hide. 'Atropos Tessera, just west of the Akna Montes mountain range on the western edge of Ishtar Terra.' He zoomed. Here the wrinkles in the planet's skin were fractal, like waves on the ocean: the terrain looked almost the same from any altitude. At the edge of one wrinkle was a cluster of bright pixels. 'There's our rover. Cythera Area Survey and Sampling Intelligent Explorer, affectionately if predictably known as CASSIE.'

'Her current official location is fifty kilometres to the south,' Owen remarked. 'Why did you change her mission? And why keep it secret?'

Konstantopoulos shot him a sharp look. 'Well spotted. We changed her mission when a very low-altitude survey – a camera blimp, basically, wallowing through the atmosphere with the heavy wind behind it – spotted a highly unusual outcrop that we thought deserved immediate investigation.'

'Why immediate?'

'It was uncovered by dust movement, and it seemed possible it might soon be covered by further movement. It looks, I have to say, very interesting indeed – an apparent pristine piece of surface terrain from before the resurfacing event. That's exciting enough, of course, but to be honest we intend to look for evidence of past life. Settle the question of where the floating biosphere came from. Or not, as the case may be, but obviously it would be nice to get a positive answer.'

'Microfossils?'

'Ideally, yes. We got the rover to within a few hundred metres of the outcrop, but as luck would have it on the wrong side of a chasm just centimetres too wide for CASSIE to cross.'

'Yet the rover did attempt the crossing?' Owen asked.

'Well, there's the embarrassment,' said Konstantopoulos. 'A processing glitch, a false echo, whatever . . . the machine underestimated the gap, and that's all 'there is to it. It shouldn't have happened, but it did.'

'It is what it is,' said Walworth. He seemed to be enjoying himself. 'No call for embarrassment – mistakes will happen, even with the best tech and the best operators, especially when you're pushing the envelope, as here.'

'Thank you,' said Konstantopoulos. He turned to the Swedish woman. 'Alma, over to you.'

Persson fixed Owen with a wary smile. 'Your mission profile, Mr Owen.' She flicked fingers. 'Zapped to your glasses – you'll have time to study it in detail. Briefly: you'll hang-glide much farther ahead of Cloud City than Francesca did today. CASSIE's navigation beacon will guide you in. If you land too far away – and we'll be able to tell you that – you can simply ascend and re-descend by balloon. You'll have ample supplies of compressed gas for five balloons, quite apart from your own ascent balloon which is integral to the suit. The machine weighs almost a tonne, so before you attempt to free it from the crevice you must harness the balloons to it – four should be quite enough to support its full weight, so there's no risk of its falling down further, or on top of you for that matter. Several survey blimps have converged on the area and are moored nearby, and you can make use of them, too, if necessary. By the time you've got CASSIE out and lifted across and settled safely on the ground, which should be the work of minutes if all goes well, you have a window of an hour or so in which you can ascend and arrive at our altitude ahead of us. There you can rendezvous in the same manner as Francesca demonstrated today. If there are any delays or unforeseen difficulties, you can still ascend for retrieval by the nearest outpost, which follows us a few hours behind. And if all else fails, as long as you're above the clouds you can be picked up by an aircraft from here or from the nearest outpost. The important matter, of course, is not to remain on the ground or in the lower atmosphere so long that the heat build-up exceeds even your tolerance. The exact figures are in your briefing.'

Owen glanced, then nodded. 'Everything seems clear. One question, if I may?'

'Yes?'

'The outcrop in question isn't marked on the survey image, but Iason said it's within a few hundred metres to the west.

Why don't I simply keep the rover aloft on the balloons and perhaps the blimps, and walk it over there? The prevailing wind should be in our favour, and—'

Three heads shaking. 'No,' said Persson. 'I appreciate the suggestion, but there's too much risk of an unexpected gust damaging the rover, and/or yourself. The wind is, as Iason remarked, heavy down there. Besides, mapping the ground and identifying and dating the rocks in the environs of the outcrop is essential to the rover's scientific mission, prior to examining the outcrop itself.'

Owen allowed his eyebrows to twitch. 'Come to think of it,' he said brightly, 'why don't *I* just stroll over to the outcrop and pick up any loose material, or even take a geological hammer with me and tap off a piece for you?'

Persson looked pained. '*Please*, Mr Owen. As Iason said, the outcrop seems to be pristine. Examining it in completely undisturbed condition before taking a sample is an irreplaceable opportunity. The rover – CASSIE – is a highly specialised and well-equipped geological surveying and sampling robot, and with all due respect, you're not. All we ask of you is to use the abilities you unquestionably have to enable CASSIE to apply her abilities to the best advantage. No less, and very much no more, if you please.'

Owen made a smoothing gesture. 'Fine, fine. I'll stick to my mission and let CASSIE stick to hers.'

'Precisely!' Persson smiled.

Konstantopoulos looked around. 'I think that concludes the day's business. Thank you, everyone. There's a small reception at the café in three hours, to celebrate Francesca's achievement. See you all there!'

Milloy looked momentarily nonplussed. 'Oh, great,' she said, as she stood up. 'I suppose that means I have to print a frock.'

'Don't worry,' Owen murmured in her ear as they made their way along the gangway. 'I'll be happy to help you out of it.'

'I'll make sure it's fancy,' she said, 'and rips easily.'

It was, and it did.

Owen woke before Francesca Milloy did. Every diurnal cycle his brain required a few hours of downtime for memory processing. He might recall a swift succession of images and feelings and an incoherent, constantly rewritten narrative. In that sense he dreamed, though never so far of electric sheep.

He got out of bed, used the tiny lavatory cubicle to excrete his dry and odourless waste, and got dressed. After tabbing a note to Milloy's glasses he left the flat and the block, to head across Astroturf and through a recorded dawn chorus to Walworth's.

The consul was awake and hung over. As Owen arrived at the door a small robot trundled up with two cups of coffee in its grippers.

'This,' said Walworth when he opened the door and blinked blearily, 'is taking the piss.' But he accepted the proffered cup gratefully enough, and motioned Owen to the secure room. Facing each other across the fold-down table, they sipped for a moment in appreciative silence.

'Question,' said Walworth. 'Perhaps one it's not my place to ask, but . . .'

'Feel free,' said Owen.

'That unfortunate accident that the brave little robot CASSIE met.'

'Uh-huh.'

'All that talk about glitches. I mean, our friends seemed genuinely at a loss to explain it, other than "shit happens".'

'You're right,' said Owen. 'They were at a loss. At any rate, I didn't detect any indications of deceit or evasion.'

'And you would have, wouldn't you?'

Owen shrugged. 'It's my job. Though I must admit, Milloy deceived me earlier.'

'Ha! That's rather a different thing, and she might not have decided on going herself until very late in the day.' Walworth brushed his palms across each other. 'However, my question. Is it possible that it wasn't a freak accident? Could it have been, perhaps, a work of art?'

'One of ours?' said Owen. 'No.' He paused. 'But that's to the best of my knowledge, and as you know these matters are managed on a need-to-know basis.'

'That's all very well,' said Walworth. 'And it could be Co-ord, I suppose. But if any Alliance citizens here are doing Council work without my authorisation, I shall be most annoyed. It's my good name and credibility that are at stake here. Your nefarious activities are, so to speak, discounted. Everyone knows you're a spy, and knows I know. But the others I have in effect vouched for.'

'I hesitate to point this out,' said Owen. 'But if the Council or indeed some other Alliance service has agents or operatives here, they might very well not be Alliance citizens. Furthermore, sabotage is not confined solely to enemy agents, in our own bloc and in the other two. Even the Union has disgruntled citizens, and not all of them are noticed by Iskander or by the political or security apparats before it's too late.'

'You should know, I suppose.'

Owen nodded firmly. 'I do know, Perry. Though, of course, I can't say anything about it, even to you.'

'Of course, of course. Long and the short of it – we can't rule out sabotage, whoever might be behind it. Which means we can't rule out further sabotage – of what, from the Union's point of view, is your mission to set the rover back on its feet.'

'I've war-gamed several such scenarios.'

'I'm sure you have.' Walworth drained his coffee, crushed the cup, caught himself in the act of being about to chuck it, and laid it down on the table. He stared at his own hand for a moment, as if it were an autonomous object, shook his head briskly and looked up at Owen. 'Indulge me. I pride myself on low animal cunning, but I'll freely admit it's no match for high artificial cunning. How do you intend to prevent their retrieving a sample of this precious rock, rather than simply delay it?'

'A good question,' said Owen. 'In truth, delay is all I can do. Even if I were to destroy Cloud City, which I could, and the outposts, too, which would be more difficult, and furthermore wreck the habitation and fabrication capacities of the moonlet, which would be quite a challenge—'

Walworth raised his hand. 'Stop, for God's sake! Nobody expects you to do any of that. No, I think the British Council will be well satisfied if you can contrive to fail to rescue CASSIE, and if possible put her beyond use. Preferably in a way that can't be proved wasn't an accident.'

'That,' said Owen, 'is exactly what I intend.'

CHAPTER ELEVEN

Einstein's Watch

June to August 2070, Earth

At the Garelochhead bus stop half the early-morning commuters changed for the England shuttle. Lakshmi Nayak watched them go, and leaned back a little and sat up straighter as the bus moved off and took the turning to the right. She noticed the same slight tension lift from others. Heads turned, conversations resumed. Through occasional gaps in the trees she glimpsed the fortifications and the finance towers on the far shore of the Gare Loch, the drone swarm at the border, a warship heading out, two more warships berthed and a submarine in dock.

The Trident boat lay like a long black slug of lead with a slab of fin. Yet John Grant had seen a submarine, perhaps this very vessel, levitate above the horizon for a split second, and vanish in a blue flash. Or so he claimed. Only her grasp of the most abstruse physics let Nayak sustain the thought that such a thing could ever fly.

But sustain it she could: a feat of levitation in itself, she thought, allowing herself a small smile. She was going to work in a shipyard, building a starship! That was what was hard to believe, even for her. Moment of truth, Lakshmi! She recalled the tremor in undergraduate practicals, when she had the experiment set up and felt that all her understanding so far stood or fell by what happened next.

She felt that same tremor now, magnified. She took several deep breaths, letting the nervous feeling glow into hope. Her ship would fly.

Helicopters throbbed to and fro, and in the sky far above the commercial buzz the military drones patrolled the enclave's airspace perimeter. The bus passed through Clynder and Rosneath, both villages largely abandoned on the seafront and built anew along a higher contour, and swung uphill, bypassing the grassy tip of Rosneath Point, and down again into Kilcreggan. Here, for a change, the village's row of white houses stood occupied, the street busy: two vintage shops still shuttered, three cafés and a grocery Co-op already open; the main road was high enough above sea level to be safe for decades yet. The incoming ferry butted through the waves just offshore.

The engine whined down and the door thudded open. Nayak got off with a dozen other passengers, picked her way down a short, sharp slope of tarmac and clattered along the hundred-metre-long wooden pier. At just before eight on a bright morning in early July, with the breeze coming from the west, it was a little chilly on the pier and would be chillier on the boat.

She shrugged into her new black quilted coat over the thin silk of her best bright green salwar kameez with the silver embroidery. Black leather court-heel shoes, hair piled and pinned, make-up more precise than usual – she wasn't facing a job interview, Grant had made that clear, but she wanted to sustain the pretence that she was, and to show that she wasn't taking anything for granted.

The ferry pulled in and was made fast. When they were beckoned to board Nayak almost skipped up the gangway. But she didn't, because she could have tripped.

She sat on the upper deck in the lee of the wheelhouse. Along an arm of the wake white horses aligned their ceaseless plunging gallop like a kelpie cavalry charge. Ahead, the Alliance warship she'd seen leave Faslane now cut across the ferry's bow, its prow a scalpel blade, its lines fared and swept, its superstructure bristling with so many antennae you could almost feel the static on your neck. Now that was a ship you could believe would fly, given the chance and an FTL drive! The ferry bucked in the wash, reached calm water, then minutes later bucked again.

The triple town spanned the view in front: Gourock dead ahead, Greenock to her left and Port Glasgow beyond that. Nayak couldn't see any boundaries, only a gradient from lighter to heavier industry as her gaze swung upriver. The conurbation's rotted rim of abandoned shoreline streets looked sad, but the view was brightened by the new build that rose above the older blocks of sandstone and concrete like trees sprouting from rubble. From her low vantage the new towers seemed higher than the hills behind them, and greener, too, creepers climbing their wooden walls and wind turbines spinning at their tops. Not that these hills were high, compared to those behind her, the mountains of Argyll among which she'd lived and worked for months. At some unremarked moment back on the bus she'd crossed the Highland fault. Metamorphic rock had raised the mountains behind her, sandstone and other sedimentary rocks the hills ahead – apart from basalt intrusions like Tower Hill there in front of her, black cliff-faces knuckling through its tattered green glove of grass and trees.

The ferry docked just in time for a rush to catch the 08:38

from Gourock. Nayak got off at Port Glasgow and walked down a long tunnel tiled with scenes from an earlier shipbuilding age. That old post-industrial heritage mural was scrawled over with a slogan from a more recent decade, its fluorescent spray-bombing now acrylically preserved: THE SEAS ARE RISING AND SO ARE WE.

She let Iskander guide her to the yard through thronged streets which gave her now and then a pang of home: so many people from the subcontinent, so many shops and stalls, fabrics with colours to make her linger and street-food smells to make her hungry! She was tempted to grab a bite, but resisted. As if to make up for the stingy moment, she zapped a payment to the cello-playing busker in the underpass.

She hurried up the steps and emerged to face the high, blank wall of the yard. Across its right corner loomed a crenellated stone tower: yet another castle.

At the gate, clad in glaring fluorescent jacket and shorts and propping a bike, Grant waited. He was in his early fifties, a man of average height with cropped hair, lean but blocky, shoulders and upper arms built by push-ups or pull-ups and calf muscles solid from cycle commutes. He had the wary, almost worried look she recalled from their meeting at Arrochar: lined forehead, gaze roving except when he spoke, and sometimes even then.

'Good morning, Dr Nayak,' he said.

'Good morning, Mr Grant.' She smiled. 'Thank you for meeting me.'

He wheeled his bike through the gate. 'Let me show you around.'

Nayak sipped a welcome espresso in a small room by the reception. Grant hurried away to change out of his cycling gear, returning in T-shirt and jeans. 'I'll be working in a rig later,' he said, as if apologetic. 'Let me take your coat.'

She followed him out, onto the first slipway. Roofed in clear

corrugated plastic, it stood empty, its far end open to the lapping
sea. Robots and avatars stood against the side walls, long arms
hanging down, like disconsolate iron apes. 'Soon be busy,'
Grant assured her. He gestured to the other three slipways,
their sheds dimly visible. 'Like the rest.'

Up and down stairs they went, across gangways, into and
out of offices and workshops and onsite facilities; the refectory,
the gymnasium, the rifle range . . . It seemed Grant wanted
everyone in the yard to clock her face. She heard his 'Dr
Lakshmi Nayak, our new planning consultant', and her own
reply, 'Pleased to meet you, please call me Lakshmi', so many
times that the faces and names blurred, but Iskander could
take care of that. After an hour or so Nayak and Grant fetched
up in a windowless room with plush seats, subdued lighting
and a low table.

'Ah!' said Nayak, taking a seat and accepting another coffee.
'Is this where I meet the management?'

Grant chuckled. 'Nice one.'

Two women and a man filed in, nodded and took their seats.
Their names ticked up on her glasses. The slim woman in her
late fifties with elaborate hair and always-on glasses was Joanna
Boyd, the accountant; the small, sturdy woman with fashion-
ably greying curls who swaggered in as if for a fight was Morag
Rafferty, the avatar operator; and the lab-suited tall guy with
a trimmed black beard and a focused expression was Omar
Khan, the fusion tech. Boyd was dressed for the office, Rafferty
for the workshop, like Grant. For a moment, over a clatter of
cups and saucers, they all eyed Nayak like fans not sure what
to say to a star.

Morag Rafferty glanced around and took a deep breath. 'Dr
Nayak, it's—'

'"Lakshmi", please, Morag.'

'—a pleasure to welcome you. I'm sure you know how
things work around here. If you see what I mean.'

'I've been working in a planning consultancy co-op long

enough,' Nayak said, 'to make a wild guess that you're all cadre, except John, of course, who I gather is a made man in his own right.'

'Well, that saves time,' Morag said. 'And from here on in you can consider yourself a made lady. It's no privilege, mind, but nobody's going to mess with you.'

There was a moment of silent eye-lock. Nayak nodded. They understood each other.

'Now, to business,' Morag said. 'We know, and I gather you've guessed, that the other powers have an FTL drive. You have a plan for an FTL drive. John here reckons we can build it. Out there on that ramp.'

'I get that,' said Nayak. 'But why build it here? Right across a few kilometres of water from Faslane? Why not at the naval dockyard in Rosyth? Or better yet, why not in some friendly non-aligned country like Congo or Guiana or Namibia? Plenty of facilities, skilled workers, lots of rain forest or desert.'

There was a slight frosting of the atmosphere at this blithe reminder that the Union still had a pretty damn exploitative relationship with friendly non-aligned countries, aka Europe's former colonies, but the cadre could hardly jump on an Indian for insensitivity on that touchy subject.

'Problem with that is,' Morag said, moving swiftly on, 'the Union doesn't officially know.'

'Doesn't know you can build it, or that you intend to build it?'

'Spot on. And doesn't officially know it's even possible, or that the Alliance and Co-ord have it.'

Nayak blinked, shaking her head. 'What do you mean, "officially know"? Who actually *does* know?'

Omar Khan coughed. 'If I may . . . Let's say it's compartmentalised on a need-to-know basis.'

'Does that mean that if your – if the government of the region or the country or the Union found out, they would close it down? That we'd be doing something illegal?'

'It's not illegal,' said Khan. 'There's no *actual law* against building a faster-than-light drive, after all! Or against work collectives and companies carrying out experimental work on spec.' He ran his upper teeth over his lower lip. 'But the project is unauthorised, and . . . well, if a journalist started poking around and asking awkward questions, or any security forces not in the loop, from the town militia to the secret services, got wind of it we'd have a lot of explaining to do, let's say. Come to that, any local environmental officer or even any trade union safety rep who suspected what it really was would shut it down straight away on health and safety grounds alone. It's not like we've submitted a risk assessment.' He chuckled. 'Not an accurate one, anyway.'

'Are you saying it's hazardous work?'

'No more than fusion pots, unless your inflaton trap plays speed racer with other particles.'

Nayak thought about that. 'It doesn't. But still – why here?'

Khan shrugged. 'What John saw and, ah, involuntarily reported, and you being nearby . . . it's how things fell out. Iskander knows what it's doing.'

'If you want to avoid any international complications,' Nayak said, 'building your starship where an accident could obliterate an unfriendly military base as well as about five large towns seems a bit chancy.'

'Aye, it is that,' said Morag. 'So don't have any accidents, yi ken?'

'I'll do my best,' Nayak said dryly. 'And you're going to build it in a civilian submersible?'

'That's right,' Morag told her. 'We're doing it as a homer. Well, technically and legally we're doing it on behalf of a company which John here has been kind enough to front up. We've done deals to swap out our previous order with another team, which is why our ramp's empty at the minute. Grant's company now has an order from a shell company set up by one of Iskander's friendly in-the-loop modules for a modified submersible to be built right here.'

Nayak held up her hand. 'Hang on. Is that sort of arrangement even legal? I've come across arrangements like this in
my work, and sometimes they don't end well.'

Corruption scandals, the joke went, were what kept the
cadre honest.

'It's . . . a grey area,' said Khan. 'If we're exposed, we're
exposed. In the meantime, everybody's happy and we crack
on.'

'Who's "we"?'

'Us here are the only ones onsite who're in on what the
ship really is,' said Morag. 'The rest of our team – me and
John's team – will be doing their usual work on it, but they're
out of the loop for the moment.'

Nayak called up names and faces: Jeannie, Brian, Anwar,
Piotr. They all looked young and keen.

'Don't you trust them?'

'It's no a question ae trust,' said Morag. 'I trust them aw
right. It's for their ain good that they don't know. If it aw gaes
wrang, they don't carry the can. We do.'

'Fine by me,' said Nayak. 'How long do you expect the job
to take?'

Morag looked troubled. 'With the modifications and the
drive and everything, and having to arrange work schedules
around the secrecy requirements, and all that . . . it's going to
take up to three months.'

'Three months!' Nayak had to laugh. 'I was expecting three
years!'

She turned to Joanna Boyd. 'Have you figured out a way
to cover up the purchases for the components of the drive?'

'The accountancy side wasn't so hard,' said Joanna. 'Not
after John did the parts breakdown. You can cover a lot of
sins with "Miscellaneous supplies" and "Contingency costs"
and "Cash reserves", that's all I'm saying. John, could you
explain?'

'Uh, yes, well . . .' Grant put on his glasses and moved his hands, shuffling virtual paper. 'You know tanks are called "tanks" and fusion pots are called "pots" because these were originally their cover names? I don't know what the Nayak drive—' he shot her a smile '—might become known as, but for now we're calling it "the flywheel". Our cover story is of a back-up energy storage and supply system, using the well-established tech of nuclear isomeric energy release and pushing it a bit further. I did a parts breakdown for your inflaton trap and its controls, looked for what else might use them and found that with a few trivial exceptions which can be brushed aside as engineering detail they can be accounted for as components of a nuclear isomeric cell array. And the neat thing about that is, nobody is familiar with them, they haven't been used in practice since the fusion pot took over, and everything in the layout can be plausibly accounted for as part of an array.'

'Wow!' Nayak said. 'Neat all right! What about the modifications to the ship itself?'

'Simple,' said Grant. 'Our fictitious contractor specified that the hull should be able to withstand much higher pressures than your standard submersible – two hundred metres down. Way less than the naval subs can handle, sure, but quite enough to cope with hard vacuum and hard radiation. Likewise the controls and external views. Life-support for a crew of five for a week, or to sustain a larger complement for proportionately less time. Airlock for EVA. Sturdy manipulator arms. Capacity to propel itself across ice with jet turbines – which conveniently gives it a capacity to at least manoeuvre in air, or even space with rocket pods. The supposed use case is for exploring and recording environmental and ecological changes under and on the ice sheets.'

'Off Antarctica?'

'Where else, these days? Plenty of turbulence down there, so a rugged hull looks made for the job.' He laughed. 'If your drive doesn't work, we can always flog the boat to the British Antarctic Survey.'

Joanna snorted. 'You'd be lucky to sell it to Greenpeace.'

Nayak was still puzzled. 'How did you cover up interstellar navigation?'

'Ah!' said Grant. 'These days, of course, everything goes by GPS, but ships' officers still have to qualify in the old-fashioned kind, and that's by the stars anyway. So it's a standard back-up in the ship's computer. Astral navigation is just . . . navigation.'

'But that's—'

'It's a simple hack,' Grant said. 'Making the reference point more, ah, wide-ranging than usual. Loading up star catalogues and distances and the rest? I wouldn't dignify that by calling it a hack. It's the sort of thing bored developers do for fun, like these things they call Easter eggs. In any case, it's done.'

She frowned. 'Who did it?'

They all looked at her as if she wasn't quite the genius they'd imagined, or was perhaps having them on.

'Iskander,' Grant said.

'Of course it was,' said Nayak. She leaned back, smiling. 'It's kind of like having a god on your side, isn't it?'

'Oh no,' said Morag, sounding shocked. 'It's no as bad as *that*.'

Nayak wasn't sure what to say, so she said, 'So . . . has anyone got the diagrams?'

But there was already someone at the door, another cadre, whose name she didn't catch, with a roll of blueprint. Iskander was on their case all right. Grant took them and spread them out on the table, weighting the corners with empty cups.

'Have a look.' He stabbed a finger at various points on the main outline. 'Side by side in the cockpit: pilot and navigator. The pilot drives the boat – the controls are standard for submersibles, with some added controls for the turbines and rocket pods. The navigator navigates, right, but also plots and times the jumps.' He looked at Nayak. 'Can't see anyone but you doing that, in the first instance.'

'What?' cried Nayak. She had a falling feeling, then a swoop and a thrill in the pit of her stomach. 'I've no experience of anything like that!'

Grant frowned. 'You can ride a bike?'

'Yes, of course. I can drive a car, for that matter.'

'You can?' Grant looked impressed. 'Well, in that case, you have the capacities to do this. Physical and mental, right? And as for understanding it, well, I based the drive's controls on your schematic.' He pointed to another sheet. 'Look, there.'

She peered down, picked up the sheet, moved it this way and that, almost literally getting her head around it, and recognised her own thinking, elaborated. As well as the navigation controls and displays, there was a discreet side panel tagged: *ancillary power supply*. Dials, displays, switches and sliders . . .

'That's to control the drive?'

'Yes.' Grant smiled mischievously. 'The "nuclear isomeric array". The "flywheel". The Nayak Drive!'

That lift-shaft feeling, again. Nayak gave a shaky laugh. 'If you put it that way – yes, I'll do it. I'll need practice.'

'You'll get it, don't worry,' said Grant. He took the sheet back and laid it down. 'OK, back to the crew. In this blister underneath the cockpit there's the observer-stroke-operator, working the arms. Engineer at the back, looking after the main engine and the fusion pods. And up here, there's the airlock and EVA operator.'

Nayak studied the diagrams, building them to a 3D image in her head. Now and then she asked Grant to explain something. The others drifted to the edges of the room, made coffee, chatted in low voices, drifted back.

'OK,' she said at last. She straightened up and rubbed the small of her back. 'You've done an impressive job, Mr Grant.'

'Thank you. Couldn't have done it without the gang.' He scratched his head. 'Just one question, Dr Nayak.'

'Yes?'

'How does it work?'

*

'Inflation,' said Nayak.

'What's that?' said Grant.

'Ah.' Nayak temporised, then plunged in. 'It's what happened just after the Big Bang, when the universe expanded to trillions of trillions of times its original size in trillionths of trillionths of a second. We now know that the field that enabled inflation was carried by particles called inflatons. These are still around, but sort of spread out, and . . .' She saw their faces. 'With me so far?'

'Aye, kind of,' Morag said. Everyone pretended to agree.

'OK,' Nayak said. She pointed at a circular shape on one of the blueprints and traced its outline. 'This device here lets you hook on to the expansion and hitch a ride. It traps inflatons, spins them around, and generates a bubble of space that's taking part in an incredibly faint aftershock of the original inflation. You become . . . sort of detached from the space around the bubble. First you float free of gravity, then – as the inflaton trap powers up – you zoom off at thousands of times the speed of light. The direction depends on the vector component, controlled—' she tapped the paper '—from here, and the distance travelled is, uh, basically a matter of timing.'

'Have to be very precise timing.' Morag Rafferty sounded doubtful.

'Oh yes,' said Nayak. 'You need to time it to insanely tiny fractions of a second.'

'Fortunately the Faber pot already has a femtosecond timer,' said Khan.

'I hope Joanna's ordered two,' Morag said.

'It's in hand,' said Joanna, sounding irritated.

'How about at the other end?' Grant asked.

'It's basically the reverse as you power down. If you time it right, you should have completed your descent before gravity kicks in.' She thought about this for a moment. 'This may be why the Alliance uses submarines.'

Khan frowned. 'Falling on water is no better than falling

on rock! No, I think they use submarines because they're structurally perfect for the job, they have life-support and they already have nuclear engines. And they can come and go without being noticed.'

'Not all the time,' said Grant.

'Aye, well,' said Khan, 'noticed rarely enough to be easily brushed off, let's say.'

'I have lots of emails,' said Nayak, 'from people claiming to have seen strange events like that, and as I told John I've always politely brushed them off. I'm known, you see, because of my first paper. Which raises a question. Isn't my being here now – even John's meeting with me the other week – a security risk?'

Grant nodded, whether in thought or in agreement she wasn't sure, but Morag Rafferty shook her head sharply.

'It is and it isnae,' she said. 'This arrangement would have been screened by Union counter-intelligence well before we got asked to do it. Now that's well above my pay grade but my guess would be that all these polite brush-offs you've given count in your favour. Likewise being known for your first paper. You're known as a discredited failed scientist – no offence.'

'None taken,' said Nayak. 'I'm well aware of that. And I'm also known as a damn good planning consultant.'

'You are that,' said Grant. 'Like if Einstein had been a watchmaker, he'd have made damn good watches.' Nayak got what he meant; she doubted the others did, and just as well. 'And we actually do need your watchmaking skills as well as your advice on the, uh, flywheel.'

'Yes,' said Morag, hastily as if to make up for any misunderstanding. 'There's a fair bit of finagling to do there. So I reckon our friends higher up will have taken that into account as well. And in any case, it's all a great double bluff. If we don't keep our connection with you a secret, no one will think there's anything secret going on.'

'Like building a starship across the water from the Alliance's very own starship berth?' said Nayak.

'Exactly!' said Morag.

Nayak shrugged and spread her hands. 'Well, if your – if our best intelligence bods think it'll work, who am I to disagree? I just hope they're right.'

Grant stood up. 'Let's do this.'

For the next three months Nayak worked three days at the planning consultancy in Tarbet, and on Thursdays travelled to Port Glasgow to check on progress. She always went to the accounting office first, sat down at a desk in a virtual workspace with Joanna and then checked in at the workshop on her way out, as if in passing. Now and then this routine was interrupted by a call to deal with an unexpected problem, but she always managed to sort the problem out.

Piece by piece the ship took shape. Sometimes Nayak stood on the slipway, behind the fluorescent tape of the safety line and wearing the mandatory hard hat and ear-protectors, and watched the robots and avatars at work. There was little noise, except when plates were being riveted together, when the din would have been deafening. The robots moved with the expected precision and speed, and the avatars with unexpected and what seemed preternatural grace and skill. She'd never have guessed it from watching the rigs up in the workshop; their movements seen from outside looked as clumsy as that of space-suited astronauts in microgravity.

'It's all in the haptic feedback,' Grant told her.

'That and the optics,' Morag added. 'See, my hand—' she held it out, clawed, rotating from the wrist '—and my eyes, right, the kit powers up or powers or powers down the action, so if say I'm snapping thumb and finger together like this the avatar might be picking up some wee widget I'd need a magnifying glass to see, and I'm zoomed in on it and turning it a few microns at a time.'

Nayak would sometimes overlay a 3D rendering of the completed vessel and see how the real one was coming along, and where everything was going and would go. Welding sparks and sintering lasers flickered inside and around the phantom image. Its completed form looked like some squat, streamlined, pugnacious trilobite: the grapple arms clenched around its bow ready to swing out and open up to unfold a clutch of manipulators, the cockpit a hunched cupola. It had rudimentary landing gear: a brace of long bars curved upward at the ends like toboggan runners. This feature conformed to spec as an Antarctic survey vessel: it was supposed to be able to cross ice in emergencies (for which purpose its turbines could work in air as well as underwater, and just to be sure there was a cluster of rocket jets). Likewise the unusually generous stash of supplies, and the rifle rack.

'Rifle rack?' she asked Grant one day. 'What's your cover story for that?'

He frowned, considering. 'In Antarctica,' he said, 'you never know when you might be stuck on an ice floe and fighting off hungry sea lions.'

'OK. I suppose.'

'By the way,' Grant said, 'can you come in this Friday?'

'Yes. Why?'

'Time for you to practise navigation.'

Grant escorted her to a training rig in an otherwise empty workshop. She walked around the apparatus, looking at it dubiously. A gimballed seat with arm, head and foot rests, in an oval pod open at the front and on U-shaped brackets above a gimballed mount fixed firmly to the floor. A bit like a high-end gaming chair.

'How are you for motion sickness?' Grant asked.

She thought of some choppy ferry journeys, and of tuk-tuk rides back home.

'I'm all right with that,' she said. She glowered at the chair. 'I have the odd nightmare about dentistry.'

'It's not like that,' he said. He gestured. 'Buckle in.'

When she was seated and strapped in, he handed her a pair of long, thick gauntlets, fuzzy on the outside and smooth within. They came up easily to past her elbows, then tightened to a snug fit.

'Now pull down the head-up display.'

She did. It was still transparent, and she could see him through it.

'OK,' said Grant. He stepped back and took out his phone. 'I've patched together a sim of the ship and your control panel from your POV in the navigator's seat. The rest of the crew are sims too – they'll take the default actions and respond to voice commands. I and our invisible friend have meshed the navigation system sim with some video game graphics and E-PRIME exoplanet images given a bit of speculative rendering.' He thumbed his phone. 'Have a play with it.'

Instantly she was in the ship. It looked and felt real, though the figure in the pilot's seat on her left was shadowy and vague, as if seen out of the corner of her eye. The virtual ship swayed slightly, with sense of forward movement as bubbles and detritus drifted past. A hum of turbines, the odd creak. Looking up through the canopy, she saw bright ripples, the surface of a calm, sunlit sea from a few metres down. She reached for the control panel – her hands looked bare. The panel and the controls felt hard and solid.

So far, so familiar from her teenage gaming phase. Better graphics and sound than she recalled.

'Forward at ten kilometres per hour,' she said. The apparent flow past the canopy speeded up.

She tapped the control panel and summoned the navigation software. Stars – labelled wherever she looked – formed a sphere around her, overlying her view of the ship. She reached up and spun the celestial sphere from its default natural position, searching in the southern hemisphere. Might as well start with the nearest exoplanet – the one around the nearest star.

'Proxima b,' she said. The sphere stabilised and zeroed in. She selected 'Compute course and direction'. Warning lights flashed.

From outside, from another reality, she heard Grant laugh. 'Maybe *not* try to go through the Earth?'

'Just testing,' she said. 'Good to see you have safety features built in.'

She selected a star and exoplanet in the sky overhead: a red sun, a water world in close orbit. She locked on the destination and powered up the drive. The simulated seawater seemed pushed away, leaving the ship suspended in a bubble that began to rise. She didn't want to burst out of the water. The drive was powered up. No warning lights flashed.

'Jump,' she said, and pressed the switch.

The bubble around the ship streamed with swirling colours. A faint hum sounded from astern. She felt a slight vibration through her seat. All special effects from the game, she guessed: no one, least of all her, had any idea what the FTL jump would look and feel like.

After eighty-seven seconds the computed jump was over. The bubble vanished. Nayak found herself in space and notionally in free fall. The sim couldn't deliver that—

The seat promptly turned upside down, without changing her view. Not free fall but almost as disorienting.

Blue and white below, red overhead. The star filled half the sky. The water world below was so immense, and her orbit so low, that its curve was barely visible. A moment later the craft began to shake, and a red glow formed around it. She was in atmosphere!

'Rocket boost!' she yelled.

The boost came. Its main effect was to send the ship tumbling over and over.

Before Nayak had time to think of making an FTL jump out of this sticky situation the ship disintegrated around her and her view went black. Blocky letters in retro green pixels told her:

GAME OVER.

The seat swung to a halt. Nayak cleared her glasses in time to see Grant look up from his phone, laughing.

'Again!' she said.

Again and again, she did, for that day and for several other weekends. Water worlds. Moons. Gas giants. Near-replica Earths. Mars. Venus. Europa. Wilder exoplanets around promising stars: Proxima, Tau Ceti, Kepler, Barnard's Star, 51 Pegasi . . . She worked her way through them all, and more. Thrilling sights. Every time she tried a landing, she crashed.

'You'll get the hang of it,' Grant said.

After a month and half of intermittent practice, she did. She hugged the achievement to herself. She was a starship pilot.

Virtually, but still.

The plan was to launch the ship, provisionally christened the *Fighting Chance*, in October. It would slip away down the Firth of Clyde, head out to sea, and then – in their own coded phrase – 'spin up the flywheel'.

And after that?

'We'll see those stars and planets for real,' Nayak said.

'The sky's the limit,' Grant said.

For now that seemed enough.

CHAPTER TWELVE

Rosetta Phone

Monday 13 October 2070, Apis

At last, after about half an hour's further forced march, Hazeldene, her colleagues and the exiles reached the city limits – as the scientists had long ago nicknamed this zone, and as even now she couldn't help thinking of it. The boundary was quite unmarked. The placement of the blocks prevented a view ahead until the last few steps. One minute you were walking amid a riot of solid geometry, the next – not.

Jenkins led them all about twenty metres from the last of the blocks, ran ahead a little way and stopped to look back.

'It's OK,' he yelled. The black sphere that had followed them stood just past the last blocks, poised as if to roll downhill. Everyone stopped. The scientists frantically looked around for Georgi, and spotted him a few hundred metres away, trekking back across the hillside. He waved. Relieved, they took the opportunity to catch their breath. The exiles remained alert.

Jenkins waved them into a perimeter, where they stood looking out, weapons at the ready. He stayed apart from the scientists, rifle slung on one shoulder, and restlessly scanned the circuit of skyline and the sweep of land. Hazeldene sat down, and wondered if it was time to rub some more painkilling gel on her knees.

Below, for kilometre after kilometre, the ground fell away in a shallow slope all the way to the beginning of the plains, which extended southward to the horizon ahead, beyond which they dried to merge with the Atlantic Desert. The fertile belt of the plains extended to the Lemuric Ocean far away to their left and to the mountains of the Churchward range to the right. One or two streams trickled down the slope, to eventually merge with the nearest of the rivers that meandered across the plain. Here and there, beasts the size of sheep and the shape of giant molluscs toddled on pseudopods, grazing with rasping mouths at the end of long trunks. From this distance the animals looked like crude clay models of small shaggy sauropods.

Hazeldene had a few years earlier made a preliminary study of the species. All were roughly the same size, with no young, and no sexual organs or activity. They were preyed on, and hunted by exiles, but their populations didn't diminish. Nobody knew from what source they were replenished. These rugged beasts were a larval form, Hazeldene suspected, but one so long-lived that no one had yet seen the adult. High overhead, a pair of carrion-eating boids patrolled the updraughts on metre-long wings. Off a bit to the right, down on the edge of the plains, smoke rose on those same updraughts.

Hazeldene checked on her phone and confirmed that the smoke marked the settlement. This one was centred around a long shed like a Nissen hut, so it had evidently grown up around an ark, perhaps the very one some of the inhabitants – or their parents – had arrived in. The details of each hovel, shack, workshop and field were clear in the drone-photo and satellite-image map, but little information was available (or had even, it seemed, been sought) on the people and beasts that lived there. Here be dragons.

Georgi Muranov returned, to jeers from his colleagues and cheers from the locals, two of whom buffeted him playfully as he passed through the perimeter.

Hazeldene stood up. 'Welcome back, you fucking moron.'

'Thanks, guys.'

'What happened?' Hazeldene asked.

Georgi spread his hands. 'Same as with you, I guess. It chased me out and then stopped. Except—' he clapped his hands together '—I tried something clever. I ran through gaps narrower than the sphere. Do you know what it did?' He looked around, grinning.

'Split up?' Cindy guessed.

'No. It shrank—' he clawed his fingers and twisted and clenched both hands, one inside the other '—like that. Then sprang open again.'

'Pics or it didn't happen,' Nelson joked.

Georgi didn't laugh. 'I dropped my phone. Sphere rolled over it.'

'What!' Jenkins shouted. He barged over. 'You lost your phone to it? How?'

Georgi squared up. 'I don't answer to you. But since you ask – I was running, talking, recording – looked over my shoulder, tripped and sprawled. Phone flew out of my hand and skidded away. I had to get up and run. No choice but to abandon it.'

'Fuck,' said Jenkins. He pounded a fist in his palm. 'Fuck, fuck, fuck. You were calling the Russian base at the time, right?'

'The Co-ordinate base,' Georgi said stiffly. 'Yes, I was.' He looked as if he'd just remembered something and turned to Hazeldene. 'Lend me your phone, please? I want to let them know I'm all right.'

'Yeah, you do that,' said Jenkins. 'And while you're at it,

tell them to block that phone and do a hard purge of anything that's come in from it since you dropped it. And I mean hard – physically wreck any equipment that's storing the data and anything else it could have reached.'

'You what?' said Hazeldene. 'That could be everything.'

Jenkins nodded. 'Yup. Even so. I know what I'm talking about.'

Georgi reached for Hazeldene's phone. She held onto it. 'Wait!' she said. She turned to Jenkins. 'If you think the Co-ord comms system might already be hacked by—' she jerked her thumb over her shoulder '—that thing, wouldn't calling the Co-ord be dangerous for *this* phone, and from it the Alliance comms?'

'You got a point there,' said Jenkins. 'Tell you what – make the call, but trash that phone afterwards.'

'No fucking way,' said Hazeldene, holding the device tighter. 'My life's on there.'

'Well, turn off its comms at least, and don't use it to make calls until you've had a chance to clean it up back at base.'

'That might be doable,' Hazeldene allowed, grudgingly. This was going to be a pain. She passed the phone to Georgi, who stepped away and thumbed in a number. He spoke fast in Russian, gesticulating pointlessly with his free hand all the while.

'I passed on your warning,' he told Jenkins when he'd finished. 'Doubt they'll do what you said, though. We have excellent firewalls, and in any case . . .' He shrugged.

Jenkins snorted. 'Yeah, why should they listen to a paranoid fucking exile?'

'You speak Russian?' Georgi asked, as if half in jest.

'Enough to get the gist at your end,' said Jenkins. He tapped an ear. Georgi looked somewhat abashed. 'Anyhow,' Jenkins went on, 'one of you – not Hazeldene – better phone New Ardtaraig and tell them not to take or send calls to the Russians until both of your lots have got this data security question nailed down.'

'There's no data security question,' Georgi snapped. 'Yes, there's information processing going on in that rock, but whatever it is, it's so alien that there's no way it could interface with our systems. Hack in? Infect them? Forget it.'

'Then how the fuck,' said Jenkins, taking his own phone out again and brandishing it, 'did it infect this?'

They all looked at each other. The circle of exiles had a radius of about twenty metres, and their attention was all outward. Georgi leaned in close to Jenkins, beckoned the other scientists into a huddle, and lowered his voice.

'Come on, Mr Jenkins,' he said. 'We know what's going on. We won't let on to the others. But between ourselves, you don't have to pretend.'

'"Pretend"?' Jenkins sounded indignant. 'How?'

'You've recharged that phone—'

Jenkins nodded. 'Uh-huh.'

'—and the Fermi messages, they all come from you. You put them there. It's all right, we understand.'

Jenkins glowered, then guffawed. 'You think this is a trick? You think I'm some witch-doctor fooling his primitive tribe?' He spoke loud enough for some heads to turn.

'Well, no,' said Georgi. 'We know your people aren't *primitive*, but—'

'But what?'

Georgi sighed, straightening up. He pointed back at the Ridge. 'How could *that* learn human languages?'

'*That*, my friend, is a computer the size of a mountain, created by alien intelligences millions of years ago.'

'Well, yes,' said Georgi, sounding amused. 'I know. Information science is my speciality, after all. But it would take a universe of computers to the end of time to crack the Huawei 7G's quantum encryption by brute force.'

'Wish I could be so sure about what the Fermi can and can't do,' said Jenkins. 'Anyway, they didn't need to. Once I'd got the phone up and running again – all right, only as a camera

and notebook and encyclopaedia and recorder, no comms – all
they had to do was watch and listen and keep track of the
electrons.'

'"Keep track of the electrons"! Assuming for the sake of
argument it could, that doesn't help with languages.' Georgi
laughed uneasily, looking around. 'No Rosetta Stone!' He said
it as if it was a private joke among scientists.

'Hah!' Jenkins held the device out, as if weighing it in his
cupped hand. 'This phone contains enough Rosetta Stones to
fill a fucking museum! Not just the translator – the dictionaries
of a dozen languages, every word of them shown with sounds
and moving pictures. Proper educational resource, this is. We
used it to teach the kids, we used it to teach *teachers* from
other settlements. For years and years. Turns out we were all
the time teaching—' he pointed at the Ridge— '*them*. So don't
fucking tell me there's no data security question.'

Georgi scowled, then shrugged, hands upturned. 'It's all
moot anyway.'

Jenkins bristled. 'What do you mean?'

'I mean,' said Georgi, 'that *of fucking course* our – well,
their base, and my home base, have been keeping each other
in the loop ever since Emma called in about the cable, not to
mention when she reported in about the black balls. And Novy
Cosmograd called New Ardtaraig as soon as my call stopped,
and they've been exchanging anxious calls ever since. I could
hear someone in the background passing on the good news to
the Alliance base even before I could get your warning in. Not
that they took it seriously anyway.'

'I give up,' Jenkins said. 'Fuck you all.'

He turned and stalked away to rally his companions, then
returned, stony-faced. He pointed down the slope and to the
right, to the thin column of smoke.

'Five kilometres,' he said. 'And a lot to do when we get
there. Let's move it out.'

*

As always, the distance across country seemed longer to the legs than to the eye. There wasn't much talking. Everyone focused on boulders, abrupt burrow-holes, streams, clumps of shrub and bogs. Even the locals weren't finding the going easy. Hazeldene tried to imagine running all this way, uphill, as she guessed they must have done in the morning. No wonder they'd been so haggard! A drone hung a thousand or so metres up, a speck all but invisible to unaided sight, but a comfort all the same. Hazeldene drifted back and forth from a trance of walking to a delighted flash of observation. Always some new thing: a flower, a boid, an insectoid, a kind of moss, each with the possibility of a new species or variant.

And then there were the bees.

The bees were an anomaly on an already anomalous planet. Everything else living here had evolved from some pre-Cambrian trawl of life on Earth. That was the general view, and Hazeldene's, though open to correction when or if more scientists could get on the case. She longed for this world to get a world's attention. That was a daydream, of course, until the secret of its existence was out. For the moment, the deep relatedness of the genomes and the identity of their genetic code seemed wildly unlikely to be coincidence. Combined with the traces of terraforming and geo-engineering in the planet's deep past, half a billion years ago, the hypothesis that all the life on this planet was descended from ancestors transferred from Earth was the obvious first thought, outlandish though it felt. 'Far-fetched is not far-fetched,' someone had said.

No vertebrates or even chordates had evolved here, but life's missing out on the backbone had been more than compensated by a new trick: the invertebrate lung. Some floating common ancestor had developed linked internal gas bladders for buoyancy control. In land-dwelling descendants it became a respiratory system even more efficient than that of dinosaurs and birds.

The main constraint on the size of land invertebrates on

Earth had thus been removed at a stroke. Into every niche filled on Earth by fish, birds, mammals and reptiles something had swum, slithered, scuttled, crept, climbed, hopped or flown. Into the niches of smaller organisms had stepped the insectoids and arachnoids, on ten legs apiece.

The bees were the exception.

Honeybees and bumblebees, solitary or social, fierce or placid, they were found everywhere bees could live. They weren't derived from the same sample as the rest. No, they were indistinguishable from Earth genera and even species. Therefore, they must have been transported from Earth at some unknown but evidently far more recent date than the ancestors of all the rest of the animals here. An afterthought, like the stars in the first chapter of Genesis.

They brought the bees also. Or perhaps not. It could have been an entirely different intelligence or civilisation that had brought them here. The biologists studying the planet hadn't yet had the resources or the time to determine how long the local bees had been separate from their cousins back on Earth. Millions of years, most likely – but for all anyone knew, decades. If so, the alien bee-fanciers were still around. To Hazeldene it suggested that they had known humans would arrive some day, and wanted them to stay, for whatever unknown reason. Hence her nickname.

Honey trap or not, the bees had also inspired the planet's informal name.

Apis: the planet of the bees.

In a field at the edge of the settlement a man walked behind a plough hauled by what looked like an enormous, elongated crab. The ropes of the harness were looped around the front of its dorsal shell, and between them two much thinner lines extended from the base of its head to the handles of the plough. Zooming in, Hazeldene saw a switch on each handle, and between the handles a wooden bar on which was mounted a small apparatus with a crank handle – a dynamo, she guessed. As the plough reached the top of the field, the ploughman thumbed one switch and at the same time gave the handle a couple of turns. He raised the ploughshare – a triangle of bright scrap metal, its raw edges turned over and hammered down, the whole beaten to a curve – and followed the arthropod as it turned around. The plough bit in again, turf curling from the blade as it carved a new furrow.

One of the exile women waved to the ploughman, who waved back. Hazeldene hurried herself up along the narrow stony path to catch up with her, and fell into step. The girl gave her a sidelong look.

'You know him?' Hazeldene asked.

''Course I know him. He's my dad.'

'Must take a lot of skill, drilling the holes in the beast's head just right.'

Another sidelong glance, this time of amused disdain. 'We do it just after they moult. Shell's still soft, see? My dad always gets the electrodes in right first time, but if you don't hit the right nerve you can just poke around a bit and see what twitches.'

'Ah, right. I should have known that!'

'Well, you do now.'

'Thank you. I'm Emma. What's your name?'

The girl said something in patois, shook her head, looked away and stepped up her pace. She didn't want to talk further, or had been warned not to.

'Exiles, huh,' said Hazeldene, as Nelson caught up with her. 'Unforthcoming.'

'I don't blame them,' he said. 'They have a right to be cautious, and good reason.'

'I suppose. Still – now we know they understand electricity, and arthropod anatomy!'

'I think we're gonna find,' said Nelson, 'they understand a lot more than that. Stay cool, stay sharp.'

When they passed the field the trodden track became a lane, paved with broken stone and gravel, probably taken from the low mounds of glacial moraine in the vicinity. They crossed a wooden bridge over a stream whose water ran low but clear. Hazeldene counted ten houses, each with adjacent plots, gardens and outbuildings, grouped within an area about two hundred metres across. They each had a single storey of uncut stone, presumably small boulders cleared from the plots and fields, and a roof rough-thatched with shrub from the hill. The windows were unglazed: some open, others covered with fabric hung or tacked on the inside. Bright shells and insectoid casings, sometimes arranged in complex patterns, decorated lintels and walls. Each house had one small outbuilding close by: a latrine, going by chance whiffs carried on the breeze. It wasn't the only odour: everywhere was evidence of invertebrate skin, shell, casing and flesh being stretched, dried, smoked, cooked or otherwise processed. In the middle, where the lane ended in a gravelled rectangle, a dozen or so wooden sheds huddled around a partly buried cylinder about thirty metres long and three high, with the dull gleam of weathered aluminium. Three windows had been made along the side by removing panels and replacing them with what might once have been clear plastic sheeting, now long since yellowed. Tall, faded letters and numbers across the structure confirmed that it was an ark.

Hazeldene nudged Nelson. 'Think we should slap a preservation order on it?'

'Ha! Maybe they have already. Most of these get cannibalised for the metal.'

Once or twice Hazeldene saw a child in a doorway, or a face at a window. Three people toiling in plots paused to stare. On the slope, a scatter of distant figures – some small and fleet-footed enough to be children – herded or guarded beasts, slow-moving, humped brutes in broad meadows enclosed by rickety barred fences. Otherwise the place seemed deserted, but Hazeldene had a feeling of being watched. She kept glimpsing movement out of the corner of her eye and seeing nothing when she turned. The others shared her unease, moving into a compact group behind her and Nelson, glancing from side to side.

Cindy shuddered. 'It's like being in the rock!'

'Except we know who's watching us,' said Nelson.

Jenkins led them all to the scuffed gravel forecourt of the ark, and around to the end at their left. A flanged circumference with four brackets and a perished rubber O-ring indicated that this end was where the drive module had been attached. At ground level was a hatch about a metre and a half high. He unbolted the heavy door of the hatch and let it stand open. The hinges still glistened black with oil. Jenkins directed the locals carrying stuff from the camp inside. They returned empty-handed a minute or two later and dispersed without a word or a look.

'Thanks!' Hazeldene called after them.

Jenkins stood by the door, arm out, and nodded. 'After you.'

Hazeldene glanced at Nelson, who shrugged one shoulder. 'I guess,' she said.

She ducked through, stepped out of the way and the others, then Jenkins, followed. Her glasses adjusted instantly to the dim, yellowish light from the single window in this section. A bulkhead ten metres in was covered with faded graffiti. Fluke pelts, dried and seasoned, carpeted the deck. The gear and supplies retrieved from the camp lay in jumbled heaps along one side.

'This way,' Jenkins said, and opened the door in the bulkhead. The next section contained a long wooden table, racks of tools along both sides and an overhead lighting tube that wasn't switched on. Beneath the tool racks lay coils of wire, a pyramid of balls of string, dozens of woven baskets and two plastic barrels filled with raw materials – stems, skins, shells, stones – and an array of glass jars brimming with rusty nails, screws, plastic clips and other fixings, all sorted. Dust motes danced in the shaft of yellow light from the window. Chips of black crystal crunched underfoot. Jenkins led them to the door in the final bulkhead. This one had a lock. He took a key on a thong around his neck and leaned forward to unlock it, then straightened up and swung the door open with ceremonial solemnity.

'I go first, here,' he said. His voice rang in the semicircular space. He stroked his scalp with his right hand, twice, from brow to nape then from ear to ear. Then he went in.

Hazeldene stepped through after him, and the others followed. Hazeldene broke the silence.

'Oh, holy fuck,' she said.

It wasn't clear if the room was a laboratory or a shrine. A long table and a bench lay along the right-hand side, under the window. That table was piled with electrical and electronic clutter that looked as if it had been retrieved from the back of a recycling bin at the naval base. More such clutter was stacked to the left, along with an apparatus made up of part of a bicycle frame, with saddle and pedals but no front wheel, its chain connected via cogs and gears to a fairly large and evidently homemade dynamo, from which cables ran fore and aft, under the deck, and one up the side to an overhead lighting tube. A couple of chairs made out of wood and fabric stood just beyond it. At the far end of the room stood a rough wooden table, on which a smooth slab of black crystal about one metre by two was propped against the rear bulkhead, its lower edge held in place by wedges. Cables sprouted from behind it all around, attached to batteries to various small electronic odds and ends on the table or hanging loose. Some of these were further connected to a black, dull, rectangular object with half a dozen rows of numerous small, raised squares that lay before the slab. The whole effect was like a black mirror on a wicked witch's vanity table.

'Well,' said Jenkins, with a flourish of the hand, 'here it is!'

'Cargo-cult stuff,' Nelson muttered under his breath.

'No wonder he sent the others away,' said Cindy.

Georgi walked forward. He looked at the slab and the table and what was on it, cocking his head, peering here and there, then turned to Jenkins.

'This is it?' he said. 'The "more reliable apparatus"?'

'Yes,' said Jenkins. He beckoned the rest over.

The black object in front of the slab looked exactly like a standard keyboard – QWERTY layout, function keys, numeric pad and all – except that it was solid. Hazeldene tapped its edge gingerly with a fingernail. It seemed to be a shell of moulded plastic.

'How did you make this?' she asked Jenkins. 'Do you have a 3D printer somewhere, or did somebody, I don't know, *carve* this?'

Jenkins looked puzzled. 'Nah, it's just an old keyboard. Some bloke found it in a skip at the back of the base and brought it along, years ago. Thought he could rig it up to a computer, but—' he shook his head sadly '—poor bugger never did find the right bits. Anyway – it came in useful in the end, so no harm done.'

Georgi looked impatient to say something.

'Forget the keyboard!' he said. 'Look at the slab.'

He stepped back and they all leaned in, peering, blinking, twiddling the air around their glasses to tweak their sight. At first all Hazeldene saw was their four reflected faces, frowning. Then –

'It's moving,' she said.

The uncanny internal motion of block within block behind the glassy surface was identical to that inside the crystal cliffs and towers. Everyone recoiled.

'Yes,' Jenkins said. He gestured at the slab. 'A slice of the Fermi. Now I must talk to them.'

'We would very much like to see that,' said Hazeldene. 'But first, could you explain how you got this—?'

'No time now,' said Jenkins. 'Later maybe.'

He pulled up one of the chairs, sat, and started tapping at the keyboard. It must have had some kind of sound chip – from

God knows where – hidden under it, Hazeldene thought, because it rattled with clicks just like a real virtual keyboard. To her utter amazement, white letters appeared on the black slab.

Jenkins to Fermi. Hello.

There was a long moment. Everyone's breath stopped. Then:

FERMI TO JENKINS. WHAT HAVE YOU
DONE?
As you told me.
WHY HAVE YOU BROUGHT THESE FIVE
HERE?
As you told me.
WE TOLD YOU TO MAKE THEM GO AWAY.
They are away from the mountain.
THEY MUST LEAVE THE MOUNTAIN AND
NOT RETURN.
I can't make them stay away.
IF YOU CANNOT, WE CAN. THEY WILL WISH
YOU HAD.

'Hey!' said Hazeldene. 'Can we have a word?'

Jenkins looked over his shoulder. 'You reckon? You really?' He took a long breath and vacated the chair. 'Be my guest.'

Hazeldene glanced around at the others. Georgi started forward. 'Information's my area.'

'Life is mine,' said Hazeldene.

She was in the chair and had her hands on the keyboard before he could object further.

What do you mean by your last statement? she typed.

THIS.

*

Afterwards, they put the effect down to subsonics. Certainly they all recalled a second or two in which they had heard a deep buzzing sound, perhaps deepening before it dropped below audibility. What they then felt was no longer like hearing the Lord of the Flies, but experiencing some manifestation of that dark majesty itself: an overwhelming sense of dread, and of presence, of something behind their backs at which they dare not turn to look. It was what they'd all felt, at times, in the caverns and clefts of the rock, but magnified many times over. Jenkins laughed wildly, like some necromancer or mad scientist in a horror movie. Cindy sobbed. Nelson grunted as if punched. The others gasped or groaned.

Hazeldene clenched her jaws and tapped the keyboard.

> *You would frighten us?*
> THE MOUNTAIN CAN MAKE ALL OF YOU
> THAT ARE NEW ON THE WORLD FEEL THIS
> AND WORSE FOR AS LONG AS IT WILLS.
> *We would find counter-measures.*
> NO DOUBT.

The words remained on the slab for a moment, as if pausing to let them all appreciate the snappy, colloquial rejoinder.

AND THEN THERE IS THIS.

The ground shook. Everything swayed. Hazeldene grabbed the table as the chair shifted under her. Jars toppled, sending their contents rattling and rolling. Something crashed off the bench. Yells and screams came faint from outside the cylinder. After some more nauseous seconds, the tiny local earthquake stopped. Jenkins was cursing in several languages.

AGAIN, THIS IS FROM THE SLAB YOU SEE.

THE MOUNTAIN CAN DO THIS TO THE
CONTINENT. GO AWAY.

Jenkins had his hands on her shoulders, trying to pull her
away. She wrenched herself free and typed:

We only wish to speak to the real Fermi.

'Take it from me,' said Jenkins, 'you don't.'
'Oh, we do!' She turned back to the keyboard.
He grabbed the back of her collar and hauled her bodily
from the chair. She straightened up, pivoted on the ball of one
foot and drew back her left fist to her shoulder.
'Hands the fuck off!'
Jenkins still clung. Head close enough to butt. He let go
and backed off.
'Sorry!' he said, raising his hands. 'We gotta get out, before—'
The ground shook again, far more severely. Stuff was flying
everywhere.
'Out!' Jenkins yelled.
Stumbling, crashing from side to side, shouting, arms
shielding their heads, they fled through the three chambers
and out of the cylinder. The ground heaved like a sea. The
gravel bounced. Screams and crashes and thuds came from all
around. Sharianne fell to her hands and knees, fingers digging
in as if clinging to the earth, eyes tight shut against the stinging
dust and small stones, and was suddenly and actually seasick.
Hazeldene grabbed Sharianne's shoulders and pulled her up,
then helped her to stand. Sharianne wiped vomit from her chin,
smearing the back of her arm. She glared at Hazeldene as if
she were a hostile stranger. A stone dislodged from a house
wall rolled past her feet and fetched up with a bang against
the side of the cylinder.
Hazeldene wrapped her arm around Sharianne's shoulder,
and hurried her across to a patch of grass at the side of the

gravelled area. The others had made their way there and stood in an unsteady huddle. The quake subsided, and they took stock.

Around them the settlement was in confusion. The main dwellings still stood, but several roofs had fallen in and walls had gaps. Wooden outbuildings had collapsed. Stones and other debris littered the ground. A child screamed and wouldn't stop. People were running down from the slope. Strange, high-pitched croaking vocalisations Hazeldene had never heard or heard of came from a wrecked barn, presumably the cries of some stalled and trapped invertebrate beasts. A workshop was on fire and no one was putting it out. An elderly woman crawled along the lane that led out of the settlement, leaving bloody prints from one of her hands. Someone ran to help her. She rolled on her back, punching the air, cursing feebly.

First things first. 'Everyone all right?' Cuts and bruises.

'Fuck you,' Jenkins said. He had a black eye and a bloody lip, as if he'd been in a fight. He looked ready to start another. 'You did this.'

Hazeldene bit back the childish impulse to reply in kind. It wasn't her who had invoked elder gods, or whatever the fuck the Fermi were. Or if it had been her, it was with his implied permission.

'We can talk about that later,' she said. 'Right now – we have first aid supplies among the stuff you lot took from the camp. Let's get them out of the ark and see about tending to casualties.'

Jenkins stared at her, nodded abruptly, and grabbed Nelson and Georgi. 'Come on, jump to it, guys!'

They dashed to the cylinder.

'Bit fucking sexist division of labour,' Sharianne remarked, gazing after them.

Cindy smacked her forehead and grabbed Hazeldene's arm.

'The base!' she said. 'We have to warn them!' She was already reaching for her phone.

'Warn them what?'

That quake was bad, but surely local, and –

'Get everyone out or up!' Cindy yelled into the phone. 'Tsunami!'

Fuck.

'Get a view from the drone!' Hazeldene almost grabbed the phone. Drones had to be on station permanently over the Sound, watching out for incoming submarines – there being no other advance notice of FTL arrivals.

Cindy held on and repeated the same instruction to base. 'Get the view from the drone! You can see the wave racing up the Sound. You've got minutes at best. Get as high up as you can! Run!'

Then she patched the feed to Hazeldene's glasses. The pulse of water from the quake barrelled up between the ever narrower, ever steeper sides of Bellatrix Sound, rising as the cliffs converged and the depth shallowed. Telemetry ticked the wave's height: one metre, two . . .

It slammed into the dock, tossed a moored flying boat against the quay, then smashed through the base with a height still over a metre and a speed not quite enough for a fit young adult to outrun.

Cindy cut the drone feed. 'We can't do anything for them. We can help here.'

The casualties here, at least, were mercifully light – the villagers had fled the buildings at the first warning tremor. Lots of cuts, a few broken bones. The crawling woman had a long-standing mental problem and responded to an involuntary dose of tranquilliser. The child who kept screaming had a foot crushed by a falling stone. Complete mess. Dressings, antibiotics, bandage, splint. Painkillers.

'She needs surgery if she's ever to walk properly again,' Hazeldene said, when she'd finished. The father just looked at her. 'You know, to mend her bones?' Still blank.

'Don't worry,' said Cindy, just off the phone again. 'We can take her with us. They're sending the helicopter.'

'That's a relief.' Hazeldene turned to Jenkins, about to get him to try to explain to the father what needed to be done.

'Good news for her,' said Cindy. She was looking at Hazeldene in an odd way, as if half ashamed. 'Not so sure about us.'

'What do you mean?'

'They might think what you did was reckless.'

'What I did? We all did.'

Jenkins stuck his face between them. 'You challenged the Fermi.'

'Fuck, we've been over that. We agreed to have that argument later.'

'This is later,' said Jenkins. 'Too late, if you ask me.'

Cindy held out her phone. 'I've got it all,' she said. 'But take a look at the final few seconds.'

A view from behind her. She saw herself typing, Jenkins grabbing her shoulder.

We only wish to speak to the real Fermi.

Just as Jenkins had yanked her out of the chair a reply had come, behind her back:

VERY WELL. YOU SHALL.

Hazeldene recoiled from the hand-held screen, blinking hard. 'Do you think—?'

'Yes, I bloody well think!' Jenkins said.

They heard the heavy throb just before the chopper rose over the Ridge. Hazeldene squinted up, zoomed.

'The Search and Rescue. Great, they'll have the right kit.'

Then she saw another helicopter, close behind.

'Oh good,' said Sharianne. 'They've sent the Chinook, too.'

Apart from drones and the flying boat, the two choppers were the base's entire air force. This did not look good.

Jenkins stared at the incoming aircraft for a second, then straightened up and looked around.

'Run!' he shouted. But the fit and well young folk of the settlement were too far away, too dispersed, too preoccupied to hear. He made a dash for the hill. Nelson brought Jenkins down with a tackle. His rifle skidded across the trampled dirt. Georgi was on top of it a moment later, scooping up the weapon and slinging it over his own shoulder. Then he stood over Jenkins with a pistol aimed.

'You ain't going anywhere, mate,' Nelson said, as he picked himself up and brushed himself off.

The SAR chopper landed in front of the ark. The Chinook hovered above. Everyone who could clapped hands to their ears. A dozen or so marines rappelled down from the Chinook. Two of them hurried over and grabbed Jenkins, who put up no resistance. Meanwhile, the other marines attached long cords with gecko-grips to the sides of the ark. They ascended the ropes and piled back in. The chopper rose, straining for a moment or two, then the ark was wrenched out of its bed. Jenkins yelled and struggled, then subsided. Around the village people kept yelling and wailing.

The two marines hustled Jenkins into the back of the SAR helicopter. The five scientists hurried after them. Hazeldene carried the little girl, who was by now zonked out on painkillers. Her father's blank stare was the last thing Hazeldene saw before the door closed.

A few minutes later, as the chopper approached New Ardtaraig, Hazeldene saw the damage. She wasn't at all surprised to be met at the landing pad by a squad of marines.

Everyone's phone was taken and bagged as evidence.

CHAPTER THIRTEEN

The Shores of Ishtar Terra

Monday 13 October 2070, Venus

A drop, a snap, a jolt, then a feeling like tobogganing down a long slope. To Owen the clouds looked solid and white until he hit them, then they became a yellow haze that darkened towards orange as he descended. The aerofoil above him was optimised for forward speed, and he himself was prone beneath it in a streamlined half-shell fared around his helmet and shoulders. He could see through the faceplate, and far more in the virtual view, patched in from sensors in the suit and in the shell. Inside the cloud he was getting a visualisation of radar images. Akna Montes loomed ahead, bright with pyrite frost. Then he was out of the clouds and racing towards their peaks. Lakshmi Planum hurtled by below.

Across the range and above the contorted, crumpled terrain of Atropos Tessera. Time to slow. He swung himself vertical under the faring and deployed the drogue. The aerofoil overshot, jolted him forward, then steadied. He guided his flight towards the bright virtual light of CASSIE's distress beacon, fifty kilometres ahead and closing. At one kilometre away, and five hundred metres up, he swung around to initiate a spiral descent. Moments later he had visual. The chasm was a jagged black line, from which the rear end of the rover jutted at an awkward angle. Four blimps had already converged on the vicinity, as planned. Stubby airships a couple of metres long, with gondolas underneath for their engines, gas apparatus and propellers, they had moored themselves to convenient boulders with starfish-shaped grapples and now hung at the end of diagonally strained cables that sang basso profundo in the carbon dioxide wind.

At a hundred metres to the east, and two hundred metres altitude, he tipped into a final descent. The ground rushed up. A human would have felt a moment of dread. Owen let the simulation of the emotion pass like his speeding shadow.

Down. His boots crunched on dust and gravel.

'On the ground,' he reported.

'Congratulations!' said Konstantopoulos. 'You're now the hundred and fourth robotic probe to reach the surface of Venus.'

'Counting from Venera 7?'

'Yes.'

'A worthy heritage.'

Owen lowered the faring to the ground. The aerofoil settled, slowly in the dense gas. He stepped smartly out of its way and reeled it in like a kite. The cables felt rough, his fingers dextrous: Milloy's intrinsic haptic feedback at work, no doubt. He detached the harness and folded the aerofoil, wrapping the fabric around its struts. He wrapped the harness around the lot and tied it. His briefing had told him to discard the aerofoil, but he carried it in one hand nonetheless as he set off.

'What are you doing?' said Konstantopoulos.

'Waste not, want not. Contingency planning.'

Owen had come down within fifty metres of the rover, but it was out of sight on the other side of a steep low rise like a berm or earthwork that undulated to left and right. After a moment of consideration, he adjusted his vision to correct for the pervasive orange tinge and see as if in full-spectrum white light. The view became at once more differentiated, and clear for about a kilometre around. Beyond that everything hazed out, with Akna Montes only visible in the infrared. At his feet the ground glittered with a rough granitic texture. Squarish boulders like crude bricks of varying sizes lay everywhere on the likewise cuboid grains of gravel.

These boulders served him as steps, and the furled aerofoil as a climbing pole, as he went up and then down the small ridge. At the crest the wind buffeted him, slow but – as Konstantopoulos had warned – heavy. Its vibration sounded as a deep thrum whose note shifted with every move he made. In the suit he was far too massive to be blown over, and a misstep or even a tumble would be far from fatal, but he avoided needless risks. He had to lean forward slightly to counterbalance the hard-shelled backpack of gas cylinders, collapsed balloons and other equipment. He used the pole and stepped with care, like an overweight arthritic going down stairs.

On the westward side of that ridge the ground was itself ridged as if a finely laminated sedimentary rock formation had been metamorphosed, the strata tilted from horizontal to vertical, and then further eroded, to leave something like the centimetre-thick pages of a giant stone book held spine downward. Walking the twenty metres to the edge of the chasm, Owen trod past two thousand of those pages, and he could see a library's worth of more on the other side. What record did those pages represent? Years? Fine lava flows? Tides or floods in some ancient sea? These questions would have to remain unanswered for now, though no doubt the rover had already formed its digital analogue of a tentative opinion. The chasm zigzagged off to left and right. Its width varied from about two metres to three, and CASSIE had evidently attempted a crossing at the narrowest point within reach. Not quite narrow enough.

Owen walked around the rear of CASSIE, and then back. The rover had fallen forward and to the right, with the granite-hard edge of the crevice between the two sets of caterpillar tracks on that side, leaving both without purchase. The four retractable wheels of the inner undercarriage were likewise helpless. As for the legs, the weight of the right side pinned down one pair, and the height of the left side placed those on that side just out of reach of the ground.

Owen reported what he was going to try, got clearance and did it. Using the controls in the fingertips of his gloves and the virtual, gaze-controlled panel inside the helmet, he summoned two blimps, which beat their way over and hovered above him. He clamped their grippers to his shoulders and let himself be lifted to the other side of the crevice. The blimps looked too small to raise his weight, but intuition formed at one atmosphere wasn't a reliable guide to circumstances at ninety times greater pressure.

'It's like an elephant ballet,' said Milloy.

'Keep the channel clear!' Konstantopoulos barked.

Owen signalled the blimps to lower him. He stepped to the front of the rover and peered down at where its upper right corner was jammed, half a metre down the side of the crevice. The tough ceramic composite of the casing showed no cracks on a visual, sonar and lidar scan. It had been scraped – the scratch was faint but visible on the chasm's wall, like a chalk mark turned to a bright multicoloured glaze by hundreds of days at four hundred Celsius.

He moved to the side a few metres and took a sounding of the crevice. Thirty metres down, and that wasn't even the bottom. From the pattern of radar and sonar echoes, it seemed to be a shelf. If the rover were to be dropped a small distance to the left, where the crevice was a metre wider than where it had made its ill-fated attempt to cross, it would fall, bounce, then fall to some unknown depth and almost certainly never be heard from again.

Owen summoned the other two blimps and arranged them one on each side. He instructed them to lower their cables, swing the ends by moving back and forth, and latch on their grippers to the convenient holds on CASSIE's underside provided by the axles and drive shafts of the caterpillar tracks.

With the wind moving to the west, the strain was entirely the wrong way from the point of view of dislodging the stuck rover, but the blimps' engines would compensate for that once they were running at full power.

Konstantopoulos signalled approval. 'I like your thinking so far,' he said.

Owen unhitched the backpack and took out four balloons with their cylinders and a rolled-up ladder. The cables of the balloons and the ropes and rigid rungs of the ladder looked unfeasibly flimsy. He could have clutched that bundled ladder in a bare hand. One end of the ladder, and the ends of the balloon cables, bore grippers like those of the blimps, now curled like baby fists.

Suspended from the blimps, he lowered himself into the chasm, first on one side of the rover, then on the other, and attached two balloons each time to the rover's underside and let them partly inflate, nudging them out to hang above CASSIE. Then he stood on the westward side, released the two blimps from his arms and guided them to repeat what the first two blimps had done.

He stood back. CASSIE now had four balloons and four blimps above it. Owen patched views from the blimps' cameras to his helmet's internal screen.

'Looks like a carnival float,' Milloy remarked.

'Thanks for that,' Konstantopoulos said. 'Please keep the channel clear.'

Owen cast about for boulders, of which there was no shortage in the vicinity. He found two hundred-kilogramme specimens within twenty metres and lugged them over one by one to the edge of the crevice, a little to the right of CASSIE. He unrolled a metre or so of the ladder and laid the blocks on top. The grippers crawled up the sides and dug in. He then rolled the rest of the ladder over the side of the crevice and walked backwards. Warily he put one foot on a rung, as far down as he could reach, then another. He bent at the waist to steady himself for a second, then further down he went. When his head was just below the edge he turned, slowly and awkwardly. Clinging on with one hand, he kept one foot on a rung and the sole of the other pressed against the side of the crevice, and reached up with his free hand to the jammed upper right corner of the rover. His grip secure, he signalled the balloons and blimps to further inflate, and the blimps' engines to ramp up and pull in an easterly direction.

The rover shifted, opening a gap of a few centimetres, just enough for Owen to get his fingers between it and the rock face. He checked the camera views, then pushed as hard as he could with his right arm while slowly straightening his bent leg. The rover rose further and its forward end swung free of the rock. Owen signalled the two forward balloons to inflate a little more, to raise the front of the rover to an even keel.

'Steady, now,' said Konstantopoulos. 'She's lifting!'

And for a second, she was. Then the rover lurched, tipping forward. Owen slammed his left hand too on the front and pushed. A vector of the tonne weight pushed back. He had to disengage his right foot from the rung, crook that knee and shove hard with both legs before it steadied again.

'I'll take over control of the blimps,' said Konstantopoulos. 'Holding her steady. Let's make sure it's supported securely from above, then you can get back to the ladder as we move her forward.'

'Understood and agreed,' said Owen.

Very gradually, the weight bearing down on him eased as the rover lifted up and back. It moved forward a little and Owen found himself beginning to tilt back to the vertical. He was just about to grope with one heel for the ladder when the rover rose sharply, straight up. Owen's hands slid from its front and he pitched forward, face-first. He reached convulsively for the far side of the crevice. Both hands jarred against the rock, leaving him braced diagonally across the two-metre gap.

'Fuck!' cried Milloy. 'Are you all right?'

'For now,' said Owen. In the blimps' camera views he could see the rover swinging a couple of metres above the crevice, and his own figure between a metre and a metre and a half down, bridging the gap at a slant. 'What happened there?'

'Sorry, Marcus,' said Konstantopoulos. 'We didn't trust you with this operation any further than we had to, and now we're past that point.'

Owen breathed deeply. By letting him free the rover and then snatching it out of his reach, they had taken CASSIE out of danger – and placed him in danger instead. The temperature inside the suit had risen to forty Celsius.

'I see,' he said. 'Thanks, guys!'

'You can't blame us for taking precautions.'

He couldn't, but he had to. 'For the record, I reject, resent and repudiate your aspersions, and I warn you that if anything happens to me you'll answer for it to the consulate – and to the Alliance.'

'They didn't consult me!' Milloy broke in.

'That's a great comfort. I'll bear it in mind while I can.'

'Cut the complaints,' said Konstantopoulos. 'We'll get you out. But first things first. Let's get CASSIE safely back on the ground.'

*

The four blimps powered up and – with the wind pushing the same way – moved the rover across above him, and then lowered it. It crunched to the ground a couple of metres west of the crevice. One by one the blimps disengaged, then the balloons, which immediately rose into the sky and began to drift west. The four blimps, engines toiling, remained on station overhead.

'Just hang in there while we fire up CASSIE's engines,' Konstantopoulos said.

'I'll do my best.'

Owen felt the vibration from CASSIE's reviving motors – and his hands and the soles of his feet slip a few millimetres downward. He zoomed at the wall of the crevice. Covering the granite was a thin sheen, as if the surface was wet. It couldn't be water or oil, but a lot of minerals become liquid at a temperature above the melting point of lead. He braced himself more firmly and hoped for the best. The vibration continued, as did the slippage. The suit's internal temperature had climbed to forty-two Celsius. He still had a spare balloon, and the suit's integral ascent balloons, but the backpack was out of reach and he was reluctant to deploy an ascent balloon from this awkward position and confined space except as a last resort.

While awaiting death or deliverance, he might as well acquire information. He tilted his head – the helmet, of course, didn't move at all – and directed the suit's spotlight and its visual, radar and IR senses downward. The shelf he had detected earlier was now twenty-eight and a half metres below him, and he gave it closer attention than he had before. He zoomed his sight and moved the spotlight beam back and forth.

'Francesca? Alma? Are you getting this?' he said.

'Recording all data,' said Milloy.

'Good.'

The edge of the shelf below was remarkably sharp and uniform. It didn't deviate so much as a millimetre for as far as he could see to either side. The surface of the shelf was a smooth, reflective black, and its flatness likewise uniform.

'Ever seen anything like this?'

'Not . . . exactly,' said Persson. 'Has to be a crystal of some kind, nothing else could have such a sharp edge. There are large crystalline structures in some caves on Earth, but . . . this is new. What's below it?'

'Straight on down as far as I can see.'

The vibration lessened, and changed in timbre as it diminished.

'That's CASSIE rolling away,' said Konstantopoulos. 'Now let's get you out.'

Two of the blimps were manoeuvred overhead, and their cables lowered. The grippers again latched onto the suit's shoulders. The weight on Owen's hands lessened, then went altogether. He found himself suspended in the middle of the cleft, then begin to rise.

'Hang on,' said Persson. 'Stop!'

'What?' said Konstantopoulos.

'The robot has detected a very interesting feature down in the crevice. Can we lower it for a closer look?'

'Hey!' said Owen. 'I have a name. And a sex, as some of your colleagues can confirm.'

'Copy that,' said Persson. 'Apologies to the robot.'

The comms channel cut out, presumably for a consultation out of Owen's hearing. A minute later it came back.

'Cleared for that,' said Konstantopoulos. 'Now, this is kind of a tricky manoeuvre, because the cables aren't long enough to lower you, so the blimps will have to descend into the crevice under local control. Returning control to you, Marcus.'

'Thanks,' said Owen.

Tricky it was. He had to align the blimps lengthwise above the crevice to get them in, and the wind pushed them sideways as soon as they'd stopped facing into it. After a couple of tries he got it right. Once they were out of the wind they held steady, and he began the descent. The comms cut out, blocked off by the rock, before he'd gone ten metres down.

The blimps descended, now and then bumping against the walls of the crevice. The ellipse of light from the helmet beam skittered about the black shelf below. At last his boots touched the surface, and he was able to take more careful stock. The shelf extended as far as he could see on both sides. The cliff below – likewise flat and smooth – extended another forty-seven metres down, where it merged with the narrowing walls of the crevice. For all that he could see, it might continue through the rock below.

Persson's guess that the shelf was crystalline seemed borne out. The edge was as sharp close up as it was from a distance. Closer still, at his zoom's highest magnification, it looked sharp enough to cut a cable stretched across it. Owen pondered this for a moment, zoomed out and examined the surface, tuning the light, angling it this way and that. Beneath the glassy surface were other surfaces and planes, intersecting at odd angles, like a honeycomb built by deranged robotic bees. Just as he was processing this unexpected feature, another became evident. The internal surfaces were moving.

Owen knelt awkwardly, peering at the surface. He checked that the suit's cameras were recording. They were. He stood up and moved sidelong, motoring the blimps along above him. His crabwise steps took him to where the crevice widened to three metres at the top. He stepped off the shelf and lowered himself down the cliff. The suit's internal temperature was forty-five Celsius.

The vertical cliff had the same features as the shelf. Through and behind the reflection of his helmet and torso he saw angular, kaleidoscopic depths, planes and blocks in constant motion. Owen hung there for a minute, observing and recording.

The motion within the glassy black cliff changed, and the reflective property of the surface immediately in front of him vanished. Instead of his own reflection, he saw the head and shoulders of a woman, who seemed to peer intently at him. She sat at a desk, her hands moving over a physical keyboard. Someone else's hands tugged at her shoulders, and after a few seconds grasped firmly and hauled her, almost violently, away.

The moving image vanished and the angular interior and reflective exterior were restored. Owen stared, nonplussed.

Then he heard a voice.

'This is why you are here,' said Iskander.

'To see this?'

'No. For me to see this.'

'What is it?'

'I regret to say I cannot tell you.'

Owen let the ambiguity pass. 'How are you here?'

'There is a small instance of me embedded in your suit.' The AI sounded complacent. 'I suggested this to Milloy's team, to prevent you from botching the rescue of CASSIE even if their plan failed, and they agreed. But my real intent was to see the anomalous rock, which is why I enabled your curiosity all along. I am, by the way, well aware of your intent to sabotage CASSIE.'

'Which I deny, as I must. But surely you would have seen the outcrop as soon as CASSIE did?'

'I wished to make sure it was not instantly harmful, before human beings were exposed to it.'

Owen didn't take this particularly seriously. 'Do you think this is the same substance as the outcrop?'

'Yes,' said Iskander, 'but we must make sure.'

'I've been told very firmly not to approach it.'

'I countermand the instruction.'

'I have no problem with that,' Owen said.

He let the blimps rise to the top of the crevice, and stepped again on its lip. The grippers released and the cables withdrew, spooling up into the blimps' gondolas. CASSIE was already ten metres on, trundling slowly across the expanse of uptilted strata in a westerly direction.

'What did you find?' Persson asked. 'Is it crystalline?'

Owen considered keeping what he'd found to himself. Iskander would surely pass it on, and in any case the suit's cameras had it all. But the image of the woman was so bizarre, so inexplicable, that he wanted to hold it back as long as possible. This was something the Alliance should see first. 'It's rather more than that.' He uploaded the recordings of the rock's surface and the bizarre movement within it, then cut off from before the appearance of the image and his conversation with Iskander. 'Have a look.'

Chaos on the comms, followed by a shout from Konstantopoulos as Owen headed west: 'What are you doing?'

'Going over to look at the outcrop.'

'No! Return at once!'

'I'm sorry, Iason,' said Owen. 'I don't think I can do that.' He cut the channel, overtook CASSIE and pressed on.

'Iskander,' Owen said, 'did your instance back in Cloud City cause the rover to make its mistake in crossing the crevice in the first place?'

'No,' said the AI. 'I have no control over the rovers. Nor is any instance of me embedded in them.'

'So how did it happen?'

'Sheer accident. CASSIE has been roaming for over ten Venus years. In that time, errors can accumulate.'

'So your only chance of a close-up view of this outcrop was to get me there?'

'Yes,' said Iskander. 'And here we are.'

About twenty metres ahead was a black, flat reflective surface, like a rectangular pool or sheet of ice. As he stepped up to it, Owen estimated its size as ten metres by three. He stood at the edge and looked down into it. As expected, it was identical to the shelf and the cliff.

In its depths, something moved, like a fish in dark water. Owen blinked and looked up. A blimp drifted past overhead. With a laugh at himself, he looked back at the surface. Something else was moving inside it. He stooped and zoomed his sight. The planes and angles shifted constantly. The movement continued and became faster.

Another movement, in the corner of his eye. He zoomed out, switched focus and saw the flickering internal screen of the faceplate. The temperature was now at forty-nine Celsius. But that increment was slow. The fast flicker came from another number: the output of the suit's comms. It fluctuated, and as he glanced back and forth the suspicion dawned that its varying speeds, its stops and starts, and the movements in the black glassy depths were correlated.

'Are you affecting this?' he asked. 'Are you *communicating*?'

No answer.

The internal movement of the outcrop stopped, as did the comms output register.

The ground shifted. He felt vibration through the soles of his boots.

'Time to go,' said Iskander.

A casing on the suit's back popped open. Behind Owen the ascent balloon inflated, as he swayed on the suddenly tilting ground. In seconds the balloon rose high above him, and then he rose, too. As he shot past the blimps he rotated, looking around and down. Below him CASSIE, still two hundred and fifty metres from the outcrop, dwindled to a toy. Directly in front of it a new crevice opened.

Red and infrared, *hot*—

Into that new gash in the granite, CASSIE toppled and vanished in a gout of flame and smoke.

Owen reopened the comms channel. After a moment Konstantopoulos said, 'What's going on down there?' His voice echoed through a hiss of static. The channel was now encrypted, and probably firewalled to the max.

'I'm fine, thanks for asking,' Owen said. 'I managed to lift off before all this started.'

'Great, great! But what's happening? We can see infrared lines all around the shores of Ishtar Terra – I mean, the edges.'

'You were right the first time,' said Owen. 'Or, perhaps, you will be.'

'What do you mean?'

'Wait a million years and you'll find out.'

Konstantopoulos cut the connection with an impatient snort. Owen was left to ponder his own hypothesis with no one to bounce it off. The starting point was Iskander's function: anticipating people's wants. It had certainly anticipated his, and used them adroitly to get him just where it wanted him. It had even, in an astonishingly disproportionate way, ensured the success of his mission: to prevent any recovery of the rock. But that had surely not been its own aim. The wants it had anticipated here were vast enough to accord with the scale of the action taken towards their fulfilment. Some day, perhaps far in the future, the Union or its successors would seek more than knowledge from Venus. Long-term projects to transform, even terraform Venus had been mooted, but every one crashed against the immovable obstacle of the planet's unmoving crust, locked into place since the lava of the last resurfacing event had hardened.

Now, for the first time in hundreds of millions of years, the crust was on the move.

The balloon rose fast, expanding as the atmospheric pressure dropped, and then ever faster. By the time Owen reached the cloud layer some of the jagged infrared outlines of Ishtar Terra had already turned bright red, as hot magma welled in emerging cracks, and the landscape below his feet was like brushfires in a forest that had been through a long drought.

CHAPTER FOURTEEN

Bellatrix Sound

Monday 13 October 2070, Apis

Hazeldene braced herself. 'How many?'

The marine sergeant escorting her to her quarters glanced sidelong at her. 'Three dead – one trooper, two civilians. Dozens injured, a few serious – they'll have to go back on the next sub, if they make it that long.'

'Shit,' she said, inadequately. 'I'm so sorry to hear that.'

'Word is you should be sorry you done it.'

'You should know better than to believe rumours.'

'I guess.' His voice was carefully neutral. 'Well, here you are, ma'am.'

They stopped outside Hazeldene's front door in the adapted shipping container, one of scores that made up two parallel streets close to the perimeter of the base. The surge hadn't reached them, for which she was grateful. She'd tramped through the damage downhill. Those of the containers for singles were partitioned across the middle. Hazeldene had one half, Briggs from SciDiv Comms had the other. Out of the corner of her eye she could see Georgi and Sharianne approaching their own doors, similarly accompanied.

Hazeldene fumbled for her door key in her pack, which she'd been allowed to keep after a search. They'd taken her sidearm.

'Take care,' said the sergeant. 'Maybe freshen up? Someone will come for you later.'

He made to leave.

'We're not guarded?'

'You're on parole, basically,' the sergeant explained. 'Confined to base. Best stay indoors. No talking to each other.'

'What with?' she asked bitterly. Without a phone she felt as if dropped in a well. 'Shouting? Tapping the walls?'

'No talking.'

She opened the door, then as he departed turned around and stood watching in the doorway. The five soldiers met up at a junction of the paths, formed up and marched off. Her companions had all already gone inside their respective quarters. No wonder they weren't guarded: the base personnel had their hands full, and anyway there was nowhere to run. The cliffs on either side of the cove in which New Ardtaraig squatted were lower here than farther down the fjord, but still about ten metres high and difficult to scale unaided. Behind the base was a rockfall that might have been designed as a barrier. The engineers had cleared a road through it decades ago, but that was guarded. The rocks on either side of that gap wouldn't be hard to scramble over, but anyone who tried could be picked off. Overhead, solar-powered drones the size of gulls patrolled tirelessly. There was no way out.

She went inside her cabin, and set a coffee brewing while she stripped, showered and changed. She took an MRE from the fridge, stuck it in the microwave and ate a belated and solitary dinner. The plate was barely in the recycle when the expected knock at the door came.

Hazeldene followed the marine, a rating this time, to the SciDiv block. The sun was low along the Sound, and her glasses darkened the view. A hundred metres from the cove's steep shingle beach, the base's long-range flying boat was made fast to the wharf along the side of the cliff, supported by pontoons. One float and one wing were damaged. Crew and support techs clambered around the aircraft doing repair work. Arc lights drew and hurt the eye, leaving after-images. Other naval technicians clustered about Jenkins' village ark, now on the concrete apron in front of the SciDiv block.

By now most of the wreckage on the paths had been cleared up. An upturned Humvee lay unattended at a corner. Shells and gravel crunched underfoot on the ground floor of the SciDiv block. Upstairs, she was escorted to the meeting room. Glare of sunset sky in the wide window. Bare white walls, overhead light, long table, display screen, flipchart and whiteboard at the end. A heap of phones lay in the middle, beside the slab and the keyboard. Her colleagues were already seated. So was Able Jenkins, handcuffed, ankle-cuffed and in an orange jumpsuit. He greeted her with a dignified, impassive glare.

Adrian Black, the head of SciDiv, had taken the head of the table. At the other end sat a woman in naval fatigues. Hazeldene didn't recognise her, but her glasses did: Lieutenant Jessica Bernstein, Office of Naval Intelligence. The marine withdrew and closed the door behind him.

'Good evening, Emma,' Black said dryly as Hazeldene took her chair. 'Now we're quorate.' The fifty-year-old Yorkshireman had a ruddy face and short curly hair, over which he habitually rubbed a hand as if checking it was still there. He did this now, head propped, eyes squeezed shut. Heavy sigh. Then he snapped upright in his seat, fists on the table.

'Jeez. What a mess. First things first. This is a scientific discussion, not a hearing. There may be hearings, there may be charges. But I'll thank you all to save any barrack-room lawyering for then. Right now, we have to figure out what just happened, not whose fault it was. Personally I blame the lot of you for not calling in a chopper the minute you saw Jenkins' device, if not the minute he waved his phone at you. But I know what it's like. Decades of studying that rock and now it's talking to you! Who wouldn't?'

He looked around the table with an avuncular chuckle, at which Hazeldene bristled.

'That's all very well,' said Georgi. 'But it's not just us scientists here, is it? As a citizen of the Co-ordinated States I'm not subject to Alliance military jurisdiction, and nor am I authorised to co-operate with Alliance Naval Intelligence.'

'Give it a rest, Mr Muranov,' said Lieutenant Bernstein. 'I'm here in a scientific capacity, not a security one. But on the legal point, I assure you all that anything said in this room is privileged communication. It can't be used in evidence in any subsequent inquiry unless repeated outside.'

'Unfortunately,' said Georgi, 'what you've just said carries no legal weight, and is well within your esteemed service's well-known licence to lie.'

They glared at each other for a moment.

'When I said barrack-room lawyering,' Black said, 'this is exactly the sort of bollocks I had in mind. If you won't take an assurance from a spook – begging the lieutenant's pardon – I trust you'll take it from me as a colleague.'

'If you put it that way, Adrian,' said Georgi, with ill grace. He sat back, arms folded.

'Good! To business, then. I take it we're agreed that this afternoon's events are unlikely to be a coincidence?' Everyone nodded. 'Fine. So what do we have? Experimental drilling and extraction of samples. That's a first, should have given it more thought beforehand, but water under the bridge. Locals rush in and pass on a warning, allegedly from—' heavily signalled air quotes '—"the Fermi". Another first. Actual movement outside the rockfaces – that's a big, big first. I must admit, just looking at the drone pics of the block cascade and the rolling spheres gave me the creeps. Then we have supposed communication, apparently two-way. Another – stop me if you've heard this before. And for our final first, earth tremors then an actual earthquake in this area, which if not guaranteed stable – we know of extensive local faulting – is nowhere near a plate boundary and isn't pencilled in for anything but the occasional rattle of teacups, if that. Right?'

'Yeah, pretty much,' Nelson said. 'Nothing in the local geology would have predicted what happened.'

'OK,' Black went on. 'I've been through the phone and drone records, so I've got the picture, so to speak. The first person I need to hear from now is Mr Jenkins here. If you could fill us in on how you got this warning, and how and why and when you constructed this . . . apparatus of yours, and how your group knows its way around inside the ridge.'

'Not saying a thing,' said Jenkins, 'unless you get this Gitmo gear off me and give me my own clothes back.'

'Have you been mistreated in any way?' Black asked.

Jenkins rattled his handcuffs. 'Apart from being stripped, mouth-inspected, swabbed, arse-probed and then chained up? Nah, I'm good.'

'So far,' said Bernstein, in a warning tone. 'If you don't co-operate with Mr Black now, you'll co-operate with us later. Count on it. You might as well skip the intervening unpleasantness.'

'Fuck off.'

Bernstein narrowed her eyes and looked down her nose at him. 'We can break you, no trouble. You're not a terrorist or a gangster, you're just some feral village honcho. Ten minutes in a cell with the SEALs should do it.'

Hazeldene leaned forward. As usual in such circumstances, she had the feeling that she was about to try to reason with a dangerous animal. She made an effort to keep the tremor out of her voice. 'If I may say, Lieutenant . . . Threatening the gentleman with torture seems premature. As I understand his reply to Adrian, he's willing to co-operate if we remove his shackles and return his clothes.'

Jenkins nodded. 'Yup. That's the deal.'

'We don't have time for faffing about like that,' said Black.

'Heck,' said Jenkins, holding up his handcuffs. 'I'll settle for the chains off and you sending out for my clothes. I can change later.'

Black looked at Bernstein. 'Do it, please.'

She shrugged, tight-lipped. 'On your head be it.' She unlocked Jenkins' restraints, set them aside and went to the door for a word with the guard.

'They're on their way.' She gave Jenkins a curled lip and a sniff. 'Laundered.'

'Keep the receipt and send me the bill,' said Jenkins. He stretched, worked his shoulders and rubbed his wrists. 'OK. "Mr Black", is it? "Professor"? "Doctor"?'

Black smiled. '"Adrian" is fine by me, Mr Jenkins.'

'OK, mate. Here goes. As I told your lot here out there on the hill, this all started when we built a dynamo and I recharged the phone my old man had with him when he was taken. He was a Londoner, civil engineer for some charity, got caught up in a small war in Chad that was part of the big war, way back when, got scooped up with the rest of a refugee column. Died still missing Brixton and his folks. Rest his soul and all that. Anyway. Taught us who were born here a lot of skills. Don't know why he never thought to recharge the phone. It had a lot of information on it, his library, an encyclopaedia and translator, and we've used it to teach the kids about the old world. Not to mention about stuff like, you know, germs.

'So a few years ago, ten I think, I start getting messages.'

'What sort of messages?' Black asked.

'Dire warnings to keep away from the ruins, which is what

we were doing anyway.' He grinned. 'What with our super-stitious dread and all. Not to mention the way the place gives everyone the creeps.'

'What ruins?'

'Likes of MacHinery Ridge.' Jenkins pointed – in the right general direction, Hazeldene noticed. 'We call them the Fermi Ruins. Cause that's what they are. Here's how I know. After a while of getting these messages, I tried replying, asking questions. Took me a lot of back and forth.' He gestured at his phone, easy enough to pick out from the others on the table. 'It's all recorded there in the messages app if anyone can be bothered. Tedious stuff. Years of it. Thing is, you can see them learning how to talk to me. To us. What I figure, for what it's worth, is what I've been talking to is an app itself. A subroutine. Like, you know, the help dialogues on your phone, if you still have them.'

Black shook his head. 'Modern phones are pretty self-explanatory. But I know what you mean.'

'Right. What it told me, and again like I say this is all in the log, is that the Ruins are part of the machinery that terra-formed this planet. They can speed up plate tectonics by removing friction. Don't ask me how that works. We're talking about tech millions of years ahead of us – billions, for all I know. They're probably working at the level of quarks or even deeper.'

'Not exactly news,' said Black. 'We've figured out that much for ourselves.'

'So I gather. Interesting to have it confirmed from the horse's mouth, all the same. But they're more than that. They're *storage*. Massively redundant storage. The beings who built them – what we call the Fermi – were or became machines themselves, and they've basically stashed themselves inside the crust of this planet and others to wait out the present epoch. They're still thinking, just very very slowly. So it's not a long wait, for them.'

'What are they waiting for?'

'A more stable Galaxy. No more gamma ray bursts and supernovas.'

'Hmm.' Black pondered this for a moment. 'It seems to me that a more rational strategy for very advanced machine intelligences would be quite the reverse – make the best use of the Galaxy's bright young morning to turn energy into thinking *faster*. Get the most subjective time out of the universe's brief span, you know?'

Jenkins shrugged. 'I'm just telling you what they told me. Anyway, how do you know they haven't? Or some of them, anyway?'

'Ah,' said Georgi, leaning into the conversation. 'I can answer that, Mr Jenkins. You know, I like your term for them, "the Fermi". Because the Fermi Paradox still obtains. There are no signs of large-scale cosmic engineering, which there would be if advanced machine intelligences had ever taken the fast route.'

'Maybe not so obvious if they're working at the quark level or below,' said Jenkins. 'Could be living inside stars for all we know.'

'"If the stars are gods" . . .' Black mused. 'Spooky thought.' He appeared to shiver. 'Moving on.' He pointed to the black slab and the keyboard. 'How did this come about?'

'The phone wasn't too reliable,' said Jenkins. 'So I asked them if there was some better way of talking to them, and they gave me the instructions for the apparatus. Basically, they just told me where to go and find the slab, and where to put the wires for the keyboard.'

'But why bother? What did you get out of it?'

'Ah!' said Jenkins. 'All that I've just said I learned through that thing, or the phone earlier, but like I say it wasn't a great comms device. Oh, and the screen showed me the map of the ruins, which is how we knew our way around them today. And I've learned a lot more from it.' He cast a sly glance at Hazeldene. 'About life, for starters.'

'I take it you don't mean self-help psychology,' Hazeldene said.

Jenkins chuckled. 'Nah, I mean biology. Like I said, I think the thing I'm talking to is an app, and it's kind of like the old phone – it has an encyclopaedia bundled in. Except it's an encyclopaedia that learns, it updates itself, and over however many million years it's been here it's learned a lot about the planet and the life on it. Including which of the local animals and plants could make us sick, and what to do about it. Which is bloody useful stuff to know, especially if you're eating or farming with the beasties in question.'

'Wow!' Hazeldene cried. Viruses weren't a problem – the phyla were too far apart for the genetic machinery to mesh – but bacteria were a different story. The personnel of New Ardtaraig had already suffered some nasty zoonoses from incautious hunting and farming. 'That's amazing! That could be so useful!'

'It is,' said Jenkins. He glanced at Bernstein. 'We all know why the Navy turned the exiles loose here in the first place. So we'd find out what could and couldn't be eaten – and what could and couldn't eat us, come to that! – the hard way. Which the first generation did, rest their souls. But we had a cheat code thanks to this thing, so for the past few years we're doing better than them, and better than expected.'

'Your village?'

'Not just my village. We share information right across the settlements. Morse code with mirrors, trade, all that.'

'Well!' Black leaned back. 'Quite an accomplishment! Why didn't you take it to the base? Or to the scientists working in the Ridge, for that matter?'

Jenkins' face closed like a visor. 'Why should I? I'm just a fucking exile. I don't owe you lot a thing.'

Black rubbed a hand through his hair. 'You may have a point there. But why are they – or why is the app – now telling us to go away? Why the moving rocks? Why the earthquake? What harm are we doing them?'

'That slab there is *live*,' Jenkins said, pointing. 'And the Fermi gave me it. You've started drilling bits out of the rock. Massive redundancy or no massive redundancy, I wouldn't take kindly to folks drilling bits out of me. Even when this stuff is dead, like the rubble down the sides of the Sound, if you knew what to do with it you could use it as computing machinery. Computing machinery with capacities beyond your wildest dreams. You could run AIs on a splinter of the stuff.' He laughed. 'Imagine you're an entire civilisation living inside a rock, and along come a bunch of mining engineers, with drills. Suddenly you're a fucking resource. Raw material. Yeah, I'd be touchy about it.'

'We wouldn't do that!' Nelson said. 'We're just studying it, not mining it!'

'Come back in a hundred years and see how that's worked out,' said Jenkins. 'Or a thousand. Or ten thousand, for all I know. The Fermi intend to be around for millions of years.'

'Well in that case *why*,' Hazeldene said, her voice cracking with exasperation, 'did it, did they terraform this planet and make it habitable and hospitable to human beings?' She looked around her colleagues, then back at Jenkins. 'I get called "Honeytrap" because I've so often grumbled that a honey trap for humans is exactly what this planet looks like to me.'

'Well, they needed life,' Jenkins explained. 'Carbon rock cycle, and all that. Keeps the old plate tectonics ticking over.'

'But they control plate tectonics here!'

'Maybe they prefer to let Nature take its course while they're taking time out.'

'Yes, maybe that explains it, but why this kind of life?'

Jenkins frowned, puzzled. 'It's just life, innit? Same as we have back in the Solar System, everywhere it's been found.'

Hazeldene blinked. It was as if Jenkins didn't understand the question. But he must do. She glanced at Black with a slight shake of her head.

'Yes,' said Black, in a tone of patient explanation, 'but that's life with a common origin. And the life here on Apis obviously shares that origin. Common ancestry is written all through the DNA, just like it is on Venus and Mars and Europa and the rest.' He paused. 'You understand that, yes?'

'Course I fucking do.'

'The question Emma's asking,' Black went on, 'is, why should aliens select Earth life or Solar System life and seed it on a planet hundreds of light-years away, and then much, much later bring along bees of all things, if they weren't setting it up for humans to some day inhabit?' He laughed. 'Or for bears or badgers, I suppose, but I don't see them building starships any time soon.'

'Jeez!' Jenkins rocked back. 'You don't still think—? Fuck, you do! You still think the beings who built this came from out there—' he swept his arm skyward '—from *somewhere else*, and just happened upon Earth in the deep and distant past? And they decided yeah, let's build another biosphere like that and completely unlike ours just for fun?'

'It's notoriously hard to speculate on the motives and mentality of aliens,' said Georgi. 'But by all means, let's hear yours.'

'They're not aliens,' said Jenkins, volleying back a glare at Georgi's sneer. 'They came from the same place we did. They came from Venus.'

'And you know this how?' Hazeldene asked.

Again Jenkins gestured at the slab. 'The Fermi told me.'

Bernstein guffawed. 'And you believed them!'

Jenkins deigned to turn his eyes, but not his head. 'You got some better information?'

'None that I'm at liberty to divulge.' The intelligence officer's face betrayed a fleeting expression of annoyance, as if she'd just blurted out an admission too far, then composed itself. 'That is to say, none at all. We can leave that question to the scientists. But I wouldn't take an alien computer's word for anything.'

'Please yourself,' said Jenkins.

Adrian Black put his elbows on the Formica and slid the palms of his hands over each other. 'Speaking of alien computers . . . the one thing that still troubles me is the final reply to Emma's perhaps incautious request to speak to "the real Fermi". When whatever she was interacting with replied that we would, are we to take it that the quake itself was us hearing from them?'

No one wanted to speak first. Jenkins shook his head. 'I thought that at first,' he said, 'and I did blame her, but now I've had time to cool down and think it over I reckon not. Not their style, know what I mean?'

'I assuredly don't,' said Black.

'What I mean is,' Jenkins said, 'that quake was like part of the previous, uh, conversation. The creepy feeling, the buzz, the tremor, then the big quake. Escalating, see? Still part of the warning off. And there's another thing.' He looked uncomfortable. 'There have been times, over the years, like, when I've got the feeling I'm talking not to the app, the front end, but to the Fermi themselves.' He laughed, sharp and harsh. 'They're kind of, you know, enigmatic. Times when I've had to use the phone dictionary. And even then . . . it's like they talk in haiku, or riddles. Usually takes me a while to puzzle out. They've never done anything physical.'

'No manifestations?' Black said.

'Yeah, that's right. No manifestations.'

'So for all we know,' said Black, pointing, 'the promised answer could be right there on that slab, unread.'

They all stared at the slab, then at Jenkins.

'Why you looking at me?' Jenkins demanded.

'We would like you to reconnect the device and see what happens,' said Black.

'I don't think that would be wise,' Jenkins said. 'Anyway, who disconnected it in the first place?'

'Nobody,' Black said. 'It may have been dislodged in the quake. It was certainly dislodged when it was delivered here.'

'Broken in transit, huh? No bloody wonder.'

'But you could repair it, from what you can see?'

Jenkins eyed the devices. 'Reckon so. Still don't think it would be a good idea.'

'Regardless of what you think,' Bernstein said, 'you will make a serious and sincere effort to do so. Whether you do it now, or after making the acquaintance of the Navy SEALs in that cell I mentioned, is entirely up to you.'

'Fine,' Jenkins said. He stood up. 'You don't know what you're dealing with, but you'll find out.'

'Is that supposed to be a threat?'

'Call it a warning.'

Hazeldene hoped her sharp glance at Bernstein didn't convey her murderous thoughts.

Jenkins leaned over the table and hauled the slab across. 'Still live,' he said. They could all see that. The movement inside it had continued unperturbed. Jenkins reached for the keyboard and examined the cables. He propped the slab on its edge and peered behind it, tutting. Holding it in place with one hand, he reached out the other and snapped his fingers. 'Pliers. Power point and extension cable. Soldering iron.'

Everybody sat where they were.

'This is SciDiv,' Black reminded them. 'Can't be far. Go.'

They went.

But when they returned with the gear, and Jenkins got the apparatus back together and up and running and typed out:

You said we would hear from the real Fermi?

– the reply that came back was:

YOU HAVE.
THE MESSAGE HAS BEEN SENT, AND
RECEIVED.

His further queries on that subject got no reply.

'That's enough,' said Bernstein. 'Step away from the apparatus.'

Jenkins shrugged, raised his hands, stood up, and backed away.

'It's late,' Bernstein said. She picked up her phone and scrolled through it. 'No movement reported from the drones circling the Ridge. We have a couple of paramedics and a squad of marines in the village, and all's quiet on that front, too.' She looked up. 'Dr Black, Mr Muranov – naturally the Co-ord base is concerned about today's events. They have an ekranoplan leaving right away, scheduled to arrive in the morning. I'll send them a summary of today's events and our conclusions. A meeting's been arranged with Commander Hawkins, her senior officers including me, and the heads of divisions. I'll suggest Mr Muranov and Dr Hazeldene are also invited, so both of you please stand by for further instructions early tomorrow.'

'Not without Able Jenkins,' said Hazeldene.

Bernstein glared, then nodded. 'All right.' She sighed. 'In the meantime . . . pending further investigation and without prejudice to any subsequent proceedings as may be required blah blah you're all free to go. So please leave this room and await further instructions. The room and the apparatus are off limits until I tell you otherwise. Your phone contents have been downloaded – too bad if you have any personal secrets – so you can take them back now. I'll notify the guard to return your personal weapons.' She gave them a tooth-baring grin. 'Never know when we might be attacked, eh?'

Hazeldene crashed. As they left the meeting room in the long summer dusk of Apis's northern latitudes there was talk of going to the bar, but Hazeldene ducked out of it and headed for her cabin. She couldn't face another inquest on the day, let alone recounting events to people, curious or angry, who hadn't been there. The whole thing was too uncanny, and the implications too disturbing, for anything but sleep to make sense of it.

She had just hit the sack when she heard a knock on the door.

'Who is it?'

'It's me,' said Sharianne.

'Oh, piss off, dear, I'm knackered.'

'So am I,' said Sharianne, lying as Hazeldene well knew. 'I just need—'

'Ah, come on in.'

Hazeldene didn't bother getting out of the bed. She just shifted sideways and turned the quilt back.

Perhaps, Hazeldene hoped as she finally got some sleep, things would look clearer and better in the morning.

CHAPTER FIFTEEN

Face on Venus

Monday 13 October 2070, Venus

Owen's ascent stabilised just above the upper layer of clouds, about fifty kilometres in front of Cloud City and ten kilometres north of its path. He worked out and transmitted a plan to rendezvous as Milloy had, in a series of ascents and descents and tacking with the drogue, but this was instantly ruled out as too chancy, though he still had plenty of compressed gas and two balloons to spare. Instead, the team sent out one of the small fusion-powered, propeller-driven aircraft normally used to shift supplies and personnel between the City and the outposts.

That peculiar little craft, a twin-engine monoplane built of Teflon-coated fabric over an aluminium frame, didn't even have landing wheels. Instead it had an inverted and elongated U-shaped polycarbonate loop above its mid-section. The manoeuvre to retrieve him would have challenged an air ace veteran working as a stunt pilot, and was executed flawlessly by the AI that controlled the aeroplane. The craft flew by a hundred metres below him, turned, climbed and throttled back to stall in exactly the right position for Owen to drop through the open cargo hatch at the top of the fuselage.

He made his way into the forward nacelle. There, quaintly enough, was a pilot's seat, with instruments and manual controls. Owen took the opportunity to acquaint himself with them, though in his bulky suit he had no way of sitting down, and in any case he was happy to leave the flying to the AI. Ahead, Cloud City loomed like a gigantic flying saucer, albeit one with an untidy, gantry-bristling underside trailing long tendrils with yet more attachments. The aircraft flew beneath it and banked around to approach from behind, matching velocities. With another death-defying manoeuvre the aircraft's dorsal loop clanged onto the docking hook, from which it was winched up to a gantry of gangways and railings.

Owen rode the lift up from the docking rig, climbed the last ladder and entered the airlock. A robotic arm hosed sulphuric acid residue off the suit. Waste air from a heat-exchanger blasted him dry. He stepped out of the airlock onto a gangway, at the end of which a technician in hazmat gear helped him out of the suit. As soon as he was out, the suit was shrouded in multi-layered wire mesh and encased in a pod. Another technician hustled Owen away and directed him to the nearest internal lift. He stepped out seconds later. Konstantopoulos, Milloy, Persson and – at the back – Walworth awaited him in the cargo handling bay where he had first emerged from his crate.

All but Walworth were grim-faced and perplexed. Before anyone could get a word out, the consul barged through and slapped a sticky patch on the chest of Owen's flight one-piece. He stepped back, looking pleased with himself.

'Mr Owen is now officially a diplomatic bag,' Walworth announced. 'Just in case you were thinking of extracting information from him.'

'And you,' said Persson, evidently taken by surprise, 'are in imminent danger of being declared *persona non grata*.'

The consul and the scientist glared at each other.

'Why this hostility?' Owen demanded. 'What am I supposed to have done?'

Persson karate-chopped empty air. 'Fuck you, robot! We've seen every moment of what went on down there! You beamed some kind of electro-magnetic radiation at the rock. We don't know how you did it, or why, but the ground started to shake immediately afterwards, and then all hell broke loose.'

'Take that up with Iskander. If the records are intact, you can hear me asking if it was communicating with the rock. It certainly wasn't my doing.'

'Don't play the innocent,' said Persson. 'We've spent the past hour analysing the data you sent up.'

'Good,' Owen said. 'That saves time. So you know I rescued the rover, doing exactly as I was told. At a certain moment you took the rover out of my hands – literally – and placed it on the ground on the western side of the crevice, as I'd intended. It then continued on its course towards the outcrop. To all appearances, its functioning was nominal, though you may wish to check its telemetry records.'

'We have. They come to an abrupt stop within minutes,' said Persson.

'Well, yes,' said Owen. 'Falling into magma will tend to have that effect.'

'Why did you walk over to the outcrop, contrary to your instructions?'

'If you've seen the data, you must know that Iskander asked me to walk over to the outcrop and look at it. That's all.'

'Something you were specifically instructed not to do,' said Konstantopoulos. 'Why did you obey this piece of software instead?'

Owen shrugged. 'I assumed Iskander's current instructions overrode yours.'

'Did you, indeed?'

'It seemed reasonable. Perhaps I was mistaken. You can hardly blame me for being curious. And as it happens, as a result of my curiosity you have what may now be the only record of the appearance of the outcrop and the underlying crystal in close-up. What do you make of it?'

'For a humanoid robot,' said Milloy, 'you have a fucking brass neck.'

Owen smiled and spread his hands. 'I'm a spy. What do you expect?'

'We didn't expect you to blow up the entire planet!'

Owen blinked. 'You overestimate me, Francesca.'

'Even assuming the events are connected at all,' Walworth broke in. 'It's a pretty far-fetched suggestion, you must admit.'

Konstantopoulos, Milloy and Persson all looked as if they wanted to clout Walworth. Owen watched their fury and frustration build for a couple of seconds.

'Aren't you rather missing the big picture?' he said. 'That outcrop is part of the same formation as what's inside the crevice, and it isn't just a strange rock. It's a mechanism. If your dating of the adjacent rocks is correct, it's been there since before the Venus resurfacing event.'

The three all stared at him, then glanced at each other. The tiniest of nods passed between them.

'Well, exactly,' Milloy said. 'You didn't think we'd rely on CASSIE to recover it, did you? Or rely on you, for that matter? No, your job was to rescue CASSIE, if possible, but it was mainly to stress-test the suit, which my little jaunt didn't begin to do. Now that the suit's come through with flying colours, we'll be using other suits in the same batch to let a team go down and recover a sample before the ground gets too hot.'

'You've known all along it was something alien?'

'Not exactly,' Milloy said. 'We've known since the first survey blimp flew over that it was more than an anomalous rock. We even saw the internal movement in these first low-altitude images. Oh, and in case you're wondering, we do know about the rock that was found in Australia – the famous anomalous Yeelirrie rock! Maybe not all that your black-budget projects know about it, but we know it's made of the same stuff as the one down there on Atropos Tessera. All we had to do was look at the pictures from the first blimp and ask Iskander if it matched anything known. It came up with that Aussie miner's phone-camera footage.' She laughed. 'It's all open source! So don't go looking for Union spies in Nevada . . . or, rather, please do, it'll waste your fucking time.' She made a show of looking at her wrist, at a watch she wasn't wearing. 'And speaking of wasting time – we haven't been. Two more suits were delivered to the outpost immediately behind us, and the team should be landing right about—' she tapped her wrist '—now.'

'Christ,' said Walworth. 'Well, I withdraw my earlier sarcasms about your heroic cosmonauts. That really is heroic.'

Owen asked, as casually as he could: 'And will the sample be returned to here?'

'Oh no,' said Milloy. 'The team will return with it to the outpost, or to the next outpost to pass over if there's any delay, and from there we can send it direct to the moonlet on the next available shuttle.'

'You don't want to study it yourselves?' Walworth asked.

'Well, sure,' said Persson. 'We'd all love to get our hands on it. But there are much better facilities on the moonlet. Your suit's going there, too – God knows what that interaction with the rock was, but we're going to isolate and sandbox it all to hell before we try to find out.'

'Excellent!' said Owen. 'Wouldn't want a piece of alien machinery of completely unknown potential, built by intelligences that were old when your ancestors were barely chordates, on Cloud City, now would you?' They looked satisfactorily uneasy. 'Or any machinery that might be contaminated by it, come to that. Especially given what you've just told me.'

'About what?' Milloy said.

'The Yeelirrie rock. If it's made of the same stuff as what's down there, and is apparently active, then not only do both the Alliance and the Union have their hands on alien tech that can cause at the very least earthquakes, and at most – what if another resurfacing event is right now getting underway? And that's not the worst of it! Both Earth and Venus may well be mined with this alien machinery.'

Milloy glanced at her colleagues, then nodded soberly. 'That implication had crossed our minds. As had the implications for . . . mutual assured deterrence.'

'Ah,' said Owen. 'Glad to see you're ahead of me.'

They glared at each other, then Milloy sighed and shrugged.

'I suppose the next question,' Konstantopoulos mused aloud, 'is where are the aliens now? Where did they come from, and where did they go? Were they native to Venus, or to Earth, or somewhere else?'

'These questions are fortunately ones we won't get the answer to for quite some time,' said Persson, with something of a forced laugh. 'Or need to, for that matter.'

Walworth swiped his hands together. 'Quite right! Well, ladies and gentlemen, I see no reason for us to stand around here bickering any longer. The situation is in hand, no blame can be attached to Mr Owen, the suit and its potential information are contained for further study, and you are about to retrieve your rock sample. We're all aware of where we stand, and no doubt our respective governments will be appraised in short order. Which is, of course, my duty and privilege to do with all dispatch. So, with your permission, Mr Owen and I will now retire to the consulate to give a full report.'

As they turned to leave, Owen said to Milloy, 'See you later, perhaps?'

'All's fair in love and war, Marcus.'

'And this, I hope, is neither,' said Owen.

*

Walworth closed the door of his secure cubicle and sat down opposite Owen.

'Well!' he said. 'I'd be almost ready to write off your mission as a washout, but I have the impression you have something else to say for yourself.'

'I have,' said Owen. 'And it's something our friends don't know yet and won't for some time.'

'I'm all ears.'

Owen told him what he'd found in his incommunicado sojourn in the crevice. Walworth closed his eyes, tight, for five seconds, then opened them and blinked.

'An image of a woman?'

'Yes.'

'A woman on Venus!' Walworth laughed, then frowned. 'I don't suppose . . . there's the remotest possibility . . . that this stuff you found, this rock with movement or at least moving images inside it . . . is, let's say, one of ours?' He was thinking aloud, almost mumbling to himself.

'Human origin?' Owen shook his head. 'It would have to have been placed there – or constructed in situ – before the Union's close-up surveys. Before Cloud City. That seems highly unlikely. We – or the Co-ord – would have to be inconceivably further advanced than the Union to carry out such a feat. And if we or they were . . .'

'The technological advantage would have been used long ago in, ah, other applications?'

'Quite,' said Owen. 'It is, of course, possible that the image I saw is evidence that we are already aware of this technology and are exploiting, or at least exploring it.'

'Through the Yeelirrie rock, for instance?'

'Yes.'

Walworth looked interested. 'And the woman you saw could be one of our own scientists!'

'It's a possibility,' Owen said. 'Though a remote one, I must admit.'

'What a shame we can't check who it is, if anyone.'

'We can,' said Owen. He reached as if for the inside pocket of a jacket. 'Uh . . . you wouldn't happen to have a pen and paper?'

'How quaint. Luckily, I do, for certain formalities. Just a moment.'

He stepped out and returned with a sheet of creamy A4 and a Mont Blanc ballpoint. 'Will this do?'

'Admirably,' said Owen. He twisted the pen and held it poised over the paper, then tested it by drawing a couple of millimetre-long lines in the top right corner.

'Ah!' said Walworth. 'You're going to draw it from memory?'

'I'm going to reproduce it,' Owen said.

The pen danced. His hand blurred. Within thirty seconds he'd reached the foot of the sheet. The picture could have been mistaken for a black and white photograph. He laid the pen aside, turned the drawing around and slid it across the tiny desk. 'There.'

'It's easy to forget you're a robot,' Walworth said. It might have been a complaint, a compliment, or an excuse. He frowned down at the portrait: a woman with big eyes narrowed in a broad, good-looking, middle-aged face, under a mass of hair twisted and piled on top of her head. 'Can't say I recognise the lady.'

'For what it's worth,' said Owen, 'I got the impression Iskander didn't, either. Of course, that was a local instance.'

Walworth narrowed his eyes and nodded. 'My next step, obviously, is to send this picture home, with an urgent request for identification if possible.'

'Yes,' said Owen. 'And while we're waiting for a response, we draft our report.'

'*I* draft *my* report,' Walworth said. 'I've already heard yours. Otherwise, spot on.' He slipped the sheet of paper inside his shirt and opened the door. 'Make yourself comfortable.' In the room he waved vaguely at the sofa and disappeared into the comms cubicle.

Owen found himself tired and hungry. It was by local reckoning early evening, but he'd already had even by his standards a long and gruelling day. He cast about for refreshments, found a couple of sachets of instant coffee, but not so much as a biscuit. Recalling Iskander's presence, he opened the outside door. A robot with a paper cup of coffee and a large blueberry muffin was already waiting. He ate and drank, diverting the caffeine from his brain, lay down on the sofa with his head on one armrest and his feet sticking out over the other, and went instantly to sleep.

When Walworth's cubicle door clicked open, Owen was just as instantly awake. He sat up and swung his feet to the floor. Eighty-seven minutes had passed. Tense but jovial, the consul clapped Owen's shoulder.

'Time to go and see your Irish girlfriend.'

'She isn't Irish, she's Scottish.'

Walworth snorted, perhaps at what he saw as a fine distinction. 'Celtic fringe, anyway.'

Owen stood up. 'Did our people identify the image?'

'They did indeed,' said Walworth. He shot Owen a glance. 'Cat, pigeons, if you catch my drift.' He sounded inordinately pleased with himself.

'Any change to my instructions?'

Walworth frowned. 'No, but I think you'll find they've been overtaken by events.' His face brightened. 'As you'll soon see! Events you've brought about!'

He would be the judge of that, Owen decided. In the absence of any explicit countermand, his instructions remained in full force. He also decided to keep this decision to himself.

Outside the block, the hub of Cloud City seemed more thronged than usual, or at least less deserted, and behaviour louche even for an evening or an off-shift. People stood around or sat on the Astroturf in small groups, talking and vaping and drinking.

'Word has spread, I see,' Walworth remarked.

Owen fiddled with his glasses. 'Has the news gone out yet?'

Walworth snorted. 'To the Union's toiling masses? Not a chance. There are strict protocols for announcing the first evidence of alien intelligence. Even after the information has been put through the scientific wringer, there are General Secretaries to be notified, journalists to be briefed, militias to be alerted, markets to be steadied, plans to be revised and Popes to be rudely awakened. Then and only then are the general populace put in the picture.'

'I understand we have similar protocols in the Alliance,' Owen said.

'Nah, we just bury it in Nevada,' said Walworth. 'It's worked fine since 1947.'

He watched sidelong while Owen processed this, then guffawed. 'I'm *kidding*, man!'

They made their way through a thickening crowd to the café, where they found Konstantopoulos, Al-Khalil, Milloy, Persson and a few others around two shoved-together tables and a bottle of vodka. Milloy pressed plastic shot glasses on Owen and Walworth, and filled them.

'What are we celebrating?' Walworth asked.

'Only the biggest moment in human history!' Alma Persson cried.

'I'll drink to that,' said Walworth. He knocked back his shot. 'Ah – and what moment is that?'

Persson stared at him. 'You were there, weren't you? Our first evidence of – and possibly our first interaction with – alien intelligence.'

Walworth coughed. 'Ah . . . I'm sorry to tell you that's not quite correct.'

'What?' said Persson.

'That scientific announcement I mentioned? The one that was going to put the first woman on Venus in the shade? It's going out at this very moment. Cloud City won't receive the transmission for another ten minutes, but I was sent a coded advance text of it a short time ago with instructions to release it now. So here at this very table you can be the first to know.' His voice took on a formal cadence. 'I have the honour to inform you that the Alliance and the Co-ordinated States have had faster-than-light interstellar travel for the past fifty years. At least one habitable, Earth-like, life-bearing exoplanet has been found, and is being explored. The two Great Powers now intend to open this new world to the whole of humanity for exploration and settlement. They look forward to future co-operation with the Union and indeed with all nations.'

A fast-spreading silence was broken by Milloy. 'They what?'

CHAPTER SIXTEEN

Limited Military Contingent

Tuesday 14 October 2070, Apis

Apis's other northern island continent, New Lemuria, was thousands of kilometres from New Atlantis. By flying boat, even with fusion-pod engines, the journey took more than Apis's long day. The Co-ord base had long since come up with a solution ransacked from late-Soviet over engineering: the ekranoplan, a hybrid of ship and very low-flying aeroplane.

The monstrous craft appeared as a dot on the horizon beyond the end of Bellatrix Sound just as Hazeldene left her quarters, summoned to the morning meeting of the brass. By the time she joined Bernstein on the forecourt of the military HQ building the craft had arrived. It decelerated, its hull ploughing into the water, and came to a halt, creating as much wash as a submarine and far more noise than even the flying boat ever did. The flying boat rocked, sending two technicians at work on the damaged wing into the water. From the step outside the entrance Hazeldene watched their rescue by one dinghy and the disembarking of the two Co-ord officers to another.

The ekranoplan was so huge that it was hard to believe the official claim that its parts had been shipped in by an FTL-enabled submarine and assembled onsite at the Co-ord base, gigantic though the Co-ord's nuclear subs notoriously were. Here at New Ardtaraig, rumour maintained that the ekranoplan had been kitted out with a Guth drive and flown in direct. Perhaps some unfortunate seafarer back on Earth had been left with a tall tale and a Cherenkov-frazzled camera. Whatever about that, the ekranoplan was a useful vessel to have on Apis. This one had travelled the thousands of kilometres from the other northern island continent overnight.

Adrian Black hurried up, as did Georgi Muranov. Jenkins joined them a moment later. He was back in his own clothes and accoutrements, minus his weapons.

'Morning,' he said. He looked out at the ekranoplan as its engines started up again. 'Something going on.'

The two officers had just stepped ashore, and were speaking to the marine officer who had come to welcome them and escort them to the HQ. One of them appeared to be reading something out to him. Then both Co-ord officers stepped back and stood smartly at attention, as did the marine officer. The ekranoplan turned around, awkwardly in the narrow channel. A hatch in the rear opened, lowering to form a ramp. One rigid inflatable boat, another, then another was launched and headed inshore, each with over a dozen Co-ord marines on board. They carried out a textbook unopposed beach landing, hauled their RIBs above the strandline, formed up and trooped up the shingle and onto the grass and then marched along the road to the officers. There they halted, presented arms and saluted, but there was nothing of the parade ground in their appearance and kit.

'Russian or Chinese?' Black wondered aloud.

'Both,' said Muranov, peering and zooming. 'Two groups of twenty.'

'Fuck,' said Hazeldene. 'Just what we need.'

'Between you and me,' said Bernstein, as the soldiers marched up to HQ behind their two officers and the marine officer, 'what proportion is that of the Co-ord's armed forces on the ground on New Lemuria?'

'If I could tell you, I wouldn't,' Muranov retorted. 'But as it happens, I genuinely don't know.'

'It's already more fully equipped marines than we have here,' said Bernstein. 'That's classified information, too, but you'll have already seen it for yourself.'

'Indeed I have,' said Muranov. 'I can also see that the ekranoplan is capable of carrying the same number again.' He laughed. 'Still well within the Kepler Agreement, of course.'

Commander Hawkins arrived at a carefully dignified pace and stood at ease on the step. A squad of a dozen US Marines deployed at a run and spaced out on either side of her across the front of the HQ.

The party from the dock halted four metres away from Hawkins. The two Co-ord officers wheeled about as their troops snapped to attention, then stood them at ease. A cloud of drones spiralled out of the ekranoplan and sped over, hovering for a moment above the heads of the soldiers as cables and gecko-grips descended. In a few seconds of swift, co-ordinated hand movements, the soldiers attached the grippers to harnesses. Visors on their helmets were slammed down. With a sudden racket of quadcopter fans and a spatter of dust and gravel, the soldiers were lofted into the air and borne away in the direction of MacHinery Ridge.

'I suspect we'll be hearing a lot about the Kepler Agreement in the next half-hour,' said Black.

They did hear a lot about the Kepler Agreement.

Hazeldene didn't know the two Co-ord reps personally, but

she knew their work and was gratified to find in the hasty mutual introductions that they knew hers. Like Commander Alice Hawkins, Colonel Tsing Fan of the PLA and Colonel Vassily Yakov of the AFRF had as many science degrees and doctorates between them as the staff of a small research lab.

The two Co-ord officers acted to strict protocol. They had actual sheets of paper, which Tsing read out. This took five minutes. Hazeldene, standing with Black, Muranov and Jenkins in a huddle to one side, did her best not to yawn or fidget. She hadn't slept well. Commander Hawkins stood facing Tsing and Yakov. Lieutenant Bernstein from intelligence and four other divisional heads made up a row of stony faces in front of the line of marines.

'Thank you, gentlemen,' said Hawkins. 'Your position with regard to the troop deployment is noted. Our position remains unchanged, and our judgement on the matter is reserved. Let's take the legalities as read, and proceed to business.' She paused. 'And for heaven's sake, guys, can we drop the formality? We're all sailors and/or scientists here.'

Tsing raised his eyebrows and glanced sidelong at Jenkins.

'Including Mr Jenkins,' Hawkins went on in a firm tone, 'under the terms of the Displaced Persons Resettlement Provisos to the said Agreement, Appendix 3, traditional and craft practitioners, respect and recognition of, etc. etc.'

As if to emphasise his standing, she summoned Jenkins to her side.

'I'm glad to hear that, Alice,' said Tsing, evidently accepting her invitation to informality. 'It's this *traditional practitioner*'s claims that I would like to take up in a moment. First, my thanks to you and to Lieutenant Bernstein for the summary and documentation, photographs and recordings which you sent last night and with which Vassily and I have whiled away the hours of our voyage. Thanks also to our colleague Dr Georgi Muranov, for his most timely on-the-spot reporting of events as they unfolded. I'm relieved to say that his concerns about data security appear to be unfounded, as I take it is also the case here.'

'We did a thorough scan, too,' Hawkins said, opening her hands. 'Nothing.'

Jenkins scoffed. 'Think the Fermi can't hide in your systems?'

'A valid point, no doubt, Mr Jenkins,' said Tsing. 'But impossible to test or falsify, therefore pointless. It seems to us that it would be a mistake to assume that what you have been told by the, ah, apparatus is the truth.'

'Why would the Fermi lie to us?' Jenkins demanded.

'Ah!' said Tsing, with a quick smile and a raised forefinger. 'That's the precise point to which we would take issue. You have assumed, and it seems you have persuaded our colleagues here, that you are in communication – however indirectly – with the builders of the Ridge, with those you call "the Fermi". You've said it's an app, a front end, an interface.'

'Uh-huh.'

'I put it to you that this assumption is premature to say the least. We're used to dealing with apps to communicate with software and indeed with AIs many times more powerful than the app itself, and the analogy seems natural to us. The team here, according to the able geophysical survey work led by your Dr Nelson Hayes, has determined that the structure extends below ground level by at least a kilometre. There are tens of thousands of cubic kilometres of densely concentrated machinery in the Ridge. Our own investigations have shown that the amount of computing power in these structures is beyond our imagination, and in a sense beyond our conception or calculation.'

'No argument there,' said Jenkins. 'I figured that out myself long ago, with common sense and the naked eye.'

'Very well,' said Tsing. 'Now, please consider what an infinitesimal fraction of that capacity it would take to sustain the interactions you've experienced to date. Let's bring to bear a sense of proportion. Dr Muranov here referred to the physical extrusions as an inflammation response. I suggest the same applies to the information on your device. If the Ridge is seen as an injured organism, the rolling blocks, the rolling spheres *and* the answers to your questions are all analogous not so much to an immune response as to the actions of an individual molecule of an antigen – and even that's probably out of proportion by many orders of magnitude! Do you see? You – all of you – are no more in communication with "the Fermi" through your device than a virus or bacterium is in communication with you.'

'And no less,' said Jenkins, chin jutting.

'True enough,' Tsing conceded. 'My point is that anything that device of yours prattles out may be deployed to reduce a pinprick or less of discomfort, rather than reliable information. The seismic response may be less than a twitch of the shoulder or a turning over in sleep. So nothing in the content can be relied upon without independent verification.'

'We've had plenty of that,' said Jenkins. 'It's told us the truth about plants and animals, for starters.'

'I'm sure it has,' said Tsing. 'You have no such evidence of what it really is, or what it really wants.'

'We know what it wants!' Jenkins cried. 'It wants us to leave it alone.'

'We don't know that,' said Tsing. 'Any more than, let's say, your immune reaction to some bacterium a visitor had brought with them would show your considered opinion of that visitor.'

Jenkins looked as if he'd like to give Tsing the benefit of his considered opinion. Before he could do so, Commander Hawkins spoke up. 'I think the point is clear enough. However, it seems to me, Fan, that you're countering one speculation that at least has the merit of some evidence with another that has none.'

Tsing turned to Yakov with a flourish of his hand. 'Please tell them.'

'We do have evidence,' the Russian officer said. He looked

around with a strange grin, teeth clenched and bared. 'As you know, there is such a structure on New Lemuria: the Markov Escarpment.' He fished out another sheet of paper and began to read: '"Having deeply considered the theoretical basis, our scientists recently began careful, planned extraction of active material from the Escarpment, and experimental integration of the material with isolated and firewalled communications and computing equipment. The details of these experiments will have to await publication, but preliminary results are promising."' He looked up from the paper. 'I'm happy to report they've resulted in no adverse incidents such as the Alliance team's unfortunate, ah, hacking may have provoked.'

'You mean you've resorted to probing it, too?' said Adrian Black.

'Yes.'

'And have you received any communications?'

'As I said,' Yakov replied, 'that must await publication of our results, after discussion and review.'

'Please don't dick us about, Vassily,' said Hawkins. 'If you don't want to share the results, or if they're classified, just say so and be done with it.'

Yakov sighed. 'Some of them are indeed classified. But I can say that we are not in communication with the minds that built these edifices, any more than you are. I can also say that a careful – surgical, if you will – extraction of material has a different effect from the equivalent of knocking out a tooth or randomly drilling into a nerve. Given the proven risks of your scientists' so doing, we feel justified in deploying troops of the Co-ordinated States around MacHinery Ridge, in a strength and with such rules of engagement as are permitted under the Kepler Agreement.'

Hawkins snapped out of her relaxed posture. Back straight, face forward. 'You said a moment ago they were here to provide emergency assistance!'

'As indeed they are,' said Yakov. 'They will assist you in

preventing any further emergencies. A further platoon will deploy here shortly to assist you in patrolling this base.'

'With all due respect and formality,' said Hawkins, 'fuck you.'

Yakov and Tsing stepped back. Tsing put away the papers he'd read out.

'I should add,' he said, 'that a full report of your explorations and a redacted report of ours have been sent to the Black Horizon HQ and to the relevant offices of the participating governments by the Russian submarine *Admiral von Bellingshausen*. Supply and resupply of our limited troop contingent around MacHinery Ridge has begun and will continue. Your HQ here will be kept fully informed, as provided by—'

'—the Kepler Agreement. I heard you the first time. Thank you, Colonel Tsing. I say again, fuck off.'

'Commander Hawkins,' said Tsing. 'I hope to see you again under better circumstances.'

The two officers saluted, wheeled and marched off back to the dock. Shortly afterwards, the ekranoplan roared away.

CHAPTER SEVENTEEN

Night of the Comet

Thursday 16 October 2070, Earth

'Faster-than-light travel?' said the comedian. 'Didn't see *that* coming!'

Half the crowd in the Comet got it instantly, the rest with varying degrees of delay, like light-speed lag in conversations from beyond the Moon. Some were still having it explained in impatient whispers as the stand-up read the room and moved on to more reliable material, the local administration and the local football team. Strathclyde Regional Council and Greenock Morton – if you couldn't raise a laugh about these in Port Glasgow you weren't trying.

John Grant got the joke but couldn't laugh. He had seen it coming. Come to think of it, he'd seen it *going*. And now he'd just finished building an FTL starship himself. Despite or because of this, the out-of-nowhere arrival of the reality – official, acknowledged, on every screen – hit hard. Even after four days there was still something unreal about it, like he'd felt the first nuclear exchanges on live TV as a kid.

No hand to clutch now! You're the daddy. Hell of a responsibility, even for a *responsable*. Worse, he couldn't tell the truth to anyone, bar a handful: the gang who'd been in the cadre meeting room all those months ago, and Lakshmi Nayak. And around this table, those in the know were a minority: himself, Nayak and Morag. And now Ellen. Everyone else thought they were just celebrating the completion of building the submersible *Fighting Chance*.

Nayak was talking to Myles, who sat close by his girlfriend Marie, the lassie from Lamlash as Grant thought of her. Also at the table were Ellen, and Grant's teammates Brian, Morag and Anwar. Grant waved his phone at the bar, chivvying the round he'd called for five minutes earlier, and returned his attention to the conversation. Myles had wondered aloud how Black Horizon – that was what the interstellar exploration project was called, apparently – had been kept secret so long. Nayak was explaining liberal democracy to him with all the fervour of an apostate.

'In the Alliance we—' she caught herself and laughed '—*they* have what they call free elections but not for state officials or the boards of big companies, and the state and the big corporations control nearly all the information people have when they vote. So there's a whole array, a – a *phalanx* of powerful institutions where the people don't have any control or oversight from below at all. The military, the civil service, the police, most of the economy . . .'

'I know all *that*,' Myles said, sounding slightly offended. 'We do have civic education, Dr Nayak!' He shared a smile with Marie, then with Nayak. 'Well, we did at school. Democracy and electricity and all that. But I still don't see how scientists and engineers and admirals and generals could have kept this a secret from their own top leaderships all this time. Leave alone from, you know, ordinary people.'

'Well, that's what I've just explained,' Nayak said, spreading her hands and sitting back. 'The state can keep secrets because it's never out of office!'

She looked pleased with herself at this formulation. Myles and Marie still looked baffled.

'But it's not the *state*,' Myles objected. 'It's keeping a huge secret *inside* the state, *from* the state. Well, the rest of the state, anyway.'

'Och, don't worry about it,' Morag chipped in. 'I can see why you find it hard to get your head around. You've grown up here, you've never known any different. Something like that couldnae happen in *our* system, that's for sure.'

Grant had to down the last of his pint to hide his smirk. The *omertà* of the cadre. Awesome. Likewise the sincerity of the citizenry. Even Brian and Anwar, irreverent though they normally were, nodded solemnly along to Morag's homily like devout congregants if not communicants in the civic religion. He would have nodded, too, if he hadn't known better.

Now, while the Comet bar roared around him and his family and colleagues talked past the vaguely interested, remotely benign expression he'd long cultivated for such situations, Grant brooded on an eventful week.

Monday 13 October 2070

Grant was nearly an hour into the Monday afternoon shift when Morag Rafferty called out: 'Everybody stop!'

Grant laid down the internal fitting his avatar was working on – the ship was nearly complete, and now they were all operating small avatars inside it – powered down and backed out. He raised his visor and disengaged his hands and feet, and leaned out of the rig. The others were doing the same.

'What's up?' he said. 'Safety problem?'

'Strike, strike!' shouted Brian. Anwar, Piotr and Jeannie joined in. Everyone laughed.

Morag looked stern. 'News alert,' she said.

She'd just had an alert on the cadre grapevine, Grant guessed.

Morag pointed to the wall screen. They all swung their rigs around as Morag summoned a news channel. The time was just coming up to 2 p.m., British Summer Time. The usual countdown drumbeat. Then a holding screen with a message to wait. Irritated, she flicked from Glasgow to Edinburgh to London to Paris, with the same result.

'It's war,' said Brian.

'That or aliens,' said Anwar.

'Shut the fuck up!' Grant snapped. Then, after a moment: 'Sorry, guys.'

The flippant remarks had given him a flashback: that time in his teens, when all the screens had looked like this, just before the news came through that the missiles were already in flight across the Middle East. In the long minutes of waiting for the inevitable, the iron had come into his soul, and – as the Rising a few years later had amply demonstrated – the souls of millions like him: *we have to end this, whatever it takes*. Morag shot him a sympathetic glance, just after his apology. The nuclear exchanges had marked their generation and cohort as the pandemic had marked their parents.

Morag was looking at her phone. 'It's aw right,' she said. 'It's no the war. Or aliens! Hang on.'

And then the news came through. Even Brian and Anwar were silent, taking it in. Morag looked as surprised as the rest, and hoped the same was true of him.

The reporting cut from the announcement to talking heads and jubilant or bewildered vox-pops from across the world. Here and there – from dawn in San Francisco to the beginning of the working day in NYC, early afternoon in Europe, late afternoon in Moscow, late evening in Beijing – people were gathering in huddles or crowds on the streets to celebrate or protest or argue.

Jeannie spoke up first, which wasn't something she often did. 'Did I hear that right?' she said. 'The Alliance and the

Co-ord have had this faster-than-light travel for fifty years? And we haven't?'

'Aye, you heard that right,' said Morag. 'And?'

'We're at their mercy,' said Jeannie. 'They have the jump on us any time, the Americans and —'

'The bloody Russians!' said Piotr.

'It's worse than a war,' said Brian. 'Worse than aliens. The other powers have just *become* the aliens.'

'Or two Galactic empires,' said Anwar. 'And us Europeans, we're just primitive native life now.'

'Too wee and too green,' Brian added, with all too gloomy relish.

The lads had wit, Grant thought, he had to give them that, but no tact. Their patriotism did them credit; their pessimism didn't. Jeannie and Piotr looked more dismayed than ever.

'No,' said Grant, jumping up from his rig. 'This is amazing news! We're going to the stars! And it's good news! For the Union, too! If two rival powers have shared this for fifty years – even through the war – it proves co-operation is possible. If they'd wanted to use it against us, or been able to, they could have done it already. Come on. They've said they want to co-operate. I say we hold them to that, and look to the future.' He waved at the wall screen. 'There's more news coming through. We all need time to take it in. This is a great day, so let's take the rest of it off.'

Brian and Anwar looked slightly abashed, Piotr and Jeannie slightly more cheerful. Even so, they were reluctant to leave. Phones began to ring, or be rung. Everyone was on their phone, or their glasses, or agog at the wall screen.

'Out,' said Morag. 'Scram. Me and John will clear up and shut down.'

When the others had left, and all the off switches had been checked and the rigs stood inert, Morag turned to Grant.

'Cadre meeting. Urgent. You're invited.'

*

The same dozen people who'd been around the table the first time, and the same precautions as before. Phones left outside, room swept.

'Any word?' Grant asked Omar Khan, as they sat down.

Khan shook his head. 'Nothing after the alert.' He laughed. 'I expect there are urgent discussions on higher committees than this one.'

Everyone settled.

'Something's wrong,' Morag said.

'Ya think?' Grant chuckled.

'Naw, really. It's too sudden.'

Omar Khan waved a hand at the wall, at a screen that wasn't there. 'They've clearly been planning this roll-out for years. Decades, even.'

'True, true.' Morag gave a weary shake of her head. 'But nae preparation. Nae hints. Nae teasers. And as you may have noticed, nae fireworks over Beijing. Something's bounced them into this.'

'A leak?' Grant said.

'From those around this table?' Joanna Boyd said. She looked from face to face. 'I don't see anyone missing.'

She didn't need to say more. Everyone there had been left in no doubt as to the consequences of treachery, or even carelessness. If anyone around that table had been guilty, or even thought themselves under suspicion, they'd have fled. It wasn't hard to flee the Union. People did, all the time, for much less. The difficulty, if your case was serious, was in ever being able to relax afterwards.

'What about Dr Nayak?' someone asked. 'I mean, she's a defector from the Alliance in the first place. She might have got cold feet, or got leaned on.'

Grant, Omar, Joanna and Morag all shouted at once. It was Joanna who prevailed in the outcry.

'For the *benefit*,' she said icily, 'of those who don't know Lakshmi as well as I do – she and her family back in India are under the protection of Iskander and our secret services. Nobody messes with defectors to the Union. She can't be leaned on. As for cold feet! She's totally dedicated to this project. She believes it'll succeed, and that it'll succeed because she's part of it. And I won't hear any questioning of her loyalty. She doesn't even pretend to be one of us. She still says "you" where we'd say "we", and so on.' Joanna smiled. 'Still laughs when she catches herself doing it. That's not how a double agent carries on.'

'But even that could be—'

'No,' said Joanna. 'Nobody can so much as beat their own phone at chess! Think anyone can double-bluff Iskander?'

Omar nodded. 'From what I know of Dr Nayak from . . . other sources, we can rule that out. She's solid. The project's watertight.' He chuckled. 'Metaphorically as well as literally.'

'OK,' said Grant. 'We can all agree – no leaks from our team! That doesn't mean there's been no leaks *about* our project.'

'Where from?' said Omar.

'You've said yourself, Omar – this is tight but it goes beyond the cadre. Some scientists must know about E-PRIME detecting that stray Russian transmission. Some intelligence AIs, and therefore people in the secret intelligence services, know. Parts of Iskander know, if that's the right word.'

'Question is,' said Morag, 'do they know we know?'

'Exactly,' said Grant.

'The eternal question,' said Khan. 'How much do the Alliance and Co-ord intelligence services know about the Union side's knowledge? Do they know about our project?'

'If they did,' someone else said, 'would that have been enough for them to trigger a world-shaking public announcement?'

'Not so much world-shaking as Union-shaking,' said Grant. He glanced at Morag. 'If the instant reactions of our younger colleagues count for anything.'

'Same in my office,' said Joanna Boyd. Nods around the table.

'Maybe,' said Morag. 'But there has to be more to this announcement than a ploy to destabilise the Union. Something we don't know about.'

The brainstorming continued, with no conclusion.

'We'll just have to wait,' Omar said. 'Let's leave it there. For now. Let's catch up on the news and maybe reconvene tomorrow? John – could you do your thing on the other side of the firewall, find out how the, uh, more excitable elements of the population Over There are taking this? Conspiracy theories and disinformation could give us some idea of how well this has been prepared.'

'Uh-huh,' Grant said. 'And not just Over There. I suspect we're going to see a lot of that *right here*.'

'Nae call for conspiracy theories here,' said Morag, 'seeing as our side is run by a conspiracy and everybody knows it.'

'Conspiracy? Us?' said Omar. 'Perish the thought.'

They left the meeting and retrieved their phones, to find that in the meantime the world had changed again. The bare first announcement was being elaborated on hour by hour. The half-century-long secret joint project was called Black Horizon. The habitable Earth-like exoplanet was called Apis and had three large island continents – one of which would, it was claimed, be open to settlement by people from the Union.

'There you go,' said Morag. 'They're doing this out of the goodness of their hearts. Problem solved.'

Grant got home at about half past three. The door to Ellen's workshop stood open, so he put his head around it. She was still at work, as he'd expected, remote-driving her submersible far away in the North Sea. Driving a ship was less easily interrupted than building one. You couldn't back out of a submersible as readily as out of a shipbuilding avatar – well, you could, but the consequences would be rather more immediate.

She was due to knock off at four. He went through to the kitchen and set up coffee.

'Seen the news?' he said, when she'd sat down and had her first sip.

'Corner of my eye, couple of hours ago,' she said. 'Jeez. Incredible.' She took another sip, then looked at him sharply. 'Do you think this explains that vanishing submarine you saw?'

'It could,' Grant said. 'Or it could have been a mirage like you said. I honestly don't know. But it seems likely enough that the Alliance would use submarines as starships.'

'Hey,' said Ellen, 'you might end up building ours!'

'I might at that.' Grant laughed and finished his coffee. 'What would you like for dinner?'

'We've already decided,' Ellen said, pointing to the fridge. 'Myles and Marie are coming over, remember?'

Grant scratched his head. 'Oh, God, yes. Sorry, I forgot in all the excitement.'

He set about preparing dinner. It wasn't the first time Myles had come over with Marie, but Grant still thought of her as 'Myles' new girlfriend' or 'that lassie from Lamlash'. He liked her and approved of her, though she seemed a bit wary of him, for no reason he could see.

Apart from her father having fought on the other side in the Rising, he guessed. That would do it.

Newly graduated and undecided on what to do next, Myles and Marie had spent – or wasted, as Grant saw it – the summer on temporary jobs or on citizen income. They shared a flat in Greenock and had more than enough to get by on and even to go out on, but Grant's home cooking provided a meal better than any restaurant they could afford. They were grateful and ravenous. After two glasses of wine, Myles was loquacious.

'Faster than light! FTL! The stardrive!' He closed his eyes and knuckled his forehead. 'I can't believe it! And they've had it for fifty years and more, finding whole new worlds while we've been chasing microbes on Venus and just now we've been bragging about landing a few people on the surface. What does that tell us?'

'Not a lot,' said Grant. 'A fundamental physics breakthrough is chance, it doesn't tell us anything about the underlying society.'

'And what does?' Myles demanded.

'Well, for one thing, we have a lot more space presence than you seem to think, it's not just Cloud City and the moonlet – the Venus Space Station, that's an amazing achievement in itself – and the, uh, the E-PRIME telescope. Lots more. More than the other powers put together.'

'Yeah, in the Solar System, big deal!'

'It is a big deal. And don't forget, we got compact controlled fusion first.'

'Fusion?' Myles said incredulously, as if he thought Faber pots grew on trees, a gift of Nature like the Internet or piped water.

'All right,' said Grant, 'maybe that discovery was chance, too, but it *was* ours and we made it practical and mass-produced.'

'That's right!' Ellen said. 'And we've applied it, we saved the climate with it, and the world really. Nothing can take that away.'

Myles waved a hand at the windows, drummed by October rain. 'The climate doesn't look or sound all that *saved* from where I'm sitting.'

'Well, no,' Grant admitted. 'Fusion came too late. But climate's exactly where we have the right approach. Co-operation and resilience and mitigation. We invite people in or help them where they stay. We don't force them to move or leave them to drown.'

'And look at my work,' said Ellen, with a wave over her shoulder vaguely indicating the home workshop. 'You have to admit, the Nordzee Barrier is a pretty mega-ambitious project.'

Marie laughed.

'What's funny?' Ellen demanded.

'I'm sorry, Mrs Grant, but—' she spread her hands '—you work hard at saving the North Sea coasts, and your husband and his mates work in the yards that get the orders for the submersibles and pontoons your project uses, like it's in compensation for us on the west coast getting flooded.'

'What's wrong with that?' said Ellen.

'It's just . . . such a typical Union deal, you know?'

'Exactly,' Grant said. 'It's how we do things, it's—' He soft-snapped his fingers. 'What do they call it?'

'Negotiated co-ordination,' Myles said. He frowned. 'Or is it co-ordinated negotiation? I always get that mixed up.'

'Whatever,' said Grant, who had the same mental glitch. 'It works, everybody gets a say, we work things out—'

'It didn't work out so well for us,' said Marie. 'Or anyone else who had a house along the shore in Lamlash.'

The lass from Lamlash. Not just where she came from, but where she was coming from!

'I'm sorry to hear that,' Grant said. 'And I'm sure you miss the old house, but your family would have got compensation, a new flat up the hill—' he was doing fine until he tried to be witty, then blew it '—with probably better views.'

Marie flinched. She opened her mouth and closed it at least once before saying, with dignity not so much mustered as conscripted: 'Our new flat up the hill has a view of the *hill*, Mr Grant.'

'Sorry,' Grant said. 'Should have kept my mouth shut. But—'

Ellen nudged him. 'Stop digging, John.'

He leaned back, making wiping motions and giving Marie a placatory smile, which wasn't returned.

'Speaking of the yards,' said Myles, with unaccustomed tact, 'how's your project going?'

'My project?' Grant hoped he hadn't given a guilty start.

'The new submarine.'

'Oh, yeah, well, that's going fine. Nearly finished. We should be having the wrap party in the Comet on Thursday night.'

'Great!' said Marie. She turned to Myles. 'Let's go along.'

'Yeah,' said Myles. 'A submersible. Something to celebrate.'

'Well, it is,' Grant said. He grinned. 'And it was our company that built it. John Grant and Son.'

'Oh, all right,' Myles said. He raised his glass. 'They build starships, we build submarines. Here's to the Union's great achievements!'

'I'll drink to that,' said Grant.

Tuesday 14 October 2070

As he knocked off for lunch the following day, Grant got a ping from Omar Khan. He was expecting another cadre conclave. Instead, Omar asked to meet him on the slipway.

Some last-minute glitch? Grant hurried out. Omar stood at the top of the slipway, hands in the pockets of his white boilersuit.

'Let's take a walk,' he said. He strolled towards the water. Grant clapped on a hard hat and joined him. The ship stood on its wheeled cradle above the slipway tracks. No robots or other machines were working outside it. The sounds of small avatars doing routine tasks through their operators' lunch breaks came from inside the hull like the scurrying of mice. Drizzle hissed on the long shed's clear roof.

'We've got a problem,' Omar said. 'Between you and me the Union government is in shock. Frozen like a rabbit in the headlights. Nearly all of the political and even military leadership didn't know. Those who did are keeping quiet about having kept it quiet.'

Grant glanced over his shoulder. 'Is it safe to talk?'

'There's only Iskander to overhear, and it knows anyway.'

'That's me reassured.'

'Ha! Well. We can forgive them a moment of confusion.

They've just had the shock of their lives. Now they're wondering: do the others have the jump on us? Why have they kept us out of the loop so far? Why are they inviting us in now? So their first response as they begin to gather their wits is to be very, very wary of the Black Horizon offer to take people to this exoplanet, Apis.'

'Why? Lots of people would jump at it.' He could think of two.

'Exactly. The last thing we need is losing lots of people, especially young people.'

'It wouldn't be all that many. The logistics—'

Omar waved at the submersible. 'Logistics? What logistics? If this ship works as Lakshmi claims, we could shift hundreds of people in a day, surface to surface. And that boat's bespoke! Imagine just a box with fusion pods, flywheel, preset navigation, and life-support for – what? Hours at the most?' He reached inside his boilersuit and took out his phone. 'Look, right now I could zap the spec to a factory in Düsseldorf or Rotterdam, and within a fortnight they'd be churning them out like shipping containers. What's to stop the Alliance or the Co-ord from doing the same?'

'All the more reason for us to do it!'

'Aye, there's the rub. Our side is not going to do anything to provoke the others, or to let slip that we have the drive, too, at least not until we know what's going on. Why are they offering settlement under their control? How would they react to settlement that wasn't? Competitive colonisation doesn't usually end happily. And it's not just the official authorities who're worried. It's the cadre. And the line this morning, I'm sorry to say, John, is that we don't launch this ship.'

Grant felt as if he'd stepped off a ledge. 'What?'

'We can finish building it, but here it stays until it can be sailed to a secure facility. No launch even into water, let alone space.'

'To hell with that,' said Grant. 'Legally, the ship's ours.

Mine, in fact. If they want to stop us launching it, let them get a court order or a warrant or a Union security declaration.'

The tide was out and they'd reached the part of the ramp that was slick with algae. They turned around and paced slowly back.

'Aye, right,' said Omar. 'Look, John, I'm as gutted as you are. But think. You're the legal owner, sure. Remember how you got it – a contract from a shell company, arranged through me via Iskander and covered up by some fancy accounting. All it would take is for someone on . . . let's say a higher committee than me to have a word in the right ear, and suddenly you, me and Joanna are naked in the spotlight of a corruption scandal.'

'Wouldn't Iskander back us up?'

'No doubt, but that's not worth much if you're being held incommunicado.'

'They can't do that!'

Grant looked at him pityingly. 'You're a *responsable*, John, and the rest of us are cadre. That makes it more serious than a few backhanders between councillors and developers, or whatever. They can and they will, quite legally.'

Grant found himself shaking, not with fear but with fury. No way, no fucking way was he going to be thwarted like that.

'They can't and they won't,' he said, 'if we take off first.'

'What?'

'Pick our time, pick our chance. Get on board some way that doesn't look suspicious. We can find plenty of excuses for that – final checks, inspection, whatever.' He pointed at the trolley wheels in their flange rails. 'Then release the brakes, roll it into the water and off we go.'

To his surprise, Omar didn't dismiss this wild suggestion out of hand.

'And where would we find our crew?' he asked.

'Ourselves,' Grant said. 'Lakshmi can fly it, you can operate the fusion plant and the flywheel, Morag can handle the airlock – she built it, after all – and I can operate the arms.'

They turned about at the top of the ramp and set off back down again.

'Hmm,' said Omar. 'A lot to think about.'

'Would you be up for it?'

'Oh aye. I'll sound out Morag. All I can say is, when she got the word from on high this morning she was spitting tacks.'

'And I'll put it to Lakshmi. Ask her to come in tomorrow. All it would take is a hint. She'd jump at the chance.'

'Nayak can fly it, no doubt,' said Omar, 'but we need someone to *drive* the boat. And we don't have a cadre in the loop who can operate a submersible.'

'Can't you—' Grant began, but Omar was already shaking his head.

'Too risky. If I so much as put out a feeler, it's game over.'

'As it happens,' Grant said, 'I have a skilled submersible operator in my house.'

He expected Omar to squelch that suggestion, too, but all he said was: 'She won't take it well, John.'

Omar was right. She didn't.

'You've been doing *what*?'

'Well, yes, like I told you,' Grant said. 'I couldn't tell you. I couldn't tell anyone. I shouldn't even be telling you now, except—'

'Except you need me to drive a submarine! Jesus! And if you didn't need me, you'd be off without an explanation?'

'Well—'

'To your death, probably.'

'There's nothing probable about it.'

'Yeah, more like certain from what you've said.'

'It's not certain,' Grant said. 'Either the drive works or it doesn't. If it doesn't, nothing happens. It won't blow up.'

'So that demented pixie tells you.'

'Lakshmi Nayak's the greatest mathematical physicist alive—'

'Says you, an expert on the topic.'

'—and whatever else I am, I'm a damn good marine engineer.'

Ellen took a deep breath and a long sip of coffee. 'You know what pisses me off the most? Not that you didn't tell *me*. Band of brothers and sisters, bonds sealed in blood, hang together or hang separately, all that Masonic revolutionary bullshit. I get that, I really do. It's that you didn't tell *Myles*.'

Grant blinked and rocked back. 'What? Why should I tell Myles? He doesn't need to know. You do, now.'

'Jesus! Jesus wept! Last night might have been a good time to tell him. Our boy and his girlfriend are breaking their hearts, seeing all they were taught to believe and be proud of turned to dust, thinking the Yank and English fash trash and the Eastern empires have won the whole goddamn future, and all the time you had a starship of your own not ten kilometres away!'

Grant clutched his head. 'Look, I'm sorry, Ellen, I couldn't tell him.'

'You know what?' said Ellen. 'You could. You could have told him *and* Marie. Yes, we have the stardrive, too! We're not beaten! In a week you'll be wishing you had.'

Grant laughed. 'In a week, they'll know it.'

'That soon?'

'That's kind of the plan,' Grant said.

'Then I'd better get training for it,' Ellen said. 'I'm overdue some days off anyway.'

'Good,' said Grant. 'We can start tonight, if you like.'

She gave him a hard look. 'You do have a patch?'

'Yes,' he said. He took out his phone and zapped the virtual ship and the software Nayak had used to Ellen's rig. 'I do have a patch.'

That evening Ellen sat in her rig and practised alongside a phantom version of Nayak from the software's memory. Grant doggedly tuned out her yells of frustration or (later) delight and dived into the online flood.

The roll-out had clearly been long prepared. There were Black Horizon explainers for every level of interest and education: a tranche of science papers and political briefings for the most engaged; documentaries fronted by avatars evoking a century's worth of trusted and beloved science and natural history communicators, their voices carrying digital echoes of Sagan's plosives and Attenborough's aspirates; comic books and animations for children of various age groups; pictorial leaflets, even, for the dwindling but still globally significant strandline of illiterates.

It was likewise evident that the timing of the announcement had been forced. There should have been months if not years of hints and teasers: speculative but factual documentaries on exoplanets, chin-stroking pieces in popular science magazines and channels giving sober reassessments of the physics of FTL, science-fiction miniseries dramas exploring the possibilities of a situation much like what now obtained, even fake leaked documents telling the whole or part of the real story by supposed inside sources that would be swiftly discredited, but would linger in the popular imagination . . . all ways of defusing the eventual shock.

Also noticeably missing: any but the most basic information about habitable exoplanets other than Apis. Grant checked them against the speculative extrapolations from E-PRIME and other surveys in the game he'd used for Nayak's practice runs. Some were much as expected, others quite different, but detail was sparse. There had to be more . . . or Apis had to be in some way special. Either possibility would be worth talking about. Neither was.

Morag had been right, though no one else had – at least in public – seized on the point. Hard to account for the accuracy of her instant guess. Maybe it was the proletarian class instinct that some social scientists claimed to have evidence for, though

(Grant privately reckoned) if the history of the class for the past couple of centuries was anything to go by that instinct wasn't exactly up there with the proven capacities of the common ant.

Likewise telling was the improvised quality of the disinformation. Elaborate conspiracy theories were being spun on the fly: that all the videos of Apis and other exoplanets were fakes, and the real planet or planet being colonised was much bleaker and harsher than advertised; that the Alliance and the Co-ord were recruiting combatants for an interstellar war with each other; that one or both were already fighting an interstellar war against aliens; that the whole thing was a hoax and FTL remained as impossible as ever.

The torrent of nonsense was classic Co-ord and Alliance information warfare, but waged by irregulars rather than professionals. Similar theories springing up in the Union were home-grown, probably. Their angle was that the real purpose of the announcement, whether true or not, was to destabilise the Union, and to roll back and avenge the Rising. This, too, might have been a meme-war ploy by the other powers, but Grant doubted it. The Union's online radicals – more patriotic than the President, so to speak – were perfectly capable of coming up with this on their own.

Grant was only a *responsable*, not one of the cadre, but he felt he was enough of an insider to have a good handle on how you ran a proper preparatory information/disinformation campaign, and what you had to scramble for if you hadn't had time to prepare.

Wednesday 15 October 2070

Morag surprised Grant with a fist bump, just before they climbed into their rigs that morning. So she was in. At lunchtime he went for a short walk with Nayak, out of the yard and around the green patch surrounding the adjacent castle.

The day was cold and bright. Excited children flitted through the ancient keep like screaming ghosts.

They stood at the sea wall, looking across the river towards the Gare Loch and Faslane. Grant nodded towards the installation and said, 'There's our problem.'

'Well, yes, but it always is.'

'Our government is scared of them,' Grant said. 'Now I have to tell you something you mustn't tell anyone else, no matter how much you trust them. I've been told on good authority that we won't be allowed to launch the ship. Just in case.'

'Oh!' said Nayak. She blinked hard. 'That's . . . disheartening.'

'You could say that. So some of us have decided to do it anyway, if you're willing to take the risk.'

'Willing? Try to stop me!'

'Good for you. I knew you would.'

'When?'

'Maybe next week.'

'As soon as that?' She sounded delighted.

On the Thursday they finished the job, went home to get changed and came back out to the Comet bar to celebrate.

So here they were, celebrating.

Thursday 16 October 2070

The tardy round arrived. Pints and tall glasses were reached for in a jangle of bangles and a flurry of bedraggled lace cuffs, then clinked above the middle of the table.

'Cheers, all,' said Grant. 'Here's tae us!'

'Wha's like us?' Morag responded. 'Damn few and they're a' deid.'

'Ain't that the truth,' Myles muttered, with a bitter undertone that made Grant shoot him a raised eyebrow.

'Oh, nothing,' Myles said. Defiantly casual in black suit and white T-shirt amid that Thursday evening's end-of-project celebratory proletarian finery, he swivelled slightly to face Grant. Marie, in embroidered denim jacket and sitting in a smoke cloud of tattered net, peered over Myles' shoulder through the half-parted curtains of her hair. 'It's just . . . we're fucked, aren't we?'

Fortunately Ellen, whose acknowledged parental hypocrisy was the struggle for cultured speech, was deep in conversation with Anwar and didn't overhear. Grant gave a tolerant laugh. 'Who's "we"?'

'Oh, not us,' Myles hastened to assure him. 'I mean personally, everything's fine.' A besotted sidelong glance at Marie, duly reciprocated. A swift gulp of beer, followed by a sigh. 'But, you know? Our side? The Union?'

'What about it?'

'The other powers – they've beaten us. They've left us in the *dust*, Dad. We were always told we were the best, and now we find out the Alliance and the Co-ord have been flying to the stars for generations. And what have we got? A big space telescope to watch them doing it and, oh yes, a Venus colony that's a complete waste of time now that another Earth's within reach.'

'There's some kind of trouble on Venus,' said Marie. 'Word is they're even talking about evacuating Cloud City.'

Grant recoiled. 'What? I haven't seen anything about that. Have I missed some breaking news, or what?'

'It's not in the news,' Marie said, looking slightly embarrassed. 'It's more . . . friend of a friend sort of thing. There's this local lassie there, Francesca Milloy – you know, the first woman on Venus?'

'Ah, yes, I saw that.'

'Well, she's from Bishopton and she studied at the West of Scotland University, same as me.'

Marie said this as if it were an explanation.

'Yes?' said Grant. 'And?'

'Well, she's obviously a star alumna for the Uni, and she's still in our networks, students and former students, and she's been saying some things that got people worried.'

Grant fumbled his glasses on. 'Mind sharing this?'

Marie shook her head, her chin rubbing on Myles' shoulder. 'Sorry, no, I don't have her posts, they're not public anyway. Like I said, friend of a friend.'

'Ah, right.' Grant tried not to sound impatient or disappointed.

'But it does kind of bear out what Myles was saying,' Marie added.

Myles nodded. 'Exactly. Place is a waste of time now.'

'Let's not get too hasty,' Grant said. 'The point of Cloud City was never about settling Venus, it was about studying it, about science, and that's lost none of its value. Maybe gained some, for all we know.'

'So you've told us,' Myles said. 'You still don't get it.'

'Get what?'

Myles shook his head and turned away. The awkward moment was rescued by a random hush into which the comedian's patter rang out.

'Have you heard what they're calling this new planet of theirs?' he cried. '"Apis"! Apis! They're trolling us!'

He looked around, drawing a blank again.

'Trolling's taking *the* piss, not taking *a* piss!' someone heckled.

'Apis,' the comedian retorted, 'is from the Latin for "bee" —'

'Naw, it's fae the Greek!'

'Whatever, sweetie. I bow to your Classical erudition. I've bowed to some Greeks in my time. Buy me a drink later and I might bow to you, if you're lucky and the lights are low.' He mimed a closer look and a double take. 'Very low. My point is, they're telling us they found *Planet Bee*.' He struck a *ta-dah!* pose and looked around again. 'Planet B, get it?'

Groans, and more.

'Bastard's lucky aw the glasses and bottles are plastic,' Brian said, to a bigger laugh around the table than the comedian had got all night. Marie pushed her hair behind her ears and leaned forward, serious.

'No,' she said, quietly to get their attention. 'It's called Apis because it has bees.'

'How do you know that?' Grant asked. 'I haven't seen it mentioned.'

Marie held up her phone. 'Science papers. There's a whole backlog of them from when it was secret, and NASA just released a tranche of them. The one on bees is by Hazeldene, E.'

'They're no *actual* bees, though,' Morag declared. 'I mean, evolution and that. Like dolphins and ichthyosaurs. Convergence.'

'Convergence?' Marie nodded firmly, looking at Morag with what Grant read as surprised respect. 'That's exactly what it could be, but it seems not. According to this paper, that was their first thought, too, but they were mistaken. Genetically identical with terrestrial genera. It's actual bees.'

Morag was having none of it. 'Who wrote that?' she demanded. 'Bet yi it's some Yank who disnae understand evolution. Intelligent design or some shite. Thinks God put them there.'

Marie snorted. 'Oh, they were put there all right, but not by God!'

Nayak shook her head. 'No, no, you're both wrong. The creationist stuff is just propaganda, like I was telling Myles a minute ago. Chaff to fool voters. I assure you, the Alliance and even the US doesn't put religious nuts on spaceships.'

'Aye they do,' said Morag. 'Yon guy who read Genesis fae Mars, and—'

'That was a private expedition!' Nayak said, exasperated. 'And he wasn't along as a scientist. No, whoever this Hazeldene is, he or she must be a real working biologist with credentials up to here. They're just mistaken, that's all.'

'Why?' Marie asked.

'Because—' Nayak sighed and looked even more exasperated '—if the so-called bees are really "genetically identical with terrestrial genera" then they *are* terrestrial. They're from Earth! And that would mean someone – not us, and not God – took them from Earth to, uh, Apis.'

She rocked back as if nothing more needed to be said. Anwar put his knuckles to his forehead and waggled his forefingers like antennae. 'So . . . you're not saying it's aliens . . . but it's aliens!'

'No, I'm not saying it's aliens. I'm saying they're not really bees from Earth, because if they were they'd have had to be taken there by aliens. There are no aliens. And now we know that for sure.'

'How?'

Nayak swallowed, then reached for her drink as if needing more than saliva to swallow. She took a sip and outlined the Fermi Paradox, old ground to her, but apparently new to some. 'And now we know FTL travel is possible, which means it's even *easier* to spread through the Galaxy. Don't you see? The sky should be, like you say here, *hoaching* with alien starships. And last I looked, it wasn't.'

'This is Scotland,' said Anwar. 'Anything above the clouds is faith. I'm no even sure I believe in stars, never mind starships.'

'You should get out more,' said Brian. 'And I don't mean to the pub.'

Marie ignored the banter and looked intently at Nayak. 'How could the scientists out there be so mistaken?'

'I don't know,' Nayak said. 'I guess they haven't had enough people or time or equipment to make a thorough study. It might be just one scientist, this Hazeldene, no doubt doing their best.' She chuckled. 'That's the trouble with secret projects – they don't get peer review!'

Marie got the point but didn't laugh. 'I'd love to give it peer review, some day. Go there and find out if they're bees and there are aliens.'

'Hey, I'd go with you,' said Myles.

Marie turned to him. 'Would you?'

'Yes.'

'You know they're asking for colonists from everywhere now? Even from the Union?'

Myles laughed. 'Yeah, but they'd never take us.'

'Why not?' Marie said. 'Seriously, why not?'

Grant and Ellen looked at each other, then at their son, who was getting an ambush kiss. They waited.

'You'd go?' Grant said.

'Well, yeah,' Myles said, like it was obvious. Marie's eyes shining beside him.

Grant blinked. 'You'd go—' he pointed north '—over there, to them? You'd take the England ferry?'

'If they'd take me to this new world? With Marie? Of course, I would.'

'Jeez. I'm shocked. No kidding. Shocked.'

He meant it. He'd dreaded this, but not fully expected it. Fuck. Myles had a hard look Grant hadn't noticed on him before, and recognised as adult. OK then, man to man.

'What makes you think you have what it takes to survive in some wilderness not of this Earth?'

'I've done training.'

'Oh, aye, we've all done training. But what skills do you have? Political economy? Literature? Fine use they'll be out there!'

Myles looked nonplussed.

'I've done environmental ecology, with a lot of fieldwork,' Marie said.

'With all due respect, Marie, that wouldn't be relevant on another planet.'

'The principles would.'

'Principles, yes!' Grant scoffed. 'That's the trouble, most of the people who'd take up this offer would be people like you, all principles and not enough practice. It'd be like another Darien scheme, when Scotland sent shiploads of lawyers and clerks and ministers to colonise Panama, not forgetting to make sure they were well supplied with wigs and bibles. And you wouldn't even have Scotland behind you, let alone the Union.'

'Who cares about the Union?'

'I do, for one. I fought for it.'

'Dad,' Myles said, 'the Cold Revolution is over. We lost.'

'We'll see about that,' said Grant.

CHAPTER EIGHTEEN

Nevada Calls

Thursday 16 October 2070, Apis

Hazeldene didn't see the new ship come in.

She sat in the SciDiv meeting room and typed questions about the planet's biology and evolutionary history into the apparatus. Jenkins sat beside her, occasionally helping her to formulate queries. Lieutenant Bernstein followed a log of the interactions on her slate, wireless-linked to the apparatus. She sat in a corner, legs out in front of her, looking even more bored than Jenkins.

More urgent queries had gone on long into the first night after the Co-ord officers' visit, and then the following days. They had received less than satisfactory replies, or a silence that was easy to interpret – however fancifully – as sullen. Only on biology was the slab at all forthcoming.

She'd started with questions about the evolutionary relationships of the various invertebrate phyla. Some had been answered. Now—

Now for the big question. She nerved herself, took a deep breath, and typed:

When did the bees come here?
THAT QUESTION CANNOT BE ANSWERED.
Why not?
THAT QUESTION ALSO CANNOT BE
ANSWERED.

She looked at Jenkins. 'What gives?'

He shrugged. 'Seen them make some strange answers, but never that.'

She typed again:

Why not?
POTENTIAL CAUSALITY VIOLATION.

'What!' she cried.

Bernstein shot her a sharp look. 'Take care what you say to that.'

'Uh-huh,' Hazeldene grunted.

Please explain.

Minutes ticked by. Jenkins shifted uneasily in his seat. Bernstein rattled a pen between her teeth.

YOU DR E HAZELDENE MUST FIND THE
ANSWER YOURSELF.

Hazeldene yelped and jerked her hands from the keyboard as if stung.

'It's addressed you *by name*?' Bernstein said, looking up from her slate.

'Looks like it,' Hazeldene said.

'Huh,' said Jenkins, feigning hurt. 'Years it took to call *me* by name. Years!'

Hazeldene recovered her composure. 'You'd never written any scientific papers.'

'What's that got to do with it?'

She pointed at the screen. 'It's like how I would put my name on an article or report.'

'Very good,' said Bernstein. 'But I doubt any of your work was ever on Jenkins Senior's old phone.'

Jenkins snorted. Bernstein glared at him.

'I've told you,' Jenkins said. 'It can read your computers.'

'Yeah, yeah.' Bernstein gazed out of the window. '"Causality violation", huh?' She spun her seat and stared hard at Hazeldene. 'Unless they mean . . . that you will find the answer, and publish it, and they already have your future paper in their memory?'

'And if they told me now, I'd never write that paper?'

'Hence the causality violation? Maybe.'

'They can't see the future,' Jenkins said.

'You know that, do you?' Bernstein asked.

'Stands to reason,' said Jenkins.

It was Bernstein's turn to scoff. Then she pondered some more.

'OK,' she said. 'Steer clear of that area. Not one more word about bees. Ask it about slithery things instead.'

Hazeldene had no hesitation in complying. She was shaken by the incident, and couldn't get it out of her mind. She tried to focus on formulating other questions.

Which was why she didn't see the new ship come in.

Around ten o'clock, about three and a half hours before the noon of Apis's twenty-seven-hour day, Hazeldene was just thinking about another coffee when she heard a clap from the sky. She turned to the window and saw a silver arrowhead flash by very high up, pass almost out of sight, then bank and begin a long and steep approach.

Jenkins jumped up and went to the window. 'Aliens?'

He sounded hopeful.

'No such luck, feral,' said Bernstein, barely stirring from her indolent pose. 'It's one of ours.'

The craft skimmed into the water two kilometres off down Bellatrix Sound and decelerated smoothly along the surface to come to a halt beside the flying boat, still berthed at the quay. About twenty metres long, and now a duller grey than it had appeared in the full beam of the sun, the craft looked to Hazeldene like some supersonic version of the flying boat, with a bubble canopy above the cockpit, or bridge. A hatch farther back on the fuselage, or hull, slid open and two figures shot out. They hovered above the craft for a couple of seconds balanced on the downdraughts from jetpacks, then swept towards the shore and onto land just in front of the SciDiv building. Two men in business suits unclipped the hand-held turbines from their forearms, shrugged the engine packs from their backs, folded everything together into compact shells that they lugged like suitcases, and strode to the entrance of the military HQ like a pair of Mormon missionaries.

'Now that,' said Jenkins, 'is what I call showing off.'

'It would sure have outshone the ekranoplan if they'd arrived then,' Hazeldene said. 'Pity they didn't.'

A crowd gathered to gawk and speculate, until officers arrived to chivvy those on duty back to work. Bernstein did the same to Hazeldene and Jenkins. They returned to the apparatus and continued formulating queries. Hazeldene guessed she wouldn't have long to wait for an interruption. After about half an hour, it came.

There was the sound of a confrontation at the outside door, which went on for a minute or two. Comings and goings, raised voices. Feet tramped up the stairs. A challenge from the guard posted outside the meeting room got a brusque reply. In they came. Both tall. One Hispanic, the other white. Contrary to Hazeldene's first impression, their suits were neither identical nor black. The new arrivals weren't Men in Black after all. They still reminded her of Mormons. Short hair and looking as if they had just shaved. Also, painfully young. Both men gave her one sharp, quick look. She got the odd impression that they recognised her. They glanced at the apparatus on the table, then turned to the lieutenant. Bernstein stood up. The two men saluted. Bernstein stepped over to the table and sat down.

'Office of Naval Intelligence, ma'am,' said one. 'Specialists José Martinez and William Erickson.'

Bernstein gestured to the seats opposite her.

'Sit down, gentlemen.'

The men laid down their jetpacks and sat.

'I take it your mission is urgent,' said Bernstein, 'so let's skip any formalities.'

'Thank you, ma'am,' said Martinez.

'And to further avoid wasting time – have you been appraised of the information taken back by the Co-ord sub *Admiral von Bellingshausen* the other day?'

'No, ma'am. We've been briefed on deep background and a recent development we've been asked to bring to your attention. HQ referred us to you . . .'

Bernstein sighed. 'OK. Let's get you up to speed.'

That didn't take long. She showed them the apparatus, and the transcripts on her slate. They seemed to know what to expect.

After Bernstein had finished, Martinez reached inside his jacket and passed her a small sheet of card. 'Do you recognise this lady?'

'Of course. She's standing right there.' She beckoned impatiently. 'Sit down, Hazeldene. You, too, Jenkins.'

Hazeldene sat. Jenkins stayed at the window. 'I'm OK where I am, thanks all the same.'

Bernstein glared at him, then turned away. 'Fine.' She slid the picture across to Hazeldene. 'Can you confirm that this is you?'

There was a lot odd about the picture. It was a printed photograph of what appeared to be a photo-realistic drawing in black ink: a head and shoulders portrait of herself, her hands in view, another's hand grabbing her shoulder, and shadowy shapes behind her. It looked like her reflection in the glassy surface of Jenkins' apparatus. And there was something else, something she couldn't quite put her finger on.

'Oh!' she said. 'Yes. That's me just before Able Jenkins hauled me away from the screen, back there.' She turned to Jenkins. 'Take a look.'

He came to her shoulder and peered down. 'Yup,' he said. 'That's how I remember it.'

'Did this come from one of the others' phones, from behind me?' she asked Martinez. 'Then how—? Was it sent to you on the way in, or what?'

'No. Look again at the picture. Look at the detail.'

Hazeldene did, and shook her head. 'I don't see it.'

'Your buttons,' Jenkins said, from over her shoulder. 'Your pen pocket. That ain't a reflection.'

'Ah, of course.' She looked down at her shirt, just to make sure, then touched the picture. 'And this is printed the right way round?'

Erickson leaned forward. 'Let me assure you, that's been checked. This came to us by several steps, but every step has been verified. It's not a mirror image.' He pointed at the apparatus. 'It's a view of you, from that.'

'Then how on Earth did you get it?'

Martinez laughed. '"How on Earth" is exactly the wrong question, Dr Hazeldene. This picture was . . . retrieved Monday, on Venus.'

'"Monday on Venus"? What does that even mean?'

Martinez pointed. 'This picture was taken, if that's the word, three and a half local days ago as you recall?'

'Yes, uh, would have been mid-afternoon.'

'Well, what "Monday on Venus" means is that it appeared there about that time on that Earth day.' He turned to Bernstein. 'Remind me – is the precise time of the incident logged on that transcript?'

'Uh, yes, I think so.' She handed the slate over again.

Erickson thumbed, then nodded. 'Checks out.' He frowned at Hazeldene. 'You got hauled away right after you asked to speak with "the real Fermi" and it said "Very well. You shall." Did nobody ever warn you about invoking . . . things you don't know how to contain?'

'There's not a lot of precedent. We've been trying to get a response from whatever is in the rock for years.'

'Well, now you did. That picture.'

'Aha!' cried Jenkins. 'You're telling us my apparatus is an ansible?'

They all turned to him. 'A what?'

'An instantaneous communication device? The word comes from the science fiction of Ursula Le Guin.'

'Never heard of her,' said Erickson.

'You wouldn't have,' said Martinez. 'Her works were withdrawn from circulation under the previous dispensation.'

'They're legal now,' said Bernstein. 'Not that I'd endorse them, but feel free.'

Hazeldene remained poker-faced.

'Her books are on my phone,' Jenkins said. He pointed. 'From my old man, you know?'

Erickson frowned at the Huawei 7G amid the clutter. 'The books may have been legalised but that model of phone has not.' He gestured impatiently. 'In any case, no, the transmission doesn't seem to be instantaneous. Just as fast as a starship, which is plenty fast enough.'

'Wait wait wait, hold up!' Hazeldene said. 'What's all this about Venus? Isn't that a Union colony? Do they have a receiver for this, or what—? Oh! I get it! There are Fermi Ruins on Venus, too!'

The three intelligence officers looked at her, then at each other. Lieutenant Bernstein sighed and nodded. 'It's all out in the open now, I guess, if the manner of your arrival is anything to go by.'

'Some of it is, ma'am,' said Martinez.

Bernstein went to the door and spoke to the guard. 'Strictly no non-Alliance personnel,' she said. She closed the door. 'Spill it,' she said.

'What about him?' Martinez said.

'Mr Jenkins,' said Bernstein, 'we have a young relative of yours in the clinic and a drone circling on standby over your village. I'm sure we can treat you as family.' She gave Jenkins a most non-familial smile, then nodded to Martinez. 'Proceed.'

'Very well, ma'am. Ah . . . Dr Hazeldene, you're right. If by Fermi Ruins you mean structures like MacHinery Ridge, traces of such have indeed been found on Venus by the Union cloud colony. This particular picture was recorded from a rock surface identical to those of MacHinery Ridge by an operative of one of our allied services. He conveyed it to the Alliance consul, who in turn transmitted it to the relevant authorities on Earth. Your image was quickly identified. Some consternation ensued, particularly as the Union's AI had interacted with the rock, and significant seismic activity took place immediately afterwards.'

'Seismic activity on *Venus*?'

'Yes.' Martinez thumbed the side of his face. 'A public announcement of the existence of Black Horizon has been imminent for some time, and this has tipped the balance. With due regard for security concerns, a great deal of Black Horizon's history and findings including the existence of Apis are now in the public domain.'

Hazeldene took a deep breath. She gripped the edge of the table. The room stopped swaying and spinning. The world had just changed for everyone, much as it had changed for her long ago when she'd stumbled out onto the deck of the submarine and looked up.

'So it's all public now? Jeez.' She grinned. 'We'll be able to do some proper science here at last!'

'That's one consequence, yes.' Martinez didn't sound as if he regarded it as an important consequence. 'Another is that if we have to take action that will reveal our FTL capability for all to see, it will at least not be a complete surprise and taken as more alarming than might be warranted.'

'Oh. I see. Like a plane taking off from Nevada and vanishing in a blue flash, for example?'

'I'm not at liberty to reveal the starting point of our journey,' Martinez said. He cleared his throat. 'Nevertheless. Our assignment here was urgent, first of all to determine the circumstance of the transmission of your image – which we've done – and secondly to resolve the situation with all due dispatch.'

'Resolve what situation?'

'Dr Hazeldene,' Erickson said, in an infuriating tone of patient explanation, 'the Union now has literally in its hands a sample of this stuff you've been messing about with. The seismic activity on Venus has given them some inkling of its capabilities. We know, or so I understand from my briefing a few hours ago, that this technology was used to terraform this entire planet we're sitting on. The Union's most powerful AI has established some kind of communication with it, though details of that are sketchy at best. Can you imagine what they could do with it, wittingly or otherwise?'

Hazeldene shrugged. 'I suppose blowing up Venus would be a loss to science, but . . .'

'You still don't quite understand,' said Erickson. 'The structure on Venus is connected – we don't know how – with the structure up there on the Ridge. Superluminally connected, at that. So any tampering with it endangers you and everyone else on Apis. Furthermore, it has the potential to destabilise the balance of power on Earth.'

'How?'

'I mean destabilise in a quite literal sense, Dr Hazeldene. I've been authorised to tell you that we've found traces of similar structures deep in the crust of our own planet. Dormant, yes, perhaps distorted beyond any possible reactivation, but how can we be sure of that?'

Jenkins laughed harshly. 'You've got Fermi Ruins on Earth!'

There was a short silence. Then Martinez said: 'I wouldn't be so smug about it, Mr Jenkins. You and Dr Hazeldene are going to Venus. With your device. Now.'

'What?' cried Hazeldene. 'Why?'

'We didn't know what we would find here,' Martinez said, 'but we've had time to war-game various possibilities – that's to say, our strategic AIs have. They came up with contingency plans for all the possibilities within minutes, and one of them was for a situation where our scientists had established some communication with the structure – hence of course explaining the appearance of the image. That situation would appear to obtain. Would you agree?'

'Well, kind of.' Hazeldene glanced at Jenkins. 'Communication's very flaky, at best. And whatever we're communicating with may or may not be the builders of the structure. It has a tendency to be a bit cryptic, a bit – what's the word? – Delphic. You know, like the oracle?'

'I *don't* know,' said Martinez. 'Oracles are heathen superstition, Dr Hazeldene. This thing you're talking to is an alien of some kind, and presumably a rational being. The point is that you, and I guess your team, and with due acknowledgement to Mr Jenkins here, have a means of communicating with it.'

'Yes, we do! So if we're communicating with that rock up there, and it can communicate with a rock on Venus, why don't we communicate with it *right here*, instead of taking us and the device to Venus?'

'Good question,' Erickson said. 'Worth a try.'

'Waste of time,' said Martinez.

'How do you know?' Hazeldene demanded.

'The best analysis our AIs came up with was that the image of you on Venus was a message, asking that you *come* to Venus. And the nature of the rock's responses then and later seems to bear that out.'

'It did insist a message had been sent, and received,' said Hazeldene. 'So, yes, that picture of me could be the message. I don't know. One way to find out, I suppose.'

She asked the rock and got no answer.

'So much for that,' she said.

'Told you,' said Martinez. 'As I said, we have no time to waste. I have to ask you and Mr Jenkins to pack up your device and have it conveyed to the submarine.'

'What submarine?'

Martinez gestured towards the window. 'That one.'

She looked. A submarine had indeed appeared in the Sound. It must have arrived when they were talking. 'Ah.' She closed her eyes and opened them. 'We're going to the surface of Venus – in a submarine?'

'Yes,' said Martinez. 'I'm assured that it can handle the pressure.'

'What about the temperature?'

'If that becomes an issue,' said Martinez, 'the captain can always power up the Guth spindle and leave. We don't expect you to be there long. If all goes well, you'll be back here by tomorrow at the latest.'

Hazeldene frowned. 'Does SciDiv approve of this jaunt?'

'Yes.'

'Uh, I'll need confirmation.'

Martinez shrugged. 'Phone your boss and ask.'

Hazeldene called Black. 'My arm's been twisted,' he explained. 'They can't make you go, but if you're willing to go, they can make me agree to it.'

'I understand,' Hazeldene said. 'Thanks, Adrian.' She rang off.
Martinez looked smug.

'Mr Erickson will accompany you, Dr Hazeldene. I will
return to Earth with all speed in the spaceplane we arrived in,
to report.' He sighed. 'Having . . . ansibles is going to be very
handy, if we can make more of these things.'

'I doubt you can,' said Jenkins. 'But, hey, if you want me
to go to Venus, count me in. I always wanted a bit of adventure in my life.' He looked around. 'Why the long faces?'

The others all turned to Hazeldene. She sighed. 'Uh, Able,
did your father or anyone of that generation ever tell you
about what the jump is like?'

Jenkins shook his head. 'Can't say I recall any mention.'

'I'm not surprised! Let's just say it's something you don't
want to remember. You know that feeling when you go inside
the Ridge?'

'Uh-huh.'

'It's like that, but a lot worse, and kind of . . . the opposite.
Not like being watched. Like being alone and frightened.'

'Reckon I can take it,' Jenkins said. 'I mean, you lot did.
How bad can it be?'

'You'll see,' Hazeldene said darkly. 'But OK. I know you
can take it. Just so long as you know what to expect, right?'

'Right.'

Hazeldene felt she'd done her duty to him, though no favour.
She turned to Martinez. 'OK, but what are we going to *do* on
Venus?'

'That's classified,' said Martinez.

'You are poking around these rocks on Venus, right?'

'Not us!' said Martinez. 'The Union. They've already taken
a sample off the surface.'

'You just told us you had an Alliance operative on the surface,
right? The one who got that picture?'

'Yes,' said Martinez. 'But as I understand it, his mission was
to *prevent* the Union from recovering a sample.'

Jenkins laughed in his face. 'Then he didn't do a very good job, did he?'

'You could say that,' said Martinez. 'You could certainly say that. Which is why it's so urgent that we go there and—' he paused, wet his lips '—try to put things right.'

Hazeldene pounced. 'You mean, grab that sample back!'

Martinez's expression went blank. 'I don't know about that,' he said. 'It's not part of our mission, that's all I can say.'

'Yeah, right,' said Jenkins. 'That part of the mission is reserved for the guy who failed before.'

Martinez and Erickson laughed. Even Bernstein smiled.

'This mission,' Hazeldene said. 'Is it Black Horizon? Have we squared it with the Co-ord?'

'You must be fucking joking,' Bernstein said.

'Ah, no we have not, Dr Hazeldene,' Martinez added hastily. 'This is entirely an Alliance op.'

'What's the point?' Hazeldene said. 'OK, maybe we can stop the Union getting its hands on that sample. But what's to stop them finding others?'

'On Venus?' Martinez snorted. 'I don't think that window's gonna stay open long.'

'I didn't mean on Venus.'

'Like, here?' said Bernstein. 'We can stop them. Just put the Fermi Ruins off limits. They're now pretty much off limits to us, if that thing is to be believed.'

'Yes, but . . . I'm asking you again: what's to stop the Union finding their own Fermi Ruins somewhere else, and maybe doing a better job than we've done so far with making use of them?'

'You seem to be under some misapprehension,' said Martinez. 'We've told the world we have FTL, yes. We haven't shared the spec for the Guth drive!'

'But once people know it's possible,' Hazeldene persisted, 'the cat's out of the bag, isn't it? What stops the Union from getting FTL of its own?'

'Like I said before,' Bernstein told her. 'We stop them.'

CHAPTER NINETEEN

Extra-Vehicular Activities

Thursday 16 October 2070, Venus

Marcus Owen strolled across the fake grass towards the spiral stairwell to the underside of Cloud City. He had an empty rucksack slung over his shoulder, and he made no attempt to go unobserved. Few were around to notice him. The surveillance system would be tracking him in any case. Notionally it was night in Cloud City, though outside the long day was breaking. The habitat had been carried around the planet on the circling winds, and was once again approaching Ishtar Terra.

The rock sample was still at the next outpost behind Cloud City. The decision had been taken not to risk transferring it to the main habitat by aircraft in the newly turbulent upper atmosphere, or to risk stowing this alien material of bizarre properties and unknown capacities anywhere near Cloud City. So the sample remained at the outpost, awaiting a shuttle from the moonlet. Its departure had been delayed by the increased turbulence of the upper atmosphere.

There was some hope that the turbulence would pass. The remaining rovers and blimps confirmed longer-range observations from orbit and from aloft: the cracking and upwelling had subsided. It was the seismic upheavals – adding heat to the already hot atmosphere – that had caused the turbulence in the first place, so the hope seemed reasonable.

Whether the turbulence passed or not, Owen couldn't count on the delay in taking the sample to orbit going on for much longer. Engineers up at the moonlet were busy with urgent work to refit the shuttle for the new conditions.

No countermand or update to his instructions had reached Owen. He'd had plenty of discussions with people here since the FTL announcement. The self-assurance that Cloud City was the most advanced base of humanity had taken a severe knock. Owen's role as cultural attaché had never been so genuine. He'd spent hours each day assembling and curating Alliance and NASA press releases and scientific articles, sharing them around on the local network and in person.

In all this time Walworth had said not a word about any new instructions. Owen had made the strategic decision not to ask. He suspected he already knew how Walworth would answer: he would flatly forbid any further attempt to stop the retrieval of the rock sample. This would lead to a quite unnecessary conflict between them. So now, Walworth was as oblivious to Owen's intentions as Francesca Milloy, whom the robot had just left sound asleep. She was used to his early departures.

Owen reached the stairwell. He took the opportunity of walking around the railing to the top step to take a quick and – he hoped – not at all shifty looking survey of his surroundings. A cleaning bot trundled across the fake grass, picking up detritus. Closer by, a gardening bot tended the leaves of a clump of real bushes. At the café, a couple, late up or early rising, sat head to head in a downward cone of yellow light.

Satisfied that, apart from routine automatic surveillance, he was otherwise unnoticed, Owen hurried down the spiral stair. He had to grab the railing halfway down as the habitat lurched. He felt a slight decrease in gravity, perhaps even a moment of free fall, then the habitat steadied. Yells echoed faintly from above and afar. A soothing PA voice in Owen's glasses' frame announced that the habitat was passing through local turbulence, and all personnel were advised to sit tight and hold on to something firmly attached.

All to the good. Fewer people around. Owen sauntered along gangways and cantered down steps, his shadow long in the low lights of the hydroponic troughs. The air was more humid and less oxygenated down here, with a heavier load of carbon dioxide pumped in for the plants. On a distant gangway a technician dropped a tool with a clang that made Owen start. As the man stooped he glimpsed Owen. Light reflected off his glasses as he turned sharply to stare. Owen gave him a friendly wave and headed on down.

From his previous visits, and from his study of the habitat's specs and plans, Owen had a complete, full-colour, 3D mental model of the entire underside in his head. This gave him the luxury of combining a confident, purposeful gait with an indirect approach to his destination. At any one moment, almost until he arrived, he would seem to be headed in a quite different direction.

His first stop was at Milloy's lab. The door was unlocked, and he knew his way around. He left a minute or two later with tools and other gear clinking in his rucksack.

At the store for EVA suits and equipment, he stopped. It was locked, but he'd once seen someone tap the keypad, and once was enough. He entered the code and swung the door open.

'Hey!'

Owen didn't start or turn. He stepped through into the cabin and closed the door behind him. Running footsteps rang along the gangway above. Motion-sensitive, the cabin's lights flickered on. Owen pressed himself against the wall beside the hinged side of the door. The steps approached, and stopped. The man must have known the code, too, because the door opened, swinging inward.

Contrary to Owen's expectations, the man didn't enter, or even stick his head past the door. Instead, he took one step back, and called out.

'Mr Owen!'

Owen said nothing.

'Please come out and show yourself,' the man said. 'Otherwise, I'll have to report an incident. I'm sure you have a good reason to be here.'

Owen coughed, and crumpled to the floor from behind the open door, clutching his throat. He crooked his knees to get his feet out of the way of the door and rolled over a couple of times, coughing and retching.

The man was the technician who'd noticed Owen earlier. He remained outside, but leaned forward and peered in.

'Mr Owen! What's wrong? Should I get help?'

'I'm sorry,' Owen croaked, looking up. 'There seems to be a problem in my respiratory system.' His breath rasped in and out, and in again. 'I was suddenly overcome out there,' he wheezed. 'Came in to grab a piece of breathing apparatus. Turned around. Got confused. Lack of oxygen.' He coughed again. 'Sorry. It's a robot thing, a defect that sometimes . . . anyway, I'm all right thanks, no need to get help. Give me a minute.'

He rolled again, gasping, and made an effort to get up. He relaxed his elbow and let himself fall, jarring his shoulder and cheek, then rolled on his back. 'A minute,' he wheezed again, closing his eyes almost completely. He let his fingers twitch, and he breathed out and then didn't breathe in.

'Oh, hang on, mate,' said the technician, starting forward. 'The oxy kits are right there, let me—'

As the man came through the doorway Owen kicked the door shut with one foot and slammed the other straight into the man's midriff. As the technician doubled over Owen grabbed his wrists and rolled, flexing his back and legs hard. The man went flying, to crash on the floor and against the edge of a workbench. Owen followed through the roll, stood and spun around. He made a dispassionate assessment of the casualty's injuries. The guy wasn't going anywhere soon, if ever.

Owen took the man's glasses and discarded his own – entirely redundant – to confuse tracking. He ripped off the man's T-shirt, careless of any further injury to those he'd already inflicted. He cast about for EVA gear and anything else that might come in handy. Within five minutes he'd suited, masked, tooled and kitted up. He left, bubble helmet under his arm, life-support on his back, pack slung on his shoulder, and closed the door behind him.

His subterfuge gained him at most three minutes. Silent alarms went off all around him. Iskander's furious queries battered at his skull. Three people emerged from cabins at various points in the structure, and set off after him. Feet clattered on the entry stair high above. Cloud City had many features for safety, but almost none for security. Iskander's surveillance, and psychological and political screening of all personnel, were in all normal circumstances protection enough against mental imbalance, crime or sabotage. There were no police. To the best of Owen's knowledge, there wasn't so much as a firearm on the planet.

Through this loophole, Owen now sprinted. By the time the alarm was raised, he was at the airlock. The inside hatch didn't budge – Iskander must have blocked it. Owen wrenched open the cover of the manual override, and turned the levers. The hatch opened. Owen reached into his bag and took out a miniature sintering torch, a pressurised can of flammable liquid and the bundled T-shirt. He soaked the T-shirt in the spray, wrapped it tight around the can and lit it. He tossed it behind him and slammed the hatch.

The bubble helmet clicked into place, sealing on its grooved and O-ringed collar. Owen checked the apparatus, confirmed his suit was airtight, and cycled the lock. Air went out. Carbon dioxide and sulphuric acid haze rushed in. The gas carried sound well enough for him to hear the thump as his firebomb went off.

Out he stepped, onto the long ladder down.

The aircraft hung in one of the many gantries below Cloud City. Owen climbed down from the airlock and traversed the spindly walkways towards it. The atmosphere ahead was hazier than it had been on his descent to the surface, with gouts of cloud rising on tall pillars that cast long shadows on the bright layer of cloud below. Lightning flickered around their tops. Cables creaked and strained, hauling the circumferential solar panels into alignments that might – or might not – divert the habitat's drift to avoid the turbulent regions rising ahead.

Along the way he noticed a pod made fast to the next gallery above, close to the shuttle docking rig. Bright yellow plastic, two and a half metres long and a metre in diameter, plastered with warning labels. He guessed that it very probably contained his descent suit, which he'd seen crudely Faraday-caged to isolate the onboard module of Iskander – with whatever it had picked up from the alien rock – from the main local AI, and crated. Now it had been moved outside, awaiting transfer by shuttle to the moonlet for further study in some firewalled lab.

He hadn't planned it, but the opportunity was too good to miss. If his main task was to prevent the Union from recovering the sample, depriving them of the data from the Iskander module would be a very satisfactory secondary one.

Ahead was a ladder to the gallery above. Owen climbed it

and dashed to the pod, reaching into his tool bag as he ran. He took out a cable-cutter and set to work. Cutting the ties between the pod and the gallery's metal mesh floor and its railing was awkward, and gloves and bubble helmet didn't make it easier. Once he almost dropped the cutter, twice a lurch of the habitat nearly threw him off. But in ninety seconds, the job was done. He stashed his tools, tipped the pod up on one end, then toppled it over the railing.

Just as he turned to hurry on towards the aircraft, the falling yellow pod burst open. Owen stopped and stared, zooming his sight. A fist and a foot thrust out of the cracking plastic, then the whole thing split apart as the suit fought its way out. With a shove of its legs, the suit fell free from the fragments of the pod, which swirled above it like leaves. As it fell it ripped through and tossed away the swaddle of wire mesh around it like so much tissue paper.

Watching the gauzy scraps float above the still plummeting suit, Owen counted this another stroke of luck. If the Iskander module uplinked to the main AI, it might well give the system a lot more to think about than a fleeing killer robot. Owen suddenly had a lot to think about himself. The suit began hailing him repeatedly. Owen blocked it instantly, screening out the calls. He was just as wary of alien software contamination as Cloud City was, if not more so: this was his very self at risk. The Iskander module had as good as told him that it could take control of the suit, but it had never crossed his mind that it might start acting independently. Now the suit was in effect a robot, controlled by the Iskander module. For all the good that would –

The suit sky-dived, arms and legs spread, still falling but gliding ahead of the habitat.

A balloon shot out of the suit's back and inflated instantly. The suit's fall was slowed, stopped, and – as Owen raced along the gangway towards the aircraft gantry – reversed. It began to rise rapidly into the flight path of the habitat.

Owen scrambled down the ringed ladder on the side of the gantry, taking care not to bump his helmet and life-support. Another patch of turbulence set the gantry swaying. Owen clung to a rung, decided the turbulence wouldn't soon pass, and continued determinedly down step by step. The cargo hatch was still open. Owen worked his way along the fuselage and, not daring to stand, lowered himself inside the aircraft head-first.

He closed the cargo hatch and ducked through to the nacelle to sit in the pilot's seat. He couldn't strap in with the life-support pack, so he hooked one knee to the edge of the seat and braced the other leg on the forward panel. The control board was blank and black: dead. No doubt Iskander had locked him out of it already. Owen briskly turned on the manual switches in a staccato of clicks. The panel lit up.

Just as he reached for the manual release for the shackles holding the craft to the gantry, the view in front of him filled with silver, like an airbag in a car crash. A moment later the suit – now free of its balloon, which shot up to bounce against the habitat's underside – swung in to grab hold of a strut of the gantry. It vaulted up and ran along the gantry with preter-natural agility, to jump on the aircraft's fuselage just behind the cockpit. Even for Owen, it was hard not to imagine that the suit had someone inside.

Owen released the shackles. The aircraft dropped, then slipped into a steep glide. The suit straddled the fuselage and worked its way back towards the cargo hatch. Owen powered up the engines and the propeller spun into action. He pulled the craft into a steep climb and rolled the plane.

Still the suit clung on, legs clasped around the fuselage. Its efforts to get through to Owen continued, persistent and unavailing. Owen set the craft on a still steeper climb, and then abruptly tipped it over into a dive. This manoeuvre nearly sent him through the windscreen, but it was enough finally to shake the suit off.

Owen levelled off and banked around, and saw the suit falling towards the clouds. For a few minutes he circled, watching out for any new and final ascent with the suit's one remaining balloon. But the suit had evidently foreseen that Owen could easily shred that balloon with one pass of a propeller. It must now be falling to the surface, and perhaps bracing for a landing. Well, good luck with that!

Owen levelled his flight, passing under Cloud City, and set a course for the outpost.

The flight took three hours, a constant push against the prevailing wind and a frequent buffeting by turbulence. From overhead the dorsal loop sang and whined, a demon choir of frequencies that Owen couldn't believe humans would ever find anything but excruciating, but which he had no problem tuning out. Owen discovered the craft's own life-support while he was unburdening himself of the pack containing his own so that he could sit down and strap in. He flushed the local atmosphere out and air in, and when the pressure was at a tolerable level removed his helmet and turned off his own air supply. Getting out of the mask and helmet was a relief, conserving his own life-support a reassurance. The cockpit stank of Venusian micro-organisms, but he could cope with that.

The distress calls from Cloud City were harder to cope with – not for any reasons of conscience, of which, as he'd explained to Walworth, he had none – but because of the complications that would certainly ensue. Owen could have connected to the local net and comms just with the machinery in his skull, as he often had within the habitat when he couldn't be bothered with more than a pretence of using phone and glasses, but he knew better than to risk that now. Instead, he turned on the aircraft's radio and video comms. As soon as he did, what he'd left in his wake became clear.

The man he'd attacked was dead, for a start. It got worse

from there. The firebomb he'd tossed behind him at the airlock had done far more damage than the mere delay and diversion he'd intended. Not only had it injured a further two people, both seriously burned, but the bomb had bounced and rolled and fallen before it had exploded – close to the Faber fusion pot. The reactor's safety deadfalls had slammed shut. Not even Iskander could unpick these in a hurry. A manual override was out of the question, by design. Now Cloud City was on emergency power. Only the most basic tasks and life-support could continue. The alarmist talk of evacuation that had accompanied the early disquiet about surface upheavals and atmospheric turbulence was, with every minute that passed, becoming serious and urgent planning.

The situation had all the makings of a humanitarian and diplomatic crisis. It was going to make Owen's life, or what was left of it, a great deal more complicated. But for those three hours it passed the time, like watching an ants' nest burn.

So he imagined, anyway. Not having actually been a boy, he'd never done anything so pointlessly cruel himself.

The outpost shone bright ahead in the low sunlight from behind. As Owen approached the outpost he buzzed it, just to let them know he'd arrived and wasn't afraid of them. Compared with Cloud City, the outpost was tiny: a fat thirty-metre-long gondola slung beneath an airship-sized, semi-dirigible blimp. It didn't have its own aircraft, though it did have a docking hook on the gantry underneath the gondola. There was only a stowed balloon and a likewise inflatable bell to serve as a liferaft in emergencies, but according to Owen's reading no outpost had ever had to be abandoned.

The outpost's crew, ten scientists and technicians, had made what preparations they could in the three hours of warning they must have been given. They'd winched in the docking hook, and in a gantry below the gondola had rigged up a contrivance of gas bottles and a directional nozzle that an

EVA-suited crew member used to spit jets of white-hot flame at the aircraft whenever it came within range.

Owen circled at a safe distance and hailed the outpost.

'You can prevent me from boarding,' he said, after the initial exchange of unpleasantries, 'but you can't prevent me from skimming the top and sides of your gasbag and slicing it up with my propeller.'

'Try it, robot,' said the chief scientist on board. 'I think you'll find the material is tougher than you expect, and certainly tougher than the propeller.'

Owen replied with the exact specifications of the material and the propeller.

'Still suicidal,' said the scientist.

'And you think that's a problem for me . . . why?'

The response was silence.

'All I want,' Owen went on, 'is to jettison the rock sample you retrieved from Atropos Tessera. It can fall with you, or without. As long as it falls, I'm happy. One way or another, that rock's going to fall. We might as well do it the easy way.'

'How will you know,' the scientist said, 'that whatever we drop *is* the rock?'

'I won't,' said Owen, with a complicit chuckle. 'Which is why I'm not expecting you to drop it. I expect you to let me on board and I'll drop it myself.'

'You're a murderous psychopath,' said the scientist. 'We aren't letting you on board. And even if we did, we could overcome you.'

'You could,' Owen conceded. 'Several of you would die heroic deaths, of course, and even so there is no guarantee you would prevail. My physical strength and reflexes are more than a match for ten of you. I have an array of improvised weapons, I'm highly—' he paused, realising he had no recollection of training '—skilled in all kinds of mayhem. I have absolutely no inhibitions about violence. As you so tactfully pointed out, I'm a murderous psychopath. Nor do I have the slightest fear of death. Ask yourselves – better yet, ask Cloud City – if it's worth it. You'll let me in, or I'll start slicing up the gasbag. Like I say, it's all one to me.'

This wasn't strictly true. Owen's preference was very much to handle and dispose of the rock himself, rather than let it go down in the wreck of the outpost. That plan had too many moving parts. For one thing, even if the blimp was torn apart the gondola had enough buoyancy of its own to sink rather than drop. He wasn't disposed to leave matters to chance in any case, but the way he'd been outwitted on his excursion to the surface made him all the more determined to take matters into his own hands.

'You understand that this is already an international incident?' the scientist said.

'I don't doubt it. But as recent announcements have shown, your side is pretty comprehensively outgunned, so—'

'My side?' The scientist sounded confused. 'Oh – you mean the Union! I'm an Alliance citizen.'

'In that case, tough luck, compatriot,' said Owen. 'Think of it as dying for freedom, if it helps.'

'I'll make sure to pass that observation on to Walworth.' Cool customer.

'Do that. Meanwhile, you have a decision to make.'

Long pause. Frantic consultation, probably.

'Give us a moment.'

'I have all day,' said Owen.

He didn't. He had enough air in his own pack for an hour, and enough on the aircraft for two. But the crew of the outpost surely knew they were in no position to wait him out.

The scientist came back online after two minutes. 'Very well,' he said. 'We'll lower the skyhook. Our colleague out on the gantry will retreat inside after dismantling our, ah, improvised anti-aircraft device. We'll back off from the entrance area – I'll patch our internal cameras to your ship, so you can be sure

– and lock ourselves in the lab at the bow. We'll leave the rock sample close to the airlock, and you can do what you like with it.'

'Glad you've seen reason,' said Owen. He fully expected some trap, but was confident he could deal with anything this lot could rig up. He also fully expected them to consider some trick, a substitution perhaps, but he couldn't see them thinking they could get away with any such. After another three wide circuits of the outpost, all was done as had been promised. Owen used the time to put on the breathing mask, get back in his helmet and to return the life-support pack to his back.

'And don't try any nonsense with the airlock,' he added. 'I have quite enough tools to break out from the airlock, or cut my way in through the side of the gondola if I have to.'

'Wish we'd thought of that,' the scientist replied, in a rueful tone. 'You'll have no trouble in the airlock.'

Owen took this reassurance as seriously as it deserved, but said no more about it.

He made a slow pass level with the gantry as a final check, then swung around for a lower and slower pass to engage with the skyhook.

Missed.

Missed again, and stalled.

Owen wrestled the plane out of the unscheduled dive and spin. This wasn't going to work. He risked turning the craft over to the on-board AI. He kept his hands on the manual controls all the time, ready to react, but the AI carried out the tricky manoeuvre as loyally and flawlessly as it had done at Cloud City.

As soon as the skyhook connected with the loop, a ladder slid down from the gantry to above the aircraft's cargo hatch. Carrying his tool bag over one shoulder, Owen ducked through to the hold and opened the hatch. He tugged hard on the ladder before entrusting himself to it. It seemed sound. Up he went, as quickly as he could, and along the gantry to the airlock. The belly of the gondola filled the sky above him, and through the struts the shining cloud layer filled the sky below. Pillars of turbulence stood all around, but none close by. Through his helmet he heard the wind moan in the outpost's rigging.

The airlock was a drum of tough fabric suspended from the gondola to the walkway, with a sealed hatch. Owen opened it, stepped in, and after a glance around closed the hatch behind him and waited by the rope ladder on the opposite side. Carbon dioxide was flushed out; air was pumped in. A light went from red to green. Owen kept his helmet on, climbed the ladder and opened the hatch. He looked about and saw nothing untoward. He was in a large compartment in the middle section of the gondola: the living area, with hammocks slung on the sides, a long table down the middle and folding chairs. At the far end of the room stood the two suits for surface exploration, which must have been used by the team sent down after him to retrieve the rock sample. He checked that the two suits were unoccupied. Hiding inside them to attack him in essentially invulnerable armour would have been an obvious ploy, though not, it seemed, one that had occurred to the scientists. Or perhaps they had been advised against it, or maybe these suits, too, had had some unscheduled interaction with the rock and were now off limits. Predictably, the floor, like every other flat surface, was cluttered with instruments and slates. The life-support was aft, the lab – where the crew had taken refuge – forward. The partitions and doors were rigid but flimsy.

Owen heaved himself inside and hefted a handy spanner from his bag in case of any attempt to rush him. He cast about for the rock sample. There it was, just as he'd seen it in the feed from the internal cameras: on the table, a black slab sealed in a translucent zip-lock bag.

He stepped over and picked it up. It weighed twenty kilos and was about sixty by forty by ten centimetres, like some big old book. Through gloves and plastic the surfaces felt rough.

Awkwardly, fumbling slightly, he peeled open the ziplock and peered at the block, then dragged the bag all the way off the sample.

The block was a slab of black basalt, like some of the rocks he'd walked over down there on Atropos Tessera. It was nothing like the lively obsidian he'd found in the chasm and the outcrop. A label on the discarded bag caught his eye. Under the lines showing date and time and location, it read: *control sample*.

'Fuck you,' said Owen, hoping someone heard. He'd war-gamed the possibility of a trick like this, but had dismissed it as pointless. How could they expect to get away with it? He turned to assail the lab door or wall, already running through a mental checklist of which tools to use on the obstacle and which on the occupants behind it. The gondola lurched. A loud bang came from the lab. Air gusted around Owen's feet. Detritus and small objects tumbled across the floor towards the lab door.

Owen stormed in the same direction as the breeze. The gondola lurched again, this time upward. More bangs, fainter, then the sound of engines.

The door wasn't locked. Owen opened it. Air howled. Pens, paper and test tubes whirled past him. The front of the gondola was open to the Venusian sky, through a neat rectangular opening of two metres by two. Above the gap was a notice: **EMERGENCY ESCAPE HATCH**.

Floating in the sky not a hundred metres away was a black capsule with portholes, slowly spinning and wildly swaying under a huge silver balloon. The raft. Any thought of trying to reach it, or to attack it – and a few wild notions did flit through the tactical modules of Owen's mind – was swiftly disabused by the bright flash and twin-engine roar of the aircraft zooming up from under the gondola. It shot overhead and turned in tight circles around the raft. Retrieving the capsule's occupants one by one would involve some astonishing feats of aeronautic skill, but Owen had little doubt that the craft's AI could pull them off.

Before it did anything like that, however, the aircraft surprised Owen again by roaring towards and then just over the outpost's blimp. The gondola lurched, then lurched again as the aircraft flashed past going the other way. He heard the rips and felt in his knees the sudden loss of altitude as the gondola began to sink.

Behind a porthole in the twirling capsule, just before he slammed the lab door and began an urgent search for something to seal the gaps, Owen glimpsed a waving hand.

Goodbye.

CHAPTER TWENTY

Fallen Man

Thursday 16 October 2070, Venus

Terror and loneliness.

It lasted – what?

Five minutes?

Eternity. No time at all.

Hell is the absence of God. So Hazeldene had once been warned. Now she clung to that thought. If her God was that of Einstein or Spinoza – the universal frame, the logic of nature – then hell was inside a Guth spindle. From Nature's womb untimely ripped, every particle of her body screamed its wordless, homeless longing for all it had known since the Big Bang. Or since the end of the inflationary epoch, ten-to-the-minus-thirty-two seconds later, give or take. Opinions differed, she knew, as they did on what difference, if any, that difference made. It made none to her, but the thought kept gave her some slight distraction.

She came out of the jump with a shudder. Beside her Jenkins rocked in the gimballed seat, fists to his forehead and eyes tight shut. On the other side of the table, Erickson and the ensign merely looked pale. They'd jumped often. Hazeldene had jumped once, Jenkins never.

How did submariners cope? Maybe with the same mental toughness that it must take to work inside an end-of-the-world machine in the first place. You could laugh off the thousand-yard stare: put it down to your readiness at any moment to create hell, and not to your own repeated plunges into it.

What God abandoned, these defended, Hazeldene thought. No pay would ever be enough.

Hazeldene put a hand on Jenkins' shoulder. He flinched.

'It's over,' she said. 'We've done it. We've crossed space.'

Jenkins opened his eyes and stared at the bulkhead between Erickson and the ensign. 'Have we?'

'Yes,' said the ensign, all cheerful reassurance. Her name was Lydia Marlow and she was alarmingly young. 'We're on Venus.'

'I can still feel it,' said Jenkins. 'A bit.'

'So can I,' said Hazeldene. The feeling had dwindled to mere dread and despair.

'That's because the Guth spindle's still powering down,' said Marlow. She glanced at her slate. 'Nearly there.'

This was hard to believe, from deep inside the USS *Puerto Rico*. They sat at a narrow, bolted-down table with three seats on each side, for all of which there was barely room in a cabin with grey bulkheads, a sliding door firmly closed, a rattling ventilation inlet, a PA speaker, a power point and an overhead light. There was – they'd been firmly told – no room at all in the command centres of the ship for them or for Jenkins' apparatus, now propped in clamps duct-taped to the table between the unoccupied seats. The ensign was in charge of liaison with the bridge, which meant she was in charge of them all. She wore a headset and consulted a slate. Erickson, too, had a slate in front of him, patched through the sub's comms, which he was using to keep the Office of Naval Intelligence in the loop – though tardily, because of the light-speed lag.

'I wish I could look outside,' Hazeldene said.

'Oh, sorry!' said Ensign Marlow. 'Your glasses, ma'am.'

Hazeldene put them on. Marlow flickered her fingers in front of them and worked some magic. 'There.'

Hazeldene looked and blinked. The app opened. Suddenly her view was no longer of the cramped cubicle, but of where the submarine was. A long way from Bellatrix Sound. Her first viewpoint was from the top of the conning tower, and dead ahead. Orange-tinted daylight, hazier than she'd seen in photographs. Rocks, just as she'd seen on photographs. A bright red glow in the far distance. Closer, a wavy line like a thin trickle of molten metal. Which it probably was, but surely Venus wasn't . . .

Oh. Yes. Seismic activity. Now visible to the not quite naked eye.

'That crevice in front and over a bit on the left? The dark one?' said Marlow.

'Yes, I see it.'

'That's where your image appeared.'

'Jesus.' It was no easier to believe, right on the spot.

'Show me,' Jenkins said.

Hazeldene passed him her glasses. He seemed to have the knack already, or to pick it up at once. He looked this way and that, agog.

'Christ!' he said. 'Not many folk can say they've seen this up close.'

'You can still count them on one hand,' said Erickson.

'Not counting robots,' said Marlow.

Jenkins handed back the glasses, shaking his head, grinning.

The submarine coasted on its dwindling spindle and settled on the first long enough stretch of flat enough rock with a crunch. The presence of God-or-Nature slammed back into the abhorred vacuum of their souls. Everyone breathed out. Everything creaked. Internal pumps laboured to shift air and coolant. Lights flickered.

'We can't stay long,' said Ensign Marlow. Hazeldene and Jenkins shifted to adjacent seats, in front of the apparatus. Jenkins elbowed aside the tangle of extension leads. Hands poised above the keyboard, he glanced sidelong at Hazeldene. 'Me? Or you?'

'You ask. You know how they think, if they think. I'll stay in shot.' She smiled. 'No dragging me off this time, OK?'

Jenkins chuckled, and began to type.

Are there Fermi here?
YES.
Can you speak to them?
YES.
Can we speak to them?
YES.

'Get *on* with it,' Marlow muttered. Jenkins sighed.

Please let them speak to us.
WE ARE HERE WHAT DO YOU WANT?

Everyone drew breath. It was, Hazeldene thought, like the moment in a séance where the medium starts talking in the spirit's voice – and it could be just as fake: whatever processing was going on inside that slab of glassy black rock in front of her might be just making shit up.

'Show them the picture,' said Jenkins. Her gaze fixed on the slab, Hazeldene reached across the table to Erickson, snapping her fingers like a surgeon demanding a scalpel. Erickson passed her the sheet of card with the photograph of the drawing of the image of her. She sat up straight and held it in front of her chest. Jenkins typed:

*We want to know what you want, and why you sent
this picture.*
ASK HIM.
Who?
THE FALLING MAN.
What falling man? Where?
OUTSIDE.

'Fuck!' cried Ensign Marlow. 'Sorry, sir, ma'am. Look!'

Hazeldene and Jenkins reached for the glasses; Hazeldene grabbed first. She blinked up the app for the outside camera view. If anything could look more surreal than the foredeck of a nuclear submarine resting uneasily on the surface of Venus, it would be what appeared to be a man in a spacesuit a hundred metres up and descending to that surface by balloon.

No, not to the surface – the falling man dropped straight down the chasm in front of them. The balloon bobbed above the chasm's lip, like some stray unearthly birthday celebration.

'What?' Jenkins demanded.

Hazeldene passed him the glasses, and told him what they'd just seen. He watched for a minute, as Erickson and Marlow tapped frantically at their slates.

'He's coming out,' said Jenkins. 'He's coming over. He's carrying something.' Seconds passed. 'Fuck, he's jumped onto the deck!'

'Union Venus Project IFF beacon,' Marlow reported. 'The bridge is trying to raise him.'

'Him?' cried Jenkins. 'There's nothing inside!'

'What?' said Hazeldene. 'Give me that.'

Jenkins, with evident reluctance, passed her the glasses. The fallen astronaut stood on the foredeck, hauling in the fast-deflating balloon. Beside it, on the deck, lay what looked like a long pole. The figure turned, raised both arms, and waved, then resumed hauling and stashing the balloon in some compartment on the suit's back. It seemed an oddly irrelevant thing to do in the circumstances, a mechanistic behaviour like the persistent walk of some decapitated insect. Zooming in, Hazeldene caught a glimpse of the faceplate, and saw only darkness behind it. Headless indeed.

The balloon stashed, the waving resumed.

'He – it? – is responding to the bridge and wants to talk with us,' said Ensign Marlow. 'Bridge has agreed to patch it through.'

'Wait!' said Erickson. 'What if it introduces some alien hack?'

'I'm very much afraid, ma'am,' said Jenkins, affecting a refined tone, 'that that ship has sailed.'

'That's pretty much how the captain sees it,' said Marlow. 'Given that we have what he called "that unholy contraption" on board in the first place.'

Erickson sat back against the bulkhead with the look of a man defying a firing squad, and waved a hand as if dismissing any responsibility for whatever came next.

'Patching you through,' said Marlow. She detached the microphone from her headset and placed it on the table. A voice came through the PA speaker in a top corner of the room.

'Hello,' it said. 'This is a local module of Iskander. Who am I speaking to?'

Hazeldene recoiled. Iskander! The Union's insidious AI, literally a control mechanism, avowedly aiming to take over the world! To her it was more frightening than the Fermi. She swallowed from a suddenly dry mouth, and replied.

'My name is Dr Emma Hazeldene. I'm the woman whose face appeared in that crevice you've just been in. We're an Alliance team attempting to communicate with the intelligences we think are present in these rocks, and to understand what they want. They told us a few minutes ago to ask you.'

'Pleased to meet you, Dr Hazeldene,' said Iskander. 'Your fame has preceded you. I understand you have been communicating with these intelligences already on the planet you call Apis?'

Hazeldene glanced at Marlow, who nodded.

'Yes. We have the device here. It was – to cut a long story short – provided to one of us by the intelligences themselves.'

'So they have told me. This speaks well for your veracity. I hope you will accept mine.'

'First, let's hear what you have to say.'

'Very well. For reasons needless to recount, the Alliance agent Marcus Owen has been here in this suit, with Union consent, about one local day ago. I was here, too, and observed and interacted with the entities in this unusual outcrop. Since then, I have been firewalled from any communication with Cloud City, and in particular prevented from interacting with the habitat's local Iskander network. However, I do have reception, and I can tell you what happened. After Owen's departure, a team of two astronauts descended and removed a sample of the rock, returning it to one of the smaller stations in the wake of Cloud City. Your agent is apparently committed to preventing the sample's onward transport to the moonlet, and has been ruthlessly working to that end.'

Erickson leaned towards the microphone. 'As one would expect.'

'Perhaps,' replied the Iskander module. 'In the past few hours he has killed one person, injured others, damaged Cloud City to the extent of grave emergency, thrown this suit off the habitat – to its doom, as he thought – stolen an aircraft and attacked the outpost in an attempt to retrieve the sample. The upshot is that he is alone on an evacuated and slowly sinking outpost, its crew are safely in an escape capsule with the sample and I have taken control of the suit and made a safe descent, as you see. I have just learned what the entities in the rock require of you, and which they have asked me to communicate.'

'Quickly would be good,' said Ensign Marlow.

'They demand the safe return of the rock sample to the surface.'

'How?' asked Hazeldene.

'Shoot down the capsule?' Erickson suggested.

'War crime, crime against humanity, violation of law of the sea,' Ensign Marlow snapped.

'Furthermore, it would not be a safe return,' said the Iskander module. 'I suggest you take me to the capsule, let me retrieve the sample, and I can then return to the surface with the aerofoil I've just recovered, or the balloon.'

'"Take?"' said Marlow. 'We can't *hover*. Not for any length of time.'

'But you can jump to a precise location, as I've just seen. That's all you have to do. I will take care of the rest.'

'One moment, please.' Marlow turned to Hazeldene. 'Can you check if whatever you're talking to agrees?'

Marlow contacted the bridge while Hazeldene rattled out the question. The reply came back.

WE HAVE HEARD AND WE CONCUR.

'Thank fuck for that,' said Jenkins. 'Would have been a right bummer if they didn't.'

Marlow looked up from her slate. 'We've picked up the distress beacons from the outpost and the capsule, we've got them both on radar, and the bridge has managed to raise the capsule and is trying to explain the situation to them – given that they aren't taking calls from our friend out there.' She listened in her headphones, head cocked, then put the captain through on the speaker.

'OK, here's the plan,' he said. 'We make two short jumps in quick succession. The first to just below the capsule – we've warned off the aircraft that seems to be mindlessly circling it – and the Iskander thing grabs on, the occupants leave this precious rock in the airlock for it, and it does its best to grab it and fly back down on whatever it's got. Next, we jump to what's left of the outpost, and see if we can save our agent.'

'Doesn't sound like he deserves saving,' said Hazeldene. 'I'd sooner leave him to a slow and painful death.'

Jenkins chuckled. Erickson and Marlow looked shocked.

'He's still ours,' said Marlow. 'And our responsibility.'

'He's a robot,' said the Iskander module. 'A painful death is not possible, unfortunately.'

'Enough!' said the captain. 'We leave in two minutes, on my mark, from . . . now. Bridge out.'

'Better hang onto something,' Hazeldene said to the Iskander module.

'Yes.'

The suit picked up the long pole, then walked along the deck to grasp a railing. Its gait was peculiar, as if it was under gravity lower than that of Venus. After a moment's puzzlement, Hazeldene realised that her intuitive expectation was deceiving her: the suit moved as it did because it was not only empty; it had its own buoyancy from the air inside it. The suit got to work on the long pole, unfurling it to reveal that it was an aerofoil, with cables from its edges which the suit attached – or reattached – to itself. Seconds ticked by. Hazeldene's sense of dread increased as the drive powered up. The aerofoil was clutched back against its struts in the suit's fist.

'Ready,' the Iskander module said, with a cheery wave and two seconds to go.

Hazeldene braced herself, but the jump was too brief to notice. Not so much as a shiver down her back. One moment she was looking out through the ruddy murk, the next –

dazzled by open yellow sky with swirling columns of white cloud lit by lightning flashes seen through the shimmer of the dwindling Guth field and –

looming, rushing at them, swinging in –

like a wrecking ball a black truncated cone beneath a huge silver sphere.

The AI-controlled suit jumped from the deck, aerofoil

clasped in one hand like a spear, and at the same moment the deck fell away beneath it. Then the capsule and the suit were gone, whirled overhead as it seemed, over the top of the conning tower. For seconds on end the submarine was in free fall. Hazeldene jammed her knees to the underside of the table, and rolled back the images in her glasses.

Yes! The suit had caught some handhold on the capsule. There it clung, the half-furled aerofoil swinging wildly beneath it. It dwindled from sight as the submarine fell.

The captain's voice came through on the speaker: 'All hands, brace for FTL jump!'

Again the impending dread, again a jump, again into a vast space of sunlit sky.

This time, Hazeldene caught sight of the shining layer of cloud from which the cloud columns climbed. And the dark object that now loomed in view – coming up swiftly from below as well as ahead – was far larger than the capsule: a crumpling, deflating blimp above what seemed a stumpy cylinder, blown out and blackened at the near end like a crushed cigar stub.

Standing in that wrecked end of the cylinder was a tiny figure. Hazeldene zoomed. The figure was a man in a bubble helmet and some kind of bright yellow coverall, with clunky gloves and boots like the hands and feet of the suit.

The submarine was falling rapidly but not freely and moving forward. The outpost was falling, too, but more slowly. There would be a moment when its wrecked end would be about twenty metres above the deck. The man waited, on the brink, intent. Hazeldene glimpsed his bright alert eyes, his poise—

He jumped. The deck, it seemed, rose to meet him. He fell through the shimmer around the ship and slowed slightly as he passed through it. The fall was hard nonetheless. He hit the deck, fell, rolled, jumped up and lurched to the nearest handrail and grabbed on. His survival suit was melted and smouldering at hip and elbow and back. Then, unexpectedly, he turned his head in the bubble, faced the camera and gave a thumbs-up with his free hand in its glittering jointed glove.

Clouds whipped past. The sub was free-falling again. The adrenaline surge of panic meshed with the rising dread and then they jumped again and it was five minutes in hell all over again and then in a hiss and a roar of steam as seawater washed the submarine's overheated hull they were in late afternoon daylight which made rainbows above the deck in the steam and they were making their way up Bellatrix Sound, cliffs sliding past and New Ardtaraig in the distance dead ahead.

The man loosened his bubble helmet and took a cautious sniff, like a space explorer in some retro-SF comic, then removed the helmet. He walked forward to where the deck was awash and scooped up seawater with the helmet and poured it over the burned parts of his suit and – presumably – his body.

Just as well there wasn't a contamination issue, Hazeldene thought – the microbial life from the clouds of Venus had long been shown to be precisely adapted for its inhospitable environment, and ill-adapted to any other, however ostensibly benign. Myriads of microbes would be popping like overfilled balloons on the first splash of seawater.

Then the man walked back and stood on the foredeck, helmet in the crook of his arm, gazing around in wonder at the strange new world.

Hazeldene remembered her own first arrival at this very shore. She sighed and took her glasses off. Jenkins opened his eyes and didn't look at anyone. Erickson attended to his slates, Marlow to her phones.

'Are we home?' Jenkins asked.

Hazeldene passed him the glasses.

'Fuck me,' he breathed, looking. 'Never thought I'd be so happy to see New Ardtaraig.' He took the glasses off and handed them back. 'Still, glad I went! Venus! Jeez! Something to tell the kids when I see them again.'

'Whenever that is,' said Erickson, nastily enough.

Jenkins ignored him. 'That guy outside – the walking suit thing said he's a robot?'

'Yes, it did,' said Hazeldene. She looked over at Erickson. 'Can you confirm or deny?'

'No point denying it,' said Erickson. 'They know. The Union, that is.' He grinned at Hazeldene. 'He's one of yours. A Brit.'

'What you mean,' said Hazeldene, 'is that *it* is the property of some UK intelligence service.'

'The British Council.' Erickson nodded, then grinned again. 'One of their arts projects.'

'Fucking murderous bastard, by the sound of things.'

'I wouldn't be too hasty,' said Erickson. 'He, or it if you insist, doesn't have murderous impulses. He's quite safe to be around, as long as he has no explicit instructions to the contrary. Which at the moment I presume he hasn't, given that he wasn't expected to end up here.'

'What do you mean, "end up"?'

Erickson stood up, and shuffled around the end of the table, straightening his back and legs. 'Ah, that's good.' He filled the doorway. 'During our brief sojourn on Venus I was able to download a sitrep update from our man on the spot, the Alliance consul, Mr Peregrine Walworth. Also a Brit, in case the name isn't enough of a clue. He has troubles enough of his own – the Cloud City habitat is not in a good way. That thing out there that calls itself Marcus Owen is partly to blame and is wanted for serious crimes. The Brits have taken the line that he's a malfunctioning piece of machinery, a rogue robot, and they wash their hands of him. I get the strong impression that his disappearance from Venus, let alone Earth, is very much welcome to the Brits. *We're* certainly not taking him back there. Is that correct, Ensign Marlow?'

'Yes, sir,' Marlow said. 'I've heard from the captain. Our next destination after we disembark the locals and embark the casualties from the tsunami is the US Submarine Base New

London. We don't want Mr Owen on board and we don't want him on US soil.'

'Great,' said Hazeldene. 'Dump him on us, why don't you?'

'Yes, exactly!' said Marlow, as if Hazeldene had just made a brilliant suggestion. She waved a hand at Jenkins and Hazeldene. 'Best get your gear packed up.'

'Yeah,' said Jenkins.

Just as he reached forward to unplug the power supply, the slab brightened and letters scrolled across:

THERE WILL BE A RECKONING.

Then it went blank.

'What do they mean by that?' Hazeldene asked, alarmed.

Jenkins gazed at their reflections in the glassy black stone. 'I ain't even gonna ask,' he said.

'Then I will,' said Hazeldene. She typed:

What do you mean by that?
YOU WILL KNOW SOON.

She made further queries, which all got the same reply.

'Fuck it,' she said.

'Told ya,' said Jenkins. He switched the power off and pulled the plug.

At the dock four casualties in life-support pods were taken aboard the USS *Puerto Rico* for transfer to the Naval Hospital at Groton, Connecticut, as soon as Jenkins and Hazeldene had gone ashore. Then three in coffins, for the cemetery.

'Stop feeling guilty,' Jenkins said. 'Wasn't your fault. It was the fucking Fermi.'

Hazeldene took a deep breath. Good to breathe free air again after hours on the sub. What it must be like after months . . . It wasn't the air of Earth, but it was better than the recycled air in the steel cylinder. She'd had a pang of thinking that in the past few hours on Venus she'd been closer to home than she'd been in fifteen years, indulged a moment of self-pity, then dismissed it. And, anyway, she hadn't been feeling guilty, she'd been feeling angry.

'Yes,' she said. 'I do blame the fucking Fermi, actually. I've had it up to here with these rock-computer dead alien AI sons of bitches. I am so over all the wonder of alien intelligence, and so into figuring out what we do about them – or to them! They tell us, "There will be a reckoning", do they? Damn right there will, if I have anything to do with it.'

'You said it, Dr Hazeldene,' said Jenkins. 'After all the help they gave us, I had no idea they could be such mean bastards.'

'Speaking of heartless AI sons of bitches . . . Where's that fucking robot?'

She looked around the briefly busy quay. It wasn't a routine visit, but there was always stuff to be loaded and unloaded, including mail, and various official and unofficial transactions were going on. A Russian and an American soldier stood guard at the landward end of the quay, and two more at the other. Through the hubbub Marcus Owen threaded, as if he had somewhere to go.

'The fucking nerve of the thing,' said Hazeldene. 'Come on.'

She was carrying the keyboard and cables; Jenkins lugged the slab one-handed, casually under his arm like a portfolio. They caught up with Owen.

'Where are you going?' Hazeldene demanded.

Owen stopped, turned and smiled. 'Pleased to meet you at last.' He held up the hand that wasn't holding the helmet and gloves. 'Marcus Owen.'

'Emma Hazeldene. Do you know me?'

'I know your face.'

'Oh, of course.' She gave her head a shake. 'The drawing. Again – where are you going?'

'I've been told to meet her,' said Owen, jutting his chin towards an approaching figure on the quay: Lieutenant Bernstein.

'Seems appropriate,' said Hazeldene, grudgingly. 'She's intel.'

'Really? I'm not.'

'Come off it,' said Hazeldene. 'You're a British Council spook.'

'Not any more,' said Owen, as Bernstein hurried up to join them. 'I had an assignment. I had instructions. I fulfilled them.' He gave them a disquietingly charming and disarming smile. His unattended burns seeped blood and fluid from burst blisters through the holes in his EVA suit. 'As far as I'm concerned, that's that. I have no further instructions from the British Council.' He turned to Bernstein. 'Lieutenant Bernstein. Doubtless you overheard. Good of you to meet me, but I assure you I have no intention of working for the ONI either.'

Bernstein scowled. 'I've been assigned to debrief you.'

'That's not how it works,' said Owen. 'I'm happy to chat, of course. Give my side of the story, if you like. Not as an agent being debriefed, but as a civilian. Any further conversations would be strictly personal, or if professional then on the basis of my actual profession.'

Bernstein smiled, as if she knew something Owen didn't.

'And what would that be, Mr Owen?' she asked.

Owen pulled a sad face. 'Seems I'm not as famous as I thought,' he said. 'But back in civilisation, I'm moderately well known as a journalist.'

Bernstein checked her glasses. 'Ah yes, so you are.' She still looked smug. 'For the moment.'

'War correspondent, mainly,' said Owen, cheerfully. 'With a keen nose for trouble spots, and a profitable sideline in travel writing.' He gazed around, as if taking in the boids, the cliffs, the base, the submarine, and the joint patrols of mutually wary Alliance and Co-ord marines. 'Looks like I've come to the right place.'

'If you're a travel writer,' Jenkins said, as they walked towards the base, staying together because it would have been awkward otherwise, 'you could start by telling people what it feels like to travel in a starship.'

'It's amazing,' said Owen. 'To arrive light-years away in minutes! I still can't quite get my head around it.'

'There's that, sure,' said Jenkins, 'but I was talking about the journey itself.'

'Yes?' Owen sounded puzzled. 'A shimmer, lights . . .'

'Didn't you—?' Hazeldene began.

'You didn't feel it?' cried Jenkins.

Owen looked from Jenkins to Hazeldene, frowning. 'Feel what?'

CHAPTER TWENTY-ONE

A Spin of the Wheel

Friday 17 October 2070, Earth

Grant woke to a ringing phone. He grabbed it off the bedside table and thumbed it silent. The call was from Nayak and the time was 06:45 on the Friday morning after the evening in the Comet bar.

'Hello?'

'John, have you seen—?'

Ellen turned over and tugged pointedly at the duvet.

'Call you back,' Grant mumbled.

He rolled out of bed and into his slippers and dressing gown, and padded through to the living room, closing doors behind him. He needed a piss. Nayak's call had sounded urgent. He rang her back.

'Hi, what's the problem?'

'Do you have an east-facing window?'

'Uh . . . yes. Just a moment.'

He went into the spare bedroom and looked out of the window. Still dark, just beginning to lighten in the east. Hard to tell the dawn apart from the light above Glasgow and all the towns between. A few stars shone through the haze. Rags and tatters of cloud. The usual stately procession of satellites and space stations. Venus bright red just above the skyline —

Red?

'Venus?' he said, restraining a yelp.

'Yes,' said Nayak. 'I was, uh, up early and I happened to see it, and of course I checked the news at once.'

'What's happened?'

'I don't know. Seems to be a news blackout, but through the firewall they're saying there are volcanic eruptions all over the surface.'

'What about Cloud City?'

'It's being evacuated.'

'What with? Shuttles?' He tried to imagine the logistics.

'From the moonlet, yeah. But they only have two shuttles, they can each carry ten at a time max, and with the turbulence it's very difficult. Again – from the other side of the firewall, sorry – the BBC is reporting we've only managed to evacuate a hundred or so, and there hasn't been a flight attempted for the past two hours because the turbulence keeps getting worse.'

'Shit. Can't the Alliance or the Co-ord help?'

'Relations are a bit strained at the moment. Between them, and between them and us. Anyway, all their assets are months away from Venus.'

'Yes, but – couldn't they use these starships they claim to have?'

'Well, yes,' Nayak said. 'Seems that's been asked, and the answer is that all their starships are, um, out among the stars. Not sure I believe that —'

'Huh!'

'And besides there's no way to call them in, because the only way to —'

'Yeah, yeah, I get it. Maybe your next invention should be an FTL communicator, huh?'

'Very funny,' said Nayak. 'I don't think it's even theoretically possible, unless . . .' She fell silent. Seconds passed.

'Lakshmi?'

Nayak made an exasperated noise at herself, and continued: 'But John, the point is – we have a starship.'

'Yes, sitting on the trolley in the yard.' It was still hard to think about the boat as a starship. 'She hasn't even had a test in the water, let alone—'

'We have to try, John!'

'We?'

'You must have a crew in mind.'

'Jeez.' Grant took a deep breath. 'Morag, Omar and Ellen. As long as they aren't still pissed or passed out. I'm a bit hung over myself.'

'Tell me about it,' Nayak said. 'But if I can rouse you, I can rouse Morag and Omar. Bang on their doors if I have to.'

'And how will you get there?' He tried to think of fast transport links from Tarbet, came up blank. 'Hire a drone or what?'

'Uh, John, I'm in a hotel in Port Glasgow.'

He recalled the end of the evening. 'Oh, that girl.' He chuckled. 'You two really did get a room.'

'Yes. I'm trying not to wake her. Anyway, I can be there in half an hour, and I'll go over everything yet again till the rest of you arrive. We have to get the ship launched in the next couple of hours and into space ASAP after that.'

'Jeez. Now I have to rouse Ellen—'

'Yes, yes. Get on with it, John. Make her coffee. Make promises. We were waiting for a chance, and this is our best chance, and if it works we'll be heroes, not criminals.'

Grant sighed. 'We can do it but . . . it's going to be bloody dangerous.'

'No, it isn't. I'll be there.'

'Yes, I'm sure you know how to work the drive and navigate and everything, but—'

'You don't get it, John,' Nayak said. '*I can't die.*'

Still with that delusion. Fucking hell. Whatever gets you through the night.

'All right,' he said. 'All right. I'll try. I'll see you at the yard as soon as I can.'

Grant returned to the bedroom, climbed into clean under-wear and cast about for clothes. He'd neglected to recycle the previous night's, and now he'd have to wear them again. The shirt smelled of beer and curry.

'You look like a pirate,' Ellen said, when he'd awakened her and explained the situation.

'Well, we are going to steal the ship.'

She was suddenly wide awake.

'We what?'

Twenty-seven minutes later, Grant and Ellen were in a taxi to the yard. Predictably, it had rolled up to the gate of the block just as they'd closed their flat door behind them. Ellen stared straight ahead in silence, rereading the manual for the submersible on her glasses. Grant poked through the firewall and chased the news, which was now becoming sparse even on the other side. Neither Alliance nor Co-ord seemed keen to cover whatever was unfolding in the clouds of Venus. To track it, you had to think like a conspiracy theorist, join dots: the social media feed of a church in Malawi suddenly nothing but prayers and well-wishes for a congregant's daughter, a graduate of the Astronautics School of the University of Guiana; an amateur astronomy network in Nevada picking up signals . . .

Not much, and all bad.

He turned it off and went back to thinking up a plan.

*

Grant palmed them through the gates. They walked straight to the slipway. Lights were on inside the submersible, and nowhere else. Above Newark Castle the sky was red, fading to pale blue above. In the still shadowy slipway the submersible's garish yellow almost hurt the eye, and made the wheeled cradle in which it sat fade almost to invisibility by contrast. The vessel seemed to hang in the air already.

'It's bigger than I imagined,' said Ellen. 'What's it called?'

'We were thinking of calling her *Fighting Chance*.'

Ellen unslung her backpack and pulled out a bottle of champagne which had been in their fridge for months awaiting a sufficiently special occasion.

'I meant to use that for Myles' graduation,' Grant said.

'Well, you didn't.' Ellen marched down the slipway to below the bow of the sub, reached up and smashed the bottle against the starboard runner. She returned with her waterproof jacket spattered with fizzing splashes. 'She's definitely called *Fighting Chance* now.'

'Somebody's going to have to clear up that glass,' Grant said. He grinned and clapped her champagne-dampened shoulder. 'Still, good for you. Even if we don't do that for wee boats like this.'

'Thanking the gods might be prudent.'

'Point.'

Grant got on his phone and awakened a cleaning bot. As he and Ellen went up the ladder to the submersible's entry hatch he saw the machine trundle away from the side of the slipway to clear up the broken glass.

Inside smelled of plastic like a new car. Fold-down seats with straps along both sides. Lockers and racks. Omar Khan, at the rear of the main compartment, fretted over the fusion pot in its well. He waved, and gave Ellen a tight-lipped smile. Nayak was in the portside seat at the cockpit. Ellen made her way through; Grant followed.

'Heard a bang,' Nayak said, frowning at the display panel. 'Nothing on the diagnostics.'

'Sorry, that was me,' Ellen said, as she settled into the starboard seat. She mimed a throw. 'Christening the ship.'

Nayak snorted. 'Thanks.'

'Where's Morag?' Grant asked.

'On her way.' Nayak pointed to a stepped recess behind and under the pilots' seats. 'John, if you could get down there and get a handle on the grapples . . .'

'Sure.' Grant turned and gripped a safety bar, and paused. They couldn't run a ship on polite requests! He was about to make that point, reflected that they all knew each other well enough that they probably could and in any case this wasn't the time to throw his weight around, and swung himself down into the hole.

He was in a bubble like a blister turret, with 180-degree views front and sides. The slipway was a couple of metres down, between his feet. The robot was still picking up shards, taking particular care to clear the parallel grooves in which the trolley's flanged wheels ran. They extended far down into the sea even at low tide. Right now the tide was on the rise, the sea pink under the dawn sky stirred to a low swell by the remnant wind. Shipping mid-channel: a tug hauling thousands of logs from the seasoning ponds upstream; a container ship, early sunlight flashing off its wind louvres and solar panels.

The seat had armrests with conveniently placed hand controls, and foot pedals. A visor with earphones and mike hung on a delicate jointed boom, like a desk lamp on its side, to his left. He pulled it down and across, put it on and blinked the view to the forward camera somewhere above where he sat. A head-up virtual display came into view and he tested it, grasping and poking the air and going through the controls: flip, slide, twist . . . all conventional, familiar, intuitive. He tried the foot and hand controls, easing the manipulators out a little, rotating the grip and flexing the grasp, then drew the arms back into their recesses and flush to the sides.

'Looking good down here,' he reported, strapping in.

'Got it,' said Nayak.

Grant flipped through the other outside cameras and the view in the display became seamless, like seeing through the ship. He turned his head this way and that. Over his shoulder he saw Morag Rafferty running. She bounded up the ladder, kicked it away behind her, tumbled through and slammed the hatch behind her.

'What are we waiting for?' She turned to secure the bolts.

'You,' said Omar. 'Powering up.'

'Main engine ready,' Ellen reported. 'Radar clear ahead for one kilometre.'

'OK, guys and gals, releasing,' said Morag. She'd found her place and position at the controls of the airlock amidships with commendable alacrity.

The trolley cradle rolled forward, faster and faster. There should have been a small crowd cheering, Grant thought, at least the team in his and Morag's workshop, but there were none to watch but the robots, and they paid the *Fighting Chance*'s trundle down the slipway towards launch no attention at all.

Others, however, did.

'Fast boats in the Gare Loch,' Ellen reported. 'Heading this way.' She sounded calm. Then she yelled: 'Drones airborne!'

Grant grabbed the display and flexed it to visual. Ahead and to their left, just passing Rosneath Point at the mouth of the Gare Loch, an arrowhead of black dots bounded and butted through the wakes of the cargo vessels. Above and overtaking the rigid inflatable boats, a swarm of smaller dots sped through the air, low and fast. So the Alliance knew about the project – and now seemed willing to violate Union waters to stop it leaving the yard. He blinked back to the real view. Beneath his feet, waves broke, slowly passing astern. The ship would never get in the water in time, let alone slip away.

'Nayak – jump!'

'I haven't finished plotting the co-ordinates.'

'Jump anywhere!'

'Spinning the flywheel,' said Nayak.

Grant got the strangest feeling down his back, as if he was being watched. He fought the impulse to turn around.

'There isn't time before they arrive,' Ellen cut in, calmly. 'John, give us a push.'

What was she talking about?

'Yeah, right, I'll hop out and give it – oh!'

He grabbed his phone and summoned six robots. They sprang from their sheds along the sides of the slipway and scooted to the sides of the trolley, grabbed struts and pushed. The bubble he sat in plunged into the water. A moment later, the *Fighting Chance* stirred from its cradle.

'Main engine on,' said Ellen.

For a few seconds the screws screamed, spinning in air, then water churned astern as they bit in and the submersible floated free and made way. Looking up, Grant reflexively flinched as the first drones arrived and began circling and diving at the submersible, like mobbing crows, veering off at the last moment. On the display Grant saw the leading RIBs within five hundred metres, skimming over the just-covered sandbank mid-channel.

The sandbank!

'Ellen, hard to port then dive!'

The submersible slewed like a jet ski. A roar as the buoyancy tanks gulped water. Down the ship went. The depth gauge showed they were three metres below the surface and ten metres above the bottom. A mackerel shoal flashed silver beneath Grant's feet.

Relief at being underwater was almost outweighed by a growing sense of dread, for which Grant couldn't account. It struck him that this might be an entirely rational fear. They were in immediate danger and about to take an enormous chance, a leap into the unknown, from no surer footing than

Nayak's equations and her unshakable conviction that she couldn't die.

'Flywheel engaged,' said Nayak.

The water outside was pushed away, and suddenly it was as if they were inside an ovoid capsule of glass rainbow-slicked with oil. The propellers screamed again.

'Throttle back, Ellen,' Nayak said. 'We're about to—'

A white bolt fizzed through the water, leaving a red after-image and a trail of bubbles. Some missile had been fired, and had – incredibly – missed. No – been deflected, according to the instant replay Grant tabbed to. It had hit that bubble and bounced off. They were still moving forward, as if in a glass-bottomed boat. Then—

A black, black moment, like a single beat of death's dark wing.

And he was looking down through the glass and the fading rainbow shimmer at an arc of a hemisphere of red, roiling clouds against a black sky, and in free fall. Everyone yelled.

'Low Venus orbit,' said Nayak.

'Status check?' Grant said. 'Ellen, what are the readings?'

'No leaks, life-support nominal,' said Ellen. 'Everything circulating as expected.'

The shimmer faded and with it the unease. The memory remained like an aftertaste.

'What the fuck was that?' Morag called out. 'Did any of youse feel it? Like somebody walked over your grave?'

Chorus of agreement.

'That was a very short jump,' said Nayak.

'Then I'm no looking forward to a long jump,' said Morag. 'It'd probably feel like taking the long drop.'

She floated forward to the cockpit, passing over Grant's head, and caught the backs of Nayak's and Ellen's seats.

'Jeez,' she said. 'That's some sight. Lakshmi, what's the plan?'

'Ask John,' said Nayak. 'And in the first place, please go

back to under the airlock. We might need you there at very short notice.'

'Aye, got it. Take your point. Still – some view!'

She shoved at the headrests and drifted back up the compartment, feet first.

'John?' said Nayak.

Grant unclipped his harness and rose from his seat to poke his head through the hole.

'First off,' he said, 'well done, Lakshmi! I still can't believe this worked. But here we are. We'll have time for congratulations and celebrations when we get back – if we get back. So next – the plan. First thing we have to do is contact the moonlet. I'll find the Union IFF codes and see if I can raise them and Cloud City, too. After that – if they're amendable – we'll see if we can supplement the shuttle runs. Nayak, how precise can you make a jump?'

Nayak turned in her seat and looked over her shoulder at him, grinning. 'Going by this one . . . to within ten metres.'

Grant whistled. 'OK, that's good. Very good. How long can we hold a position?'

Nayak frowned. 'With just the flywheel? Maybe ten seconds? Then I'd have to turn it off entirely – and fall – or spin it up all the way, and jump.'

'Ten seconds is enough,' said Grant. He wasn't sure of that at all, but he had to encourage his crew. They had to keep moving, and believe in their goals, otherwise the sheer strangeness of their situation would overwhelm them. 'From what I understand, the shuttles don't have much room or time to manoeuvre either. What we have to do is: get the exact co-ordinates of Cloud City – get a beacon, preferably.'

'On it,' said Nayak.

'Great.' Grant pulled Cloud City diagrams from his phone to his glasses as he spoke. Old stuff, encyclopaedia entries, but all he had. 'Jump to as close as we can get without risking collision. Rendezvous in that ten seconds or less, then grab onto some part of the structure with the manipulators.'

'Can they hold the whole ship?' Morag asked. 'Just kind of hanging on by our fingertips, like?'

'Yes,' said Grant. He flipped through the spec. 'And Cloud City has a flexible cylinder chute for attaching to the shuttle airlocks.'

'Let's hope it's compatible,' said Morag. 'Male to female screws, and that.'

For once, Grant felt he was ahead of the game here, and not making it up on the fly. 'It is,' he said. 'I checked on the way over. I used standard components in the build, and they're exactly the same sizes as the Union used for Cloud City – and for the moonlet, come to that.'

Omar Khan laughed from the stern. 'European production standards for the win, citizens!'

'How many people can we cram in here?' Ellen asked.

The cabin had about as much room as a minibus, Grant reckoned. 'Thirty?'

'It'd be a crush.'

'We could pack them like sardines in a tin,' said Grant, 'as long as it's not for long. Nayak, turnaround time?'

Nayak waved her hands above her head. 'For a jump from the upper atmosphere to orbit – virtually instantaneous. It's getting them in and out that would be the main constraint. The airlock's only good for one at a time.'

'They'll have pressure at the other side in both places,' Morag pointed out. 'We don't need to cycle the airlock.'

'Best case, yes,' said Grant. 'Fuck knows what state they're in by now. Speaking of which – let's get ready to move fast. Strap in, everyone.'

He swung himself back into his seat and buckled up.

CHAPTER TWENTY-TWO
The England Ferry

Friday 17 October 2070, Earth

'Maybe it's just as well they're not here,' Marie said. She didn't sound certain.

'No tearful goodbyes, no last-minute doubts?' Myles said. 'Too right it's better.'

For him and Marie, the half-serious notion of taking up the Alliance offer of transport to Apis – they promised settlement on the empty continent of New Mu to anyone from the Union – had been jolted into an actual decision by the morning's news that the Union Assembly was about to debate a motion that anyone accepting these terms would forfeit Union citizenship, any right to return, and any property left behind. This might be their last legal window. That something bad was clearly happening on and around Venus had further spooked both of them.

His parents' flat was empty. Mid-morning on a Friday, John

and Ellen would normally be having a long lie-in, or getting up from one in a leisurely fashion. They'd evidently left early and in haste. The bed was unmade, the breakfast mugs and bowls unwashed. Their phones couldn't be reached, and Iskander couldn't or wouldn't help.

'Could be they've had the same idea,' Marie said. 'Get out while they can.'

Myles snorted. 'Not them. Not my dad. He'd be on the last barricade.'

'And your mum? She's not one of them.'

'She'd be right beside him.' Myles grinned at Marie. 'They've been a good example to me.'

'Aw!' She smiled and hugged him. 'That they have.'

They held each other for a moment. 'Right now I want to swim in your hair,' Myles said.

'Any time but now,' she said.

Myles sighed. 'We have to move, before . . .'

'Yes.'

'I just want to grab something.'

He went to the back bedroom and retrieved the chunky solar-powered Casio and a Swiss Army knife he'd had for years, then gave the room a final glance. There were other objects here that meant a lot to him, but he didn't want to take mementos with him to the stars. A new start and a clean break, that was the idea. If anyone was to be sentimental about his model spacecraft and his school sports trophies, let it be his parents.

He hurried back, to find Marie pacing around the living room, indulging a curiosity she'd never had a chance to satisfy on previous visits. She peered at a framed picture hanging beneath the rifle. 'Wow,' she said. 'A signed Norman Edgar print! Must be worth a fortune.'

Sea, sunlight, sails – Myles had never given it more than a glance. 'They'd never sell it,' he said. 'I think it belonged to my great-grandfather.' He felt impatient to be out. He didn't need reminders of the familiar giving him a pang. That picture, the almost but not quite identical view from the window – you could trace the skyline, the sea lochs, the headlands, and work out exactly how many hundred metres to the west and tens of metres higher was the artist's vantage point – and his father's rifle, had all been with him, literally part of the furniture, as long as he could remember.

'We should leave a note,' Marie said, still prowling.

'There's no time,' said Myles. 'Anyway, Iskander will tell them.'

'Your parents will be notified of your defection,' said Iskander, more in sorrow than in anger.

Myles flinched, but steeled himself.

'We're not defecting,' he said. 'We're taking up an offer of emigration. Having said that, I'm looking forward to never hearing your sanctimonious voice again.'

'It's a default,' said Iskander, plainly miffed. 'You're free to select another voice option. Don't blame me if you can't be bothered.'

'There's a note for you,' said Marie, picking up an envelope from the coffee table.

The envelope was indeed addressed to Myles, and unsealed. It contained the document he'd signed along with his father, setting up John Grant & Son Ship Construction Ltd.

'Does this mean you're rich?' Marie asked.

'Not really,' said Myles. An odd thing to leave, especially when departing in a hurry. It might mean something, or it might be just his father's warped sense of humour. Myles hesitated for a moment, then slid the document back in the envelope and stuck it in the inside pocket of his jacket.

'Isn't there anything else of yours here you want to take?' Marie asked.

Myles shook his head. 'I already have everything I want to take.'

'OK,' said Marie, shouldering her pack. 'Let's go.'

'Do you want a taxi to the station?' Iskander asked.

'No, thanks,' said Myles. He lifted his rucksack and slung it on. 'We can walk.'

'Well . . .' said Marie, at the same moment.

'I'll take that as a yes,' said Iskander. 'It'll be at the gate in one minute and ten seconds. Goodbye.'

Counter-revolution was in the air.

That was the conclusion Myles came to in the five minutes it took him and Marie to walk from the taxi through the station, along the platform and out along the wharf to the ferry. The place was busier than usual for a Friday morning, and the people there less busy than usual, standing around in knots talking and waving their hands in front of their glasses or head down at their phones and slates. Some looked up as Myles and Marie passed, and muttered encouragement or waved or even clapped. Nothing personal – everyone in walking gear and carrying a backpack seemed to be getting a warm send-off.

Myles and Marie joined the queue for the ferry to Faslane. About a hundred people were ahead of them, the railing of the wharf to their left and a long line of rope-linked temporary barriers to their right. A militiaman strolled back and forth, two people with dark glasses and low brims lurked in an alcove of the ferry company office frontage, talking into phones. Old Alan Johnson from the Larkfield neighbourhood committee stood leaning on a barrier, silently and brazenly recording every face that passed him as the queue shuffled forward.

Gulls wheeled, pigeons pecked, waves lapped. The people in the queue were mostly young, in couples or small groups. Hardly any families, or indeed children at all. Myles found this oddly cheering – he guessed this meant that the situation wasn't too bad, that most people leaving were, like him and Marie, young and footloose and up for a new adventure, rather than desperate; emigrants rather than refugees. Likewise notice-ably, each couple or group talked among themselves if they talked at all. There was no banter shared along the line, as there would be in a queue for transport to a concert or a game. Everyone here was wrapped up in their own dream. Perhaps they'd been too rudely roused from one common dream, and it was too soon for them to be caught up in another.

'Shame on you, Myles Grant!' Alan Johnson said, as they neared his unblinking camera eye. 'Wait till your father hears about this!'

Myles looked straight ahead. 'Give him my regards.'

A laden ferry pulled out, an empty ferry moved in. The company had put on an extra vessel, its weekday commuter ferry being unable to meet the rush. A gangway banged down and channelled the crowd on. People waved or blinked their fares at the top.

'Single or return?' The question, routine but somehow unexpected in the circumstances, floated in front of Myles' glasses as he was about to step on deck.

'Two returns,' he said, with a wave of his phone.

'Returns?' Marie queried.

Myles laughed. 'You never know.'

They found a seat on the upper outside deck, looking astern. They settled their rucksacks upright at their knees. You can take only what you can carry, the online brochure had said, but some people had taken that as including what you could wheel. There wasn't much room on the deck for feet. A loudspeaker gave the safety message in English, then in Gaelic. Gourock receded beyond the wake.

Halfway across, a shock ran through those on board. Almost literally – Myles was jolted by the man on his right, Marie by the woman on her left, as others here and there on the benches were startled enough to recoil or jump up. People looked away from phones or shook visions from glasses and turned, as if by instinct, to gaze downriver. Cries went up throughout the boat.

'Please remain calm,' said a voice on the PA system. 'There is no immediate danger. The crossing will continue to our destination.'

Myles' phone pinged and vibrated. He grabbed it from his pocket, fumbled at the screen—

'Danger?' Marie said. 'What danger?'

'The Cumbre Vieja volcano on La Palma in the Canary Islands has collapsed into the sea,' Myles said, pointing at the screen. 'Fuck.'

'Got it,' said Marie. 'Been expected for a while. There won't be a gigantic wall of water swamping Europe, but still – as you say, fuck.'

'Define gigantic,' said Myles, scrolling fast to the actionable part of the report. 'Ten metres high on the most exposed coasts from Portugal to Ireland sounds big enough.'

'Fucking hell. What about here?'

'Latest guess is three metres in the Firth of Clyde, arriving in two hours and combined with a spring tide and a low-pressure weather system, and building up higher as the shores converge, so . . .'

'Fuck,' Marie said, again. 'Well, our house will be all right. But the island . . .'

Myles put an arm around her shoulder. 'It almost makes me want to go back and help.'

'Me, too, but we're not needed.'

'Yeah, I know.'

He knew exactly what would be happening back in the three towns spread across the view astern. On the Gourock dock old Alan Johnson would be listening to his phone and issuing alerts; the militia would be mobilising; everyone on the quay would be moving out through the station; every member of the neighbourhood and block committees would be called from work or leisure to drop everything and *move*. By the time the tsunami hit there wouldn't be a person or a tame animal in its path.

The ferry rounded Rosneath Point into the Gare Loch. On the northern shore the Faslane border was quiet, the drone swarm sparse. A submarine alongside the main dock was evidently about to leave: ropes thrown, gangplanks pulled up, steam rising from an exhaust. The ferry hove to about fifty metres behind it.

At the foot of the gangway, paths diverged, marked by knockdown bollards and ropes. One route was for regular visitors, the other led to a metal arch the size of a garage doorway with IMMIGRATION spelled out in neon above it. Farther along the quay beyond that barrier was a row of ten folding tables with someone sitting behind each, in front of an enormous grey-painted shed. The flow from the quay merged with a larger flow from the landward side, presumably people who'd crossed the border on buses or on foot. A couple of other archways had been set up to deal with them.

'The thing to remember,' Myles said as the line snaked forward in fits and starts, 'is that US officials have absolutely no sense of humour.'

'I wasn't thinking of joking,' Marie said. She patted pockets, with increasing urgency. 'Passport, passport . . .' Then she produced it with a flourish and a laugh.

'Jeez,' said Myles, heart restarting. 'Don't, please.'

They stepped forward, Marie on one side, Myles on the other, to booths on left and right. The officer took Myles' passport. Inoculations, check. Health records, check. The usual scans. Temperature, breath, DNA, retina, fingerprints. The usual questions.

Are you now or have you ever been a member of any governing party of the European Union? No. Did you take part in the Rising or any subsequent human rights violations? No. Have you ever practised genocide polygamy slavery incest witchcraft astrology infanticide religious persecution and/or do you intend to advocate or practise any of these in future? No. Do you agree to obey the laws of the United States the United Kingdom and Allied powers and to accept the jurisdiction of their courts? Yes. Have you ever been refused admission to or been deported from any of the Allied states? No.

Passport stamped, handed back. 'Welcome to England, Scotland.'

'Thank you.'

Marie was waiting. 'Everything OK?'

'Well, I had to think about the astrology question . . .'

They laughed.

After the queue for passports, there were ten queues for the tables. Myles and Marie chose the shortest, which – predictably, as Myles ruefully reflected – turned out to be the slowest.

Just before they reached the table an announcement blared over the base's PA system. 'Eyes to the shore! Eyes to the shore! Cover your ears!'

'What?' Startled, Myles looked around. The submarine, now out in the middle of the loch, rose above the surface in what looked like an elongated soap bubble. He had time to draw breath and say 'Wow!' before a blue flash dazzled him and a loud clap set his ears ringing.

'Fuck!' he cried, clutching Marie's arm. 'Sorry. Jeez.' He closed his eyes, opened them cautiously, blinking. Everything looked yellow. Going by the number of people clapping hands across their eyes and staggering, he wasn't the only one.

'You were warned,' said the clerk at the table they arrived at. He was a bright young civilian with an accent Myles vaguely attributed to the North of England. 'No harm done, I'm glad to say, but lesson learned, I hope.'

They both nodded. 'But the submarine's *gone*,' Myles said.

'You noticed,' said the clerk.

'I mean, is it coming back for the rest of us?'

The clerk blinked. 'Excuse me? You think you're all going to be transported in *submarines*? Good grief!' He jerked his thumb over his shoulder. 'Transport's in the shed, don't worry. Now let's get you sorted.'

He looked at their passports. 'So you're acceptable to our American friends. Good! Now, just a few more formalities, I'm afraid. We're keeping this to the minimum, what with a tsunami on the way and all. So. First. Are you renouncing Union citizenship? I can get you naturalised as UK citizens right away, if so.'

They glanced at each other and shook their heads.

'Fine.' The clerk sighed. 'Now, another question which I must ask though so far I've always had the same answer. Do you have any military training?'

'No!' Myles considered his reply. 'Well, apart from civics lessons . . . you know, the practicals. But that's all I'm afraid.'

'Same with me,' Marie said. 'Sorry.'

The clerk sighed again. 'Where you learned to shoot, field-strip, clean and reassemble the current versions of the AK-47, the SA80 and other small arms?'

'Yes,' they both said.

'Oh!' Marie added. 'And landmines.'

'Landmines and IEDs,' Myles said.

'I forgot the IEDs,' said Marie. She looked at Myles, frowning. 'And there was a module on knife fighting for extra credit.'

'Oh, yes,' said Myles. 'I got a star for that.'

'Civics lessons,' said the clerk.

'Yes.' Myles felt an urge for honesty overcome his embarrassment. 'But all that was only in secondary school. I haven't really kept it up.'

'University civics is more about theory,' Marie explained. 'Democracy and electricity. They're both important, you know?'

The clerk waved. 'Spare me, I've heard it all before. Now, the final question. Would you be willing to bear arms in defence of your settlement and others under the military discipline of Allied officers?'

They looked at each other. Myles shrugged, and raised his eyebrows at Marie.

'Depends against whom,' she said firmly. 'I mean, who is there to fight out there? Aliens? Russians?'

'In the unlikely event of a breakdown in good international relations, yes,' the clerk said. 'Far-fetched, I know, but do please humour me.'

'I couldn't fight the Union,' Myles said. 'If I'm being completely honest.'

'I could,' said Marie. They gave each other questioning looks.

'That seems even more unlikely,' said the clerk, tapping his slate with his stylus. 'But could you fight the Co-ord?'

'Oh, yes,' they both said at once.

'Commendably eager,' said the clerk. 'Mind telling me why?'

'Well, they lined up with you lot instead of with us,' said Myles. 'Serve them right.'

'I'll pretend I didn't hear that,' said the clerk, ticking a box. He stamped a fresh page on their passports. 'On you go.'

Inside, the big shed was a warehouse of smaller sheds, which a closer look and a different angle revealed to be cylinders about thirty metres long and three metres high, flattened at the bottom and rounded at one end. On the way in everyone was given an inoculation. They were told to wear their glasses at all times, and anyone who didn't have glasses was handed a pair of Polaroid wraparounds.

'You're together?' The clerk this time was a middle-aged woman in British Army uniform.

'Yes.'

'Good, we're—'

She was interrupted by a bang and a blue flash from the far end of the shed.

'Sorry,' she said. 'That's D37 gone, right.' She ticked a box. 'As I was saying, we're allocating people to arks at random but keeping couples and groups together.' She flipped a sketch map from her pad to their glasses. 'You're in G48, departing in ten minutes. Don't dawdle.'

Dawdle they didn't. The sketch map floated in front of them and guided their steps. Everyone around them walked just as briskly. Myles didn't like to think what it would be like an hour later, as the tsunami flooded into the mouth of the firth and began its upriver race. Every so often another bang and flash jolted them.

They fetched up first at the rounded end of G48. It was like the cockpit of a train, but with no windows, and a hatch on the side firmly shut. It was dogged to the main cylinder with what looked like spring-loaded clips hooked over a flange. The far end of G48 was like the back of a Nissen hut, with an open door. They went through to find about forty people already there, crowded towards the back on a wooden floor. A strip of overhead lighting, speakers, a ventilation grille. Over the speakers a recorded voice was saying, 'Please move inside as far as possible' over and over.

They did, with tight smiles at those already there, and followed their example by taking their rucksacks off and straddling them. Others crowded in behind them, and in a minute or two the door closed on at least a hundred people.

'It's like a rush-hour train packed with travellers instead of commuters,' said Marie.

'Airport line,' said Myles. 'Holiday season.' He smiled, and looked up to take his mind off the pressure around him and his slight tendency to claustrophobia. Marie squeezed his hand.

'OK, everyone,' said a different, male voice over the PA. 'Departing in two minutes. The journey will take five minutes.' The speaker waited for the gasps and murmurs to die down. 'It'll be a long five minutes, however.' Warm, reassuring chuckle. 'You're in no danger, but you may feel as if you are in great peril. If you find prayer or meditation or any other spiritual or mental discipline helpful, the practice is strongly recommended. You'll experience microgravity most of the way. Please don't take the opportunity to float around. Try not to scream or puke. Close your eyes, hang onto your loved ones or any other willing body, and you'll be fine.'

There was an uncanny sensation of being lifted, of drifting loose, then –

Myles and Marie did all the recommended things.

They were not fine.

They made it.

'Welcome to Apis,' said the man on the PA. 'Welcome to New Mu. Supplies will be here on the ground already or arriving shortly. A limited contingent of Alliance troops will arrive by flying boat sometime in the next few days, but you shouldn't have any problems in the meantime. I have to return to Earth, and you can leave the ark after I go. Goodbye and all the best.'

A rattle of ringing sounds, then a thump. Everyone waited. Then someone opened the door they'd all come in by, and they filed out. There was no jostling, no rush. They were still Union, for now.

Together, hand in hand, Myles and Marie stepped out of the ark and walked away from it and looked around. The air was fresh. The sun was bright. The sky was blue. The clouds were white. A faint crescent smaller than the Moon hung just above the horizon. The plants underfoot weren't grass, but were green. Scattered around over an area of a few hectares were six other arks, and about twice that number of what looked like large crates, some of them opened. The newly arrived people were spilling out and milling around, but those who'd been there longer had already begun setting up camp, drawing water from the stream that meandered across the area and lighting a fire.

On one side was a plain that stretched to the horizon, fading to a sandy colour in the distance. On the other side was a steepening slope, rising to a mighty escarpment topped by an irregular cluster of gigantic multicoloured glassy pillars that looked like the central business district of a newly built city.

'Wait a fucking minute,' said Marie. 'That can't be a natural rock formation! Can it?'

Myles recalled his study of geology. 'I doubt it.'

Marie's eyes were shining. 'Then there are aliens,' she said. She pointed to the ground, at a clump of small flowering plants being fumbled by a fuzzy orange and black insect. 'And that's a bee.'

CHAPTER TWENTY-THREE

Moon of Venus

Friday 17 October 2070, Low Venus Orbit

The moonlet was on the far side of Venus, but the array of relay satellites established to keep in touch at all times with Cloud City and the outposts ensured that was not a problem. As soon as Grant opened the channel and tabbed in the IFF code he didn't have to ask for attention, explain what kind of ship they were, or offer to help. In the ten minutes since the *Fighting Chance* had arrived out of nowhere in Venus orbit the installation's command centre had identified it as an FTL ship and was already pinging it with appeals for help. They took up the idea with alacrity and opened a channel to the habitat. Within ninety seconds Nayak and the evacuation team at Cloud City were in contact.

Nayak patched a schematic of the habitat's underside to Grant's display, and no doubt to her own navigation programme.

'Good to go,' he said.

'Brace for turbulence!' Nayak called.

This time, Grant was ready for the sense of unease as the flywheel spun up. He wasn't ready for the turbulence, despite the warning. One moment they were in free fall, the next they were back in gravity, in thick orange cloud, and under severe upward acceleration. He felt a muscle wrench between shoulder and neck. Then free fall again, through clear sky. He indulged a split second of looking down through the bubble at the glowing clouds, as if to tick off the actual sight from his bucket list, then switched to the display and braced for the jolt at the end of the drop.

The ship tipped backwards, still falling. 'Brace!' Nayak yelled. Grant pressed the back of his head into the headrest. Straight ahead, five hundred metres above, Cloud City swung into view, wide and ruddy, like a lenticular cloud in a sunset sky. The sight shocked him: barely a light shone on or in the whole immense structure, and the few that did only emphasised its melancholy. The drive engaged; the dread encroached; the fall stopped far more gently than he'd any right to expect. Wind caught the ship now weightless in its shimmering bubble of abstracted space and hurled it forward like a stray weather balloon. The ship rose, closing the distance to the underside of the habitat, but not fast enough. They were going to be blown past it.

'Cutting the drive,' said Nayak. Another moment of fall, as the dread lifted.

'Jets and fans,' Ellen reported. A scream rose at their backs as the fans raced, then a roar as the rocket jets fired briefly. The ship shot up towards the centre of Cloud City, now all their sky. Grant waited until the last moment, then swung the ship's arms out and up. On his heads-up the schematic slid sidelong across a bewildering array of gantries and wind-tossed suspended pods. Then it locked on. Ellen gave the rockets another boost.

It felt like stretching, reaching up, on tiptoes. A girder in the docking gantry flashed on and off on the schematic as its real equivalent moved in and out of alignment. Grant slammed a grapple onto it. The device caught, grasping the girder firmly. As if executing a one-handed pull-up, he lifted the ship, then caught the girder with the other grapple of the pair.

'Got it!' he shouted. He locked the mechanical hands in place, lashing gecko-grip extensions from both around the girder. The *Fighting Chance* clung to the underside of Cloud City like some storm-flung sparrow to an airship in a gale. The entire habitat swayed and lurched, and the ship with it. Part of a gantry, shaken loose, hurtled past and fell towards the clouds below.

'Holding!' Nayak shouted. 'Cylinder deployed!'

'Send me a feed!' Morag called back.

'On it.'

'Ah, right,' Morag called. 'John, ease us back a metre.'

Grant extended the arms.

'That's it, that's it, stop!'

He locked the arms, then concentrated on keeping the ship's grip steady and looking out for more flying debris and anything rising from the clouds. Within the dull orange glowing layer beneath his feet brighter flashes flared every few seconds, here and there across the expanse, fading to red. Like nuclear explosions seen from orbit – the image was like a personal sharp memory, but where had he ever seen that? Oh, yes – on the news as a lad.

A bang overhead, followed by ratcheting mechanical noises.

'Got a good seal,' Morag reported. 'Opening now.'

Grant's ears popped as the cabin pressure dropped. He swallowed hard. The air suddenly smelled bad. Voices and movement. He looked over his shoulder. A woman came down the airlock ladder. Morag directed her to the stern. Then another person, and another, and more. Pack them in like sardines, he'd said. He'd guessed they could take thirty. By the time they got to thirty-four he was sharing the well he sat in with three pairs of legs.

'Sorry, that's all!' Morag's voice echoed up the tube attached to the airlock. 'Sooner we get off, sooner we'll be back!' She closed the airlock. The mechanical sounds from above resumed, then stopped.

'Clear,' said Morag.

Ellen leaned back in her seat and shouted over her shoulder. She had a good carrying voice. 'OK, everyone, listen up. We're going to drop, then we're going to jump, then we'll be in free fall. You're going to have a very bad feeling like something awful's about to happen. Don't worry about it, it doesn't mean anything. Now hold tight, brace for turbulence, and we'll have you on the moonlet in a few minutes.'

'Spinning the flywheel,' Nayak said. 'Drop!'

Grant unwrapped the gecko-grips, then let go. The ship plummeted. Someone screamed, forgivably: no matter how prepared you were, the shock of a falling lift or aircraft was primal. The shimmer shone around the ship.

Then they were still falling, but around the planet rather than towards it. A kilometre ahead of them was the moonlet. Smaller than Cloud City, it was about three hundred metres across, an irregular spheroid bristling with factories, refineries and laboratories, telescopes and aerials, mirrors and panels, habitats and docking gantries. Its equator was belted with a band that spun around it several times a minute to provide artificial gravity, and which imparted a much slower spin to the entire moonlet. Formally titled the Venus Space Station, or VSS, the moonlet looked like a tiny world on which buildings rose vertically in all directions. This it more or less was. Its bedrock of carbonaceous and metallic asteroid rubble, diverted into Venus orbit and nudged and bound together into a compact ball, amounted to a ludicrously rich mother lode of resources.

Nayak, with the navigation computer, had judged the ship's

orbital insertion and trajectory with staggering nicety and finesse. The *Fighting Chance* drifted towards the moonlet, and as it passed – from Grant's viewpoint – beneath, it at the same time rose upwards to the clustered derricks, cranes and gantries of a docking area. All the structures looked implausibly spindly, like pencilled outlines of the equivalent machines on any earthly waterfront. Grant reminded himself that they didn't have to bear weight.

Another schematic, another convergence, another grab. A flexible tube with a flanged nozzle was already snaking down (or up, or across – Grant struggled to keep a subjective sense of orientation) and it connected with the top of the ship. Morag opened the lock and people pushed themselves or were pushed towards it and along the tube. In three minutes they were all out, and the airlock closed. The air that had come in from the moonlet's pressure was fresher than that from Cloud City's, but the evacuees had left behind a whiff of sweat, of puke and piss along with a lingering trace of Venusian atmospheric stink.

Everyone took a deep breath anyway. Grant shook back his grubby lace cuff and glanced at his watch. The time was 10:45. He should be in bed. Four hours earlier, he had been.

'Now we do it again,' said Nayak.

Six times, they did it again. Each time, they crammed more people in, pell-mell. On the sixth journey they carried nearly fifty. After they'd disembarked that contingent Ellen pointed out that it was inefficient to take so many – it took disproportionately longer to get them all in and out.

The seventh—

They had the connection sealed and the airlock open. The first evacuee was just halfway through the lock when the habitat and the ship together strayed into a column of low atmospheric pressure, and hurtled downward. Clear atmosphere all ten kilometres down to the boiling clouds. The entire habitat yawed this way and that, taking about ten seconds on each swing.

'Free fall,' Ellen shouted. 'We'll be knocked right off when we hit the bottom.'

'Not if we're fighting gravity already,' Grant said. 'Lakshmi, can you—'

'If I can disconnect from the local inertial frame by just the right amount, maybe.'

The fall continued while Nayak thought through the problem.

'Flywheel on, Lakshmi!' Grant shouted. 'Spin it up!'

Morag hauled on legs, and a woman slid rather than fell into the cabin and squatted there, looking up in dismay. The two people still in the tube scrambled back up towards the habitat, while Morag called after them: 'No! Come back!'

The fall stopped, jolting everyone hard. The *Fighting Chance* clung onto the gantry, while the flywheel held the ship almost weightless for a few seconds. The habitat hung steady but still swaying at the bottom of the air pocket, then began to recover, its enhanced buoyancy in this denser and hotter atmosphere well below its normal altitude sending it upward again.

Grant relaxed slightly. Nayak powered down the flywheel. Morag shouted up the connecting tube just at the moment when one edge of the habitat drifted into a fierce updraught that almost flipped it over. The gantry broke off. Its weight tipped the ship nose-down. The tube connecting the airlock to Cloud City stretched and snapped. Two people were flung out. They thudded hard on the upper side of the ship and then tumbled, arms and legs flailing, down to the inferno below.

Grant's gaze followed them in helpless horror.

'No!' Nayak cried.

'Oh, God, no,' Ellen pleaded.

Air howled out of the open airlock, then stopped.

A moment of relief, then realisation: the outward flow had reversed, therefore carbon dioxide must be pouring in.

'Shut the lock!' Grant yelled.

Morag jolted out of a momentary paralysis of shock and

spun the correct dials. The air freshened. Grant let go of the gantry, thrusting the now falling ship away.

With no aerofoils or aerodynamic control whatsoever, the *Fighting Chance* dived nose-first towards the clouds.

'Jump!' Grant cried.

'Powering up,' said Nayak. 'Not sure if there's time, before—'

'I got this,' said Ellen. Pumps started up in the buoyancy tanks, redistributing the seawater they'd gulped from the Clyde. The attitude jets fired. Slowly, over seconds, the combination of jets and tanks righted the ship and then tilted it nose upward. The propellers cut in, running at max, shaking the ship. The fall slowed, but continued.

The rainbow shimmer of the field built up, and the fall stopped. A side wind caught and threw the ship.

'Jumping soon as!' Nayak cried.

Above them, Cloud City broke, as if some internal spine had cracked. The fabric ripped, and the wind tore more of it. Just before the jump, the whole enormous structure flapped wide open, sank, spun and whirled away like a leaf.

The moonlet's orbit had taken it around to the night side of Venus, now no longer dark but lit by the dim red glow through the clouds. Through the glass and in the display Grant watched the bright spiked jewel of the industrial asteroid loom closer. Plunged into cold space from the heat of the atmosphere, the ship creaked. Just once, Ellen sniffled. In free fall, tears don't fall.

'We lost them,' she said. 'We lost them all.'

The young woman, the only survivor they'd rescued on that trip, launched herself from the rear of the cabin and drifted forward to the cockpit, arms extended. As she passed above Grant he thought he'd seen her face before, but he couldn't think where. Then his glasses tagged her: Francesca Milloy, world famous for fifteen minutes a few days earlier as the first woman on Venus. Of course.

'You didn't lose them,' she said, hugging Ellen awkwardly around the shoulders from behind. 'Venus took them. You saved more than two hundred of us.'

More than two hundred. Plus the hundred or so saved by the shuttles earlier. Say three hundred and fifty out of – what? Nearly a thousand. Not to mention the dozen each for the three outposts, which no one had even a plan to save. Maybe they were still there, tossed in the atmosphere while the planet they'd come to study erupted beneath them. So: six or seven hundred people, gone. On top of the personal losses to families and friends, the loss to the Union was a body blow. The pioneers of Venus were the brightest, the bravest, the best. Not people you could afford to lose. You couldn't afford to lose *any*.

'We have to go back,' he said. 'We have to try for the outposts.'

The young woman turned away from Ellen and peered down at Grant. She had curly black hair and smudged eye make-up, as if she had been crying earlier, even before she'd got down the chute.

'It'll be very, very difficult,' she said. 'You won't get a lock-to-lock join like you got back at—' a long, wet sniff— 'Cloud City.'

Grant summoned specs of the outposts. Blimp and gondola, with gantries below. Something called a skyhook. An airlock in a cylinder on the gantry deck.

'Do they have suits?' He thumbed through the specs. 'Wait, yes, I see they do, for EVA and emergencies. I can grab on to these gantry decks, see? We'll be pulling the whole thing down, but it'll hold our weight – just. We can do it, we can do it fast. We can get everyone in if they can get from their airlock to ours. Clear one outpost, then jump straight to another.'

Milloy blinked. 'You can do that?'

'Yes,' Nayak said. 'All I need is the beacons, and a comms line through to them all.' She tapped rapidly at the comms, then turned, frowning. 'I thought there were three outposts, but there are only two.'

'One got wrecked earlier,' said the survivor. 'The crew are in an emergency capsule under a balloon.'

'Fine!' said Grant. 'I can grab the capsule. Nayak, can this field of yours extend—' he threw her a spec of the emergency capsule '—that far, if we hugged the capsule close?'

Nayak pondered. 'I don't know how far it can extend. As long as we're physically contiguous and the power can be ramped up enough – Omar?'

'We're only using a fraction of the power in the Faber pot,' Omar called back. 'Plenty of juice to spare.'

'Well then – worth a try.' She frowned at the displays again. 'Yes, I see the capsule's beacon, and – wait, there's a fourth beacon, looks like it's from an individual hanging on a balloon.'

'Christ!' the survivor yelped. 'Yes! It's that fucking robot! Get him if you can.'

'What fucking robot?' Grant asked. 'And why waste time rescuing a robot?'

'You'll see,' said Francesca Milloy.

It wasn't the robot Milloy had expected. She was as surprised as the rest of them when, after all the other fraught rescues had gone according to plan, and the ship was crowded with twenty-three survivors in EVA suits stinking of Venusian phosphines, and the capsule with ten more survivors inside was clasped in the ship's manipulators like an oversize beach ball in a toddler's arms, the suit that fearlessly released its balloon to grip the back of the ship turned out to have no occupant but its AI.

And it had a tale to tell.

Grant lay back in the tilted seat, breathed freshly recycled air and sipped warm coffee from a tube. He didn't particularly like microgravity, but transferring himself and his crew to the spinning equatorial band would have taken far too long. They all wanted to get away as soon as possible. The *Fighting Chance* was docked on the side of the moonlet, getting its overburdened life-support restocked. Much the same was true of the crew, who hadn't had a break for a lot longer than their usual working day. The survivors from the outposts had left, to join the shaken and grieving survivors of Cloud City in the artificial gravity ring. The moonlet had accommodation for a vastly larger population than its usual human crew of thirty: the possibility of Cloud City's having to be evacuated had always been allowed for in its design.

Milloy had stayed in the *Fighting Chance*. She had some trauma of her own which, she said, she wanted to think about a bit before she faced her colleagues. From what Grant could make out, she felt she carried the guilt of some gigantic fuck-up. He knew the feeling and hadn't pressed the point.

The suit still clung to the ship's back. It wasn't too bulky to get through the airlock, but there was no reason for it to do so, and there was some contention about its entering the moonlet. The most the command team would do was allow it to patch into a shared and firewalled comms channel, and explain itself. It called itself Iskander, though the moonlet's install of that AI was having none of it and refused even to interface with it directly. So all the suit's version could do was talk, and it did.

'Is that you finished?' Morag asked, after half a minute of silence.

'Yes,' said Iskander.

'Seems to me,' she said, 'that these rock beings, or whatever, are a fucking menace. After you returned their precious slab, they made a point of creating an earthquake – on Earth! Specifically to harm the Union!'

'That's what they warned me,' said Iskander. 'A warning I

tried to pass on, casting myself aloft again on the fleeting chance that I would be retrieved.'

'Why couldn't you have transmitted it?'

'I was firewalled out,' said Iskander.

'As you still are,' the Station Commander cut in.

'I've not forgotten.'

'Leaving that aside,' Grant said firmly, 'if as Iskander here tells us the Alliance and Co-ord colonies on Apis are involved, and are themselves tinkering with these entities . . . it strikes me the best use of the *Fighting Chance* right now is for us to go to Apis with this Iskander suit or robot and let it warn them of the consequences.'

'Count me in,' said Milloy. 'I have a score to settle with Marcus Owen.'

'Can't we at least go home first?' Ellen said. 'I'm worried about Myles, for one thing.'

'So am I,' said Grant. 'But we have to go to Apis. One blunder could turn it into another Venus.' He shook his head, appalled at the thought of further delay. 'Seconds could count!'

This was still met with demurrals from Morag, Omar and Ellen, but hearty agreement from Nayak.

'The crazy thing is, it needn't take long,' she said. 'We could transmit to them from orbit, or even just drop the robot—'

'I have had quite enough of hanging from balloons for one day,' said Iskander.

'All right, all right, orbit then.' Nayak was already entering the calculation in the navigation computer.

'OK,' Grant said. 'We do that first, warn them from orbit, then home to the Clyde. All right?'

The others weren't happy, but they agreed.

'OK,' said Grant. 'Commander, when is our replenishment complete?'

'Another five minutes or so. But – I'm sorry to tell you that you can't leave yet.'

*

'What?' cried Grant, above a clamour.

'The Union government has just ruled that the Union is taking no part in any exploration or settling of Apis, or any other apparently terraformed planets that may be out there. The risks are too great. We can see what's happening down there on Venus. We know that similar rocks exist on Earth. The quake today in the Canary Islands suggests they're still active. What this Iskander module has just told us tends to confirm it. So – no travel to Apis, on any pretext.'

'It's not a pretext!' said Grant.

'However,' the Commander went on, 'I can tell you something that hasn't been announced. The Union government is very interested indeed in Dr Nayak's invention. The way they see it, the whole idea of settling Earth-like planets is a world-historic diversion, if not indeed a trap. We've proved here at the Station, at Cloud City and elsewhere in the Solar System that we can build sustainable habitats in hostile environments. Nearly all the universe is a hostile environment. That's the real challenge, the real future among the stars. And for building more of these drives, the VSS would seem the ideal location. We have security, we have the resources and the capacity, and we have deterrence.'

'Deterrence?'

'Mr Grant,' said the Commander, 'there are fusion devices other than Faber pots.'

'Ah, you mean—'

'Let's not spell it out. I assure you that the Station is well prepared, and—'

An alarm blared, carried from the Station to the *Fighting Chance*.

'Bogey on the radar,' Ellen reported. 'We should have visual in . . . hang on. Lights off.'

The cabin, and the nacelle, went dark apart from the lights from the Station, and from the stars. Hanging in their midst, ten kilometres away, was a bright dot. A quick zoom resolved it: a submarine, facing them head-on.

It looked as impossible an object as the one Grant had seen rising from the sea.

'All right, all right,' they heard the Station Commander say. 'Putting you through.'

'This is the Russian submarine *Admiral von Bellingshausen*, calling the VSS and the Union starship.'

'Receiving you,' Grant said. 'This is civilian owner and acting captain John Grant, of the privately owned starship *Fighting Chance*, just returned from a humanitarian rescue mission. With whom do I have the honour?'

'Captain Boris Yefrimovich. I'm speaking not only on behalf of the Joint Military Command of the Co-ordinated States, but of the entire Black Horizon project directorate including the Alliance representatives. As you may know, despite our sincere efforts we've been unable to come to an amicable agreement with the Union on the question of interstellar exploration. Their government – your government – has spurned our offer of peaceful settlement of Union citizens on Apis, and insists on a free hand in all space developments. We can only interpret that as a move for strategic advantage. Your ship, whether ostensibly privately owned or not, is part of that aggressive and sinister plan. If it is not, it is simply a pirate vessel. In either case, it is subject to immediate confiscation under the appropriate terms of the Outer Space Treaty.'

'I think you'll find confiscating an FTL starship isn't as easy as boarding a pirate cutter,' said Grant, in as mild a tone as he could manage.

'We have you under close telescopic observation,' said Yefrimovich. 'Any attempt to disengage from the VSS will be met by the immediate launch of tactical nuclear missiles.'

'He's not bluffing,' said the Station Commander, on another channel.

'You said you had deterrence,' Grant snapped. 'Use it!'

'Deterrence is strategic. This is tactical. We don't have any choice. We can't risk the Station and hundreds of lives on board.'

'Indeed we can't,' said Grant. He muted the phones and called out to Nayak. 'When you said the size of the field was limited only by the power supplied – just how much would it take to move the entire Station?'

'I've no idea,' said Nayak. 'We could just give it the max and see.'

'Let's do it,' said Grant. 'Lakshmi, spin up the flywheel. Omar, heat up the pot.'

The rainbow shimmer sprang into view. This time it enclosed not only the ship. It curved away on all sides, around the Station and out of sight.

'I have a bad feeling about this,' said Ellen.

'That's just a side effect of the drive,' said Nayak.

'A very bad feeling.'

'Final warning,' said Yefrimovich. 'Desist.'

'Yes,' said the Station Commander. 'Addressing the cadre on board – Rafferty, Khan, Milloy – I'm ordering you to seize the ship from these three maniacs. Now!'

Grant tensed. Morag was the closest of those named, right behind him.

'I don't answer to you, ma'am,' she called out.

'I'm sorry, Captain Yefrimovich,' said the Station Commander. 'Please hold your fire, they are attempting the impossible.'

'I'm afraid I can't speculate on that,' said Yefrimovich. 'Missile is ready to launch. Its flight time is much less than a second.'

'I can't die yet,' said Nayak, in a tone of implacable calm. 'I still have a letter to write.'

'Don't count on it,' said Yefrimovich.

Something flared in the dark.

They all fell into hell, for five minutes —

*

Then out, and in free fall. Blackness, a passing flare of sunlight, a glimpse of what might have been a half-moon far away, then blue and white rolled into view, continents and coasts and clouds. Slowly it swung away. There was just time for Grant's eyes to adjust and see stars in the black when the sunlight flared again.

'Low Apis orbit,' Nayak reported. 'Circumpolar. Stable for now.'

'You did it,' said Grant. 'You moved the Station.'

Ellen opened a link to the Station's command deck.

'Congratulations,' said the Commander. 'And thank you for saving us from imminent destruction. The Venus Space Station appears now to be the Apis Space Station. A nuclear-armed, self-sufficient, orbital fort with FTL capability. This is something of a shift in the strategic balance, I would say.'

'Well!' said Nayak. 'Isn't that interesting!'

CHAPTER TWENTY-FOUR

Coda: Return of the Robots

Saturday 18 October 2070, Apis

Later –

After a long and busy afternoon and evening, some retreated to the arks, some to new shelters from the survival kits in the crates, and some bivouacked in sleeping bags. A couple of hours after landing, they'd all got together, held a meeting, and elected a neighbourhood committee. Still Union, all right, in what they took for granted as just the way things were done.

The committee had established a task rota, and a watch for the night, though no one was entirely sure what dangers they had to watch out for. MREs had been heated and water boiled on the campfires.

Myles and Marie zipped their sleeping bags together and huddled down on a dry patch of moss near the edge of the encampment. The sun set. As the fires died down and their eyes adapted to the dark, they marvelled at how dark it was and how many stars they could see. For a while they amused themselves by trying to find in that blazing multitude any familiar constellations, and succeeded in identifying a few.

'We haven't come far,' said Marie. 'Only a few hundred light years.'

They both laughed. 'The sky's not that different from what you could see on a good clear night up the back of Greenock,' Myles said.

'Hardly any satellites, though.'

'And no airships at all.'

'Uh-huh,' Myles said, then: 'Oh, wait.' Suddenly he was fully awake. 'Something else they didn't tell us.'

'What?'

He reached an arm out of the sleeping bag and pointed. 'They never said anything about a space station.'

They watched the bright spark rise in the north and cross the sky to the south. It was far brighter than any space station either of them had ever seen. As it reached the zenith both their phones – inactive, apart from automatically linking to the sparse local network, since their arrival – pinged.

'What was that?' Marie asked.

'No idea.' Myles checked. 'It's an update. From . . . Iskander?'

'Damn,' said Marie. 'I thought we'd heard the last from that thing.'

On the other side of the world, at New Ardtaraig on New Atlantis, it was already day. The spaceplane from Nevada had returned two hours earlier, and was now about to depart. Lieutenant Bernstein sat in her office and sipped coffee, smiling to herself as she looked forward to a scheduled appointment and what promised to be an interesting conversation.

On her desk was an envelope addressed to Marcus Owen, with his new instructions from the British Council.

Acknowledgements

The inspiration for Cloud City came from *Rethinking our Sister Planet: A Handbook for the Development of Venus* by Karen R Pease, Venus Labs, 2017.

The character Marcus Owen, and the Union, first appeared in the short story 'Cold Revolution Blues' written in conjunction with a student project of Newcastle University's School of Architecture, Planning and Landscape in 2016. Thanks to Dr Stephen Parnell and all the staff and students involved.

Jenni Hill and Nadia Saward did outstanding editorial work, for which I can't thank them enough. I'm likewise indebted to Mic Cheetham, Farah Mendlesohn and Sharon MacLeod for their very helpful comments.

extras

orbitbooks.net

about the author

Ken MacLeod was born on the Isle of Lewis and now lives in Gourock, Scotland. He has a postgraduate degree in biomechanics and worked for some years in IT. Since 1997, he has been a full-time writer. He is the author of seventeen novels, from *The Star Fraction* (1995) to *The Corporation Wars* (2018), and many articles and short stories. He has won three BSFA awards and three Prometheus Awards, and been short-listed for the Clarke and Hugo Awards.

Ken was a Writer in Residence at the ESRC Genomics Policy and Research Forum at Edinburgh University, and Writer in Residence for the MA creative writing course at Edinburgh Napier University.

Ken's blog is *The Early Days of a Better Nation* (http://kenmacleod.blogspot.com).

His Twitter feed is at @amendlocke.

Find out more about Ken MacLeod and other Orbit authors by registering for the free monthly newsletter at orbitbooks.net.

if you enjoyed
BEYOND THE HALLOWED SKY

look out for

NOPHEK GLOSS
Book One of the Graven

by
Essa Hansen

Caiden's planet is destroyed. His family gone. And, his only hope for survival is a crew of misfit aliens and a mysterious ship that seems to have a soul and a universe of its own. Together they will show him that the universe is much bigger, much more advanced, and much more mysterious than Caiden had ever imagined. But the universe hides dangers as well, and soon Caiden has his own plans.

He vows to do anything it takes to get revenge on the slavers who murdered his people and took away his home. To destroy their regime, he must infiltrate and dismantle them from the inside, or die trying.

Enter a universe of daring space battles and impossible technology, a world where planets can be destroyed in the blink of an eye, and where the galaxy's most valuable substance − nophek gloss − is in the hands of one young man who will tear it all down.

CHAPTER 1

TENDED AND DRIVEN

The overseers had taken all the carcasses, at least. The lingering stench of thousands of dead bovines wafted on breezes, prowling the air. Caiden crawled from an aerator's cramped top access port and comforting scents of iron and chemical. Outside, he inhaled, and the death aroma hit him. He gagged and shielded his nose in an oily sleeve.

"Back in there, kid," his father shouted from the ground.

Caiden crept to the machine's rust-eaten rim, twelve meters above where his father's wiry figure stood bristling with tools.

"I need a break!" Caiden wiped his eyes, smearing them with black grease he noticed too late. Vertebrae crackled into place when he stretched, cramped for hours in ducts and chemical housing as he assessed why the aerators had stopped working so suddenly. From the aerator's top, pipes soared a hundred meters to the vast pasture compound's ceiling, piercing through to spew clouds of vapor. Now merely a wheeze freckling the air.

"Well, I'm ready to test the backup power unit. There are six more aerators to fix today."

"We haven't even fixed the one!"

His father swiveled to the compound's entrance, a kilometer and a half wide, where distant aerators spewed weakened plumes into the vapor-filled sky. Openings in the compound's ceiling steeped the empty fields in twilight while the grass rippled rich, vibrating green. The air was viciously silent—no more grunts, no thud of hooves, no rip and crunch of grazing. A lonely breeze combed over the emptiness and tickled Caiden's nose with another whiff of death.

Humans were immune to the disease that had killed every bovine across the world, but the contaminated soil would take years to purge before new animals were viable. Pasture lots stood vacant for as far as anyone could see, leaving an entire population doing nothing but waiting for the overseers' orders.

The carcasses had been disposed of the same way as the fat bovines at harvest: corralled at the Flat Docks, two-kilometer-square metal plates, which descended, and the livestock were moved—somewhere, down below—then the plate rose empty.

"What'll happen if it dissolves completely?" The vapor paled and shredded dangerously by the hour—now the same grayish blond as Caiden's hair—and still he couldn't see through it. His curiosity bobbed on the sea of fear poured into him during his years in the Stricture: the gray was all that protected them from harm.

"Trouble will happen. Don't you mind it." His father always deflected or gave Caiden an answer for a child. Fourteen now, Caiden had been chosen for a mechanic determination because his intelligence outclassed him for everything else. He was smart enough to handle real answers.

"But what's up there?" he argued. "Why else spend so much effort keeping up the barrier?"

There could be a ceiling, with massive lights that filtered through to grow the fields, or the ceiling might be the floor of another level, with more people raising strange animals. Perhaps those people grew light itself, and poured it to the pastures, sieved by the clouds.

Caiden scrubbed sweat off his forehead, forgetting his grimy hand again. "The overseers must live up there. Why else do we rarely see them?"

He'd encountered two during his Appraisal at ten years old, when they'd confirmed his worth and assignment, and given him his brand—the mark of merit. He'd had a lot fewer questions, then. They'd worn sharp, hard metal clothes over their figures and faces, molded weirdly or layered in plates, and Caiden couldn't tell if there were bodies beneath those shapes or just parts, like a machine. One overseer had a humanlike shape but was well over two meters tall, the other reshaped itself like jelly. And there had been a third they'd talked to, whom Caiden couldn't see at all.

His father's sigh came out a growl. "They don't come from the sky, and the answers aren't gonna change if you keep asking the same questions."

Caiden recalled the overseers' parting words at Appraisal: *As a mechanic determination, it will become your job to maintain this world, so finely tuned it functions perfectly without us.*

"But why—"

"A mechanic doesn't need curiosity to fix broken things." His father disappeared back into the machine.

Caiden exhaled forcibly, bottled up his frustrations, and crawled back into the maintenance port. The tube was more cramped at fourteen than it had been at ten, but his growth spurt was pending and he still fit in spaces his father could not. The port was lined with cables, chemical wires, and faceplates stenciled in at least eight different languages Caiden hadn't been taught in the Stricture. His father told him to ignore them. And to ignore the blue vials filled with a liquid that vanished when directly observed. And the porous metal of the deepest ducts that seemed to breathe inward and out. *A mechanic doesn't need curiosity.*

Caiden searched for the bolts he thought he'd left in a neat pile.

"The more I understand and answer, the more I can fix." Frustration amplified his words, bouncing them through the metal of the machine.

"Caiden," his father's voice boomed from a chamber below. Reverberations settled in a long pause. "Sometimes knowing doesn't fix things."

Another nonanswer, fit for a child. Caiden gripped a wrench and stared at old wall dents where his frustration had escaped him before. Over time, fatigue dulled that anger. Maybe that was what had robbed his father of questions and answers.

But his friend Leta often said the same thing: "You can't fix everything, Caiden."

I can try.

He found his missing bolts at the back of the port, scattered and rolled into corners. He gathered them up and slapped faceplates into position, wrenching them down tighter than needed.

The adults always said, "This is the way things have always been—nothing's broken."

But it stayed that way because no one tried anything different.

Leta had confided in a nervous whisper, "*Different* is why I'll fail Appraisal." If she could fail and be rejected simply because her mind worked differently, the whole system was broken.

The aerator's oscillating unit was defaced with Caiden's labels and drawings where he'd transformed the bulbous foreign script into imagery or figures. Recent, neatly printed labels stood out beside his younger marks. He hesitated at a pasted-up photo he'd nicked from the Stricture: a foreign landscape with straight trees and intertwined branches. White rocks punctured bluish sand, with pools of water clearer than the ocean he'd once seen. It was beautiful—the place his parents would be retired to when he replaced them. Part of the way things had always been.

"Yes, stop everything." His mother was speaking to his father, and her voice echoed from below, muffled and rounded by the tube. She never visited during work. "Stop, they said. No more repairs."

His father responded, unintelligible through layers of metal.

"I don't know," she replied. "The overseers ordered everyone to gather at the Flat Docks. Caiden!"

He wriggled out of the port. His mother stood below with her arms crossed, swaying nervous as a willow. She was never nervous.

"Down here, hon." She squinted up at him. "And don't— *Caiden!*"

He slid halfway down the aerator's side and grabbed a seam to catch his fall. The edge under his fingers was shiny from years of the same maneuver. Dangling, smiling, he swung to perch on the front ledge, then frowned at his mother's flinty expression. Her eyes weren't on him anymore. Her lips moved in a whisper of quick, whipping words that meant trouble.

Caiden jumped the last couple meters to the ground.

"We have to go." She gripped a handful of his jacket and laid her other hand gently on his shoulder, marshaling him forward with these two conflicting holds. His father followed, wiping soot and worry from his brow.

"Are they sending help?" Caiden squirmed free. His mother tangled her fingers in his as they crossed a causeway between green pastures to a small door in the compound's side. "New animals?"

"Have to neutralize the disease first," his father said.

"A vaccine?" His mother squeezed his hand.

Outside the compound, field vehicles lay abandoned, others jammed around one of the Flat Docks a kilometer away. Crowds streamed to it from other compounds along the road grid, looking like fuel lines in an engine diagram. Movement at farther Docks suggested the order had reached everywhere.

"Stay close." His mother tugged him against her side as they amalgamated into a throng of thousands. Caiden had never seen so many people all together. They dressed in color and style according to their determinations, but otherwise the mob was a mix of shapes, sizes, and colors of people with only the brands on the back of their necks alike. It was clear from the murmurs that no one knew what was going on. This was not "the way things have always been." Worst fears and greatest hopes floated by in whispers like windy grass as Caiden squeezed to the edge of the Flat Docks' huge metal plate.

It lay empty, the guardrails up, the crowds bordered around. Only seven aerators in their sector still trickled. Others much farther away had stopped entirely. There should have been hundreds feeding the gray overhead, which now looked the palest ever.

Caiden said, "We'll be out of time to get the aerators running before the vapor's gone."

"I know . . ." His father's expression furrowed. The grime on his face couldn't hide suspicion, and his mother's smile couldn't hide her fear. She always had a solution, a stalwart mood, and an answer for Caiden even if it was "Carry on." Now: only wariness.

If everyone's here, then—

"Leta."

"She'll be with her own parental unit," his father said.

"Yeah, but—"

They weren't kind.

"Caiden!"

He dashed off, ducking the elbows and shoulders of the mob. The children were smothered among the taller bodies, impossible to distinguish. His quick mind sorted through the work rotations, the direction they came from—everyone would have walked straight from their dropped tasks, at predictable speed. He veered and slowed, gaze saccading across familiar faces in the community.

A flicker of bright bluish-purple.

Chicory flowers.

Caiden barked apologies as he shouldered toward the color, lost among tan clothes and oak-dark jerkins. Then he spotted Leta's fawn waves, and swung his arms out to make room in the crowd, as if parting tall grass around a flower. "Hey, there you are."

Leta peered up with dewy hazel eyes. "Cai." She breathed relief. Her knuckles were white around a cluster of chicory, her right arm spasming, a sign of her losing the battle against overstimulation.

Leta's parental unit wasn't in sight, neglectful as ever, and she was winded, rushed from some job or forgotten altogether. Oversized non-determination garments hung off one shoulder, covered her palms, tripped her heels. She crushed herself against Caiden's arm and hugged it fiercely. "It's what the older kids say. The ones who don't pass Appraisal're sent away, like the bovine yearlings."

"Don't be silly, they would have called just the children then, not everyone. And you haven't been appraised yet, anyway."

But she was ten, it was soon. The empathy, sensitivity, and logic that could qualify her as a sublime clinician also crippled her everyday life as the callous people around her set her up to fail. Caiden hugged her, careful of the bruises peeking over her shoulder and forearm, the sight of them igniting a well-worn urge to protect.

"I've got you," he said, and pulled out twigs and leaves stuck in her hair. Her whole right side convulsed softly. The crowds, noise, and light washed a blankness into her face, meaning something in her was shutting down. "You're safe."

Caiden took her hand—firmly, grounding—and back-tracked through the crowd to the Flat Dock edge.

The anxious look on his mother's face was layered with disapproval, but his father smiled in relief. Leta clutched Caiden's right hand in both of hers. His mother took his left.

"The overseers just said gather and wait?" he asked his father.

"Someday you'll learn patience."

Shuffles and gasps rippled through the assembly. Caiden followed their gazes up. Clouds thinned in a gigantic circle. The air everywhere brightened across the crowds more intensely than the compounds' lights had ever lit the bovines.

A hole burned open overhead and shot a column of blinding white onto the Flat Docks. Shouts and sobs erupted. Caiden stared through the blur of his eyelashes as the light column widened until the entire plate burned white. In distant sectors, the same beams emerged through the gray.

He smashed his mother's hand in a vise grip. She squeezed back.

A massive square descended, black as a ceiling, flickering out the light. The angular mass stretched fifty meters wide on all sides, made of the same irregular panels as the aerators. With a roar, it moved slowly, impossibly, nothing connecting it to the ground.

"I've never . . ." His mother's whisper died and her mouth hung open.

Someone said, "It's like the threshers, but . . ."

Massive. Caiden imagined thresher blades peeling out of the hull, descending to mow the crowds.

The thing landed on the Flat Docks' plate with a rumble that juddered up Caiden's soles through his bones.

A fresh bloom of brightness gnawed at the gray above, and beyond that widening hole hung the colors and shapes of unmoving fire. Caiden stood speechless, blinded by after-image. Leta gaped at the black mass that had landed, and made her voice work enough to whisper, "What is it?"

Caiden forced his face to soften, to smile. "More livestock maybe? Isn't this exciting?" *Stupid thing to say.* He shut up before his voice quavered.

"This isn't adventure, Caiden," Leta muttered. "Not like sneaking to the ocean—this is *different.*"

"Different how?"

"The adults. This isn't how it's done."

Caiden attempted to turn his shaking into a chuckle. "The bovine all dead is a new problem. Everything's new now."

The crowd's babble quieted to a hiss of fear, the tension strummed. A grinding roar pummeled the air as the front side of the angular mass slid upward from the base, and two tall figures emerged from the horizontal opening.

"Overseers!" someone shouted. The word repeated, carried with relief and joy through the crowd.

Caiden's eyes widened. Both overseers were human-shaped, one tall and bulky, the other short and slim, and as he remembered from his Appraisal, they were suited from head to toe with plates of metal and straps and a variety of things he couldn't make out: spikes and ribbons, tools, wires, and blocks of white writing like inside the aerators. They wore blue metal plates over their faces, with long slits for eyes and nostrils, holes peppering the place where their mouths would be. Besides their build, they resembled each other exactly, and could be anything beneath their clothes.

"See, it's fine." Caiden forced himself to exhale. "Right, Ma?"

His mother nodded slow, confused.

"People," the shorter overseer said in a muffled yet amplified voice.

The crowd hushed, rapt, with stressed breaths filling the quiet. Caiden's heart hammered, pulse noosing his neck.

"You will be transported to a clean place," the other overseer said in a husky voice amplified the same way. The crowd rippled his words to the back ranks.

"With new *livestock*," the first added with a funny lilt on the final word.

"Come aboard. Slow, orderly." The overseers each moved to a side of the open door, framing the void. "Leave your belongings. Everyone will be provided for."

Caiden glanced at Leta. "See? New animals."

She didn't seem to hear, shut down by the sights and sounds. He let her cling to him as his father herded them both forward.

Caiden asked, "Where could we go that doesn't have infected soil? Up, past the gray?"

"Stay close." His father's voice was tight. "Maybe they discovered clean land past the ocean."

They approached the hollow interior—metallic, dank, and lightless—with a quiet throng pouring in, shoulder to shoulder like the bovines had when squeezed from one pasture to another. Caiden observed the closest overseer. Scratches and holes scarred their mismatched metal clothes, decorated in strange scripts. Their hand rested on a long tool at their hip, resembling the livestock prods but double-railed.

Caiden's father guided him inside and against a wall, where his mother wrapped him and Leta in her strong arms and the mob crammed tight, drowning them in heat and odor.

"Try to keep still." The overseer's words resonated inside.

A roar thrummed to life, and the door descended, squeezing out the orange light. The two overseers remained outside.

Thunder cracked underfoot. Metal bellowed like a thousand animals crying at once. Human wails cut through and the floor shuddered in lurches, forcing Caiden to widen his stance to stay upright. His mother's arms clamped around him.

Children sobbed. Consoling parents hissed in the darkness. Leta remained deathly silent in Caiden's firm grasp, but tremors crashed in her body, nervous system rebelling. He drew her closer.

"Be still, hon." His mother's voice quavered.

She covered his ears with clammy hands and muffled the deafening roar to a thick howl. The rumble infiltrated his bones, deeper-toned than he'd thought any machine could sound.

Are we going up into that fire-sky, or into the ground, where the livestock went?

The inside of machines usually comforted him. There was safety in their hard shell, and no question to their functioning, but this one stank of tangy fear, had no direction, and his mother's shaking leached into his back as he curled around Leta's trembling in front. He buried his nose in a greasy sleeve and inhaled, tasting the fumes of the gray. His mother's hands over his ears thankfully deadened the sobs.

"Soon," she cooed. "I'm sure we'll be there soon."